This Transient Life

An Inspector Vignoles Mystery

Stephen Done

British Library Cataloguing in Publication Data:
A catalogue record for this book is available from the British Library
ISBN978-1-9164010-5-1

1st published 2021

The Vignoles Press
Stephen.done@gmail.com
FB: The Vignoles Press
www.inspectorvignoles.ukwriters.net

Set in Garamond
Cover paintings: Stephen Done
Cover design: Bill Citrine
Editor: Peter Elson
Printed in Poland by booksfactory.co.uk

'And we most humbly beseech thee of thy goodness, O Lord, to comfort and succour all them, who in this transitory life are in trouble, sorrow, need, sickness, or any other adversity.'

The Communion, Book of Common Prayer

MARCH 1957

In Memorium
West London

The cemetery was on a grand scale. Row upon row of stone memorials of differing heights, shapes and states of repair stood like so many teeth amongst the fresh spring grass and encroaching weeds. Some were polished black or dazzling white marble with gold-leafed incised lettering, but most were just grey stone, now slowly greening and stained. Sculpted angels stood high on plinths looking downcast with wings folded, whilst assorted evocations of the Virgin Mary, hooded and gowned, stood quietly, their impassive faces appearing tear-stained thanks to the sooty rain. There were a few sinister Victorian Gothic creations made all the more uninviting by unpleasant accretions of moss, cobwebs and dead leaves. Broad roadways bisected these serried ranks, the greensward studded with fine specimen trees that swayed and rustled in a raw wind. Pink and white cherry blossom tumbled in gentle drifts against the tyres of the makeshift hearse that stood beside the open grave.

The glossy black police van had at least been freshly washed for the occasion and was of a type popularly known as a 'Black Maria,' and perhaps the nickname had never seemed more appropriate. The rear doors stood wide to allow the coffin to be removed by four men in police dress uniform. Their lower faces were tightly masked with cloths tied at the napes of their necks and each wore leather gloves and police

1

caps pulled low on their brows.

They hefted the coffin onto a wheeled gurney, eyes staring blankly, some glassy, their breath sucked in through the cloth of their masks to form an indentation with each inhalation. They rolled the gurney towards the oversized hole in the ground. Six was the usual number for bearing a coffin upon broad shoulders, but Government restrictions and a crippling shortage of men fit and able for duty, rendered this impossible. Hence the bone-shaking ride as they urged the wheels to negotiate the gravel pathway. They tried to maintain a level of dignity but when a wheel caught in a grassy hole, they were forced to heave and lift and grunt until it ran freely, the coffin swaying dangerously on its short journey.

A priest stood waiting. His face also masked across mouth and nose. His surplice teased by the wind. A Book of Common Prayer in one gloved hand, a thumb marking the place. Text underlined in red pencil to highlight the few lines still allowed in the apology for a service limited to no more than ten minutes from start to finish. His eyes were lowered, staring in horrified incomprehension at the enormous void recently excavated by the mechanical digger parked at one edge, the scoop now unbolted and put to one side and replaced by a metal hook hanging from a chain. It bore an unfortunate and unintentional similarity to a gibbet. The mass grave was on a scale the priest had only seen on newsreels in the Odeon back in the days when he could still visit the cinema with his wife. Like so much else, the cinema was closed for the duration with posters of films as yet unseen fading outside as litter gathered in front of the glass and chrome doors chained shut.

There were twelve caskets already stacked to one side of the communal grave with room for at least the same number again.

'Piled on top of each other like so many peas in a pod…' The priest had complained to his verger. 'Not even afforded the dignity of space between each coffin. Just the thickness of the cheap pine they use, thanks to yet another Government edict.'

He noticed that one or two caskets had been rendered less utilitarian by some artful wood staining. The coffin now being fastened onto the metal hook by the men in blue using hefty cords placed underneath had also been given this special treatment. It was polished and buffed to a semi-gloss finish. It contained someone with status, the dark oak colouration and metal plaque instantly conferring importance amidst the dehumanising surroundings.

Two workmen helped the coffin make its deep descent as the digger fired into action, the ugly sound of the churning motor and the diesel fumes that stung their eyes robbing any last vestiges of dignity from the spectacle. The coffin came to rest on top of a plain pine offering already in place. The policemen stared into this unholy man-made crater. The wind worried at the pages of the prayer book as the priest's voice, muffled by his mask, was rendered indistinct. Few caught the exact words, but the meaning was clear.

A widow dressed all in black stood a few yards away. She was alone. High heels, stockings and a fine Italian wool coat with a silver and pearl brooch pinned to the collar. This had been a wedding anniversary present from the man now being laid to rest. Her hat was small and simple. A handkerchief was held to her mouth as a temporary replacement for the obligatory face mask. Gloves sheathed her arms almost to the elbow.

A handful of earth was thrown, and the priest winced as it fell short, so great was the size of the open grave. The woman took a few steps forward and tossed down a bunch of flowers which fortunately landed on the coffin lid. It was all over in less than eight minutes. The policemen looked at the woman in black, saluted, then turned and wheeled the gurney, noisily, back to their van and soon were driving away, leaving behind a trail of blue exhaust.

An Army truck now growled its way forwards. Time was tight and another ten had to be buried that morning. The truck was bringing in the next four. There was no time for reflection, no time for sentiment, no time for tears. No time for goodbyes.

Even before the woman in black had reached the cemetery gates her husband's wooden box would be lost to view. She had been reassured that one day when some sense of normality returned, the Corporation would erect a memorial plaque listing those buried in the communal grave. Would they carve it in stone and gild the letters? Or use some man-made plastic in chocolate brown with cream paint as a highlight? Her eyes pricked as she imagined tracing the incised letters with her finger.

Chief Superintendent John Badger.

He'd died in office, and she felt it important that if anyone bothered to look, they would at least know his rank and gain some sense of his working life. It had taken some string-pulling by DCI Vignoles to evade the draconian restrictions regarding access to the body, but her husband had been buried in his dress uniform complete with cap, gloves and favourite swagger stick. John would like that. She hoped they might allow her to place flowers in a vase beside the promised plaque, but even that simple request was impossible at present.

The sound of distant gunshots echoed in the distance. It had become so commonplace these last weeks, that Mrs Badger took less notice than she did of the blackbird singing gaily from a branch nearby.

She found it hard to cry. The swift and impersonal death of her husband, alone, in a virus ward she was forbidden to enter, followed by the hurried burial preparations had stripped away all meaning and left her numb. It was as if she'd given a shot of morphine. She'd watched his burial impassively. This was not a funeral for a friend, for a lover, for her dutiful and fiercely loyal husband but a moment of efficient civic waste disposal.

Mrs Badger leaned her back against the brick wall of a shuttered clothes shop and closed her eyes. The weak March sun beat on her face and with the wall sheltering her from the wind and the bricks having soaked up a little heat, it felt soothing. It was good to feel the sun on her skin. The papers said the virus didn't like sunshine, that everyone should try to get as much of it as they could - restrictions allowing.

As yet another ambulance clanged its bell and hurried into view across a distant intersection, she wondered if she cared about keeping safe and observing the ever-changing lists of what she could or could not do. If the virus didn't get her, then a bullet from a crazed looter might.

At least the bullet would be quicker.

JANUARY

Chapter One
Leicester Central

The telephone jangled and when DCI Charles Vignoles picked up the receiver, he heard the honeyed tone of Chief Superintendent Badger's new secretary with the unspellable name of Karolina Smolej.

The young Polish emigre had been recommended by a recruitment agency and met with approval. Miss Smolej advised Vignoles the Chief Superintendent wished to speak with him urgently. Before Vignoles could say a word, there was a moment of silence whilst the extension was connected.

'That you, Vignoles?'

'Sir?'

'Get yourself here on the next train. If my watch is correct and the timetable running as it should, you have a fast service due in the next few minutes. Make sure you're on it!'

Vignoles spun about on his old and beloved swivel chair and looked through the bay window of his office on to the broad expanse of the covered platform at Central as the gleaming form of *Isinglass* glided effortlessly into the platform at the head of the fast London train. Badger's timing was impeccable.

'May I enquire what this is about?'

'You may not. You're needed for a top-level meeting. Attendance is essential. Alone. Now jump to it!'

Vignoles just had time to sweep up his hat, scarf and gloves and with a hurried, 'I'm off, London's calling…' rushed outside whilst waving to the stationmaster to attract his attention. 'I need to be on that train at all costs.'

'Right you are, sir.' The formally dressed and top-hatted stationmaster was used to the hasty and sometimes unconventional demands Vignoles and his team placed on the railway and swivelled about heel to find the train guard.

Departures on the former Great Central Railway were briskly managed and passengers expected to board and close the carriage doors as quickly as possible. Vignoles was no slouch, however, and needed no ticket as his rank conferred freedom of movement across all British Railways services, passenger and goods, even to the extent of having the power to commandeer trains and halt or redirect services if dire necessity demanded.

He was soon seated in a compartment occupied by two others, with a freshly minted copy of the Leicester Mercury on his knee. He'd snatched this from the WH Smith's kiosk, calling 'I'll settle later!' to the startled vendor.

Isinglass, the powerful Brunswick green-liveried engine which had arrived buffed and polished to perfection, now snorted into action in response to the guard's terse whistle. The train, composed of carriages in a mixture of the new all-over maroon and others in ageing 'blood and custard' livery, smoothly pulled away onto the long stretch of the viaduct that spanned the city streets and river.

It was a dour January day that made steam billow past the carriage windows and so offering only imperfect views of factories with their slim-fingered chimneys. He glimpsed the shoe and clothing warehouses and bustling wharves, busy roads and myriad brick terraces with their thousands of chimneys issuing smoke that combined with the steam rising from the surface of the River Soar thanks to the power station outflow. Clouds hung heavy in the sky, corralling this smoke and steam into a noxious sickly fog. 'The Clean Air Act' passed just the year before had a way to run before it would improve the skies above this particular East Midlands city.

The young woman seated opposite sneezed and reached hurriedly for a handkerchief. Her nose was pink and her eyes puffy.

'Bless you.'

She nodded thanks but had to concentrate on blowing her nose before eventually balling her handkerchief in one hand and flopping backwards against the seat cushions in a posture of lethargic tiredness. These winter colds were everywhere, thought Vignoles. The local paper agreed, running a short article on page four about 'The Menace of Winter Colds' and repeating the good practice necessary to help ward them off. Some GPs in the southern counties had reported a spike of influenza cases and on a day thin on county-based news, this had been picked up by the Leicester Mercury. Perhaps to better pad out a story sketchy on detail, the picture editor had found an illustration of the old wartime Ministry of Health poster that warned '*Coughs and sneezes spread diseases,*' showing graphically a man spraying an underground carriage occupied by infuriated passengers with his uncontrolled and very wet, sneeze.

Vignoles buried his head deeper into the opened paper as the young woman had a fit of sneezing and nose blowing. At least she knew the drill.

Arrival in Marylebone was on time thanks to some smart running by the A3 class engine on the front, and Vignoles hurried to his meeting.

Miss Smolej, who turned out to be as disarmingly attractive as her voice over the telephone implied, met Vignoles. He had the impression she'd been anxiously awaiting the arrival of his train and was eager to hurry him along with barely an exchange of polite greetings. She offered to take his hat and coat and trotted off on clicking high heels along the linoleum floored corridors, her pretty behind swaying enticingly in perfectly tailored tweed. Vignoles made a mental note to keep DS Mellor away from HQ.

Idle considerations of the secretary's obvious physical attributes were instantly erased by the surprising presence of a man in Army uniform standing guard outside Badger's office. The guard sprang into life upon seeing their approach and without so much as an explanation, rapped his knuckles on the door and ushered Vignoles inside. The door closed behind and he found himself looking at five men seated around the conference table in Badger's office. None stood up, merely observing him impassively whilst Badger spoke from his position at the head.

'Ah, DCI Vignoles. Your timing is impeccable.' A thin smile followed that tried to convey warmth, but it was brief. 'Take a seat, we must start at once.'

A chair stood empty on the unoccupied side of the table. Badger offered introductions as Vignoles sat down.

'Mr Lombard from the Ministry of Defence, based in the Microbiological Research Department; Colonel Broadbent, British Army, Royal Engineers and chair of the meeting; Doctor Urban, MOD, Chemical Defence Experimental Establishment at Porton Down and seated at the end, Mr Wellbeck from the Common Cold Unit, Harnham Down, Salisbury.'

Each man gave a slight nod of the head in response. A weighty silence seemed to fill the room along with the smoke from the cigarettes each man was smoking. A large ashtray in the centre of the table showed evidence they had been ensconced for some time.

'Light a pipe...' Badger again tried to sound friendly, but Vignoles could detect a nervous quality in his voice. 'We have a delicate matter to discuss.'

Vignoles took out a tin of Redbreast tobacco and tamped some into his pipe whilst looking at each man facing him, trying to gauge what was coming. This was a very curious group with no obvious connection to the railways. The mention of the secretive Porton Down establishment where deadly and virulent microbes were actively encouraged, made him illogically thankful they had not shaken hands.

Badger's seat at the head of the table was in deference to this being his office, but he was not running the show. 'Colonel...?'

Broadbent took over. 'I've been advised you're the best man for this job. The link to your field of policing is tenuous, but there is a logic behind our thinking.' He paused a moment to give Vignoles a hard stare. 'You come highly recommended, although your file makes curious reading, inspector. Some would find holes to pick, others might question your methodology.'

Lombard exchanged a worried glance with Badger, but otherwise remained stony-faced and tapped ash from his gold banded cigarette.

'Be that as it may, we require someone to finesse a delicate operation. It needs a deft touch and a man who can apply his intelligence to the task with the sole purpose of delivering the expected outcome. Achieving the objective is paramount.'

Vignoles wondered where this was leading.

Broadbent leaned on his forearms and locked eyes with Vignoles. 'The paper in front of you is an Addendum to the Official Secrets Act. You will sign it before I continue.'

Vignoles frowned whilst concentrating on getting his pipe alight. It bought him a few moments to think. The official document was a single sheet of typed foolscap. Someone had thoughtfully placed a fountain pen beside it. They were accepting no excuse for delay. 'I have already signed the Act...'

'I repeat, for clarification, this is an addendum. An enhancement to the parameters of the original act, if you prefer.' Broadbent was a man not used to having to justify his actions. 'You will be privy to matters of national security with the potential of impacting severely upon two of the most discreet establishments in the United Kingdom. There shall be no breach of security.'

'Just sign it, Vignoles,' Badger growled, before retreating behind his cigarette induced smokescreen whilst contemplating the highly polished surface of the table.

'It's nothing you are not familiar with, Inspector. Just another level of co-operation and understanding between departments,' Mr Lombard from the Ministry of Defence added in a humourless voice.

Vignoles, with pipe jutting from one side of his mouth, dutifully signed and it was collected by Lombard who immediately secreted it in a file lying on the table before pinning this down with his elbow.

'I want you to take a look at this.' Colonel Broadbent now slid across a single sheet of pale blue writing paper. 'Don't worry, it has been fumigated.'

Vignoles raised a questioning eyebrow at this surprising comment but took the private letter without a word. It was written in blue ink in a spidery hand that wavered across a page pock-marked by several blots and over-large full stops as though the writer had paused with the nib pressed to the paper for too long whilst the ink continued to flow.

January 18th
Longmoor Downs Barracks

My dearest Phyl,

I'm not well. But am resting in hospital in good care as the doctors here are the best and the nurses make me comfortable, so please don't fret.

I got the Flu! A real bad dose. Typical me, isn't it! A special type. Remember I said some of the boys would be ginny pigs in a test and be paid for just catching colds? Forty of us lads agreed and took it, but I've not reacted well. High fever and arms so heavy I can hardly write. They said it would make me poorly, not kill me so that is good, but God knows I feel like it at times.

Soon as I'm better I'll ask for leave off and see you.

Love you always,
Ian.

Aside from the misspelling and evidence of having been written by someone with a high fever, Vignoles could not fail to notice the letter had been rubber-stamped in red with the single word 'Censored.' He looked up. 'Ian made a full recovery, I trust?'

'Regrettably, Lance Corporal Mordon did not. He passed away.' Broadbent silently took the letter back and placed it in the folder from whence he'd extracted it. Vignoles had registered this file was stamped 'TOP SECRET'. 'There were compelling reasons why the letter was not delivered to his wife. Widow.' Broadbent narrowed his eyes as he spoke. 'Mordon was in danger of spilling the beans on a sensitive subject he had no right to share with a civilian.'

'She was his wife.'

'And a civilian,' Broadbent was unsmiling.

'Mrs Mordon has been informed of her husband's death?' Vignoles asked.

'An official communique was drafted and sent to her.'

'And the reason for his death?'

'Influenza. To be specific, flu' that lead to pneumonia, exacerbated by Mordon having an undetected asthma condition,' Broadbent explained. 'It was a mild affliction, but the silly fool managed to keep his asthma hidden from our medical staff and the consequential reaction was unfortunate.'

'What was the nature of the test the forty men took part in?'

'You do not need that level of information for your task, inspector.' Urban now spoke. 'The details are classified and on a strictly need-to-know level.'

'And I need to know what you are asking me to do. I need a proper grasp of the situation. Without that, my work will be compromised.'

'We define the terms of the mission around this table, Vignoles,' Broadbent responded irritably, but then collected himself. 'Look, the teams from the CDEE and MRD are conducting a carefully monitored clinical trial of a mild flu strain. Lance Corporal Mordon developed unforeseen complications and died. Awkward, but it was neither negligence nor irresponsibility on our side that killed him. The specifics of the test are classified and certainly not for his wife's ears. We deem it better you have only the lightest overview of the trials so you cannot accidentally give away more than we would wish.'

Vignoles bridled at the implication. 'She has a right to know how her husband died and not fobbed off with veiled half-truths. Or lies.'

'That is an insulting insinuation...'

'She has been informed of the circumstances of her husband's death,' Professor Urban interjected, cutting off the colonel. 'Respiratory failure has been recorded by the coroner. The PM report confirmed this without ambiguity. Neither unusual nor a rare occurrence in cases of influenza. Is that not so, Wellbeck?'

Terence Wellbeck was suffering the effects of a head cold and trying to discreetly wipe his nose when addressed. 'Yes...' Sniff. 'Many thousands die from influenza each winter. A sad fact, but demonstrably true. There is evidence of a new and rather nasty *Asiatic flu* doing the rounds and so one can expect many more similar casualties.' He looked sad, possibly because of his cold, but Vignoles sensed he was also ill at ease, more so than anyone else around the table. Perhaps less comfortable with the objectives of this curious meeting?

'Should we expect a similar death rate from this new strain

of flu your institutions have manufactured?' Vignoles queried.

'We did not summon you here to debate clinical trials nor indeed the scientific remit of either the MRD or CDEE,' Broadbent fired back. 'The gentlemen seated around this table represent parts of our most classified and specialised defensive capability. We cannot, I repeat, cannot have work that by its very nature is secret, broadcast to just anyone and everyone.'

'His widow is not 'just anyone'.'

Badger spoke up, 'Easy, Vignoles. Hear the Colonel out.' His voice was flat, and he was nervously fiddling with his cigarette.

'I appreciate this situation is curious to one more used to policing the railway network. We would all do well to focus on the task in hand and knuckle down to agreeing on a plan of action.' Broadbent adopted a less intimidating manner. 'We intercepted the letter because of the obvious breach of confidential information,' Broadbent continued. 'And thereby hangs our problem. The clever chaps running these tests had not realised until too late that one of their subjects failed to appreciate the acute importance of the Act you put your moniker to. Signing the Act carries significant responsibilities and severe punishment for transgressions. Regrettably, Lance Corporal Mordon fell short.'

Vignoles was gripping the stem of his pipe in an effort not to say anything unwise.

'Our concern is that Mordon previously shared information about the tests with his wife. The letter makes it clear they had prior communications on the subject. This is a serious breach of security. That Mordon died is a matter of regret, but not the reason for convening this meeting.'

'What is the reason for this meeting? And how can it concern a DCI in the Transport Police?'

'We wish you to speak with Mrs Mordon. We must understand the scale of this breach - then take appropriate steps to close it.' Broadbent's voice was emotionless.

'That sounds ominous.'

Lombard now spoke. 'We cannot make light of the matter nor ignore it. However, it may prove less serious than it appears. We just need to establish if he wrote another letter. Or perhaps the information was shared over the telephone?'

'Or face to face?' Vignoles added.

'That's not possible. Mordon, and indeed the others involved, only learned about the trials once they returned from leave over Christmas and New Year and have had no leave since. With swift action to recover any written evidence, some ameliorating words accompanied by a handsome cheque from the Home Office and the promise of an Army pension and we should be able to close the door on this.'

Vignoles puffed on his pipe. 'You want to buy her off?'

'I would not characterise it so crudely,' Lombard replied.

'A consoling cup of tea and the offer of a cheque in return for the last love letters from her dead husband?' Vignoles was unimpressed. 'Once again, why would a DCI in the British Railways Detective Department be the 'man for the job'?'

'Two reasons. You will have noticed the letter was written from the barracks at Longmoor Downs. I'm not sure if you are familiar with the set up there, although knowing your background as an enthusiast of railways and your professional role, I suspect you know more than I,' Lombard risked something approximating a smile.

'The Longmoor Military Railway?' Vignoles had his interest awakened. This was more like it. 'I only know what I've gleaned from articles in *The Railway Magazine*. I've never had the opportunity to see it for real.'

'Then you have missed out!' Broadbent allowed himself a proud smile. 'We run a fine operation and pride ourselves on the level of training across many skills. Mordon was working his National Service with the regiment at Longmoor. He was a fireman on the engines. I've been told he was enthusiastic and a willing worker, although we suspect the daily proximity to smoke and ash may have had the unfortunate side effect of worsening his asthma. Be that as it may, his connection to the railway whilst strong, would not be directly relevant if it were not for the fact his wife, Phyllis, also works on the railway.'

'At Longmoor?'

'No, British Railways. She's a waitress in the buffet rooms at Sheffield Victoria,' Lombard interjected.

'On the same line as the train we can hear departing,' Badger added, feeling overlooked at the head of the table. The strident whistle and deep chuffs of the engine were audible to all.

'Precisely,' Lombard smiled, although it was not heart-warming. 'Colonel Broadbent's regiment would appear the obvious people to follow this up, but they have no jurisdiction over civilians.'

'Off the record, our military police are often knuckle-headed thugs in white helmets,' Broadbent added with a wry turn to his mouth. 'I would not wish them to go barging in and scaring the living daylights out of the poor gal.'

'It would send out the wrong signals if the MOD, let alone one of the biological research institutions, were to go knocking on doors. It could set the wrong kind of warning bells ringing in her pretty little head and the next thing we know she's gone to the press to tell all...' Urban added.

Vignoles' mind was whirring. *They're worried and they're hiding something.*

'With Phyllis Mordon also part of the railway set up, albeit, in a modest capacity, this is an opportunity to utilise someone with sufficient authority whilst not attracting undue attention.'

'What about the local police?' Vignoles was not yet convinced.

'Briefing the Sheffield City men only multiplies the risk of the story leaking further. Railways were something the Mordons shared in common and your presence is likely to feel less intimidating. Just yourself in plain clothes accompanied by one of those pretty WPCs I hear you keep in Leicester to offer a light touch, and it should be easy to question her without sounding forced.'

Vignoles stared at each man in turn before speaking. 'I don't accept it. Nothing you've told me makes sense. If you want me to do your dirty work, then lay your cards on the table. What exactly do you want?'

'You warned us he had an attitude,' Broadbent darted an angry look at Badger. 'I'm used to men following orders.'

'And with respect, I don't take orders from the British Army.'

'But you *do* from the Home Office, and you'll damn well do what we ask, or you'll hand over your warrant badge!' Lombard spat the words out, his eyes were cold as those of a fish.

'Ah, hum, the Assistant Commissioner expects full co-operation from our side,' Badger added with an apologetic cough.

'If you wish me to execute this task effectively then I need to understand what underpins it. You're holding more back than you're telling me. I signed your bit of paper, so lay the cards on the table so I can see what hand I'm being dealt. What happened to Mordon? And why are you so anxious to stop his wife from talking?'

'Doctor Urban?' Broadbent looked to his right.

The doctor adjusted his glasses and stubbed his cigarette before speaking. 'As previously explained, the lance corporal died from complications. It was an accident. You should understand that the experimental virus is fundamentally safe. It was the onset of pneumonia in conjunction with asthma that resulted in his death. We were not responsible.'

Vignoles felt the hairs on his neck stand on end. These men unsettled him. They appeared emotionless and talked glibly of this man's death as though it was just an inconvenience. A mess that needed cleaning up and he was the cleaner with the mop about to be sent to Sheffield with a bucket of filthy water. 'You don't engage a DCI with my experience to travel to Yorkshire to drink tea and offer condolences. If I'm to win her confidence and retrieve anything you consider incriminating, then I want to know about how the virus was administered and what actions were taken once he started to take bad. I need to know specifically what aspect of this sorry tale you need hushing up.' There was a flicker of a muscle around Broadbent's left eye and Lombard sucked air between his pale lips. 'I have to fully understand the case, otherwise, I walk in insufficiently briefed and become a liability.'

Badger smiled. 'Vignoles makes a fair point.'

'Let me make this explicit. You are not investigating the death of Mordon,' Broadbent replied. 'This has been concluded to the Coroner's satisfaction. However, I appreciate that from an operation standpoint you require more background on the testing programme in question. Very well. Professor, this is your bag.'

Professor Urban looked along the faces ranged around the table as he gathered his thoughts. '*Operation Chinese Bird* is the name given to the active field tests of a new strain of *coronavirus* we developed. This virus exists in the wild in a great number of forms, with effects ranging from something like a common cold through to the more aggressive forms of influenza, pneumonia…'

Chapter Two
Longmoor Military Railway

The Longmoor Military Railway was a fascinating curiosity. At any one time, it comprised approximately seventy miles of railway tracks crisscrossing a north-eastern corner of Hampshire, complete with fully functioning stations and wayside halts, various bridges and a flyover, road level crossings, signal boxes controlling signals of all manner of shapes, sizes and vintages and the large engine sheds and sidings at Longmoor itself. The depot was home to a large collection of steam engines painted Royal blue or War Department brown stabled alongside several diesel shunting engines, again of varying vintages and sizes. All these could be seen most days merrily huffing, puffing or trundling all manner of trains whilst under the control of men dressed in army fatigues. It was, effectively, a full-sized Hornby model railway set built on a scale and to a standard not even the most staggeringly wealthy individual could ever dream of owning.

It might have looked like a play-thing from the air, especially with the tail-chasing trains having the ability to loop around in giant circles without the need to enter the termini at Bordon, Liss and Longmoor Down, but was operated with such professionalism that anyone lucky enough to travel upon it would soon realise this was no plaything.

The railway tracks were regularly lifted, sometimes in short sections violently and destructively using the captured Nazi 'Schienenwolf' plough that had been designed to tear railway sleepers apart as the retreating Wehrmacht sought to prevent the Red Army following their retreat. At Longmoor, once the vicious plough had done its worst, sappers from the Royal Engineers would be ordered to make good and relay the track they had only just destroyed. These operational tasks might be repeated many times over, sometimes using explosives or other sabotage techniques. Tracks were slewed to new alignments and sets of points inserted or removed and signals hastily re-rigged to reflect the new layouts, whilst trains hauled steam cranes and wagon loads of sleepers, rail and ballast. All part of the rigorous training for The Royal Engineers in how to construct, reconstruct and disable a railway during wartime or crisis.

Trains of provisions and victuals were regularly run by the young soldiers as the railway served the large barracks located at Longmoor Downs. The impressive stations were not mere stage sets either, as the general public were sometimes allowed to travel as passengers and in the spring and summer months, many enjoyed stopping off for walks through the attractive woodlands that flanked much of the line by disembarking at the wayside halt at Liss Forest Road or perhaps take a stroll to the pretty hamlet of Woolmer from the station of the same name.

Lance Corporal Ian Mordon loved everything about the LMR and considered himself to be one of the luckiest men alive and frequently heard voicing this opinion. Whilst some of his comrades rolled their eyes and grumbled, he 'should try spending all day shovelling ballast and see how he liked it then,' others shared this opinion. As Royal Engineers they had one of the better assignments in the British Army. Mordon could think of no finer regiment in which to work out his National Service. The men got the chance to work with magnificent locomotives pulling rakes of venerable but attractive coaching stock, operate powerful steam cranes and set their minds to the task of how to build a bridge or gauge the materials needed for a track-laying project or studying the complexities of the signalling systems used by various European countries. If called to war they would still be in danger, but at least some distance behind the chaps driving tanks and placing themselves in the firing line. It was the job of the engineers to repair damage from aerial bombing and find logistical solutions for moving vast quantities of supplies using whatever equipment they could lay their hands upon. As Mordon memorably observed to his driver as they backed one of the giant 2-10-0 engines onto a rake of coaches which for that day's exercise was to be considered as an ambulance train, 'We get to fix up what they blow up, then ferry the dying back from the front line. Got to be better than being one of the poor bleeding buggers in the train!'

Mordon had a youthful zest for life, and his bubbling enthusiasm for the railway quickly endeared him to his superiors. He was always willing and never shied from a task.

'Why would I, sir? Firing and driving one of these lovely machines and keeping them in tip-top condition is a dream for a working-class lad like me!'

Ever since he was small, Mordon had loved trains and some of his fondest memories were from the tail end of the war when his mother or elder sister could be persuaded to take him to watch the endless succession of filthy black steamers slogging through Sheffield's bustling main station. If the women were in a good mood, they might buy him a platform ticket and leave him there for a few hours, safe and content whilst they made forays into the city to queue for scarce goods. Otherwise, when free from school, he would run down to the smoke-blackened and polluted environs of the Lower Don Valley at Tinsley to watch even grubbier engines hard at in on unfeasibly long coal and ore trains or hauling wagons laden with forged steel from the rolling mills. It often made for dramatic scenes as these locomotives battled with over-weight trains in their attempt to supply the insatiable war effort.

It was therefore unsurprising he grew up wanting to work on the railways, preferably as a fireman, with the expectation of working up to becoming a driver. He also wanted to be part of something more than just a peacetime railway. During the war years, he'd envied the men working all hours trying to get vital supplies through despite constant hold-ups and delays, bomb damage and failing engineering. It was a romantic notion of man and machine pitted against the odds, but it sowed a seed in his mind, so when National Service beckoned there was only one place he wanted to be.

He argued his case convincingly, demonstrating an aptitude for mathematics and physics and a good understanding of mechanics and machinery learned through borrowing every book he could find in the local library. His single-minded objective of learning his trade on the Longmoor Military Railway made the recruiting sergeant's job easy. It was rare to find someone so enthusiastic and passed through the process without delay. His occasional breathlessness was mild and infrequent. His explanation that the filthy Sheffield air heavy with iron dust and fumes from the smelting ovens was responsible was accepted without question. The war was over, but the country still needed willing young men.

Almost coincidental with his move into barracks for his first months of basic training, was a blossoming romance with the pretty lass in the Sheffield Victoria station buffet. Whilst not his favourite of the Sheffield stations, Mordon nonetheless made regular visits there to take locomotive numbers, and when possible, speak with the crews to gain insight into how they nurtured and operated their engines. When it was time for a restorative cuppa in the station buffet, he discovered the smiling face and forthright manner of Miss Phyllis Langton started to pull him more frequently towards his 'least favourite station'. Whenever he'd an hour or so free, he would find himself weighing up the odds and being drawn to Sheffield Victoria as if Phyl had a magic magnet in the pocket of her white apron attracting him.

They both loved the railway. She came from a family of railwaymen and the smoke and steam seemed to be in her blood (but more probably her lungs) and this only helped romance blossom. The wedding had been simple and on a budget with a lot of help from the girls in the station buffet who provided ample fish paste or cheese and pickle sandwiches, and her sister baked and iced a nice cake. Both families believed 'the couple were made for each other' and once he was back from his time with the Royal Engineers, he'd be set fair to be signed up by the railway and make the 'top link' in no time at all. A small terrace house in blackened stone on one of the steep streets of Sheffield would surely follow and Phyl dared hope she could manage a growing family whilst still working part-time at Victoria.

Yes, when all was said and done, Mordon was content.

No more so than when he had one of his favourite engines to work on. *Gordon* was massive and painted Royal blue with vibrant scarlet lining in a surprisingly cheerful livery at odds with its military role.

Number 600 had been built in 1943 and Mordon felt an affinity with it because the date on the builder's plate reminded him of those distant days as a young trainspotter. It was a big brute of a machine, designed and assembled under wartime conditions to last just a few years and lacked any attempt at comfort or refinement. It was hammered, riveted and welded together by the North British Locomotive Company as quickly as possible, and there were times when this showed.

It was *Gordon* he was firing, alongside Sergeant Dugald Frazier on driving duties, on the first day of the trials of the new flu-virus he'd had injected into his upper arm. As with so many military operations, this came with a daft code name the forty volunteers had laughed at whilst the doctor from the Porton Down establishment smiled indulgently.

They had been gathered together the day before in one of the large wooden huts used for operational briefings and introduced to Doctor Urban and his team of scientists clad in white lab coats. All eyes in the room however were all on the two female nurses, who were causing quite a stir. The doctor was fully aware of the effect these two women would have on a room of men starved of contact with the fairer sex, and whilst both were fully trained in treating infectious diseases, the nurses were also a powerful inducement to help drum up willing volunteers.

'...the procedure is quick and simple and won't cause a room of hot-blooded lads like you even a moment's worry. And besides, you will have Nurse Jones and Nurse Simpkins to cool your fevered brows once influenza takes hold...'

The room erupted into a roar of cheers and wolf whistles which the doctor did nothing to suppress. Jones and Simpkins were long used to this kind of reception and smiled back, allowing their uniforms to stretch that bit more across their hourglass figures.

'Yes...Yes...Gentlemen! Calm yourselves... Once the injections are administered, which will take only seconds, you will return to your duties as approved in advance by your commanding officer. You will each work alongside someone who has not received the injection. This is deliberate, as part of the exercise is to establish how contagious this strain is and to monitor how quickly it takes effect.'

Oooh!' Another roar from the men, who were in high spirits. Each dreaming of lying in the crisp sheets of the hospital wing with one or other of the two nurses leaning over.

'Once again, I must reassure you. There is absolutely nothing to be concerned about. My team of expert scientists are the very best in their field, and they have created a relatively mild flu - but a very contagious one. Yes, it will make your head fuzzy, you won't be able to concentrate, your legs and arms will feel so weak you cannot stand or work and this will be followed by a short fever and a desire...'

'A desire for Nurse Jones?' More salacious cheers and whistles.

'A desire to *sleep* for about twelve hours or more! Believe me, you won't have any thoughts about anything else!'

More uproarious laughter whilst the cheeks of the two nurses coloured slightly.

'We shall be on hand at all times, day and night, to ensure everyone is given the very best care if needed. Now don't be alarmed, but from the moment we administer the injections until the time the all-clear is given we shall be dressed in protective clothing. It might look intimidating and I am afraid will do absolutely nothing to enhance the admirable figures of our two lovely nurses...'

'No-oo!'

'Shame!'

'Sorry, gents! But we must remain completely virus-free, of course. Now, there will be no public access, even to the more remote locations of the railway. We are not publicly declaring the reason for this exclusion because people will talk about the flu and undoubtedly exaggerate or invent half-truths and the next thing you know there is mass panic. Completely groundless, of course, but you know how some elements of society like to exaggerate and stir up trouble.' A perfunctory smile. 'The camp commander has declared that there is to be a 'military exercise' running over the next month of sufficient importance to exclude any civilian unless given clear written permission. Sentries will be posted at every area of public ingress and you are asked not to leave the base until the all-clear is given and the exercise completed. This will be hard, as some of your colleagues free of the infection might be granted the right to leave, but you are being compensated for your sacrifice.'

Various men gave nods of acceptance others called out they'd be happy enough if the nurses kissed them...

'I cannot promise that, but as previously explained, at the end of the exercise you will all receive ten pounds for your troubles.'

More whoops of excitement.

Mordon had been delighted. A week with a pounding head

and aching muscles was hardly a heavy price for such bounty.

As he coupled up *Gordon*, Mordon was still feeling perfectly healthy and perhaps even a little disappointed that he felt the same as he had before the injection. A view shared by a number of the others. One said his head was 'going a bit fuzzy', but this was dismissed as the effect of the beer drunk in the mess the evening before. A couple of men were coughing, but as it was a freezing January day when the air could set you coughing if you breathed deeply, nobody thought anything of it.

Back in the cab, Mordon was giving the fire some attention. They'd been given a lengthy mixed train of vans and open wagons to take to the locomotive depot. Mordon guessed the cargo would be drums of locomotive oils, refurbished brake blocks and other such essentials needed to keep the fleet operational. He needed a decent head of steam, so Mordon was swinging the shovel with practised ease, landing each load to the front, back and then either side of the white-hot fire. He was a skilled fireman and knew what kind of fire each type of locomotive favoured. His driver was busy oiling around the motion, leaving Mordon alone on the footplate. He dug into the coal, lifted the shovel and turned his upper body and then his head swam, his vision instantly blurred and the shovel clanged unpleasantly against the side of the fire door, spilling coal on the clean wooden floor and creating a nasty bend at the end of the shovel.

'Buggeration!'

Mordon had not made such a foolish mistake since his first week of training. He stood upright, cursing his mistiming and trying to clear a strange woolly feeling in his head and little stars swimming before his eyes. He staggered backwards as his legs suddenly lost their strength. 'Oh...' He leaned on the cab side sheet and took a deep breath but instantly started coughing violently. He'd probably gulped in some of the dark smoky air curling around as a result of the fresh coal on the fire.

Shaking his head and managing to control the coughing, he pulled himself upright and made another attempt with his shovel, dreading the look he would get from his driver. His annoyance was not lessened by the presence of one of the observers from the Porton Down team. They were standing just a short distance away, clad in a gas mask, thick gauntlets and a gas-suit coverall, silently watching his every move. Mordon was glad they'd been warned to expect these menacing-looking figures with the rhythmic breathing of their air filtration system.

He tried to dig the shovel into the coal, but his arms lacked the strength in one move, and he needed to slide it deeper underneath, but then struggled to lift the load. *This is stupid!* He was now breathing hard, his arms refusing to do what he asked of them. He finally got the shovel in the air, turned, and toppled backwards, the coal once again falling uselessly onto the cab floor. He lay on his back staring up at the bleak winter sky beyond the cab roof, the silver stars now brighter and more confusing behind his eyes. He wanted to get up, but his chest felt as if a metal band was around it and he was finding it hard to get his breath. He just needed to lie here a moment…

The round staring eyes of the masked medic appeared over the side of the cab, breath hissing through the filter. Rubber gloved hands reached out to help Mordon into a sitting position. Mordon tried to peer beyond the circles of glass to find the human being inside, but all he could see were reflections of his pale face.

This was not the enticing vision of raven-haired Mary with her generously heaving bosom or the lithe but equally charming bottle-blonde Alice they'd been promised. This was expressionless and impassive inhuman mask accompanied by the overriding smell of rubber.

Mordon rallied briefly in the isolation wing created

especially for the trials in the army medical centre, even managing to write a letter to his beloved wife as the sweat poured from his brow but, the effort of even this proved too much and he lapsed into semi-consciousness. He died two days later.

Chapter Three
Sheffield Victoria

Vignoles took WPC Benson with him to Sheffield Victoria on a train hauled by *Prince of Wales,* one of the now ageing 'Director' class of locomotives. The venerable engine was in shabby condition, giving the impression it was painted many shades of charcoal grey. Someone had at least rubbed a damp cloth over the cab side to reveal the faded number '62662'. It was a dispiriting sight under the lowering winter clouds and would surely bring little cheer to the notoriously unappealing Sheffield Victoria. An unlovely station with glazed platform awnings coated in coal and iron dust long congealed to an opaque layer thanks to the frequent Yorkshire rain.

Vignoles infrequently ventured this far north, and whilst preoccupied with his curious mission, he was perhaps one of the few passengers on board who could find the bleak industrial landscape compelling on this cheerless day. Collieries and steelworks seemed to dominate the hard landscape interlaced by vast arrays of railway sidings, sharply curving industrial branch lines, odd corners of tatty wasteland filled with sickly grasses and pieces of abandoned engineering trapping drifts of pale snow turning grey. Nearly every siding was occupied by lines of coal or iron ore wagons, often attended by black locomotives whilst compact industrial engines in the service of the collieries or steelworks shunted and pushed and pulled ancient wagons, some heaped with steaming ash.

As the spinning wheels of the pit head winding gear of Nunnery Colliery drifted into sight, Vignoles knew they were close. *Prince of Wales* threaded the train through yet more ranks of sidings, the scale of which prompted Benson into passing comment. 'It's all heavy industry around here. Smoke and fire and ash everywhere. It feels like we're entering a different world!'

'We are, Jane; Yorkshire!' Vignoles quipped. 'They're proud people and like to think of themselves as a bit different from the rest of the country.'

'They may have a point...' Benson was watching as the train rattled over a bridge crossing the Sheffield & South Yorkshire Navigation, which looked poisonously grey and sluggish. 'And I thought Frog Island was bad.' She tried to peer above the pungent gasometers and smoking chimneys of the Effingham Street Gas Works towards the snowy white hilltops on the edge of the city, but smog and cloud offered only brief glimpses.

It did not take them long to walk to the long run of Victorian dwellings that lined one side of Aston Street that stretched a considerable distance towards Nunnery Colliery's towering slag heaps. The Mordon's rented flat was above an electrical repair shop about halfway along the terrace with its front door leading straight onto a steep flight of stairs.

Phyllis Mordon was a nineteen-year-old with brown hair, hazel eyes and a narrow nose and chin that gave her a slightly mousey appearance. There was a youthful vitality about her, however, and if not classically beautiful, she had undeniable charm. Neither was she timid like the mouse she slightly resembled. The front door was opened wide in answer to their ring and the appearance of police on her doorstep didn't appear to cause her a moment's concern.

'Best get yer'selves inside as its raw wi' door open,' and without any further ado, trotted up the creaky stairs with a shout to 'shut it behind yer! Give it a slam, as frame's warped!'

Mugs of strong tea in hand, they sat in her sitting room that overlooked the rear of the property. A gas fire fizzed and kicked out a fierce heat. Benson looked out of the soot-stained window at a sunken railway cutting. This was crossed by an ugly metal bridge carrying yet more rails, with both sets of tracks immediately burrowing into dark tunnel mouths that were slowly exhaling spent locomotive smoke as if from open mouths. In the far distance, a soap and grease factory belched noxious steam into the air from behind the massive box-like shape of a railway warehouse. The air in the room felt stale and humid, but as yet more puffs of dirty smoke rose from a train passing below, she could appreciate why she kept the windows closed.

'That why I 'ad me shift changed, so yer could see me at 'ome?'

'Yes. I telephoned through last night. We felt it more appropriate to talk with you in private.'

'Aye, well it makes no odds when I work...' She sipped some tea and gave Vignoles a firm stare across the top of her steaming mug. 'Let's face it, I've no one to answer to now, 'ave I? Worst luck...'

Expressions of condolence were offered.

She shook her head is if rejecting their well-intended words. 'What d'you want me to say? Thanks! You reckon that makes me feel any better?' She closed her eyes for a moment. 'Sorry, that weren't fair...' She took a breath then addressed Vignoles. 'You going to tell me wor 'appened to my fella? I've had next to nowt from the Army. Just a few lines in a letter and a telegram. Not much for losing an 'usband, is it?' She lit a cigarette and flopped back into the one armchair the flat was provided with.

Vignoles steadied his voice and launched into the carefully prepared statement Doctor Urban and Lombard from the MOD had fed him. Vignoles was no doctor let alone microbiologist, so was in no place to challenge the facts as presented, but his detective brain wouldn't rest easy. He instinctively didn't trust either man. He'd replayed the curious meeting in Badger's office and the briefing session that followed countless times in his mind, and whilst confident the basic outline of the story was factually correct, he sensed he was still not being fed the whole story. He had an unpleasant feeling the three of them now seated in the upstairs room were just pawns in a larger chess game. He was not convinced Badger was anything less than an expendable chess piece either. Vignoles felt frustrated he'd been forced to be circumspect with WPC Benson.

However, he had been ordered to give almost nothing away and so the intelligent WPC seated opposite could only privately wonder why they were making a trip which appeared to have no obvious connection to their work. The whole thing felt like a charade and Vignoles was hating every minute of it. '...and therefore, it transpires it was a tragic combination of circumstances. The medical evidence is clear in that your husband's asthma contributed significantly to his untimely death.'

'Not forgetting 'e was jabbed full of flu!'

'He willingly volunteered to the trial...'

'Well, that's as mebbe, but if they hadn't gone messing about with nature and inventing things best left alone, he'd still be right as rain. What do you say to that?' She left that hanging in the air and smoked in silence for a moment then stubbed the cigarette out with force. 'They twisted his arm. That's what they did. Got him to agree to summat e' knew nothing about.' There were passion and steel to her voice now. 'And 'e were not alone. They put pressure on lots o' young lads that were in no place to say no. It's not right!'

'Did your husband tell you he was coerced into taking part in the field trial?' Vignoles asked.

'He told me about it. Well, told me about the money side of it, leastways. Said 'e were gettin' ten pound for his trouble. That's a lot of money for the like of us. Look at this place! We could do with a bit extra. How could he turn that down? It's like winning the pools. Come off it, inspector, 'e was no keener on getting flu than you or I. It's not nice, flu.' She glared at the two of them in turn. 'Either of you ever 'ad it?'

'Just the once,' Vignoles confessed.

'Right. So, you'll know how horrid it is then. Nobody who's

32

had it would ask to be given it, deliberate. Just read the papers. There's more of it on the way this winter, so we don't need scientists giving out more! It's madness...' Her cheeks were gaining colour as the talked, her voice full of passion. 'My Ian had never had it, but I did when I was twelve. I thought I was going to die. I told him, but the money won.'

Vignoles nodded sympathetically. He could readily imagine the conversation. 'Did your husband tell you what the test entailed? Did he explain who was conducting the test and what the outcome was expected to be?'

'No... He said it was secret and run by scientists and doctors from some military place down in the South West.'

'Can you remember the name of it?'

'No... Something Downs. I dunno. Can't remember. Why you askin'?'

'I just want to appreciate how clearly you both understood the situation. We, that is, The Royal Engineers, wish to be sure that proper procedures were followed and that volunteers and their dependents were all made aware of the risks, no matter how small these are for the majority.'

'I might say different...'

Vignoles privately steeled himself for the lie that was coming. 'Of course. The Army appreciates your feelings.' Phyllis Mordon shook her head and looked away. 'The Army wishes to compensate you for your tragic loss once I have established that your husband was correctly briefed and advised about the potential risks in advance of the trials commencing.'

'Compensation? You can start by handing a couple of fivers over for starters!' She snorted with derision. 'Paying me off, is that name of the game, then?'

'It is only proper that the Army ensures you are looked after financially. It won't bring your husband back, of course...'

'Bloody right!' She looked down at the threadbare carpet. Red spots appearing on her pale cheeks. 'Sorry, I did not mean to use language. You must think me cheap and badly brought up… I'm not like that.' She wiped a tear from her eye.

'We think nothing of the sort, Mrs Mordon.' Benson was sympathetic.

'I didn't just lose him. They didn't even let me give him a proper send-off. A funeral. His wife. And then his parents and brother an' all. No one was there. They just…' She wiped a tear away. 'They just put his ashes in an urn and said it would be brought to me next week. Why did they have to do that?' She looked imploringly at Benson. 'Could I not 'ave said goodbye one last time? What was the hurry? I would have used the money to pay for it.' Her voice was quiet and lacking the bite of a moment ago.

Vignoles felt his throat constrict and he swallowed some tea before risking speaking. 'It is regrettable. As part of the controlled testing situation, the MOD couldn't release the body and to maintain the strict quarantine conditions currently enforced at Longmoor as part of these field tests, it proved necessary to follow that line of action.' Vignoles was hating this even more than he'd feared. Just speaking the words made the whole situation reek of deceit. There was something wrong and he was being ordered to create the cover-up.

'But it were just flu?'

'Is that what he told you?' This was the heart of the matter and Vignoles had to follow this up. 'Mrs Mordon, Phyllis, what exactly did your husband say about the trials?'

'He just said it was a new type of flu. I can't remember anything more.'

'If you could please just tell me as accurately as possible everything he said - or perhaps he wrote to you?'

'It was not long after the New Year. He'd gone back after a few days together here. He telephoned and told me about it. But 'e was more excited about the money than the jab. He didn't want to talk about what he had to do to get the money.'

'Did he write to you and tell you more?'

'No, I told yer. I just got one postcard and nowt else since he went back. He was never a great one for letters.'

This was a relief. They were not going to have to take precious letters away only for the MOD to destroy them. Lance Corporal Mordon's infrequent letter writing was a blessing in disguise.

Vignoles outlined the Army widow's pension she would receive, then handed over a cheque for thirty pounds. Phyllis Mordon looked overwhelmed. Tears gathered in her eyes. 'I suppose I should be thankful. It's 'ard to feel it, though.'

It was a relief to escape into the bracing air once again.

Vignoles and Benson hurried back to Sheffield Victoria, eager to take refuge in the station buffet and tuck into some warm food. Vignoles also wanted to gently sound out Phyllis Mordon's colleagues in the pleasingly warm and steamy buffet and gauge how much they'd been told about the death of her husband.

'Sir, what exactly are we doing here?' Benson could no longer curb her curiosity.

Vignoles tucked into his plate of bacon, sausage, eggs and fried bread having decided that having skipped a decent breakfast it was perfectly fine to have a large one now. Comforting food was something he was craving in the hope he could replace the unpleasant sensation in the pit of his stomach. He considered his answer to Benson's query.

'Honestly, Jane, I'm not sure. I know what I was *instructed* to do, and this has been executed as ordered. Hopefully to the satisfaction of Badger and some other persons who must remain nameless.'

'Others?'

Vignoles liked Jane Benson and respected her intelligence and ability as a valued WPC. It was a matter of chagrin there were many within the Home Office and the Transport Police, who did not wish to see women, no matter how able, climb the ladder and make a detective grade - perhaps beyond. Benson had all the attributes of a fine detective sergeant and he wished he could help her achieve this position. Vignoles didn't like withholding even basic operational information from her it would be professionally dishonest and potentially dangerous to share restricted information with her.

'We are helping the Army and some other agencies. The Royal Engineers agreed to the testing of a new flu-type virus being developed - that much you already know. I have been reassured it is as benign as flu can be. In other words, it is pretty rotten to catch, but won't in itself, kill you...'

'Enough people seem to be catching it at the moment. The news keeps mentioning this *Asiatic flu* that's arrived. It sounds like a nasty one. Some experts claim it's lethal.'

'And it's mid-winter. These seasonal outbreaks are common and when the news is thin the papers like to make more of these stories than perhaps is deserved. Viruses favour cold weather - and slow news days.' Vignoles smiled and tried to make light of it. 'One extra strain trialled at The Longmoor Military Railway probably won't make much odds. This poor chap died due to unforeseen complications and it is also true any dose carries some danger. I just think the Army is smarting over an embarrassingly awkward situation and eager to keep a lid on it.

'And keep the widow quiet?'

'The money and pension will at least see her right. The settlement is generous.'

'I liked Phyllis Mordon,' Benson replied, tactfully choosing not to challenge her superior over his avoidance of the question. 'She's a character and bright with it. She knew she was being paid to say nothing; she just has to put up and shut up. You're right, sir, thirty pounds will go a good way together with a pension. But why not send someone from his regiment to do this? They could at least pretend they knew her dead husband.' Vignoles said nothing. 'You were quizzing her about how much she knew of this trial, but there was little to engage someone of your ability...'

Chapter Three

Vignoles continued to eat his late breakfast. What could he answer? What was he allowed to say? He was however enjoying the plate of fried food in the gentle bustle of the buffet.

Rivulets of condensation running down the windows offered a distorted view of the platform outside and Vignoles peered through to watch the life of the station unfold. It all felt pleasingly normal and inconsequential, and yet ever since leaving Marylebone he'd carried with him a low-level sensation of unease. A nagging feeling that something was wrong and whatever it was, it was bad.

What was he missing? What could be prompting this feeling? He'd been summoned to odd meetings before and confronted by plenty of 'top brass' calling the shots and demanding he obey and not ask too many questions, so surely this was not enough to stir this sense of unease. Vignoles listened as someone across the room erupted into an unstoppable coughing fit, finally forced to stand, scraping their chair across the floor and retreat outside.

His skin felt itchy, probably because of the contrast between the January cold outside and the humid warmth inside, but he suspected it was also because one of the things he had especially disliked about the meeting in Badger's office were the establishments represented. The Microbiological Research Department and the Chemical Defence Experimental Establishment were secretive places. Their names alone carried with them all manner of rumours and unsettling stories of blood-curdling experiments with dangerous microbes. Almost certainly unfounded tittle-tattle of the kind generated by a place deemed 'top secret,' and yet, even the descriptive titles alone made the hairs on his arms and neck stand up. Toxins, deadly viruses, the bubonic plague and Sarin gas… He'd heard enough over the years to appreciate these were not establishments he wished to visit out of choice. Nor would anyone want any of these organisms to escape the confines of the laboratories.

That was the crux of the matter. Porton Down had taken what he thought was an unusual step of carrying one of their ungodly conceptions out of the intense security of their building - and let it loose. The so-called experts and politicians could give any number of reassurances, but these virulent organisms cared nothing for human life. They followed their course and listened to nobody.

Vignoles shook his head to clear away this disturbing thought and was aware that Benson, whilst busy polishing off her own fry-up, was giving him a curious look. He changed tack. 'I rarely see these…' He waved an empty fork towards the steamed-up window, beyond which could be seen the shape of an electric locomotive that had pulled, almost silently, into the station.

It was as glossy black as a raven's back and attractively lined out in thin red, cream and grey lines. As a piece of industrial design, it was perhaps more akin to a shoebox than a locomotive, but its alien appearance was so very different from the familiar steam engines that this made it intriguing. It sat motionless like a giant cubic toad, making little odd clicks and clacks in sequences that held no obvious logic. It was impossible to tell how it moved, only that it issued strange sounds.

'I've never seen one before. Do they go to Manchester?'

'Yes, through the Woodhead Tunnel and across very difficult and steep terrain. This type haul passenger trains, but most of the traffic these DC electrics locos haul are heavy coal trains.'

Vignoles continued to look at *Aurora* for a few moments longer, enjoying the calming sensation of harmlessly studying a locomotive, but then broke his silence by speaking quietly, so only Benson could hear.

'I am constrained in what I can say. Hence the motive behind today's adventure has been kept vague.' He offered her a friendly smile. 'We need fresh tea and coffee and so I'd like you to strike up a conversation with the two ladies behind the counter. They work with Mrs Mordon. Gently does it but see if you can get them to offer an opinion on what befell their friend's husband.'

'Righty-ho, sir!' Benson was glad to have something to do. She'd suspected there was more to this than met the eye and eager to do her best.

Chapter Four
Leicester Central

'That you Vignoles?' The voice bellowed down the telephone.

'Speaking...' He was trying to place the voice.

'Bernard Minshul. Northern Division, Sheffield!'

'Of course, DI Minshul. It has been some time since we last spoke.'

'DCI now! Just like you!' He laughed generously. 'Enough of the small talk. I heard you've been up my way?'

'You heard correctly.'

'My sources are impeccable. I even know you brought that buxom WPC with yer an' all. Now, aside from being mortified you denied me the pleasure of making her reacquaintance, I'm trying not to 'ave my nose put out of joint because you didn't see fit to tell me you were about my neck o' the woods.'

'I assure you I meant no offence.'

'Mebbe not, but you were making enquiries about railway personnel on railway property without so much as a thought you were treading on my size 10's. That can't be right, Vignoles.'

'My apologies. I was following orders that demanded strict levels of discretion. WPC Benson was only given the sketchiest outline and my sergeant has been effectively cut out. It is an imperfect situation.'

'Didn't stop your lass asking questions of the girls in the buffet...'

'It did not.' Minshul's sources were indeed impeccable. 'They were low-level queries that revealed nothing.'

'Look, we work for the same people. It's not my job to muscle in on summat that's come from a stuffed shirt in Marylebone, but if you don't ask the men on the ground for help, you're liable to miss a trick or two.'

'I appreciate that, but my orders were explicit. The Official

Secrets Act was quoted, and I even had to sign some kind of extra security addendum.'

Minshul whistled low. 'Well, I signed the OSA an' all, so you can trust me not to go blabbin'. Sorry, I don't mean to chew yet head off, but cut me some slack, will yer?'

'Sorry, Bernard, my hands are tied.' Vignoles was trying his best to mollify the blustering Yorkshireman.

'I'll come at it another way then. We're on a phone line that's probably as leaky as the sieve my missus uses to strain the veg, so we'd best be circumspect -.'

'We had.'

'I know your interest was a lass by the name of Phyllis. Phyl, to everyone who knew her. She served food in our cracking little buffet. It does an absolute joy of a breakfast fry-up.'

'I tasted it.' Vignoles was gripping the telephone that bit tighter. He didn't like the use of the past tense.

'We need to meet. Somewhere in the middle. Nottingham Vic will do fine. Get there as fast as you can.'

'I could do with more information as to why?'

'You need more? That's a bit rich. You've not been listening to me rabbiting on these past five minutes? The young girl in question has just been dragged out of a canal. Stone cold dead. I'll see you in the bar at Vic. We'll both need a drink.'

The line went dead.

* * * *

As he was leaving the office, Vignoles asked Mavis Green, who acted as secretary, gatekeeper, message carrier and main biscuit provider for the Detective Department in Leicester Central, what had happened to DS Mellor.

'At home with a bad cold. Lots of people are going down with it.'

'Not the *Asiatic flu*, I hope?'

'I doubt it. Mind you, being a man, he'll make out it was as bad!' She laughed. 'Blocked nose and sneezing. A head cold. Told him to stay away or we'd all catch it.'

'Very wise.'

This played out well. Vignoles was not comfortable shutting his DS out of…out of *what*? Whatever it was he found himself in, Mellor was as yet unaware and uninformed. It was not ideal, but with Mellor at home for another day it bought Vignoles a time to assess what was going on and by the sound of it, things had just taken a very nasty turn for the worse.

With a grim set to his face, Vignoles boarded a slow all stations 'stopper' to Nottingham Victoria with a sinking sensation that however the MOD might wish it to be defined, was fast turning into something dark and sinister. But shocking though it was, a dead body made Vignoles feel like he was at least stepping into familiar territory.

* * * *

DCI Bernard Minshul was perhaps a touch fatter around the waistline since they'd last met. His lank oily hair was still combed over in a few desperate strands that fooled nobody but himself. He was practically bald. He still smoked like a chimney, had a bellowing voice and a pleasing twinkle in his eye. He was a man who knew how to unwind after a busy day and was always ready to take advantage of a pint whenever the licensing laws allowed and not averse to occasionally twisting a landlord's arm if these hours didn't fit his need. Vignoles suspected Minshul was on his second pint when he joined him in the moodily lit bar in the station.

'I'll get these, Vignoles. I've found us a quiet corner where nobody can overhear.'

Vignoles was happy to accept the pint which he recognised as a symbol of goodwill from his peer. Minshul was a blustering type with a reputation for bawling out junior officers and with mannerisms that annoyed others, but his heart was in the right place and he could be generous and forgiving.

'Tell me about Phyllis Mordon. I'll listen and then judge what I can offer in return.' Vignoles supped some beer and started to fill his pipe.

'She was fished out by the Sheffield City boys, first thing today. A cyclist along the canal path spotted her sometime after 6 am. I know this because they came to Victoria making enquiries, although with less grace than your lovely WPC managed. I got wind there was summat going on and called a detective I'm pally with.' He sucked on his cigarette, then continued speaking whilst blowing smoke out at the same time. 'Face down in the water, so there was no mistaking she was dead.'

'Where was this?'

'Just a step from Victoria. The rail tracks cross the Navigation and she was lying in the water not far from the bridge. She'd got a foot tangled in some rubbish in the water so had not floated away.'

Vignoles remembered Benson commenting whilst looking down on the oily waters from their train.

'They hooked her out fully dressed and as far they could tell, unmolested. After a bit of poke around in the bushes close by, the plod found her handbag, house keys and her address on an envelope, so within an hour were able to give her a name.'

'A robbery?'

'Her purse was still in her flat, so maybe someone snatched the bag and pushed her in the canal at the same time but got bugger all for their trouble.'

'How was she dressed?'

'Blue dress, stockings, winter coat and scarf and hat. None of that would have helped her get out of the water. Her hat was found downstream.'

'She was wearing a blue dress when we visited...' Vignoles

observed. 'She was dressed as one would expect for someone taking a walk, for a bit of fresh air perhaps. She took her handbag but no purse, as she was not planning on visiting a corner shop?'

'I agree, but here's the thing. The City lads are now saying this is pointing to suicide. You don't need your purse if you're out to drown yourself.'

'Nor house keys.' Vignoles took a deep swig of beer, brow furrowed.

'Aye, that's true.'

'Was there a suicide note?'

'Not that they found.'

'There won't be.'

'Why d'you say that?'

'Because Mrs Mordon didn't kill herself. I sat and talked with her on the same day. She had a strong personality and made of sterner stuff than to walk out of the house a few hours later and throw herself in a canal.' He could visualise the unappealing water and someone would need to be in a desperate state to even consider that an option. Turning on the gas oven and leaving the windows fastened tight would surely be preferable. 'She was upset about the death of her husband - it would be strange for her not to be. But she was coping and back at work. She shed a tear but no waterworks and far from a broken woman.'

'I trust your opinion.' Minshul tasted his pint, dragged on his cigarette and gave Vignoles a beady look. 'But there's more…'

Vignoles had his pipe lit. 'Tell me.'

'They've already done the PM and had a preliminary chat with the coroner, who's decided he'll move for suicide.'

'So quickly? But surely they've hardly started looking into the circumstances?'

'I know. And if you ask me, there's summat wrong. I smell a rat. They've been too quick. It's too neat. The family have already identified her and been sold a story about how distraught she was, blah blah blah. Case closed.'

'She was not distraught. I cannot accept suicide. I share your misgivings. We talked about how her husband died at the Longmoor Military Railway -.'

'- I hadn't heard he was based there.'

'Lance Corporal in the Royal Engineers. Part of my remit was to advise her she was to get a widow's pension and a golden handshake from the MOD.'

'What kind of money are we talking?'

'Thirty pounds and a decent monthly income.'

'Blummin' 'eck, I'd have someone bump my missus off if you were handing me that kind of money!' Minshul drained his pint. 'Thirty smackers and a pension on top and she wanted to drown herself?'

'Exactly. Hush money they call it in pulp fiction.'

'Easy come, easy go...'

'They gave with one hand...'

'...and took with the other.'

The two men stared at each other in silence for a moment.

'They never intended her to cash the cheque nor claim that pension.'

'A suicide or a mugging that turned nasty. Either way, these are easy cases to close.' Vignoles felt that cold chill down his spine again. 'We need another pint.'

Minshul nodded assent. His bluster had transformed into something more introspect and thoughtful. Whilst he waited for Vignoles to return from the bar, he smoked and observed who else was nearby. All were men, as to be expected and he gave each scrutiny. He was sure he'd made the correct decision to meet somewhere where two men could sit and talk and not attract suspicion whilst remaining in a public space. It felt safer like this.

'The implication of what we just shared is too extraordinary to be credible. If true, it would imply State-sanctioned murder.'

Vignoles spoke quietly. Not only to ensure he could not be overheard but because he could hardly bring himself to speak the words.

'Bloody Hell!'

'No, we must be wrong. We're making assumptions based on almost no evidence about the crime. There is undoubtedly another explanation.'

'Aye, we're working on second-hand data. Unsafe and unwise,' Minshul was also trying to convince himself they were barking up the wrong tree.

Both men lifted their glasses and drank.

'Tell me something you know as fact. Tell me about the husband. It was because he died you and your bonny lass paid her a house call, so he's got to be part of the story.'

Vignoles weighed up the odds. 'Be careful how you handle what I tell you. I suggest the City are kept in the dark.'

Minshul looked surprised. 'Fine by me. They treat us like second-rate coppers anyway.'

Vignoles outlined what he knew about Lance Corporal Mordon and his part in the experimental field trials at The Longmoor Military Railway.

'He died of flu?'

'Combined with asthma which he'd developed and hidden during his time on the engines.'

'An' you believe that? There's summat more to this. There's nowt odd about him kicking the bucket over a dose of flu. Have you not been reading the papers, Charlie? There's an outbreak down south. Typical soft Southerners, can't handle it and dropping like flies, so what's the big deal about one more? Sad, but daft.'

Vignoles stared into his beer, mind racing. 'It was a new strain. A man-made virus.'

'Give over...'

'I really shouldn't tell you this, but I need an ally. Someone I can trust and someone not to a part of the more secretive wings of the Ministry of Defence. Give me your word you'll treat this with the utmost caution?'

'You've my word.'

'Mordon was injected with a new strain of virus developed for military purposes designed to incapacitate an enemy army.'

Minshul stared at Vignoles for a moment. 'But it killed him?'

'Indirectly.'

'And pigs might fly! Then they sent you up to Sheffield to pacify his missus and pour a heap of gold into her lap to keep quiet?'

'I fear that might be true.'

'But was it enough? They needed her silent. Forever.'

'We cannot say that, Bernard. She knew very little. I was instructed to press her on what she'd learned. Her husband had broken orders and spoken to her, but she knew nothing more than the men were offered money for their part in the trials. I reported this back. There was no reason to doubt her word.'

'Others thought different.'

'It could be a coincidence. Look, what do I know about her true mental state? Perhaps she was closer to the edge than I imagined?'

'You're an experienced DCI and that means you can read someone and read them accurately.'

'But if she was not a security risk it makes no sense to kill her.'

'Where exactly is this military railway?'

'Hampshire. It runs between Liss and Bordon and a few places between.'

'Anywhere near Haslemere or Farnham?'

'I'm not exactly sure of the geography, but I think it cannot be far away. Why?'

'Ten people died in Haslemere yesterday. From a sudden flu outbreak. This young lady didn't know the specifics, but she knew her hubby died from a man-made virus in Hampshire.

People have suddenly started to contract it and now dying in towns and villages in the same county. Makes we wonder.'

Vignoles nodded thoughtfully as he chewed this over. 'In time she would have talked to her friends and family. About the life-changing income, the Army had gifted her. She said it herself, that we were buying her off. She was no fool,' Vignoles gulped down more beer. 'A senior military figure showed me a letter they intercepted that Mordon had tried to post to his wife. As he passed it over, he told me they'd disinfected it. That sounded odd, but I didn't question why they felt the need.'

'Taking no risks.'

They sat in silence again and smoked.

'What do we do now?' Minshul felt stunned.

'Could you get the PM report on Phyllis Mordon?'

'It'll be hard. She died close to railway property, but far enough away to cut me out of the investigation. Unless I can wangle some reason why we need a look-see. I'll try to convince my pal to let me take a look. Could you do the same with the soldier's PM? It might make interesting reading.'

'I doubt I can. The brick wall of the top brass and secretive scientists I faced will be a hard defence to breach. We'd best keep this under our hats and reconvene in a day or so and see how the land lies?'

'I'll drink to that!' And Minshul drained his pint.

Chapter Five
Leicester Central

Vignoles had been in a pensive mood on the trip back to Leicester Central and now sat alone in his office idly doodling on a notepad. Jotting down odd words and short phrases and making connections between them with arrows and looping lines. He didn't like what he saw. The implications were disturbing. He sat upright, pulled out a box of Swan Vesta's and burned the page in his desk ashtray until it was ash.

'Benson! Could you step in here?'

WPC Benson stood almost at attention on the far side of his desk, looking smart in her uniform. Her impeccable presentation and attentive demeanour brought Vignoles some welcome reassurance that his own team were trustworthy and decent coppers who didn't indulge in sinister assassinations.

'Sir?'

'At ease, Jane. Take a seat.' Once settled, he continued. 'Phyllis Mordon. We discussed her on the journey back, but after a night to chew everything over has your assessment modified?'

'No, sir. I still believe she's a pleasant, self-assured young lady. Tough, but not hard, if you take my meaning?'

'Do you mean mentally strong?'

'I would say so. She's feeling the pain of her loss and it's heartfelt, but she's hardly about to throw in the towel.'

Vignoles nodded. 'Did you observe anything that suggested she was severely depressed?'

'Far from it. She shed a tear and gave us a piece of her mind. But I liked her for that.'

'Not bottling everything up?'

'No?'

'If I told you she walked out of her flat that evening,

dressed as we saw her but with a winter coat and hat and handbag then drowned herself in that slimy canal, what would you think?'

'Impossible! I cannot believe she would do that.'

'Neither can I. I'm sorry to say she was found face down in the water this morning. Presumed to have died the evening before. Her handbag was discarded close by. The Sheffield City Police are moving for suicide.'

'If she fell into icy cold water weighted down with her winter clothes, it *is* plausible. A tragedy.'

'Do you believe that, Jane?'

'Given the facts as you present them, I must. But you think differently?'

'She could have gone for a walk to clear her mind and met an unsavoury character.'

'She chose to walk beside that horrid canal in the dark? Perhaps unwise.'

'That industrial environment surrounded her home in all directions, so she had few obvious options.'

'A misplaced step in the dark? Or a sudden push by a cold-hearted mugger who refused to help her once in the water would both fit what you've told me...' Benson was processing the information.

'I am seeking complexity when the simplest explanation is usually the correct one. Thank you.'

Once Benson had left, he telephoned Badger.

'Vignoles?'

'Have you heard Mrs. Mordon was found dead this morning? Drowned in a canal. The Sheffield force consider it suicide.'

'That is a surprising development. Or perhaps not? The recent loss of a husband could have prompted such an action.'

'With a good pension and golden handshake. She had plenty of life left to live and an income to ensure a far better quality of life. Neither Benson nor I considered her a suicide risk.'

'What are you implying?' Badger's voice was level and cold.

'I spoke with DCI Minshul. He shares the same opinion. Some aspects of the investigation by the Sheffield City force appear rushed.'

'Are you implying improper procedure from Sheffield City Police?'

'I have insufficient information to consider such an allegation, only that the speed of the PM and advice to the coroner to move for suicide through drowning feels hasty and there are significant points unexplained by that interpretation.'

'You would be wise to stay your hand casting aspersions on another force.'

'May I ask we get sight of the PM report for Phyllis Mordon? Minshul will be telephoning you asking the same.'

'I can't see the why we should get sight of it.'

Vignoles ignored the reply. 'I would also like to see the PM report on Lance Corporal Mordon.'

'You will need a very strong argument to support that request.'

'I would feel happier if we had a clearer grasp of the facts of this case. Not the version filtered through the MOD.'

There was a silence on the line for a moment. 'I will accept we have been left short in regard to the information they shared. We should however trust that the best people in their fields are dealing with this.'

'And they have vested interests in reaching a certain conclusion. A neat and tidy job of keeping Phyllis Mordon quiet.'

'I do not like that implication. Not one bit!' Badger's voice was icy cold.

'Neither do I, sir. I urge you to bring what influence you can so, at the very least, we can see the specifics of how this couple lost their lives. It would settle my mind and lay to rest what are probably just unfounded misgivings.'

'Let me see what I can do.' That was as far as Badger would

go, and Vignoles considered it a minor victory. 'Until then, I advise you to keep your mouth firmly shut. Loose talk could play out very badly for you.'

Chapter Six
Leicester Central

Vignoles and his wife, Anna stood together on the platform at Leicester Central waiting for the train on the short run to Belgrave & Birstall station that lay on the northern edge of the city.

They were both wrapped up against the chilling east wind whipping under the platform canopy before clawing its way through even the heaviest winter coats. Tiny flakes of icy snow peppered their cheeks like grains of sea salt tossed by a malevolent spirit. Vignoles's vision was becoming impaired by larger snowflakes catching on his spectacles but he decided to wait until inside a warm carriage before attempting to clean them.

'*When the wind is in the east, 'tis neither good for man nor beast.*'

'I'll agree with that, Anna.' Vignoles had timed their rendezvous on the platform to ensure they stood outside for the shortest time possible. He was looking expectantly along the elevated main line for the approach of their train and silently cheered at the swish and twang of signal wires and heavy clunk of a signal arm lifting.

'Bank the fire up when we get in. I'll make us some chicken soup.'

'I like the sound of that, though you normally reserve chicken soup for when one of us is ill.'

'Prevention, not cure.' Anna was huddled in an elegant green Italian woollen coat with a contrasting scarf tied around her chin. Her office in Goods Dispatching was notoriously draughty and the small fire grate never offered sufficient warmth for those seated at their desks all day.

A welcome toot, almost immediately whipped away by the

wind, announced the spirited arrival of their train hurrying into the platform hauled by an L1 class tank engine running backwards, as it was designed to do. The fireman was leaning out of the cab of number 67756, face almost black with the dust flung up from the coal bunker built into the back of the locomotive cab. His eyes and teeth glowed white in the lamp light making him look like one of the Black & White Minstrels currently playing in a variety show at the Floral Hall in Belgrave Gate.

Anna and Charles stepped into a narrow compartment and squeezed into the last spaces available on the bench seats. It was hot inside and the windows steamed over by the combined effect of the steam heating and the breath and cigarette smoke exhaled by the other commuters. Anna was glad of her scarf to help filter the foetid air that smelt of damp wool, stale tobacco, engine smoke and competing brands of scent and aftershave. Newspapers were refolded, throats cleared, and coughs and sneezes punctuated the rhythmic panting of the L1 and the gentle tum-tiddly-tum of wheels on rail joints.

Anna was reading the headlines on the paper held high by a formally dressed city gent opposite and squeezed next to her husband. The headline news was typically downbeat with more concerns raised about the suspected Asian flu outbreak in the south which had claimed another four lives. She narrowed her eyes to try and read the smaller type below and learned that doctors in the Hampshire area were urging citizens to take extra care to cover their mouths and if they felt poorly to take to their beds with plenty of aspirin and a hot water bottle. Their family should steer clear for a day or so until the 'contagious phase had passed.'

A young man sneezed violently in the far corner of the compartment and only then searched for his handkerchief. Papers rattled as others communicated their displeasure. Anna looked at the grubby floor with its pools of water and smeared footprints and tightened the scarf across her nose and mouth.

Chapter Six

A couple of hours later, they were enjoying the comfort of a generous measure of a Highland malt whilst Vera Lynn sang from the expensive valve amplifier and speaker cabinet of their elegant Cossor Radiogram.

'Vera? We've not heard her in a while, Charles.'

Vignoles swirled the golden liquid around in his heavy crystal glass, enjoying the powerful aroma it released. 'I thought she might fit the mood. My mood at least.'

Anna looked quizzical. 'You seem preoccupied. Is it work?'

He nodded. 'I'm sorry. I try to set work aside when I come home, but sometimes it's not easy. An odd case is puzzling me.' He paused and looked deep into the whisky, enjoying how the light refracted from the fire and from the standard lamp behind his chair. 'I have unresolved questions about this case - or perhaps it's two separate, yet related cases?' He shook his head as if that might help make more sense of the puzzle.

'Would it help to try some ideas out on me?'

Vignoles sighed sadly. 'I think it best I don't. I'm concerned that some of the thoughts running around in my head hint at troubling conclusions. They are probably best left unspoken until such time as I can back them up with hard evidence. Sorry, I'm speaking in riddles.'

'That sounds ominous. I presume this is a murder investigation. You don't have to give any details...'

'Is it murder? Ah, now that is the question. Two *deaths* for certain. Two people; man and wife, who both died a short time apart but a long way apart geographically - and in quite different ways. Both can be explained away as misfortune of one kind or another. One was perhaps a mugging that misfired, but some claim was suicide.'

'Oh dear. The couple were living apart?'

'Yes. The husband was working his National Service on a rather interesting railway The Royal Engineers have built in Hampshire, but he fell ill and died due to complications. She survived him a short while but perhaps lost her footing in the dark and plunged into a canal in Sheffield. However, the local police are convinced she threw herself in deliberately, unable to accept the loss of her husband.'

Anna shuddered. 'I think it would take a very disturbed person to attempt - and succeed - in that form of suicide.'

'I agree. To hold one's head under such foul water and allow it to fill the lungs, yet her handbag was found on the bank some distance away. Perhaps a mugging that went badly wrong.'

'Horrible. But why should either cause you to formulate questions of a dark and brooding nature?' Anna queried.

'Yes, just one of those sad events that occur all too often...' Hail rattled on the windowpane and the fire lifted as a gust of wind pulled air through the grate. 'These two events could just be happenstance, and yet I sense they are connected. One leading to the other in sequence. Cause and effect. I hope Mellor is back in the office tomorrow. His refreshingly cynical and questioning nature will pull me back down to earth. He's a thorny personality in some ways, but a decent detective and I appreciate him as a sounding board. My hands are somewhat tied, however. I am not talking about the usual protection of privacy that any case demands.'

Anna raised a questioning eyebrow.

'The Official Secrets Act...'

'For a husband who took ill and a wife who fell in a canal?' Anna was sceptical.

Vignoles put down his tumbler and walked across to flip the record over. 'Everything feels out of proportion. And that niggles me. If there really is something bigger behind what on the surface looks so depressingly ordinary - as many deaths are - that would explain the enhanced secrecy.'

Vera Lynn sang about apple blossom in springtime...

Were those men in Badger's office playing some kind of lethal game? Or had he read too many Ian Fleming books for his own good? There was no 'licence to kill' in the Home or Foreign Office. That was pure fiction and the idea that a governmental office had 'arranged' for Phyllis Mordon to drown was absurd. As wind-born hail clattered around their cosy home he reminded himself that on such a night there was only Coleridge's 'secret ministry of frost' at work.

'What caused the husband to die?' Anna asked. 'Can you say?'

'A short illness.' Vignoles reined in any idea of spilling the beans to Anna. She and her Italian mother had an obsession with common colds, chills and fevers and the draughts they claimed brought them on. If he told her Mordon's death was linked to a new strain of military-grade flu designed to be virulently contagious, he would never hear the end of it. They were due over at his in-laws on Sunday for one of their lengthy and highly enjoyable meals but feared it would descend into an interminable discussion on all things 'influenza,' and the proper avoidance of colds. He smiled reassuringly at Anna as Vera Lynn advised them that there were now 'Bluebirds over the White Cliffs of Dover.'

Chapter Seven
Ashby Magna

DS Mellor was still struggling to shake off his 'bloody awful cold' but when they talked on the telephone that morning, reassured Vignoles he'd be back in the office the following day.

For his part, a good night's sleep had seen Vignoles awaken in a better mood and less preoccupied. He'd barely glanced at that addendum to the Official Secrets Act but could be sure it promised draconian repercussions if he broached the silence it demanded of him. He'd sailed dangerously close to the wind with Anna, but in the privacy of his own house, he felt secure.

Vignoles also appreciated he needed more information before he should risk discussing any of this with his sergeant. He hoped to get news about either of the PM reports today. These might at least give him a clearer understanding of what had happened to the couple and possibly quell the unsubstantiated concerns Minshul and he managed to stir up between them. But when the telephone rang into life it made him jump, and he realised he was still more on edge than he'd given himself credit. Perhaps Badger had managed to pull some strings?

'Detective Chief Inspector Vignoles?' It was an unfamiliar voice.

'Speaking.'

'Wellbeck. Terence. From the CCU.'

Vignoles thought hard. *Who was Wellbeck? And what on earth was the CCU?*

'We met in Marylebone House.'

It came flooding back. . .from the Common Cold Unit.

'Are you alone in the office, Inspector?'

'I am...'

'Good. Listen, I've been chewing things over and think it necessary we speak, *privately*.' Wellbeck's nose was blocked and he abruptly stopped to sneeze. 'Apologies. One of the less attractive sides of working where I do is that we get to test out every new strain of the common cold.'

'I can imagine. We can talk now...'

'No, no, no. Not on the telephone. We need somewhere away from work and other people. A walk in the country would be ideal.'

In this weather? The sky above Leicester was leaden with the threat of snow and the east wind continued to blow with a vengeance.

'It has to be outside. Far safer.'

'As you wish. Ashby Magna. I know a walk beside the railway and only a step away from the station. It is always quiet. Do you know the village?'

'No, but if it's on the line from Marylebone I can find it.'

'Where are you now?' Vignoles could hear the perfectly enunciated tones of a woman's voice amplified so it echoed around a vast space.

'Marylebone. I shall board the first train that stops there and await your arrival, no matter how long that takes.'

'So soon?'

'It is imperative we speak as soon as possible.'

'St Mary's is on top of a small hill, easily visible. We can rendezvous inside the church. It will be unlocked.'

The line clicked and went dead.

Vignoles sat holding the receiver for a moment, then slowly replaced it. What had got into the man? Wellbeck had been part of that extraordinary meeting in Badger's office and that could only mean he wanted to discuss something pertinent to Mordon's death and the field trials. Wellbeck was surely risking everything. That would explain the secrecy. Was Wellbeck even aware that Phyllis Mordon was also dead? Things were starting to take an even more curious twist.

But could this a trap? Vignoles felt a strange prickling sensation on the nape of his neck. He needed to tread carefully and keep his council. A set up to catch him out and evoke the OCA and have him, even if only temporarily, out of action in a prison cell?

Thinking about the brief conversation, the names Ashby Magna and St Mary's church were clear road signs to anyone listening in on the line, although he'd not heard any suspicious click before putting the handset back on the cradle. There again, MI5 would surely be more sophisticated and subtle in their techniques. MI5? What was he thinking? This was no fanciful Cold War thriller. He needed to calm his fervid imagination.

However, as he picked up his hat and shrugged on his overcoat there was the inescapable fact that the man who dabbled in cold cures was in a desperate hurry to tell him something. Vignoles chose to be vague when advising Mavis Green of his whereabouts.

* * * *

'There is something you should understand about the virus that killed Mordon. I won't bore you with technicalities, of which there are a great many.'

Vignoles looked visibly relieved. The intricacies of three-cylinder valve motion on a Gresley V2 locomotive fascinated him, but microbiology left him cold.

'I have obtained more information about those tests Porton Down is conducting at Longmoor.' Wellbeck continued. 'Some of this was obtained by using – some might say, *mis*using - my position to wheedle out more than some should have shared. If it is discovered I've been prying where I shouldn't, I'll be for the high jump.'

'That sounds alarming.'

'Retaining my job is nothing when others are losing their

lives...' He waved this away. 'I am uneasy about what I've learned.'

'The tests were mismanaged?'

'No-o...That would be an unfair allegation. I believe the scientific team on the ground are conducting themselves with commendable professionalism. I would expect no less from the CDEE. They handle some of the deadliest toxins known to man and their methodology is scrupulous. However, the decision to conduct field trials is perhaps the moot point.' Wellbeck looked pained.

'After what? The investigation into Lance Corporal Mordon's death was hastier than I would have preferred but has been concluded. Case closed.'

'After this outbreak runs its course.'

'The *Asiatic flu*? What's that to do with Porton Down? Is this not just a typical winter problem?'

'You have been reading the papers and listening to the radio like everyone else.'

'My wife talks about little else...'

Wellbeck smiled, rather sadly. 'The Asiatic strain is a concern and proving virulent and unpleasant. But, as you say, every year we fret about our hospitals being overrun when so many go down with one or other variant of the flu virus. A fact of life - and death. That is why we receive generous public finding to find vaccines against this ever-present problem.' Wellbeck looked anxious as he paced around in circles like a caged zoo animal. 'I keep reminding myself that a few cases in one small geographic location are hardly proof of anything.'

'But you think there is something unusual going on?'

'There has been a sudden spike in numbers catching a flu-type virus and associated deaths. Concentrated - for now - in Hampshire, and more specifically in and around the towns and villages through which the Longmoor Railway operates.'

'What are you implying?' Vignoles could make the connection but wanted the expert to voice it.

'It would be wrong to make definitive statements about which strain is causing these incidents without setting my eyes on the test results of those infected within the camp and those affected outside the camp. But I have my suspicions. I don't believe the Hampshire outbreak is Asiatic Flu.'

'I cannot profess to know anything about the topic although the papers are full of editors, doctors and other specialists weighing in with their pennyworth of theories. It seems as though the only topic of conversation is debating if it is 'type this' or is it 'type that', so why are you worried?'

Wellbeck nodded with a tight-lipped expression. His face was drained of colour, but perhaps this was a combination of the chilly air inside the church and his head cold. 'Don't make light of it, inspector. Determining the exact strain and sub-variant is crucial. There are a considerable number of different strains and new ones crop up each year, all of which makes it a challenging adversary.'

'My point precisely...'

Wellbeck blew his nose, then took a few uneasy gulps of air. He didn't look well, with a slight sheen on his forehead. 'I am still in two minds about being here now. I asked to meet you, but I have grave misgivings.' He paced once again in a tight circle then stopped and faced Vignoles, looking him in the eye. 'Can I trust you? Perhaps a better way of framing that question is to ask how *far* I can trust you?'

They were standing close to the varnished wooden board mounted on the wall listing the succession of incumbent vicars of St Mary's, each spelt out in gold leaf. Vignoles by way of an answer pointed towards this with a gloved finger.

'Rev Vignoles? An unusual name...'

'My father. He brought me up to follow a strict moral code. I'd like to think my position of DCI also confers weight. I can keep my counsel. I handle dangerous situations without sharing the details to just anyone who'll listen and speak to the press only when circumstances demand a formal statement.'

Vignoles paused a moment, before continuing. 'We both signed our lives away to absolute discretion. We are joint signatories to the same 'problem' - I don't know how else to best describe it - so I see no reason why we should not share information on the subject.'

Wellbeck wiped his nose and nodded. 'I suspect the others will take a less magnanimous viewpoint.'

'A risk we shall have to take. I respect the need for discretion in much of our work and of course respect the rule of law. I won't however allow such constraints to silence me or prevent acting in a manner that protects the greater good of the citizens of this nation. A viewpoint that has not always made me popular.'

'Power, money, rampant egos and the protection of the reputation of institutions all too often dictate our actions.'

'Do you think the protection of reputations is clouding judgement in this case? Or is the Colonel's ego calling the shots?'

'We cannot talk more in here...'

They walked whilst they talked, their slow footsteps raising a slight echo. It was cold inside, but at least they were out of the wind. 'The weather won't do that cold much good. We should perhaps stay inside the church?'

'No! It is safer to be in the open with a clear view around. I would be happier. We must not be overheard.'

'As you wish.' Vignoles closed the heavy wooden door behind. 'Is this why you are here? To talk about virus strains and their impact on the citizens of Hampshire? It hardly seems worthy of such cloak and dagger behaviour.' Privately, Vignoles felt like a man fumbling his way forward in the dark. He was a railway copper in Leicester, so why was he even part of this? There was only the most tenuous connection to railways.

They walked in silence through the metal gate at the end of the church path and past the war memorial. 'More people died in 1918-19 from Spanish influenza than in all those years of conflict,' Wellbeck observed.

Vignoles acknowledged he already knew that chilling fact.

'Never underestimate its potential to kill. I wonder why those who died from that particular virus did not also deserve their towering memorials across Europe? It's the primary motive for why we do what we do inside the Common Cold Unit. Attempting to eradicate the cold and all its unpleasant variants which have such an impact on human life.'

'A worthy cause.'

'Our remit is the preservation of life. To eradicate a menace for the good of all mankind. We have *no* ulterior motive.'

'I am reassured to hear that. But other agencies have less altruistic intentions?'

Wellbeck left this question unanswered as they crossed the railway bridge that abutted the station. At that moment a short train of covered vans trundled beneath them, the sprightly J39 class locomotive at the front throwing up a pungent cloud of oily steam and smoke around the parapets, smothering Vignoles and Wellbeck for a moment. Vignoles always loved the bitter tang of combusted carbon and that soft, almost downy caress of warm steam with a hint of machine oil that was reminiscent of baby oil. He was still surprised to see Wellbeck inhale deeply. 'I see you like engine smoke.'

'Old wives tales say it is good for the lungs. Complete rubbish of course, but the little boy in me can't help it.'

'I like the aroma, though more because of association than the actual smell perhaps. I would not want my wife taking up wearing it as a scent!' Vignoles laughed and Wellbeck joined in.

They were now walking high on the embankment top and watching the train hurry towards the short tunnel ahead. 'At the CCU I lead a department investigating in the common *rhinoviruses* – one of which I appear to be suffering from,' Wellbeck pulled a rueful face. 'It is my specialism and has been since I graduated. I am one of a large team of skilled scientists. Some of the best in the land and all concentrated on finding a cure for the common cold, of which we know of at least two hundred variants. For the past five years, three of my colleagues and myself have been concentrating specifically on the *human coronavirus;* a curious and especially awkward byway from the more well-known infection. I shall strip out the complexities as they will serve only to muddle and confuse a non-expert.'

Vignoles just knew how much he hated catching a cold and was wondering if choosing this exposed location was not asking for trouble. They had stopped walking and were leaning on the wooden fence running along the top of the embankment with their backs to the wind. Vignoles turned up the collar on his coat. 'Go on.'

'Put in the most simplistic terms, the *coronavirus* can be characterised as an ugly twin of influenza. Similar symptoms and effects on the body, but also its peculiar quirks and surprises. It also shares an equal enthusiasm for mutation.' He stopped and coughed repeatedly into a handkerchief. It took a while to subside. 'Sorry. The wind irritates my throat.' He turned and faced Vignoles. '*Corona* is a clever and agile organism. It has the better of us and leads the finest scientific minds a merry dance. Don't let *anyone* tell you otherwise.' His look was intense.

'Including Lombard and Urban?'

'They understand the complexities and dangers far beyond my knowledge. They are world experts. However, be wary of their promises of carefully constructed mutations and ready cures. Colonel Broadbent should know better than to voice an opinion on these matters. His specialism is building bridges and laying railway track, not fighting an almost invisible enemy.'

'Do you think Broadbent fully understands what he is dealing with?'

'He does not. Few of us do. He's an intelligent man and a

decent one, but don't let anyone convince you they have this virus tamed! No sooner do we close in on a vaccine or find something that might reduce the impact on the human body, than it transforms itself; not once, not twice but many times, skipping away from our sophisticated laboratories and Petri dishes, to infect others whilst waving a mocking goodbye to our research.'

'You speak as if you almost admire it.'

'I do. It deserves and requires the utmost respect. Think of it as the sea...' Wellbeck stared across the railway cutting at the low, gently undulating land opposite, still stained white with shallow drifts of snow that had not yet melted. 'The most seasoned mariner will always respect the sea, no matter how fine their ship and long their experience. The sea is always the master, never the mariner. The moment they fail to treat Old Man Sea with due care and attention, he will drown them all.'

Vignoles drew on his pipe. 'You believe others are not treating this *corona* with sufficient respect?'

'Forgive me for repeating myself, but this is crucially important. Our stated aim is prevention and cure. The saving of lives. However, what is not made explicit is that we are expected to liaise with other less benign Governmental institutions. We share information and data on the effects these organisms have on the human body.'

Vignoles kept his eyes on the twin tracks that lay in parallel lines along the cutting floor. He heard the distant wailing chime of an approaching train. 'And these other departments are not intent on prevention and cure?'

'They intend to kill. Or to incapacitate. And the sharing of information is strictly one-way.'

'The Microbiological Research Department?'

'In concert with the CDEE. All our research proves it is close to impossible to stay ahead and create a vaccine for every variant of *coronavirus*. It is, however, relatively easy to encourage new strains and refine these to carry specific traits of devious human devising...'

'Traits that do what?' Vignoles did not like what he was hearing.

'Creating an organism more contagious than its natural state, targeted to infect only humans. In the wild, it tends to prefer animals, with fowls and poultry especially favoured.' Wellbeck hesitated. 'If an antidote cannot be manufactured at the same time as the laboratory strains are developed, and I know that such a vaccine *cannot* be made with the scientific knowledge we have at present, then this is a dangerous game to play.' He turned away and coughed repeatedly again, bending at the waist with the intensity of the attack. 'Sorry...'

'We shall walk back with the wind behind us. The tests at Longmoor fall into this category?'

'We were sold a story about it being a relatively benign but extremely contagious strain. We were told one man died, but this was quickly explained away. But...I have heard rumours.'

'At Longmoor?'

'Two GP's in the area have registered several deaths in the community due to a strain of *corona* they were unfamiliar with. I not only fear the man-made strain is less benign than we were told, but that it is escaping the camp. As it was always going to do. You cannot fence in a virus.'

'What do you want me to do with this information?'

'Try to use your detective skills to uncover the truth. You will never get inside Porton Down, but you might be able to observe what is happening in Longmoor. I was refused permission to visit, but perhaps you might be luckier? I suggest the postmortem report on Mordon could make interesting reading.'

'I have already submitted a request.'

'You have?' Wellbeck looked cheered by this news. 'Then you are ahead of the game and I was right to talk with you. I was told it was restricted. Broadbent was adamant and none-to-nice telling me so.'

'I suspect I will get the same response for both PM reports.'

'Both?'

'You have not heard?'

'Another death?'

'Yes, but not at Longmoor. I visited Mordon's widow in Sheffield and left Mrs Mordon in reasonable health and spirits, but she was found dead the following morning.'

'My God! Was it the virus?'

'She drowned in a canal. Some argue suicide, others a mugging.'

'At least the virus has not spread north. Thank goodness for that.'

'It was an unpleasant way to die.

Wellbeck ran a hand down his face. 'Forgive me. That was callous. It is dreadful; appalling for both families. A double tragedy. But believe me, inspector, it is better for everyone it was not *coron56-N4* that took her.'

'That is the strain tested at Longmoor?'

'The same. Keep that name under your hat. Developed at Porton Down in 1956, variant N4. Hence the name.' They were now close to the gate leading down onto the station platform. 'Take this.' Wellbeck produced a bottle from his coat pocket. 'Industrial strength alcohol with disinfecting additives. We use it constantly at the CCU. Wash your hands at every opportunity in hot water and soap and in-between use this. Rub it on everything you handle. Even your leather gloves, which you should wear all the time you are at the military railway. Keep your scarf over your mouth. Don't ignore my advice.'

Vignoles took the bottle and looked perplexed. 'Is this not rather excessive?'

'It is not. I practically doused myself in the stuff before speaking with you. You cannot be too careful. If you do get inside Longmoor, keep your distance from everyone. Try not to shake hands. *Coron56-N4* is on the loose and you must avoid catching it - and it is highly contagious.'

'What do you understand it was designed to do?'

'On the face of it, nothing serious. It incapacitates. It targets younger people with the idea of knocking them out of frontline service for a week or so. Lays them low with aching limbs; hopelessly weak with debilitating headaches and shortness of breath. An enemy soldier would be fit for nothing and so allowing our troops to roll in unopposed and take control.'

'But they recover?'

'That is the idea. A benign form of germ warfare. When compared to *Sarin* gas, I suppose it is.'

'But you suspect it is behaving differently?'

'I don't know... But something is not right. My questions are being rebuffed and doors are closing about me. Frustrated at being refused sight of the Mordon's PM report, I went directly to the Health Secretary's office. I have the ears of the Secretary and he is usually helpful. But this time I was given the cold shoulder.'

Both men shivered as an especially icy blast carrying snowflakes buffeted them. As they neared the station Vignoles checked his wristwatch. 'There is a train in less than an hour and a half that will take you back to London.'

'I shall change at Woodford and make a deliberately circuitous route to Harnham Down. I mapped it out in my timetable.'

'Covering your tracks?'

'It cannot harm. I advise you to be equally circumspect.'

'A family visit to the Vicarage here is an innocent explanation for my presence.'

Wellbeck nodded approval. 'Good luck and take care, Vignoles. Use that bottle wisely.' He walked onto the platform and without looking behind, went in search of the waiting room.

Chapter Eight
Leicester Central

When Vignoles returned to his office, he was immediately accosted by Mavis Green. 'The Badger is in your office! He's been here for the last hour. Said he'd wait as long as it took for your return.'

'Something's up...'

'Vignoles! Where the devil you've been?' Badger turned from the bay window and almost barked the question. 'I saw you arrive. From where?'

'Making enquiries, sir.'

'With whom? About what? Nobody seems to know anything around here...'

Vignoles was tempted to say that he agreed. 'I prefer to keep my counsel for the time being. Discretion is the better part of valour.'

Badger snorted. 'And where's DS Mellor?'

'At home with a cold.'

'Pah! Alright, take a seat.' Badger sat in one of the two chairs reserved for visitors and fiddled impatiently with his expensive gloves whilst Vignoles shrugged off his coat and scarf and tossed his Fedora onto the top of the coat stand.

'Something urgent, sir?'

Badger surprised Vignoles by not launching into a string of commands as expected but instead sat very still, beady eyes locked onto Vignoles' for an uncomfortable length of time before he finally broke his silence. 'DCI Minshul is still bending my ear about that poor drowned woman.'

'Phyllis Mordon.'

'He's agitating about getting sight of the PM report on her death, just as you warned he would.'

'I share his wish to see it.'

'Minshul is a straight-talking chap, but I couldn't get any sense out of him. Talking and acting as though he was in a spy film.'

'We share concerns over her death. A husband and wife die in a space of days. Both investigations, although seemingly, unrelated except through the fact of their marriage, were concluded with indecent haste. Neat explanations offered with no complications. Signed, sealed and delivered. Cases closed. In my years of policing this rarely happens.'

'But tenuous grounds for rattling the bars of the cage, d'you not think? It's not enough to work on. We were given instructions following Lance Corporal Mordon's death, which were duly acted upon. You did your part of the job and that's it. I don't see why my two DCIs have suddenly become so interested in his wife's suicide?'

'I'm not sure we can call it that.'

'A mugging… an accident. She died off railway premises. It can be of no concern of yours - nor Minshul's.'

'It was Minshul who alerted me to her death, which as you rightly say, took place outside our area of jurisdiction.'

'Way off. Neither of you has any right to muscle in on the City force.' Badger spat the words out, but then seemed to rein in his anger. 'Be that as it may, what's the problem as you see it?'

'Minshul is pally with a detective on the Sheffield City Police who shared his misgivings about the hasty investigation. They often share information about cases and ensure both forces work in concert.'

'Makes sense. What of it?'

'For the record, Minshul was not best pleased I visited his patch following the orders issued at Marylebone House. He knew I had spoken to the deceased earlier the same day. You can see why he heard alarm bells ringing when the same woman turned up dead the next morning. It's hard not to imagine there is a sinister link between these events.'

'Humph.' Badger was yet to be convinced. 'Why are you unhappy about the husband's death? The Army had their best medical chaps looking into it and working with the CDEE. You're not implying incompetence?'

'Far from it. If anything, I expect their work to be exemplary in such a case. I'd wager their knowledge outstrips that of any civilian.'

'Your point being?'

'It's what they chose *not* to report. I would expect everything to be meticulously and accurately recorded, but my guess is Colonel Broadbent allowed us the sight of a heavily redacted version.'

'That is a dangerous allegation.'

'The Royal Engineers have their reputation to uphold. He is looking out for his regiment.'

Badger fished out a cigarette with a shake of his head. 'Light up if you wish. We have much to discuss.' His face glowed in the flame of his expensive silver lighter with his initials engraved on the side, tiny lights dancing in his pupils. He watched the tiny skein of cigarette smoke drift upwards for a moment. 'I'll start by saying that I got it in the neck from the colonel for asking. He made it abundantly clear railway detectives do not need to see such a document. Lance Corporal Mordon's death is a closed book and he told me to cease all enquiries on the matter.'

'Ordinarily, I would be inclined to agree. However, he seems to have overlooked the fact that we are both involved. At his request.'

Badger gave Vignoles a conspiratorial look. 'And I don't take kindly to that kind of language, no matter what colour his tunic and how many medals pinned on his chest. Darned impertinence...'

Vignoles smiled to himself and concentrated on cleaning his pipe.

'It's been a few years since I put the metaphorical shoulder to the wheel and did some detective work...' Badger's voice had mellowed considerably. The tone was gentler and less combative. 'I had misgivings the moment I was told to call that meeting. Nothing made sense. Getting a DCI in to carry a cheque to Sheffield and offer tea and sympathy was preposterous. Why not use Minshul, at least?'

'He's too close to the ground? He was aware of Phyllis Mordon. She was not a friend, but he used the buffet at Victoria and knew her. There was a personal connection, no matter how tenuous.'

Badger nodded. 'That occurred to me. I don't like it when jumped up Ministry chaps start over-ruling my authority whilst explaining next to nothing. I hated that meeting every bit as much as you did.'

'I take reassurance in that, sir.'

'I have made my own discrete enquiries.' A sly glance towards Vignoles. 'I called in a few favours.' Badger sat back in the chair and smiled. 'I don't put the hours in on the golf links for nothing. It's how the wheels of power and influence are oiled. Connections made and delicate matters discussed before the 18th. To cut to the chase, I have a poor and smudged copy of the dead soldier's PM. Those rotary copying machines are not all they are cracked up to be, but it's legible - in a good light.'

'You have Mordon's PM? From the Army?'

'Porton Down...'

Vignoles whistled under his breath. 'Dare I ask how you obtained it?'

'You may not. It's a sinister and un-Godly place. The less anyone has to do with it, the better. It gives me an unpleasant sensation touching something that came out of there.'

Vignoles was reminded of the bottle Wellbeck had handed him.

'Read it, then burn it. It is hot property.' He flapped a hand. 'But there's little in there that will surprise you.' He now handed over the sheets of paper which smelt heavily of ink.

'Nothing amiss?' Vignoles felt deflated.

'His death is exactly as explained to the coroner. They played a straight bat. The only area of interest that I could see, was the section concentrated on the microbiology angle. Rather beyond my understanding, to be frank, but they seemed interested in a virus known as *corons56-N4*. Mean anything to you?'

'It does. The person I met today offered the same name. Accompanied by their disquiet about the trials of this strain at the Longmoor Military Railway. This -,' Vignoles tapped the smudged report, '- sounds like it will prove nothing untoward. We were told they were running tests on a new virus and we now have a name for it, but that doesn't explain anything either!'

'You're losing your touch, Vignoles. Every grain of information has value.' Badger's face became animated, his eyes bright. 'Grains accumulate and gain mass, then slowly take form and shape.' He blew an extravagant plume of smoke into the air. 'And besides, I have more. The matching half of the pair,' Badger reached into his briefcase again and tossed over a few sheets of foolscap clipped together. 'Phyllis Mordon. A precis of the investigation and the PM report.'

'May I ask how you got these?'

'You forget I'm from that neck of the woods. Darnell born and bred. I know the Super on the Sheffield City Police. We go way back...'

'Don't tell me, you play golf together?'

'Naturally,' Badger chuckled. 'The moment I suggested the Army and some gentlemen from the darker corners of the Home Office were eager to ensure his men made a swift and neat job of the investigation, his hackles rose. A Yorkshire-born Chief Superintendent takes even less kindly than I do to being told how to run his shop!' Badger allowed this to sink in a moment. 'Read it. It won't take long. I've rarely seen a more succinct investigation.' His words were laced with sarcasm.

A few minutes later and with pipe puffing smoke, Vignoles looked up. 'The faint mark on her left shin could imply she was deliberately tripped forward into the water.'

'Implying assault. But the bruising is subtle and open to interpretation.'

'I note the line of enquiry moved from suicide to a mugging that saw her topple into the canal. A callous attack in the dark on a slippery towpath. Quite plausible.'

'Yes. An open and shut case. An unfortunate incident that will encourage the press to bemoan a young woman who chose to walk alone along a canal in the dark. The public must take care not to place themselves in danger, blah, blah... You can almost read the headlines.'

'Few are likely to question these findings,' Vignoles nodded agreement.

'Now get that detective brain in gear. Minshul has already made his views plain about what he doesn't like, now it's your turn.'

Vignoles was flicking through the pages looking for something. 'The pathologist found a pinprick in her upper arm. It was fresh but had not bled. He could not explain it being there other than to say it was the kind of piercing a needle might make. That is odd.'

'Go on...'

'He asked for a toxicology report on her blood, but this was refused on grounds of time and expense as they were already convinced it was a mugging.'

'We have to keep a firm grip on budgets. I know you chaps bemoan our parsimony, but we get it in the neck if we overspend.' A flash of the old Badger flared up.

'But this could be significant. Was this made by a hypodermic needle in a syringe? It needs an explanation.'

'Agreed. There is nothing materially wrong with what you read. There is no 'cover-up' as such, just lackadaisical policing and over-careful consideration of budgetary matters.' Badger smoked and eyed Vignoles wearily. 'You met Phyllis Mordon. What did you make of her?'

'Young, healthy, well presented and remarkably controlled despite her loss. She was not alarmed when we came prying into her life.'

'Minshul offered much the same. She's from tough, working class stock. She'd not be afraid of a turn around the local area every evening in the dark. It was something she did regularly. The neighbours have confirmed that.'

'Why did she not fight back? I would expect her to put up more resistance. There is nothing under her nails, no signs of defensive wounds...'

'And who just lies face down in cold water and drowns?'

'She was taken by surprise and toppled into the water? However, she was fit and healthy and even with a sodden coat and the perishing cold I would have expected her to flail about, scrabble against the canal sides and cry for help.'

'There was nothing in this report to suggest an attempt to scramble out.'

'However, if she was sedated, that would be a different story.'

'The pinprick in the arm?' Badger grinned, wolfishly. 'A passerby gives a silent quick jab in her shoulder. She may not have known what happened. A sensation like a wasp sting at worst? She feels faint, she falls. Perhaps he holds her until she passes out and gives her a shove over the side?'

'And he's there to ensure she drowns. He retrieves her handbag, which I note was discovered to be wet, and this is discarded some distance away to give the semblance of a mugging. He melts away into the dark.'

A silence fell in the office as the import of this realisation sank in. A guard's whistle blew, a metal-wheeled sack truck was trundled past the window by a porter and from behind the closed office door, Mavis Green coughed.

'That would make this premeditated murder.'

'It would.' Badger looked grim.

'But she just served eggs and bacon in a station buffet for God's sake!'

'It was not what she did, but what she knew.'

'About the trials? We were sent to quiz her about what her husband shared with her. But there was nothing. One phone call, nothing more. I reported this faithfully.'

'Nothing in writing, but nobody can make her forget what she knows, what she was told.'

Vignoles drew on his pipe, realising he was biting on the stem. 'I got the impression it was not much. But how can anyone know for certain? She was a bright girl and understood we were paying for her continued silence.'

'And paying handsomely. But what's to stop a smart girl from coming back for more? Or telling the press in return for further remuneration? Only she knows what her husband told her.'

'Someone decided she must be silenced. They first wanted to understand the level of risk. Discover if she'd spoken to others? Cleanse any written evidence, and then...'

'Don't speak it.' Badger stubbed his cigarette out angrily. He picked up a copy of a newspaper he'd brought with him. 'A local paper from the Basingstoke area.' He jabbed a finger at the lurid headline.

FLU EPIDEMIC WORST IN YEARS!
GPs and hospitals struggling to manage.

'At least eight have died in the immediate area and thirty admitted to hospitals in the county. What sparked my interest is the hint at a significant number of squaddies in the Longmoor Barracks have also taken ill. Naturally, the Army has refused to comment.'

'I'd like to visit their private railway if you can pull some strings.'

'What's your thinking?'

'The man I met today suggested it would be instructive to gauge the situation down there. I was given to understand the trials are not going as planned.'

'Is there a risk of contagion?'

'I've faced worse threats.'

'Don't be so confident.' Badger drummed his fingers on the desk. 'Colonel Broadbent can be played at his own game. He reassured me everything on his patch was, to use his own words 'business as usual and the railway running like clockwork.' In which case, he can have no reason for refusing one of the men he called into my office, one with a specific interest in the running of railways, from paying an observational visit. Oh, he'll post a couple of goons to chaperone you, but you can still learn a lot riding on the footplate or talking with a guard and keeping your eyes and ears open.'

'You can rely on me.'

'Lodge off-site, but somewhere close to where the men relax when allowed out of camp.'

'A drink in a local pub when tongues loosen with beer?'

'Precisely. If the Colonel plays it tough, the railway runs through open country and the public have some rights of access, so he cannot completely exclude you.'

'Agreed.'

'Take Mellor. You have permission to share as much of this conversation as you feel appropriate with your sergeant.'

'And DCI Minshul? I presume he is also playing his part?'

'He is making discreet investigations into Mrs Mordon's death. Look, Charles, it doesn't need me to say we're flying well under the radar. Way off limits and with no right to stick our noses in. Observe and collect information, but don't be tempted to intervene or throw your weight around. I don't know what we're involved in, but I don't like it. When innocent people have needles stuck in their arms, be it for an experiment or in the dark beside a canal and end up dead, I won't just bury my head in the sand.'

Vignoles nodded gravely. Badger could be difficult at times and a hard taskmaster, but underneath there was a man who held strong moral convictions and was not afraid to act on them.

Chapter Nine
Longmoor Military Railway

Vignoles and Mellor were standing on the platform at Bordon, close to the wooden signal box placed at the point where the platform turned a slight curve. An attractive detached house stood some way back from the platform and presumably provided for the stationmaster and his family. Across four parallel railway lines lay the opposite platform and a crudely constructed corrugated iron engine shed. Beyond the perimeter fence were copses of trees and distant views of open scrubland and fields still touched by the pale gleam of a hard frost.

In many ways, it was just a quiet country station. The sort of place that could expect a handful of passenger trains a day interspersed by the infrequent arrival of a mixed goods train hauled by an antiquated tank engine that would slowly potter around the yard, dropping off and collecting a wagon or two and perhaps loading a brace of milk churns into a box van before shuffling away. However, the sight of a soldier in fatigues and beret with a gun slung over his shoulder on the platform suggested a military presence. The soldier looked bored and was idly smoking a Woodbine. Bored or not, armed soldiers were not a sight seen in peacetime on British railway stations. Two more squaddies stood nearer the detectives, blowing on their hands in the perishing cold. They were, at least, unarmed.

Privates Walker and Denning had been assigned as their guides for the day following a lengthy briefing about the history and layout of the railway and its operation. It was a detailed and instructional lecture and no doubt laid on as part of the Royal Engineers' desire to present a positive image of their impressive railway complex. Vignoles and Mellor had requested a visit 'to study how the Army ran a railway,' and

Chapter Nine

Colonel Broadbent was dutifully ensuring they got the full works.

Their instructor had sold them an upbeat story and the impression this was a fabulous set-up, where men with the right attitude and application could learn every conceivable aspect of railway operation and management. From designing track layouts to the construction of all aspects of railway related civil engineering to signals and telegraph installation and operation across a wide selection of systems - many brought back from the recent conflict in Europe. Then there was goods handling; locomotive maintenance and the correct firing and driving of the many different types of locomotives.

'I rather like what I've seen so far.' Mellor had enjoyed the morning more than he'd expected.

'They've built a model system. As good as it gets. If I were cynical, I'd suggest a system artificially protected from the usual daily irritations and vagaries of the real railway.' Vignoles noticed their chaperones were drifting a distance away whilst awaiting the arrival of the train. 'Here's the drill. We approve of everything and admire their professionalism. Easy to do.' He gave Mellor a knowing look. 'But that's not why we're here. We win their confidence and they might slacken off the reins.'

'Ah ha, our train!' Mellor piped up loudly, with deliberate enthusiasm. 'My, what a beast that is!'

'Number 400, sir,' Private Walker replied. 'Our flagship. We like to roll this one out for passenger duties and you are in luck!' He looked with unbridled admiration and pride at the giant locomotive painted in a deep rich blue and cleaned, buffed and polished to perfection. The scarlet lining glowed in the weak winter sun.

'Only the Army would paint the wheel rims white, eh?' Mellor smiled, good-naturedly.

'Don't joke. If the sergeant major wants the coal painted white, we jump to it!'

They laughed.

'This is a War Department design, I think?' Vignoles already knew this splendid engine named *Sir Guy Williams* was of 1943 vintage and could read the builder's plate that declared it was assembled in the North British Works, but he wanted to keep the men talking and sharing knowledge and thereby 'softening' them up. Private Walker was happy to oblige and engaged the driver in their conversation whilst the fireman uncoupled the engine ready to run around three rather ancient if perfectly maintained carriages that formed the train.

The run round operation completed and the locomotive was now ready to run tender first. The fireman was topping up the tender tank with water whilst Vignoles was getting along splendidly with the driver, asking him technical questions about how his engine performed in comparison with other types. The driver was happy to share his knowledge, then explained this service was set to run to Liss via the Barracks at Longmoor Downs in a typical operation that involved as much running about and track mileage as possible to notch up experience for the crews, guard and signalmen along the way.

The platform had now filled with lines of uniformed men and the character of the station had changed. Mellor observed that it reminded him of the weeks leading up to D-Day when the southern counties witnessed great numbers of men and equipment gathering in the most unlikely places.

With the men loaded and departure imminent, both detectives succeeded in splitting up their chaperones, with Mellor glad to take up residence in the snug guard's compartment along with Denning, whilst Vignoles accepted the invitation to ride on the footplate. Walker could see no harm in Vignoles on a hot, noisy and coal-dusty footplate and as he was by his own admission 'more into the signalling side of things,' was happy to hop aboard the train to 'ride the cushions'.

Vignoles was in his element. A cab ride was a rare treat and all the more so when it was along this attractive and intriguing private railway. It might be the exclusive training ground of the Royal Engineers, but they displayed a certain panache and style in everything they did. The standard of maintenance of the railway infrastructure was high, as they relentlessly practised building, tearing down and rebuilding much of the not-so-permanent way or put successions of recruits on interminable painting, sweeping and repair duties on anything that stayed still long enough to be on the receiving end of their attention. The line itself was surprisingly busy, with sparkling tank engines huffing about with their red spinning wheels and shiny coats of blue. This deep shade and a lighter version on the coaching stock appeared to be used liberally, with plenty of splashes of brilliant white that demanded endless cleaning. They held no fear of possible aerial attack, as the Royal Engineers not only eschewed any attempt at camouflage but ensured their trains presented an unmissable sight, even on a dour January day.

Having established his driver preferred to be addressed simply as 'Bill' and his fireman as 'Jerry,' the three settled into an easy camaraderie on the footplate, but enjoyable though this was, it was time for Vignoles to ease the conversation around to more pertinent matters without betraying his hand.

Running tender first, the air blowing across the coal in the bunker was releasing plenty of friable dust into the cab, stinging their cheeks and making them squint to stop it going in their eyes. Vignoles kept his fedora tipped low over his brow and could hear little tapping sounds as larger pieces struck his hat. As their train approached a long straight stretch and driver Bill opened up the regulator to give *Sir Guy Williams* a stretch, the cab seemed to fill with choking dust. Both crewmen pulled neckerchiefs over their mouths and noses making them look like cowboys about to hold up a stagecoach in a 'Western' film.

'We came prepared!' Jerry's voice was muffled.

'Wish I'd thought of that!' Vignoles sneezed, then turned this deliberately into a passable imitation of a hacking cough to see if there was a reaction.'

'Not you as well?'

'Just the dust...'

'Hope so...' The driver gave the regulator a tweak, but his brow had creased as he'd glanced at Vignoles. 'There's a lot of it about.' The driver needed to shout to be heard above the rattle and bang of the crudely constructed locomotive. The metal fall plate that lay between the cab and the wildly rocking tender was juddering and squealing.

'Just one of the perils of tender-first running!'

'Bill isn't talking about coal, but colds!' They were shouting to make themselves heard.

'Oh?' Vignoles feigned surprise.

'Something nasty doing the rounds. Going through the barracks like a dose of salts!' Jerry replied.

Vignoles turned his back to the wind and airborne pollution and faced the fireman, who was standing close, shovel in hand. 'I read in the paper it's especially bad this year. With everyone sharing dormitories, once one gets the flu here, so does everyone?'

Jerry gave the water gauge glasses a look, and satisfied by what he saw, leaned into his corner of the cab. 'That's what they say. Feeding us the same old story about winter colds. But that's not the half of it...' He looked across at the driver, eyes appearing all the more expressive with the lower half of their faces covered. Bill just kept his eyes on the road ahead and didn't respond. 'Doesn't help that we've got some soddin' scientists here giving the lads a dose of their own special flu! Bloody ridiculous. They actually *want* us to get it!'

Bill grunted. It was non-committal but implied he was no more in favour than his fireman.

'Me and Bill are not interested. Not a flippin' chance. They can say what they like, but flu is nasty. They can stuff their money!'

'Money?' Vignoles quizzed.

'Paying the lads. A little earner for a week away from heavy duties in return for being a lab rat!'

'Steady now...' Bill broke his silence. He was closing the regulator and allowing the engine to coast and gently lose speed, but his words were perhaps directed at his fireman.

'It's true. They've told everyone in the barracks, so it's hardly a secret. Cash to have a needle in your arm.'

Vignoles adopted an expression of bewilderment. 'Surely those who agreed to the jab would just pass it on to everyone else?'

'That's the idea,' Bill replied. 'Great, innit? Test cases are paired with others to see how fast it spreads and how quickly it takes us out of action. It seems to be working, an' all.' He raised a gloved hand in salutation to a fellow driver in the cab of stubby tank engine bowling along the opposite running line with a train of goods wagons. 'See that? An ex-United States Transport Corps engine. Shipped over during the war.' Vignoles had indeed caught a brief glimpse as it passed.

The driver seemed torn between changing the subject to safer ground or elucidating further. 'Me and Jerry are sticking together. Trying to avoid everyone as best we can. These scarves are not just against coal dust.' He shrugged his shoulders 'But how long can we hold out? Lots of lads have gone down with it.'

'Sounds grim. I'm wondering if I should even be here.' Vignoles replied.

Jerry dropped his face mask as their train noticeably slowed as the train rounded a long curve, the wind direction now more favourable. 'You're a detective, right?'

'A *railway* detective,' Vignoles corrected.

'Just between us, you should get detecting. There's summat going wrong here. Needs looking into by someone who knows how to do it.'

'Jerry...'

'No, it's going wrong and you know it. They're denying

everything! Ten men have... Oh, forget it!' Jerry broke off and crashed open the firebox and started shovelling coal, furiously.

Bill had also pushed his scarf down and his face betrayed a man wrestling with a dilemma. 'We'll get a rough deal if caught speaking like this. It would be serious. Maybe thrown in the slammer. Jerry knows that.'

'Nobody can hear us here.' Vignoles replied. 'What was it you wanted to tell me about these ten men?'

Jerry continued to shovel, but his face betrayed anger. Or was it just the orange-yellow glow of the fire on his face casting strong shadows? The heat of the fire was certainly welcome in the draughty cab.

'I'm not saying anything definite. And don't tell anyone where you heard it.' Bill gently eased the brakes on as he spoke. 'There's a lot of lads in the hospital. We heard some reacted badly. Others just taken to their beds and laid up, as was expected.' His face was stony, staring forward beyond the bucking tender towards the signals ahead. 'There are whispers some of the men have gone. Off barracks. Taken away in the night.'

'The ten?'

'Yeah.'

'Maybe more.'

'Probably taken to a local hospital for specialised care, don't you think?' Vignoles replied.

'No.' Jerry stood upright, kicking the fire door closed with a clang and looked Vignoles in the eye. 'They went to a mortuary.'

*   *   *   *

At the rear of the train, cigarettes and a strong brew of tea and a cache of digestive biscuits were helping create a convivial atmosphere. The guard did not need to check tickets and aside from an occasional glance through the ducket window that offered him a view along the side of the train, he was content to sit and chat.

'So, about these nurses?' Mellor had a lascivious look in his eye.

'Ho-ho! Sultry Mary Jones and Alice Simpkins, aka *The Blonde Bombshell*. What a pair of lookers! Honestly...' Private Denning was grinning wickedly.

'Can't argue with that assessment,' the guard grinned. 'Gorgeous. That's why they chose them I s'pose? They knew we'd be desperate to get ill and have them tuck us up in bed!'

'Don't even dream about it...' Denning gave a comically mimed impression of a love-sick Romeo.

Mellor grinned. 'I wonder where they spend their evenings off?'

'You don't waste yer time!'

'I've only got this evening.'

'I heard if they can get away, they've been seen down The Greatham Inn. It's the closest local to the barracks,' Denning replied.

'Can't miss it, mate,' the guard added. 'The only pub in a hamlet of the same name. Just follow the line of lads with the same idea!'

'I keep hoping to pay a visit when the girls are there,' Denning continued. 'But getting a pass out is not easy since things started to -.' He cut himself short.

'Don't despair, sounds like there could be more nurses. I heard they just shipped in some extra from over Salisbury way to give the regulars a breather.' The guard sounded upbeat. 'It could be your lucky night.'

'You said they were chosen to win the lads over with their looks. Win them over for what?' Mellor gave a wink as if expecting something salacious.

'Not what you're thinking! Trust me, we've all found our minds wandering if we catch a glimpse. Those blue and white uniforms do it for me.' All three laughed in agreement. The guard suddenly stood up and walked to the far end of the coach then slid the connecting door open. 'Listen.'

The locomotive puffed distantly, the wheels clicked rhythmically, and the wooden body of the archaic coach creaked gently like an ancient galleon. There was a murmur of conversation, the odd laugh and a regular hacking cough that barely ceased.

'What am I listening for?' Mellor queried.

'The coughing.' He shut the door quickly as if eager to close off the carriage filled with soldiers from their own space. 'The death rattle.'

Mellor laughed. 'Christ, you soldiers have a black sense of humour.'

Private Denning looked uneasy and not found Mellor's comment amusing. 'Don't take any notice of the daft things we say.' He glared at the guard. 'Just stupid gallows talk.'

'Stupid? Come off it, Private, have you not noticed what's happening?' The guard challenged Denning.

Denning sat up straight and took a deep breath. 'Alright, so a few lads have bad colds. What of it? We all smoke like chimneys and stand around in all weathers, so what d'you expect?' He tried to keep his voice light, but he seemed to find it easier to stare at the back wall of the compartment and not look at either Mellor or the guard.

The guard sat down again. 'A medical orderly chum of mine said the cough was the start. Then you end up taken out on a stretcher.'

'You should be careful about repeating the rubbish people talk.' Denning spat the words out.

'Please yourself, chum, but try using your eyes for once. Look around and take note then tell me I'm talking rubbish.' He looked at Mellor as he was speaking.

Silence fell. Denning studied the wooden floor pensively and swigged his tea. The train rolled and rocked, and the distant sound of a cough was audible.

'Sergeant, you won't have been told this, but they're doing some trials. I can't tell you the details as they claim its top secret.' The guard was staring at Denning as if daring him to prevent him from speaking. 'I didn't like the sound of it despite tenners being waved around as inducement. I walked away, and I'm glad -.'

'Oy! Shut it!'

'I can bloody well say what I *think*! It's my opinion. I don't *know* nothing. Not really. But I don't rate my chances of avoiding this lurgy they've set loose. I don't like it. And nobody asked if I wanted to catch it.'

'A trial? Of a cold?' Mellor tried to sound innocent.

'Something along those lines. It's nothing special. I mean, stands to reason it can't be much or they wouldn't risk spreading it around, would they?' Denning was playing down the situation. Perhaps this was the official line he'd been told to communicate if the truth started to slip out. 'People always want to make up stories and think the worst. Lads sitting around in barracks love a good scare story.' The guard snorted in derision, but let Denning continue. 'Ask me what I think? It's safe as houses. It just takes you off duty for a week - which doesn't sound so bad!' Denning smoked with a studied air of relaxed nonchalance. He'd recovered from his initial reaction and was putting effort into offering a positive angle for Mellor. 'I heard the idea was to drop it from the air and incapacitate a city then let the tank boys roll in and secure the place without bloodshed. By the time everyone feels better they're overrun and have to surrender. Gotta be better than bloodshed.'

Mellor nodded agreement but did not comment. He wanted to appear as if only mildly interested whilst keeping the men talking. 'And look on the bright side, you've got those two lovely nurses here. Are they part of the team?'

'Yep. There's a whole team they came with. I can't say from where. Doctors, scientists and medical orderlies, all camped out up at… Never mind where,' Denning replied.

'I might take ill!' Mellor grinned wickedly.

The guard snorted. 'Don't jest. I want to stay alive…'

Chapter Ten
Sheffield Victoria

The light was fading fast and DCI Minshul stood with his hands deep inside his overcoat pockets, a cigarette jutting from his mouth. His hat was pulled low and a darkly patterned tartan scarf was tied around his throat. Flakes of snow were gathering on his shoulders. DS Ashbury was similarly attired and was also smoking. Both were cold and hunched their shoulders against a wind scything down from the high moors surrounding the city.

The steel rolling mills in the distance were swaddled in clouds of steam as the regular thump, thump, thump of the giant trip hammers pounded steel bars whilst rollers bearing immense weights grumbled. It felt as though the Don Valley was suffering a gentle earthquake. Steam engines sent plumes of pale vapour into the air on almost every side. The locomotives busying themselves in the goods yards and colliery sidings and also right above where the detectives were standing, as they moved along the tracks running through Sheffield Victoria. The endless noise of toiling labour was all around and steam and pungent smoke hung heavy and cloying despite the best efforts of the wind and snow. The sluggish black waters of the Navigation stewed noxiously.

A locomotive whistled and the deep throaty beats of piston signalled a heavy train making its departure as Minshul stared at the uninviting water. 'A bloody awful place to die...'

'Is there a good place to die, Sergeant?'

'Prob'ly not, boss.'

'Aye, but I know what you mean.' Minshul looked up at the massive bulk of the bridge that carried the former Great Central lines over the navigation, then back along the equally unappealing towpath. It was damp and potholed and strewn with litter, broken bricks and a bent pram wheel. 'The less time spent here, the better. We're not going to find nowt.'

'There's a set of steps close by coming down from the railway. It should have a padlock on the gate guarding it, but it's gone. Mebbe the killer used that to get down here and away again?'

Minshul walked across to where Ashbury had indicated. 'The top of the flight is a few steps from the end of the bay platform. Nip down here, lay in wait, then back to the station and boarding a train in minutes?'

'There again, there are loads of other ways onto the path…'

'Try cheering me up, will yer?' Minshul smoked disconsolately. 'We've got nowt. Bugger all.'

'Not quite, boss. We do at least know how the killer or killers worked out her daily routine. Put one of them GPO folding tents things over a manhole on t'other side of her street.'

'Nobody questions workmen down a hole for a day or two. And my guess is nobody saw 'em come or go and can't give a description.'

'Spot on. Complete blank. But the neighbour said Mordon liked a walk after her evening meal before settling down for the night. Whatever the weather, she went out for half an hour. Regular as clockwork.'

'Too easy for someone in dark clothing to loiter and jump her down here.'

'Perfect mugging spot.' Ashbury shook his head sadly.

Minshul tossed his cigarette into the water where if fizzed for a moment. They walked into the relative shelter of the bridge which roared with the vibrations of the departing train. A weak electric light on a rusty bracket cast a gentle glow in the deepening gloom. The snow fell harder. 'I've seen the PM report. It was no mugging, Paul.'

'What does it say?'

'I shouldn't have sight of it, OK? We've no mandate to be

looking into this, so you keep this to yerself.'

'I did wonder…'

'Never mind wondering. Just listen. What I'm going to tell you is dynamite. Like I said, not a word.'

'Of course, boss.'

'She had a needle stuck in her arm.'

'Eh? Do you mean it was…a medical mistake?'

'Bloody Hell, Sergeant, she's hardly coming down here of an evening to take a mumps injection!' Minshul could feel anxiety and something akin to fear making him ratty. 'No, it was cyanide. In the upper arm. Instantaneous death or near as makes no odds. Quick enough to see her keel into the water and just lie there. Gasping and taking in enough water to satisfy the coroner she drowned. We remarked there was no sign of her thrashing about and scrabbling up the sides.'

'Jesus…'

'It was a professional job.'

'She was silenced?'

'I reckon as she was. Until we work out who ordered a professional hit job, we'd best make sure no-one learns *we* know. Or it could get hairy.'

DS Ashbury shivered.

'Right, never mind invisible hit men and their syringes, let's get a cuppa in the station before we both die our deaths from the bleedin' cold.'

Chapter Eleven
Greatham

The Greatham Inn was doing a decent trade. Pass outs might be harder to come by, but there were still about fifteen Royal Engineers gathered in the public bar and spilling into the lounge. Their uniforms gave the pub the air of it being occupied and their laughter and boisterous behaviour not meeting with universal approval by some of the locals.

'There is a divide in the room. Between Army and those who enjoy their presence, and those who look almost antagonistic. I wonder if it's always like this?' Vignoles was standing in the lounge with a pint of local ale and looking across the serving area into the bar itself. 'Some of the locals are hanging back, retreating into the corners and giving the squaddies less than approving looks.'

'I noticed that. But this boozer must 'ave been serving troops for donkey's years. If you don't take to lads in uniform, go somewhere else.'

'Perhaps the distance and disapproving looks are more about not wanting to catch anything nasty? Rumours, true or not, spread fast.'

Mellor wriggled his shoulders as if he'd felt a chilly tingle down his back, although the lounge was nicely warmed by a healthy fire in the grate. He didn't like the idea of catching anything nasty. 'No sign of those nurses.'

'It was always a long shot, but this pint was needed any rate. Chin up, we still might glean something out of these men once the alcohol loosens their tongues.'

'Oh, hang on...' Mellor could hardly contain his delight. 'We just struck gold, guvnor...'

The two young women who entered the saloon fitted the descriptions given. They were accompanied by another woman dressed in an Army uniform and a pale young man with bad acne. If he was their chaperone for the evening, he had his work cut out.

'Sergeant, there are operational reasons why I condone you engaging these objects of desire in conversation. Just don't forget you *are* on duty,' Vignoles gave an ironic look at his half-empty glass of beer. 'A modest number of drinks are allowed for appearances' sake...'

'Don't worry, I know how to handle this. I need to be on my best form though, 'cos 'arf the pub 'ave the same idea.' Mellor was adopting full London swagger as he prepared to approach the women.

Vignoles could not disagree with Mellor's assessment. The nurses were as pretty as foretold and in their civilian dresses, winter coats and jaunty hats were causing a stir amongst the dominating presence of men in military khaki. A wolf whistle had come from across the bar and many faces turned to watch their arrival. The women were used to the reaction and studiously ignored everyone. It appeared their youthful male companion, despite his spotty school-boy appearance, was old enough to be served at the bar and it was his duty to fetch their drinks. He stood ignored at the bar, muscled out by burlier chaps, hoping to attract the attention of the barmaid.

Mellor, however, was a smooth operator and swiftly moved in. Vignoles had to admit the man had a rare gift. Within moments of tipping his hat and offering his most engaging smile, he was sharing cigarettes and deftly collecting their orders for G&Ts and a port and lemon, whilst politely remembering not to forget a pint of Best for the spotty teenager. A click of his fingers, a wink and a few words exchanged, and the barmaid was onto it, even smiling to herself as she started to fix the drinks. It was executed smoothly and with such consummate ease, the three nurses hardly had time to decide if this was presumptuous or charming. Or both. Disarming, undoubtedly. It also caused many of the men in the pub to roll their eyes and look away disconsolately, some grumbling into their beer, recognising the man in the sharp suit and confident way with the ladies had rendered them all but invisible in their characterless uniforms.

Vignoles realised both he and Mellor cut a different dash to most in the pub. His Italian suit, dark blue silk tie against a pale blue shirt, expensive rectangular framed glasses and a hat Anna had gifted him for Christmas (also in modish Italian styling) ensured they engaged the interest of the nurses, but also made them stand out as men who'd most probably travelled down from London.

Vignoles stood close to the group and allowed Mellor to charm his way into their confidence, restricting himself to the occasional observation to gently rein in his sergeant. There was no denying Mellor was delivering a masterclass of multiple interview technique.

After ten minutes of idle chatter about little other than the inclement weather and establishing the names of the three women (Mary, Alice and Laura) and their respective roles in the camp as nursing staff, Mellor started to ease the conversation around.

'I hear you're being kept busy in the camp medical centre?'

Mary, the raven-haired one, darted him a curious look. 'What makes you say that?'

'One of the footplate crew showing us around today said there's a nasty cold bug going about.'

'A cold?' Laura, the Army staff nurse laughed. 'It would take more than a cold to lay up the Royal Engineers!'

'That's what I thought. A bunch of tough soldiers in bed with an aspirin and hot lemon? Pull the other one...' Mellor gave his smoothest smile whilst attracting the barmaid's attention to call for another round of drinks. 'Must be bad?'

'What are you getting at?' Mary was not smiling. She was starting to put up her defences.

'Just curious why an engine driver was concerned about a

few lads catching colds, that's all...'

'Working all day outside in the snow we've had down here recently,' Laura shrugged it off. 'To be expected. It's nothing to write home about.'

Vignoles found her comment intriguing. It most certainly *was* something to write home about and a young woman was dead as a result. He drained his glass.

'Reckon that's about right,' Mellor nodded agreement and swiftly collected the tray of drinks and distributed them, handing a ten bob note to the barmaid and telling her to 'take one for herself.'

'What line are you gentlemen in? I don't recall you told us?' Mary inquired. She was observant, despite the gin she'd knocked back in quick time. Her eyes studying both Mellor and Vignoles. She was suspicious. 'You've got money to splash around and spend the day riding about on Army trains... What's the story?'

'We work for British Railways. Hence the reason for our study visit to Longmoor,' Vignoles replied. It was vague but not factually inaccurate. 'We're observing aspects of the railway operation down here. We feel there is much to learn from the British Army approach, especially when it comes to managing a crisis.'

An ambulance hurried past the pub, the doppelgänger effect making the note of the insistently clanging bell rise and fall. There was a noticeable stir within the pub and glances exchanged as if its passing held significance for those listening.

'Crisis? What do you mean?' Laura, the Army medic enquired.

'A medical emergency, for example. Something that might threaten the operational capacity of the railway,' Mellor jumped on the opportunity. 'The Army can mobilise and organise on a scale we could learn much from on Civvy Street. Or should that be Civvy Railway!' He laughed.

The spotty youth shook his head slightly and muttered

something inaudible under his breath, then attacked his fresh pint. Laura also pulled an expression of mild surprise but tried to mask it.

'You disagree with my colleague's assessment?' Vignoles enquired in a gentle voice.

'No. It's nice to hear, I suppose.' Laura gave a weary smile. 'Sorry. After a long day's slog, it doesn't always feel like we're quite the model organisation you describe.' Laura did indeed look tired. It could have been the ugly wood and glass chandelier fashioned to look like a wagon wheel suspended from the ceiling on heavy chains throwing an unflattering light, but there appeared to be dark shadows under her eyes.

'Laura…' Mary hissed. It was supposed to have gone unnoticed in the noise in the pub, but both detectives spotted it.

'It's true. I'm almost dead on my feet.'

'An unfortunate choice of words, Laura…' Spotty youth grumbled.

'Just an expression, Jeff. Don't take it seriously.'

The Blonde Bombshell beamed at Vignoles in a heart-warming yet deliberately distracting manner. 'You must appreciate ours can be a demanding job and when we unwind at the end of a long shift we tend to look and feel a bit flat. Until the drinks kick in, that is!' She attacked her second port and lemon with gusto.

'Has another died today?' Mellor was gallantly lighting another cigarette for Mary, the only one of the three who smoked. He was not letting the comment from the spotty youth slip by unnoticed.

'What sort of question is that?' Mary snapped back.

'We heard about the chap who bought it. What was his name? Morton? No, Lance Corporal Mordon.'

Mary drew heavily on her cigarette as she observed Mellor but was silent.

'How did you hear about him?' Laura's voice had a steely

edge to it.

Vignoles had his pipe jutting from the side of his mouth. 'Let me explain. His young wife - widow - Phyllis Mordon is a relative of my own dear lady wife.' It was not true but gave them a way in. 'I only heard the sad news as we travelled down today. Quite awful. Influenza, I understand?'

'Probably that Chinese one doing the rounds,' Mellor chipped in, with a bored tone to his voice.

'It was pneumonia,' Alice replied, matter-of-factly. Her smile was still delicious but looked forced.

'It's not catching, is it? This pneumonia...' Mellor made a look of exaggerated alarm.

'You'll be fine, Mr Mellor.' Mary flashed her dark eyes with something of a twinkle in them. There was a mixture of attraction and mistrust flickering across her face, rather like fast-moving clouds crossing the sun on a breezy April day. She seemed on the verge of cutting loose and talking more freely yet was aware she should be circumspect about her true military purpose for being in the camp.

'The lads in here might say different. They like looking at us from afar, but they don't come close these days. We're like lepers all of a sudden. Lepers with nice legs.' Alice joked.

'I'm sorry? What do you mean?' Vignoles queried with a delightful look of innocent curiosity on his face.

Alice drank more of her gin and took heart from it. 'This lot in here. They think we're contagious. If I walked towards the bar, they'd step back like the Red Sea parting.'

'Merely deference to a pretty woman...' Mellor responded.

'As if!' Laura gulped down more of her drink.

Vignoles and Mellor scanned the room and it was noticeable that for all the obvious attraction the three young women held, the men in uniforms were congregated in the bar or standing at the far side of the saloon as if wanting to maintain some distance. Four men from the village stood nursing pints near the door and casting curious looks towards the nurses, but their expressions were hard to read. They appeared to be pinned to the wall and made no effort to stray closer.

'Why on earth would they think something like that?' Vignoles asked.

'They know about Mordon. And the others.' Jeff was starting to assert himself at last. The second beer was taking hold.

'Careful…' Mary looked horrified.

'What others?' Mellor enquired.

'Ignore him. Look, can we change the subject?' Mary was firefighting the situation. 'We didn't come here to talk shop…'

'If the locals know, then it's hardly a state secret is it?' Spotty youth fired back.

'Are you saying others have contracted pneumonia, just like Mordon?' Vignoles asked.

'You better believe it.'

'How many?' Mellor asked.'

'Ten. At the last count. Ten *dead*, that is. There's many more gone down with it that probably won't pull through.'

There was a pregnant pause.

'I don't think you should say any more.' Alice kept her voice low.

'That's not the half of it,' Jeff continued. 'Why should I keep my trap shut? Who are we protecting? Nobody's looking out for us, are they?' He faced Vignoles. 'We might catch it. Probably will. You might. Some in the village already have, but nobody's allowed to say so.' His voice and look sarcastic. 'Nobody knows or says anything, but you heard the ambulance.'

'I heard two since we've been here,' Mellor agreed.

Mary was tight-lipped and glaring at Jeff, Mellor noticed her hand was quivering slightly.

Laura spoke very quietly. 'We'll be in very serious trouble if Jeff's loose tongue is reported. It could have unpleasant repercussions.'

'But only if we tell someone in authority at the camp,'

Vignoles replied.

'And will you?' Laura asked.

'We shall not,' Vignoles replied. 'We're here to study railway operational procedure.'

'They'll hear all the same. You can bet on it. The MPs are everywhere these days,' Mary smoked hard and looked at the ghastly carpet with its wild Paisley design in red, blue and black.

'What, the Military Police?' Mellor looked surprised.

'They barge in here most nights to spoil any fun,' Laura replied. 'I'm surprised they're not been in already.'

'They have no authority outside the camp in peacetime,' Vignoles replied, aware that neither did Mellor or he, for that matter.

'They do once we step back through the gates. They observe then wait and pounce.' Alice had lost the vivacity of a few minutes ago. Her face was pretty, but Vignoles could see that her makeup was trying to conceal lines around her eyes and mouth.

Vignoles nodded slowly, ensuring he had the attention of the four. 'If word gets out it will not be from either of us, on that you have my word. However, I suggest we had best take our leave before the men in white helmets see us together. I regret cutting the evening short.' He now gave what he hoped was a reassuring smile. 'You should know that we are detectives.'

There was a look of shock and surprise on the women's faces.

'You're here to trap us! That's underhand.' Alice was mortified.

'No, we are not. We are not working for the Army.'

'I'd not share anything with a thug in a white helmet,' Mellor added. 'I owe them nothing. Rest assured.'

'If something is worrying you, you can tell us,' Vignoles looked at Jeff, who had already said more than the others.

The four were undecided what to make of this revelation.

Mary surprised them by breaking the silence. 'It's a virus. Not unlike pneumonia in its effects. Quite harmless, so they told us. Nothing to fear. Safe to administer and everyone would be right as rain in a week or so -.'

Young Jeff sputtered into his beer.

'But then they started dying. So quickly. First Mordon, then others. We saw ten die under our care, but now they take them away in the night and even we can't be sure of how many, but there's been a lot.'

'Out of sight, out of mind.' Laura sounded bitter. 'I know of at least four other men who've been spirited away.' The others nodded in agreement. 'You hear lorries leaving in the early hours...'

'Good God!' Mellor looked horrified.

'If they get really bad, they just...vanish.' Alice was speaking so low it was hard to hear her words. 'They don't want us to see them die. We're told they go to special wards for recovery, but I don't believe it.'

Vignoles and Mellor were stunned.

The newspapers tell some of it, but what they write is so false. That this is just the Asiatic flu and it's just 'one of those things' and there's no need for alarm. But we think those who have it in the towns around here have the same virus that has escaped the camp.'

'Their desperate nobody finds out,' Jeff almost spat the words out.

'You said it was safe?' Vignoles queried.

'Scientists make mistakes like anyone else.' Mary stubbed her cigarette out and tossed back her drink. 'We have to go. We have very sick men to attend. Three hours away after eight hours rigged out in full chemical suits.' She gave Mellor a long and lingering look. 'Nice meeting you, but I doubt we'll meet again...'

'This new virus has not behaved as planned. It causes complications.' Alice looked grim. 'It kills young men.'

'And there's no cure. What a blast!' Jeff grinned ironically and gulped down beer. 'Thanks for the beers, gents. I'd like to think I'll live to repay the debt one day.'

'Listen, wash your hands in hot water and soap after touching anything and anyone. Every time. Don't forget. Wear gloves if you can. Oh, and remember to say a prayer, because there's not a lot that science can do to save you,' Alice looked away, her eyes glassy. The four walked out without further ado.

Vignoles and Mellor realised the men in the saloon were giving them hostile looks. 'Time to beat a hasty retreat. They look in a mood to turn the white helmets on us.'

Mellor agreed.

Chapter Twelve
Longmoor Military Railway

CS Badger telephoned the hotel where Vignoles and Mellor were staying.

'Needed to speak with you before you returned to camp. I shall keep this circumspect. Hotel switchboards are not private.'

'Understood, sir.'

'Don't respond, just listen. Mrs M did *not* die of natural causes. I fought tooth and nail and got her blood samples tested. A powerful toxin administered by a needle. Near instantaneous effect.' Vignoles held his breath. 'Gather what you can there but keep this under your hat. Not a whisper. I want you both out by this afternoon. Do what you can, then back to base and don't dally. Stay safe...' The phone line clicked.

'A toxin administered in the arm. Does that mean she was poisoned by an injection?' Mellor was aghast when Vignoles passed the information across.

'I take it to mean that. There was a pinprick, the kind that might be left by a syringe needle in her upper arm. She was murdered.'

'Then it was pre-meditated.'

'Expertly planned and executed,' Vignoles felt an uneasy lurch in his stomach. 'Even as Benson and I were travelling to Sheffield, someone was plotting to kill her.' He considered the implication.

Who was behind this? He thought back to that curious meeting with Wellbeck. The man had been nervous about being overheard. He chose to meet somewhere obscure and unlikely and even took a circuitous route back as might a man who feared he was being hunted.

The crew of *Sir Guy Williams* had talked darkly of their misgivings and the nurses last night had been edgy. Initially guarded, yet just below the surface, there had been an urge to talk as if wishing to unburden themselves of a weight. It was obvious they were fearful of the repercussions such talk might provoke, and perhaps they had good reason to be. Even the other drinkers in the pub had become restive and unfriendly as the evening wore on. Were they afraid of something?

'Something is going wrong and powerful agencies are working overtime to keep a lid on it, at any cost.'

Mellor chewed on his toast but now found it dry and hard to swallow. He discarded the half-eaten slice and looked out of the diamond leaded panes of the bay window in the breakfast room as yet another ambulance clanged past on an urgent errand.

'The girls said this man-made virus is worse than they were told. They reckon it's a killer, yet the science boffins let it loose. You think there's anything in that?' Mellor lit a cigarette. 'Look at the paper.' He jabbed it with a finger.

The headlines were unambiguous.

DEATHS MOUNT AS EPIDEMIC WORSENS

'Epidemic? The editors have not used that word before…' Vignoles observed as he scanned the pages.

'Newspapers enjoy exaggeration.'

'Fifteen dead in one day…' Vignoles didn't like what he was reading. 'Winchester complaining their hospital is overloaded with sickly patients showing symptoms of *Asiatic flu*…' He was reading aloud. He turned to the inside pages. 'Overseas, the situation is very grave in India and Gibraltar is closing everything and even quarantining all ships…even the naval port. And there are reports of new flare-ups in Southampton and Liverpool. Port cities. But none of this can have any relevance to what is happening here, surely? An unfortunate happenstance.'

Mellor stared back. 'I dunno. I reckon we'd best take care either way. A nasty virus is a nasty virus, whatever name you give it. Though, I'm buggered I know how to avoid something we can't see.'

'Plenty of soap and hot water.' Vignoles pushed the paper aside. It was depressing reading and serving only to blur his thinking. 'We need to take a step back and look at this coolly. The nurses were tired, perhaps a little frazzled and overwrought and imaginations can run wild when alcohol is added to that mix. There *is* Asiatic flu in the country and all these alarming stories of it spreading across the globe play on the imagination. Southampton is not so far from here, so it is plausible troops travelled here from the port with the Asiatic flu or perhaps freight brought up from a ship came into the camp? We must be careful not to make two and two add up to six. The man-made virus could be as benign as the scientists claim, just terrible bad luck the Asiatic version got amongst the soldiers and is causing all the problems, not the other way around.'

'You believe that?' Mellor was openly sceptical. 'If that's so, why inject an innocent woman with poison?'

'Fair point.' Vignoles was once again glad to have the cynical sounding board of Mellor.

'It's a cover-up job and this flu epidemic is a gift. They can muddy the waters all too easily. Make everything opaque so nobody knows which is which and offers the perfect explanation.' Mellor exhaled a long plume of blue smoke into the air. 'I reckon the locals know what's going on. They know the deaths here have sodding all to do with Gib closing its docks. They looked proper jittery last night. An' they were right in a way. The nurses *could* be carrying it. Stands to reason,' Mellor made a face. 'We might have it now...'

'A sobering thought. You might be thankful you didn't get to kiss them after all.' Vignoles gave Mellor an arch look and tried to inject some levity. 'Badger told us to focus on the Porton Down team if we can get close enough. I don't know what our chances are, but we can try, then make our excuses.'

'The quicker the better...'

'You sound worried?'

'Give me a man with a loaded gun or wielding a knife and I'll take him on. But this? It makes my skin crawl.'

* * * *

The atmosphere within the camp seemed to have noticeably altered from the day before. Yesterday, the detectives had been chaperoned but those they met during the day had been willing to talk, and quite openly, about the field trials. There had been a relaxed atmosphere to the arrangement and with some careful steering of conversations, both detectives had elicited useful information. The tip-off about the pub and the Porton Down nurses had been a gift on top.

However, a frosty greeting upon arrival at the main gate set a different tone for the day. The gate guardians were civil, but no more. The cheery smiles and laddish bonhomie had evaporated. After a lengthy telephone call inside the guard office there followed an equally lengthy inspection of their papers granting admission, all perhaps designed to make them feel very much under the power and authority of the regiment. Their documents had been perfectly in order the day before but were now the cause of delay and much head-scratching and low conversations out of earshot. They were eventually escorted into the camp and deposited close to the engine shed yard office where they were ushered into a bare room and told to wait. It was a command rather than a request.

When Privates Walker and Denning arrived, both men shook hands but appeared noticeably quieter and more ill at ease than yesterday. Vignoles and Mellor tried some gentle banter but neither soldier was in the mood for chatting and merely mumbled vacuous replies.

It was going to be a day of tightly chaperoned and pre-prepared sight-seeing around the engine shed complex, with no opportunity for unscheduled 'off-track' explorations. The conversation was restricted to harmless discussions about such things as the coal consumption of different locomotive classes, the relative merits of differing injector designs and the build quality of German 'Kriegslok' locomotives from the last war.

'They've been nobbled...' Mellor mumbled as they were escorted from one engine shed to another.

'A three-line whip,' Vignoles replied under his breath. 'Our evening in the pub has got back to the senior ranks.'

'Looks that way. One of the squaddies didn't like us buying drinks for the girls and had a word, is my guess.'

Ordinarily, Vignoles and Mellor would have thoroughly enjoyed the being shown around by the assistant shed master, who was eager to tell them everything and anything he could about the build dates, horsepower and finer operational quirks of the eleven engines he currently had standing inside or on the apron outside his sheds.

A stranger gathering of ex-War Department, industrial and almost life-expired tank locomotives could hardly be imagined. From enormous ten-coupled beasts to tiny four-wheeled 'pugs', they spanned a wide range of sizes and shapes. Some were adorned with grand headlamps, runs of external piping leading to oddly shaped valves and festooned with wire for electric lamps, all of which gave them a distinctly 'European' character despite hailing from workshops in places like Manchester or Leeds. Some wore brass nameplates declaring them to be called *Gordon* or *Kitchener*, whilst the favoured deep blue, red and white paintwork abounded.

Both detectives were itching to escape their attentive guide, whom they suspected had been instructed to keep them fully occupied on 'safe territory.' It was starting to look like a futile waste of a morning and Vignoles was struggling to find a way out of the confines of the shed. By late morning everyone was in need of refreshment and generous mugs of tea and coffee were brewed and with the weak winter sun taking the edge from the cold, they sat on a collection of oil barrels and mismatched chairs outside a typical railway man's bothy on the edge of the yard. An American-built six-wheeled tank engine named *Maj-Gen. Frank S. Ross*, shuffled wagons about in front of them.

Vignoles lit his pipe. They would make their excuses and call it a day.

It was obvious The Royal Engineers had closed ranks. They were doing it without fuss and in a manner not to cause embarrassment, but it was undeniable. Whenever he'd enquired if they could take a walk around the barracks or see how the railway ran its medical section so they could 'better understand how you deal with accidents and emergencies,' he was firmly rebuffed. They were allowed to see the locomotives being prepared for service or under maintenance, and in the afternoon had been told they would take one last trip to Bordon, riding in a separate guard's van on a goods train timed to connect with their service train to London. This almost certainly chosen to ensure they had no chance of speaking with anyone outside their small group. That was to be their lot.

Vignoles leaned back against the corrugated iron wall and allowed the sun to fall on his face and admitted defeat. The Army was a well-drilled organisation and two detectives from Leicester were not going to get through this impasse. The constant, albeit distant, presence of two military policemen with their white helmets glinting in the sun was a further reminder of the impossibility of the situation. He suspected they were being watched and at the slightest deviation from the agreed plan, these two unappealing characters would step in.

Vignoles turned away and chose instead to study the ungainly but characterful design of *Maj-Gen. Frank S Ross* with its high-slung side tanks and a cab that seemed to float, as if suspended above the small red and white-rimmed wheels. It looked alien and quite out of place deep in southern England. Rather as he and Mellor in their sharp suits, collars and ties and woollen overcoats stood out like sore thumbs. There was no possibility of slipping away unobserved in a world of men in identical uniforms.

However, even the best-laid plans of the British Army could be upset. The American tank engine came to a sudden halt opposite where they were seated, and the fireman leaned out of his cab. 'Quickly! I need help. My driver's ill!'

The fireman looked worried, and after attracting their attention he hastily pulled the bandana tied around his neck back across his lower face and ducked inside the cab.

The assistant shed master was on his feet and racing across the few feet between them, but as he drew close to the engine, turned with arms raised and urged the detectives to hold back. 'Don't come closer! Stay back!' He climbed the steps and peered over the cab floor. 'What's up?'

'It came on so sudden there was no warning.' The fireman was kneeling beside the driver who was slumped in the far corner. Vignoles and Mellor ignored the order, their chaperones calling after them to 'come back,' but unwilling to follow, their young faces a mixture of worry and uncertainty.

'What's wrong?' Mellor asked.

'I told you to stay away!'

'We need to get him down from there. It won't help being crumpled up like that,' Mellor continued.

The assistant shed master dropped back to the ground and faced the detectives. He looked pale and his eyes betrayed something akin to fear. 'The medics will take care of this. There's nothing for either of to do. They will take care of him.' He called to the two soldiers. 'Don't stand there like a pair of goons! Call an ambulance - and sharp about it!'

'What do we say?'

'Just call them!' The word was almost hissed with pent up anger. 'Get on with it or I'll have you both on a charge!'

Both men hared off into the shed. Vignoles was intrigued as it would only take one person to place the call and the other could surely be better used keeping an eye on Mellor and himself. These young men were spooked.

'What's happened to the driver?' Vignoles repeated Mellor's question.

'It's nothing for you to be concerned about. We have it under control. Now step away, please. The ambulance will be here in minutes.'

Mellor had already darted around the other side of the engine and appeared on the far side of the cab. 'He's burning up! Sweating' buckets and his breathin' ain't too clever...'

'It gets you like that.' The fireman replied in a quiet voice. 'Comes on sudden. Burning hot one moment then shivering so as you can't hold your hands steady. Then you can't get your breath.' The fireman was crouched near his pal, eyes wide across the line of the bandana that spanned his nose. 'You shouldn't go close. It's contagious.'

Mellor stared at the driver's puffy eyes and his chest rising and falling in unsteady movements as his mouth gasped for air. 'What is it?'

'The bloody virus! It's taking everyone. I'll be next.' The fireman's eyes were like those of a frightened horse with too much white showing. 'I've been stood next to Mike these last five days. No chance I'll escape now.' His voice was resigned.

A strident bell clanged and the sound of a roaring diesel engine. The khaki painted ambulance with giant red crosses in white circles hurried into view, bouncing along the cinder track beside the railway. Mellor dropped to the ground and watched as the vehicle screeched to a halt, the engine left running and two figures wearing gas masks, heavy rubber gauntlets and baggy khaki coveralls tied at the wrists and ankles stepped out. They looked like creatures from another planet, the unblinking 'eyes' of the masks rendering them impersonal and expressionless, their mouths covered by an ugly black snout holding an air filter. They approached, arms waving as they indicated everyone should move away.

Mellor was glad to join Vignoles. 'They came prepared. I don't like the look of this.'

Vignoles didn't answer, just silently watched as these unsettling figures man-handled the driver from the cab. There was a deathly silence as the medical team communicated using hand signals because vocal communications were impossible. It was like some kind of macabre silent movie.

Mellor touched Vignoles on the arm and nodded towards the ambulance. It felt inappropriate to speak. Another similarly clad figure had now emerged from the rear. The same expressionless mask, but slightly shorter in height, rendered equally shapeless in the gas suit. However, this figure also wore a small cap on top of glossy black hair that hung at the back in a ponytail.

'Nurse Mary?'

Vignoles nodded.

A stretcher was extracted and the sick driver quickly lowered on to this and carried back, the two men carefully stepping over rails and sleepers as they did so. The female figure stopped momentarily, and the blank discs of glass reflected the lemony sunlight as she stared at the two detectives. She then hurried over to help escort the visibly shaken fireman to the ambulance.

'Need to check him over. They'll quarantine him, of course.' The assistant shed master felt the need to explain.

'That's necessary?' Mellor asked.

'Essential.' He glared at Mellor. 'You fool. I told you to stay away. By rights, we should quarantine you both.'

Mellor swallowed.

· 'Maybe you'll be lucky...'

'It's that bad?' Mellor asked.

'Listen, matey, I know about engines and steam and coal, not about *that*... You saw what you saw, and I can't help that, but they don't wear those space suits for fun. Now get in the bothy and wash your hands in hot water, then take my advice and get out of here.' He sounded more weary than angry. 'Just go home. I need to find someone to look after this engine...'

A jeep occupied by the two white helmeted MPs was approaching as the ambulance crew were closing the rear doors of their vehicle and starting to reverse away.

'Too late. Looks like your time just ran out. I won't shake hands...'

Chapter Thirteen
Leicester Central

CS Badger called the meeting. 'Assemble at Central. I don't want either of you up to London. That could attract attention and I'd rather we kept our heads down.'

'Attention from whom?' Vignoles was surprised.

'I'd rather not say over the telephone. But watch your backs.' His voice was clipped. 'I shall drive there. It's safer in the disinfected rear seat of my staff car than sharing a 1st class compartment these days.'

'Are such precautions strictly necessary?' Vignoles could not help sounding sceptical. Longmoor and Hampshire just felt like a bad dream and some of the dire warnings issued whilst there were already fading. Even the disturbing scene of the gas-suited medics was turning into something akin to a surreal memory.

He lacked detailed information on the specifics of what happened that last day at Longmoor, but it could perhaps be explained away as an over-reaction by the medics in a jittery regiment. The engine driver's sudden illness, whilst real enough, had prompted a pre-agreed training exercise into action, complete with bodysuits and breathing gear. It was the kind of thing they did at Longmoor; build things up, demolish, rebuild anew and practice for a gas, biological or even nuclear fallout emergency.

Despite his misgivings, Vignoles could afford a wry smile as he listened to Badger justifying the use of his driver and petrol on personal health grounds. With the reintroduction of petrol rationing the previous November and a massive forty per cent hike in the cost of a gallon to a chilling six shillings in December, this was going to put a significant dent in the departmental budget. The Super had long championed the use of an expensive and immaculately polished Rover and never felt the need to offer a reason for its use in preference over the regular trains that departed from right outside his office window.

'Minshul has similar orders. Rendezvous in three hours, traffic permitting. And Vignoles, you might wish to take a look in *The Times*. It makes interesting reading.'

*   *   *   *

'Wellbeck is from the Common Cold Institute. He is Chief Research Officer with specialist knowledge in *Coronavirus* variants. An important position and his opinion respected.' Badger had *The Times* folded to display an article the Editor had considered significant enough to afford most of page two. The accompanying photograph showed Terence Wellbeck carefully lit by an expert studio photographer. He was dressed in the obligatory white lab coat and looking suitably studious with a test tube in one hand and a Biro in the other poised above a pad of paper.

Badger, Vignoles and Minshul were seated in an empty Royal Mail sorting van that Badger had arranged to be parked in one of the bays incised deep into the island platform of Leicester Central. The scarlet rake of coaches with their bold lettering in gold leaf was striking and offered a welcome splash of colour to a dank and miserable winter's day characterised by relentless sleety rain.

These specialised coaches had narrow horizontal slit windows placed high on their sides, offering minimal natural light and considerable security. They were otherwise almost featureless on the outside, with closely fitting loading and access doors that were usually kept locked. Nobody could see in or out and despite the eye-catching appearance, the train attracted little more than momentary interest from passengers focused on keeping warm and blowing their noses. The Post

Office mail sorters demanded a warm environment to work in and the efficient cast iron stove was kicking out welcome heat as the three sat huddled around it.

'The virus strain Wellbeck refers to in this article is the same as did for Mordon?' Minshul asked.

'It is. *Coron56-N4* is the snappy name given. Porton Down didn't want anyone outside to learn about its existence and cloaked the trials with the innocuous title of *Operation Chinese Bird*,' Badger's voice was grim.

'Hence the reason I was sent to Sheffield to buy Phyllis Mordon's silence…'

'Only for someone else to silence her forever.' Minshul had just finished sharing the details from the laboratory about how the young woman had been injected with an especially strong dose of cyanide.

'The same virus that appears to be felling perfectly fit young men on the Longmoor Military Railway. We don't have exact numbers, but Mellor and I reckon ten deaths at least. There were hints at a further four and the local press cited around thirty dead outside the camp, but this was attributed to *Asiatic flu*. Those who were prepared to speak to us were scared and I suspect told us only part of what they knew. There were unsubstantiated claims bodies were being transported off-site in the night.'

'The implication is they were dead, but officially, a fudge about them being taken to civilian hospitals,' Mellor added with a bitter note in his voice.

'We need to verify this one way or the other.' Badger sounded equally grim. 'Though I suspect we shall be rebuffed at every turn. How accurate do you believe these reports of deaths to be?'

'We witnessed a man suddenly affected by illness. He was felled with little warning. We have no information about the outcome, as we were summarily escorted off the premises by the Military Police who not in the mood for talking. He looked in a bad way. I suspect we saw the virus in action.' Vignoles went on to describe the chilling scene with the masked medics.

Minshul was aghast. He smoked heavily. 'What in God's name are we dealing with? This is not a headache and going to bed with hot lemon and honey...'

'Far from it. A contagious man-made organism that appears to have developed the ability to kill. My travel precautions don't seem quite so fastidious now,' Badger observed.

'This letter to *The Times* is startling,' Vignoles continued, turning back to the newspaper. 'I met Wellbeck. Alone.' The other two sat more upright at this news. 'He telephoned the office and was cagey. He was anxious and upon reflection, perhaps scared. He was also unwell.'

'Where did you meet?' Badger asked.

'He was insistent on somewhere away from other people.' Vignoles replied. 'We took a short walk in the country along from Ashby Magna station, not far from my parent's house.'

'A place you might be expected to visit, yet far from prying eyes?'

'That was my thinking.'

'Then it was a prudent choice,' Badger replied. 'What did he tell you?'

'Much that he has now gone public with, which surprises me. There is actually more detail in this article. Why all the subterfuge if he's going to give it to the press? I don't understand. He looked genuinely worried about being held to account by the Official Secrets Act and I felt it prudent to keep the meeting quiet until such time as I could make sense of what he was telling me. But here he is telling the whole world about *Operation Chinese Bird*! He's expanding on how the new virus was designed to be contagious yet mild in effect, then makes claims it has behaved erratically and taking on a deadly aspect. Is he crazy? He's going to land himself in prison.'

Badger took a breath before speaking. 'I can answer your

questions, Vignoles. Wellbeck sent this to the editor knowing that by the time it was in print he would be beyond the reach of the law.' Badger paused. 'Wellbeck is dead.'

Vignoles and Minshul sat in stunned silence.

'Officially he died from pneumonia, but I have learned this was a consequence of *coron56-N4* infection. Colonel Broadbent called me first thing today and hence this meeting.'

'How is Colonel Broadbent reacting to the news?' Vignoles asked. 'Longmoor is going to be in the spotlight for all the wrong reasons.'

'Hard to read the man. He's a master at controlling his emotions and doesn't indulge in chit-chat, let alone emotional outbursts. He started bullish and angry about this article, as you might expect. A mixture of fury at the situation blown wide open, offset by a genuine concern that decent people like the Mordons and now Wellbeck and the other ten or more, are all dead. He's a civil engineer at heart and a manager of men in military service, not some biochemist dreaming up deadly agents. I don't believe he indulges in Secret Service style shenanigans.'

'The Army didn't jab that needle in Phyllis Mordon's arm?' Minshul growled.

'They did not. Not their style, plus I think Broadbent's humanity is winning out. Don't forget, he's seen men lost to the experimentation of others - even if packaged with a pretty title.'

'You consider him an ally?' Minshul asked.

'That word implies an 'us and them' mentality. The good people versus a common enemy. But is it that straightforward? I don't think it is.' Badger chewed this over a moment, clearly battling with a dilemma. Vignoles and Minshul smoked in silence and waited. 'We are meeting like conspirators because I feel it prudent to be cautious. It causes me considerable pain to voice what I am about to say, but the facts, as we understand them, imply a branch of Her Majesty's Government is acting in a manner that goes against all we stand for. Innocent citizens murdered; innocent men called up for National Service being used like laboratory rats for testing biological agents.' He stopped and ran a hand across his face. He looked tired and his breath was short.

'It's not the first time it's happened,' Minshul growled. 'There was talk of a scandal at Porton Down a few years back. A soldier died. Somebody tell me I'm imagining all this. Is my mind racing as if running a fever?' But it was a rhetorical question because Badger continued before either detective could reply. 'Broadbent's a decent man who obeys orders, but if he suspects other forces are hurting his regiment, he will react. My guess is he is wrestling with the same dilemma as we. He does not, as yet, know the shocking truth about Mrs Mordon.'

'Who should we share this information with?' Vignoles queried.

'The fewer, the better. Mellor and Ashbury of course. Beyond that, pick only your very best to brief.'

'You have not counted Lombard from the MRD and Urban from the CDEE as part of "us",' Vignoles replied.

'I have not.'

'Remind me what those blinking' acronyms stand for?' Minshul added, irritably.

'The Microbiological Research Department, of which Lombard is head. The CDEE is the Chemical Defence Experimental Establishment. Professor Urban is one of their top men in the biological warfare department.'

Minshul shuddered. 'I wouldn't want either near me.'

'Nor as your enemy,' Badger replied gravely. 'I won't sugar coat this, these men and the organisations they work for, worry me. I sense they're scared they've let a genie out of the bottle and are prepared to do whatever it takes to conceal that fact. If we could get an analysis of what was injected into the poor Mordon girl, I suspect it might turn out to be an artificial form of cyanide. Another of the many vile concoctions these establishments play with.'

'Do you know what the link is between the two institutions and this virus?' Vignoles asked.

'I don't and doubt we ever will. I suspect they worked together somewhere down the line and are busy pulling shutters down and burning bridges as we speak. We won't get anything out of them. It wouldn't be prudent to try.' Both DCIs agreed. Badger lit another cigarette, but not before having an attack of coughing. 'Apologies, gentlemen. Too many cigarettes...' He quietened the cough. 'We have no mandate whatsoever, nor any legal authority to do anything. Any action is risky to our careers and perhaps our liberty. So why not just let this drop? Close our eyes and ears and ignore what is happened outside our purview? I'll tell you why, because we were roped in with our arms twisted behind our backs and I don't like it. I like even less when railway personnel, be they army or otherwise, are dying. A woman serving tea in a station has been murdered for doing nothing other than losing her husband. I want to find out who is behind all this and I want them called to account.' Badger was angry. 'If either of you wants out, then speak up and leave.'

'I'm in.'

'Just try and stop me getting those who killed Phyl!' Minshul added.

'I expected no less. Now for the last piece of information I hold. This should be treated as confidential. Wellbeck sent me a short private note. Posted the same day as he sent the article to The Times. It's hard to fathom exactly what he's getting at, but it appears some people are proving immune to this man-made virus whilst acting as efficient carriers. Remember, there is no known cure. These people have no symptoms but are highly contagious. He was also concerned the camp was not fully locked down and men were still allowed out, some of whom could be unwitting carriers.'

'And go for a drink in a busy pub in the nearby village,' Vignoles added, with some annoyance.

'Hence a 'flu' epidemic flaring up in the surrounding townships,' Minshull continued.

'It looks that way. We've all read the gloomy predictions of this *Asiatic Flu*, but those spikes around Hampshire, London and some other places shout *coron56-N4*,' Badger replied. 'But there's worse. Broadbent admitted that since the outbreak they've had a high incidence of men absconding without leave. Running away from the place.'

'Can you blame them?' Minshull observed.

'They are trying their utmost to hook these chaps back, but a number remain unaccounted for. They've gone to ground and making a decent fist of evading the clutches of the military police.'

'Has Broadbent offered an opinion on why so many have gone AWOL?' Vignoles asked. 'Presumably, he suspects more than just the usual homesickness or kicking against National Service?'

'There could be several reasons. There is always low-level absenteeism, although they fare far better than some regiments. He implied there was growing dissatisfaction with a system which some believe is letting them down over *Operation Chinese Bird*. A moral revolt against the use of what is effectively a biological weapon. He admitted a number of these missing men could be carriers. Men who are scared and confused. Panicked by a dreadful realisation they are pariahs in society. The colonel wanted our help to find them and bring them in. Whatever their motives and whatever their physical well-being, we need to find these absent men as quickly as possible. Every hour they are at liberty they potentially spread this deadly virus. They could be holed up in houses and beyond our reach, but none owned cars and the railways are their usual means of transport. If they show their faces on the railway system, we have to be ready.'

FEBRUARY

Chapter Fourteen
Bristol Temple Meads

Sergeant Alan Winter carried a tray bearing mugs of tea and plates with rounds of triangular cut cheese and ham sandwiches over to where Private Tommy Clawson was seated. He placed them on the Formica-topped table and sat down, eyeing with approval the copies of Bradshaw's railway timetable Clawson had been sent to purchase whilst he got the refreshments in.

'Good work. Hope you spent time choosing them.' His soft West Country burr betraying his origins in Barnstable.

'You bet. Fondled nearly every magazine in the Smith's stall. Picked all the shiniest ones as I think they'd be the best to transfer it. I went from *Practical Householder* right across to *The Lady*.' He laughed. 'So even the rich ladies are going to get it as well!' He laughed.

Winter grinned, rather as a shark might. 'Nice touch.'

Clawson took a sip of tea. 'These cups are shiny. Bound to carry it back to the kitchen.'

'And this,' Winter's eyes had a wicked glint in them as he ran his hand over the tin tray. 'Right, let's have a shufti...' He took one of the timetables and whilst munching hungrily, expertly flipped the pages back and forth until he found the page he was looking for. 'What I'm thinking is, we both head down west for starters. One of us to Penzance, which is as far as the rails will take us, and the other work across to cover some of the coastal towns. Places like Ilfracombe and

Minehead, not forgetting to stop off in my hometown. Then work our way back to London using different routes to cover as much ground as we can.'

'Get the major stations in London covered...'

'Right you are. A day or two would have them licked, then maybe go east.'

'To the channel ports? We send it to Europe?'

'Good thinking. Maybe take a ferry to France for the day?'

'I've always fancied the South of France. Hot sun and those pretty French girls in their little swimsuits in the hot sun...'

'I heard they don't always wear them!'

'Get away!'

'But that's for later. Just travelling on the boat trains will be enough... We've got a lot of ground to cover back here, so never mind trying to work out how to buy tickets and get around France. I can't handle the lingo... We can just send it on its way over the channel and let others do the work.'

Clawson was also attacking his sandwich, making a point of wiping his sticky fingers on the Formica. 'There's pages and pages of trains in here.'

'And that's why we're using them. A car's too private. It would be just us and the odd petrol pump attendant or cafe. That's no use. This way we can cover more miles and the whole time we're on board or waiting at a station we're spreading the infection. Walk along the train touching every door handle, sit in every compartment.'

'Genius.'

Winter laughed and swigged tea, running a finger across a page of departure times.

Sandwiches consumed, Clawson lit a cigarette, tossing the packet onto the table towards Winter so he could take one when ready. He sat back in his chair and ran his eyes around the small refreshment room.

It was busy and noisy with chatter and the clatter of crockery and the whoosh of the coffee machine making the now popular Italian style 'frothy coffee' that students and posh intellectuals preferred these days. Clawson had never been to a jazz club and had no desire to, but he'd been reliably informed that in places like London and Bristol - where they were presently awaiting a change of train - you could tell the 'Jazzers' by their black-rimmed spectacles and college scarves tossed carelessly around their necks, a preference for turtle neck jumpers and also for this funny coffee that came in clear Pyrex cups.

He felt his face forming into a sneer as he watched a young couple exactly fitting this description stand at the counter. They'd just stepped off the suburban train that pulled into the platform outside, having come down through north west Bristol.

The young woman had a ponytail and wearing glasses. Now she'd unfastened her duffle coat he could see her purple turtleneck that emphasised an impressive bust line. A posh bird studying at the University. Clawson felt an odd mixture of desire and contempt course through his veins.

Was he envious and longing to trade places with the beardy intellectual paying at the till? Or did he hate them both and their awful taste in music and their intellectual mannerisms? He felt his fingers itch and started to move them as if warming up before playing the piano. He wanted to walk up to the girl and take hold of her, squeeze her where he shouldn't and kiss her on those bright red lips, then punch that pathetic lanky streak of a man on the nose and send his glasses flying. He'd infect them both - and most probably kill them after a few days of incubation.

The woman turned to walk to a table, and for a brief second their eyes met. She gave an instinctive smile. It was polite and meant nothing, but her face lit up with youthful innocence. He turned away as he felt a jolt of guilt run through him like an electric shock.

'Sarge, we're doing the right thing, ain't we?'

'We've been over this.'

'I know. It's just...' Clawson dragged on his fag and narrowed his eyes. 'Looking at those two. What they done to deserve to get it?'

'She's a cracker. I can see why you want to get your hands on her. There's a lot to handle...' He sniggered and smoked, but there was nothing sympathetic in the cold light in his eyes and the soulless emptiness in his voice. 'A few weeks ago, I'd be fighting you over her. Not she'd give us squaddies a second glance.'

'She smiled at me!'

'Don't fool yourself.' He leaned forward across the table. 'We're lepers now. She'd run a bloody mile if she knew what we had. We're outcasts. Nobody wants us now. We're alone.'

Clawson smoked and stared at the table. 'It's horrible. My girl down Southend way, won't be happy...'

'Happy? She and her family would run you out of bloody town. Push you away with brooms or chuck stones at you. They won't let you near them for all the tea in China. An' what about me?' Winter took a cigarette from the carton. 'My wife and kid? I so much as touch her or kiss her and she's dead. I'm a walking-bloody-death sentence.'

'Like that king? What was 'is name?'

'Dunno who you mean...'

'You know the one, he turned everything to gold and thought it were brilliant until he got his hands on his queen's knockers and she was just a dead lump of gold...'

'King Midas. Except we don't even get the bloody gold either. Ten sodding pounds for this.'

'And they were going to lock us up.'

'Better believe it. I heard that blonde nurse talking with the creepy doctor. Said we were carriers but couldn't get ill. They had some fancy word I didn't know for it, but I understood what they were getting at. They were talking about what to do about us. They needed to prepare a secure place to keep us locked away for months. Years. As long as it took to find a cure.'

'It's horrible. We probably caused some of the lads to die.'

'We can't know that.'

'But we must have. Stands to reason. Tom, Mike, Sammy, Dicky, Arthur and the others I never knew the names of... all gone.'

'You heard they've taken to shipping the bodies out at night and saying nothing. Nothing! Good men dead and they don't even get a farewell. Like lumps of cold meat. God knows what they do with the bodies.'

'Mass grave?'

Winter subbed his cigarette out with a shudder. 'Well, they're not locking us up in solitary. That's what they were lining up for us. Make us live alone with just a barred window to look out of like bloody criminals and we've done nothing wrong.'

'Like animals in a zoo. Stared at by those Porton Downers wearing breathing apparatus inspecting and testing and writing stuff down but never letting us get a taste of freedom. It makes my skin crawl just imagining it.'

'Mine too.' Winter jabbed his index finger on the page open in front of him. 'Right. The 1.25 ex-Paddington should be due any time. We both go to Kingswear, then split and work our way around and about and back to London to rendezvous, OK?'

'Time for some payback!'

Winter was eyeing up the attractive student in the turtleneck again. 'Like I said, my wife is lost to me now.' He shrugged his shoulders. 'Life's a bitch, but those dammed scientists can't help me either. They don't know what to do. They created a monster and can't kill it off. But there'll be others like us. On the other side. Untouched and healthy when the rest are dead. Some of them will be girls. Maybe that looker in purple will be one of 'em, eh? Only one way to find out. When this bug has finished its job and left millions dead, we look around and have the pick of the girls who are immune.'

'I see what you mean! And go to the south of France to live a life of luxury...'

'If you want. Bound to be a few nice Frenchies who escaped.'

There was a short toot of a whistle and a stirring of people making for the mock-Gothic shaped door of the Temple Meads buffet. Winter and Clawson looked out of the stone mullioned windows that looked like something from a grand country house as the gleaming shape of *King Charles II* in Brunswick green hauling a long train of coaches rolled into view. The copper and brass of the engine was freshly polished and caught what it could of the low winter sun dipping beneath the pointed arch of the grand vaulted train shed.

The two men hefted their kitbags onto their shoulders and marched onto the platform. They walked beside the carriages looking in each to select a suitable one to board, Winter's hand idly stroking each brass door handle as they walked. Once settled on a compartment both men stowed their kitbags in the net luggage racks and flung themselves on the seats, stroking the armrests and fiddling with the little metal foldaway ashtrays. Clawson stood up again and opened the narrow windows above the vestigial table that extended from below the picture window. He poked his head out to gaze at a locomotive steaming and hissing against the far platform. Also painted green, this was named *Novelty* and bore cream painted numerals on the cab side. Clawson had been a fireman at Longmoor and was interested to watch the crew expertly busying themselves for departure, oblivious of the invisible enemy just a few feet away.

There had been some discussion in Longmoor that proximity to the intense heat of locomotive fires and inhaling the pungent smoke gave some level of protection. It was a disinfectant for the lungs, so they said. Men had started gathering in groups around the engines in the morning whilst the engines were being made ready for the day's work and the chimneys were belching especially noxious coils of smoke. Everyone was inhaling deeply and holding the fumes inside their lungs. He'd even seen a few of those odd figures in gas masks and suits take off the apparatus for a few moments and take their fill.

Both he and Winter had been footplate men until yesterday. Untouched by the virus and yet unwilling carriers, they were soon to be the most reviled men in the land. They were 'Asympto-Something-Or-Other' as the gorgeous nurse had explained to him using a word he didn't know. Asses, more like. Maybe the men in their engine men's 'blues' checking pressure and water levels before steaming *Novelty* towards Worcester and Birmingham might escape it? But why should they? Winter had seen too many of his mates die, so why should he care about these two?

He pulled his head back in and closed the window making sure he rubbed his hands over the glass and handles. 'Once underway, we'll walk the length of the train and back. No time like the present.'

The whistle blew and the 'King' made a stirring start towards the West Country with its terrible cargo. The big reporting numbers on the front of the smokebox door declared the train to be identified as '149'. In time, it would be remembered notoriously, if somewhat melodramatically, by the tabloid newspapers as 'The Plague Train'.

Chapter Fifteen
Paddington

WPC Jane Benson had booked the weekend away and travelled up to London on Friday.

With DS Mellor's permission, she departed Leicester Central late afternoon and was looking forward to a delightful round of socialising, including drinking what they were now calling "expressos" (to the apparent horror of Mrs Vignoles, who argued it should be 'espresso') in one of several 'cool' coffee shops.

These were usually filled with excited students and Teddy Boys or even some of the louche gangs of 'Mods' just starting to appear in their slick togs. Whatever their affiliation, they would all feed 'tanners' into the Jukeboxes to spin Rock 'n' Roll 45's and ensure the atmosphere was loud and crackling with excitement despite the lack of alcohol. In the evening she would dance to live music played in one of the jazz clubs springing up across the city. The mornings however would be spent staying deliciously late in bed in the arms of Max Hawkes; her rakish, if rather charming, trumpet-playing lover.

Escaping to London took her away from the confines of her rented room in Mostyn Street and irritating landlady; West London offered her the chance to breathe at least a different brand of smog-laden air and a break from inhaling the insidious reek of over-boiled greens and cauliflower at home. London was the place to be these days and if you knew where to go (and Max inevitably did) they could take in the fascinating displays of strutting Ted's in the lime greens, blues, canary yellows and reds of their outrageous drape coats, marvel at their garishly printed ties and the drainpipe jeans with enormous turn-ups that so scandalised letter writers to *The Daily Telegraph*. The West End and Soho cafes now rang out to the makeshift 'skiffle' sounds of Lonnie Donegan riding his 'Rock Island Line' and the thrilling beats of Tommy Steele, Bill Haley & His Comets and Elvis Presley.

All of which, to a lesser degree she could enjoy in Leicester, especially in The Locarno Milk Bar on Loseby Lane that Lucy Lansdowne and she frequented together, but what Leicester could not offer was the hustle and bustle and excitement of the metropolis with its bright lights and swanky shops filled with enticing new goods and modish fashions she could only occasionally afford. However, window shopping for unobtainables was still a thrill.

Perhaps the highlight for Benson was sampling the novel flavours and aromas of the West Indian cooking that Max's band members concocted in their mouldy and decrepit three-storey townhouse, typical of so many in the most run-down areas of Paddington and Notting Hill. The house was the best anyone of West Indian origin could hope for. Living like squatters whilst terrorised by an aggressive Polish landlord and his thick-necked enforcers with their slavering dogs on chains, was unsettling and lacked all creature comforts except hot and delicious food that set the taste buds dancing. These shared meals washed down with generous glasses of dark rum and cola and accompanied by vivid tales of life 'back home' on their sun-baked but poverty-stricken and hurricane-ravaged islands were a continual delight to Benson.

The stories were frequently punctuated by song and sometimes dancing despite the ominously groaning floorboards, and Benson often felt as though she was being transported across the ocean to an almost unimaginable world even as mucky sleet slammed against the soot-dribbled windows and dripped through the many holes in the roof into a succession of zinc pails.

These recently arrived immigrants, in the main from Barbados, all seemed to have traditional English Christian names such as Arthur, Malcolm, Lawrence and Gerald and despite the dreadful living conditions always managed to remain immaculately turned out in dark suits and white shirts and sober ties or bright sports jackets with a polo shirt buttoned to the neck or even a thin V-neck sweater when the weather turned cold. Actually, the weather was 'always cold, far *too* cold!' for the like of Malcolm and Lawrence, but they never managed to buy the right thickness of overcoat and their preference for thinly soled formal shoes with smooth leather soles made their ability to navigate icy streets a constant trial. Benson had tried knitting thick woollen scarves in the brightest colours she could obtain, but whilst enthusiastically received these were worn simply draped across the neck hanging loose, thereby minimising any potential benefit. Their hats were of the 'pork pie' or narrow brimmed style and this look had been adopted by Max, especially when playing his trumpet or saxophone. He now considered it virtually 'impossible' to play without a hat on his head.

The women were more colourful. Benson had formed strong bonds with the 'girls' and found them disarmingly attractive, able to wear orange, yellow or red and even lime green in any possible combination and never look anything less than 'knock-out'. Benson felt dreadfully mousey despite her recent love-affair with wider skirts that flew outwards to reveal an expanse of petticoat and leg when dancing and evening dresses that hugged and shimmered in bolder colours than she'd ever dare approach before.

'Hey, gurl, you one bee-yoo-tee-ful woman! My, you sendin' all the men craa-zy...' Miriam, one of her closest new friends and the girlfriend of Malcolm the band's drummer, was not accepting that Benson was a 'typical boring Englishwoman.'

'Max got a good eye. He knows what side his bread is buttered an' no mistake! It ain't for nothin' we call you 38c!' Miriam's voice and laugh could travel halfway across the street and it was infectious.

This cheeky nickname was symbolic of how Benson's

London life was far removed from her working week in her formal police uniform and the disapproving looks from her sour-faced landlady with her typed list of strict house rules pinned to the wall. Life in west London was changing her outlook.

Max and Jane shared a large room in this rambling terrace that once must have been very grand. The whole area was one of faded glory; a once desirable area lined with villas and terraces of Georgian or early Victorian design now surrounded by untended streets with intermittently functioning lighting and abandoned cars. Scrappy gardens overgrew with dusty ground elder and stands of nettles in the springtime and fly-tipped litter abounded, whilst boarded bomb sites lay neglected and ignored, gathering more broken sofas and prams missing wheels as each month passed. It was within this mouldering part of West London that Jane Benson could shrug off her WPC uniform and accept the outrageous nickname Max had once given her.

To her mortifying dismay, he'd shared this with the band, and consequently, their wider circle. Max discovered Benson spent time at work visiting Leicester North engine shed, more usually known simply by the code of 38c. This exactly matched her bust measurement, much to his delight and he was not going to let her forget it.

'Visiting 38c for the weekend...'

'Making a stopover at 38c for the night...' and other, far ruder, versions abounded and caught on like wildfire. Since Miriam was quite unabashed about envying both the description and the reality of Benson in a daringly low-cut dress, and as some of the other girls more than matched her God-given hourglass figure, Benson was finally learning to be happy with her looks and discover a quiet satisfaction in the outrageous moniker. It felt just a bit naughty. She only prayed the name would never get back to the Detective Department.

However, when she arrived at Marylebone that Friday, she

immediately felt that the atmosphere was markedly different from the moment she stepped off the train. Hawkes was there to greet her, wearing a long coat and ever-present hat, but she noticed new leather gloves and a bandana tied across his face which he only lowered to kiss her lipsticked mouth.

'New gloves?'

'Yeah.' He sounded apologetic. 'Best to wear 'em all the time now, doll. You know…'

'I kept telling you to wear them when it's cold. You can't go getting chilblains then expect to play the trumpet in a hot club.'

'It's not the cold. It's this flu thing. We've been told it carries by touching things. Anything. And sneezing and coughing.'

'Oh?' Benson was pulling on her own gloves whilst Max took her case. She adjusted her scarf to cover her lower face. 'Is it that bad?'

Hawkes also had his bandana back in place. This alone was surprising as he would usually chatter relentlessly with an unlit cigarette bouncing on his lower lip. 'Just best we're careful, doll. You'll see some things are not the same around here. The mood's changed…'

They walked, as always, because it was not far to wend their way down narrow cobbled and weed-infested streets and along broad avenues of blackened crumbling stucco and yellow London brick. There was little traffic on what would have once been grand roads through Paddington into Notting Hill. This had been an affluent and desirable location in the years before the incipient rot set in and those that could, to had fled to the greener and far healthier suburbs of 'Metroland' out west.

Benson noticed long queues outside the few shops still trading. These were mainly poor affairs desperately needed a lick of paint and new stock to fill the window displays, so Benson found it surprising to see lines of shoppers outside, all wearing scarves across their noses and mouths. A large lady staggered out of a corner shop door laden with four bulging shopping bags of immense weight filled with tins of what looked like corned beef and soup.

A skinny black youth with a determined look on his face and hat on the back of his head pushed a pram along the road laden with packets of toilet paper stacked so high he could barely see over the top.

'What's going on, Max?'

'Hoarders. Bloody madness. You can't buy nothing these days. The queues are worse than in the war. It's worse than the war because there's no rationing. Look at them. Taking everything they can get their hands on and have money to buy! By the time you get inside, there's nothing left.'

'Why are they doing this?'

'The bug. Virus. Whatever they call it. Going through the city like a dose of salts. The new Prime Minister seems a waste of breath and said nothing about how they're going to try and stop the spread and doing even less to stop this craziness on the streets. But the killer is in the city and it's felling people fast.'

'I hadn't realised it was so bad...'

'That's because the Prime Minister won't say or do anything. He's not warning the whole country because he doesn't want to spread panic.' An ambulance clanged past at high speed. 'All day and night you hear them.'

'People with the virus?'

'Yeah. It gets people bad. Just cuts the legs from under you and then you can't breathe nor lift even a finger. It wrecks your lungs. Something like the Spanish flu after the Great War. Whatever it is, it kills the same.'

A second ambulance trundled past at a more sedate pace. Hawkes pointed towards it. 'They'll have someone inside, but it's not rushing. There's no hurry because they know...'

Benson felt a cold finger down her spine. 'You mean they're dead?'

'Or as good as. I spoke to a few nurses the other day who was taking a fag break outside the hospital in Paddington. They say once it gets a hold the oxygen does nothing and as there's no cure, racing them into a hospital bed won't help. They're going to die either way.'

They walked on in silence, more shoppers weighed down by bulging bags passing them without so much as a word, their eyes appearing exaggerated and enlarged by the face coverings and the failing twilight. Snow started to fall.

'What are these red marks?' Benson had noticed daubed crosses and angry sweeping brushstrokes of glossy red house paint on some house doors and splashed on ground floor windows.

'Marking out the immigrant houses. There's a rumour going around town claiming West Indians are the carriers. Racialist idiots claiming they brought the flu over on their boats. How do people fall for this cheap propaganda? Our friends ain't carriers - they're victims. They rarely have flu in the Windies, so it gets them doubly hard. They need help, not mindless racialists pointing fingers, and worse...'

'Violence?'

'Yep. Gangs stalking the streets like vigilantes ensuring our 'dark friends' stay locked away inside. Making them frightened to go out. Teds flashing switchblades and swinging bike chains and not scared to use them. But they're not the worst. Not by a long chalk. There's the East End Boys with lengths of lead pipe, even longer and sharper knives and some have guns.'

'But how can this be allowed to happen?' Benson was in shock.

''Cos the Met and City police turn a blind eye.'

Benson gave him a reproachful look, hurt at the implication.

'I'm not sayin' they approve. Not all of 'em, any road. Just they've got enough on their hands keeping order across the city. There's the looting of warehouses and goods sheds and shops cleaned out all over, so they can't be bothered to worry about a few lads frightening the coloureds.'

Benson was tight-lipped behind her scarf. Anger brewing inside, although she was not sure towards whom it was directed. There was too much to process too quickly. This was so different to how it was in Leicester where they read, then promptly forgot, the headlines in the national newspapers or perhaps exchanged a few words about the 'pandemic' in unimaginably distant places like India and East Pakistan.

As they approached the street Hawkes lived on, they passed an old Austin car jacked onto bricks with the wheels removed. It had been there for a least a year, slowly disintegrating through vandalism and unsleeping rust. It was almost like an old friend and passing it was a sign they were nearly home. However, Benson was surprised to see a London Corporation tar wagon shrouded in steam occupying the middle of the road.

Four workmen were busy shovelling and raking fresh tarmacadam tipped from a flatbed lorry into a succession of potholes that had been the bane of what traffic was brave enough to venture along the desolate road. Steam and the powerful odour of liquid tar filled the street. A gaggle of young children in a ragtag collection of filthy clothes stood close, each taking deep inhalations of the fumes. Hawkes also pulled his scarf down. 'Breathe it in.'

They walked closer and the smell was intense but not unpleasant. 'Supposed to kill the germs.'

Benson took in a lungful. 'We heard steam engines are the same. The guvnor recently went down to the Longmoor Military Railway and the drivers there were telling him it was the best cure they knew. Some people stand on railway bridges and inhale.'

'Got to be worth a try. Better than going down with it.'

One of the lads started coughing. He reeled away and bent almost double, face blotchy with the agonising racking coughs that he could not stop. An older girl wearing little more than a grubby summer dress and cardigan and who was probably his sister put a consoling arm around the boy. She looked up at Benson. 'He'll be all right. Honest, miss. It takes him like this 'cos he breathes in the tar too deeply...' Her eyes were filled with fear and hope in about equal measure. The boy's breathing was shallow and fast.

Hawkes steered Benson away, although she was eager to offer help. As if reading her thoughts, he spoke quietly. 'You can't. He's got it, doll. And she will soon enough. We can't do anything except catch it ourselves. I'm sorry.'

Benson walked on in silence, mind reeling. She thought of London as somewhere delightfully different and almost an exotic oasis, but now it had altered to something darker and unsettling. Everything was so much more intense than it was in Leicester, where the news still referred to 'the usual Winter outbreak of flu',' but there was no mention of this panic-buying, the constant hurrying ambulances, the stalking menace of angry mobs turning their own fears and prejudices upon others and young children dying amidst tar fumes. She looked at the dingy gas-lit street they thought of as home and realised that it now appeared ugly, mean and dangerous.

It was going to be a very different weekend from the one she'd imagined.

Chapter Sixteen
Marylebone

Colonel Broadbent had requested an urgent private meeting with Chief Superintendent Badger in Marylebone House.

The colonel appeared greyer than the last time they'd met; the lines on his face etched deeper, eyes rimmed with a trace of red that betrayed lack of sleep. However, his officer's cap lay on the corner of Badger's desk, looking as good as new and the colonel's immaculately laundered and pressed uniform with a leather belt and buttons polished to a gloss helped exude an aura of quiet control and order.

It was an image to which Badger could relate as he sat facing the colonel in his own tailored uniform. Both men long practised in the skill of maintaining an exterior that betrayed nothing of their inner feelings and perfect practitioners of the famous British 'stiff upper lip.' Knowing when to fall back on the art of speaking in economically clipped sentences that allowed no room to betray weakness or doubt. It was therefore all the more startling to hear the colonel admit his concerns to someone outside the regiment.

'Chief Superintendent, thank you for agreeing to meet at such short notice, and on a Saturday. I'm sure you are a busy man, so I shall cut straight to the chase.' Badger merely gave a slight nod, pleased his rank and position were being acknowledged. 'Things are taking a worrying turn at Longmoor. The situation has been worsening since we last met. It was barely a trickle at first, much as the regiment had been given to expect and manage. It was in line with the projected outcomes of *Operation Chinese Bird*.'

'A trickle of what? Men falling ill?'

'Yes. However, it far worse than we were advised to expect. A particularly ugly type of pneumonia caused by something called *coronavirus*. I'd never heard of it. Whatever the damn thing is, it's fatal. The trickle has turned into a veritable torrent.' He accepted a cigarette offered from the silver-plated box Badger offered across the desk. 'I should give you some background. *Operation Chinese Bird* was planned as an exercise to prove the viability of a new method of removing as many fit and able men from operational service as quickly and efficiently as possible. Designed to strike fast and to be transmitted readily by inhalation and touch, thereby immobilising as many persons of combat age as possible in a matter of hours. It was designed to be temporarily disabling and within two to four days anyone receiving a dose would recover and suffer no lasting effect. We considered this an acceptable level of risk and agreed it would be instructive to monitor how a railway would be affected by the field use of this virus. We put measures in place to expect a significant, albeit temporary, reduction in our operational capacity.'

'This is biological warfare dressed up with a pretty title?' Badger's voice was emotionless.

'Porton Down chose the name,' Broadbent waved this away. 'Look, call it whatever you wish, but this was sold to the Regiment as an effective, short-term virological method of removing the threat of a hostile enemy with no lasting effects. I stress the last point. Unlike guns and bombs, *Chinese Bird* was reversible. Full recovery in all but an acceptable number of those infected.'

'An acceptable number? Is the loss of even one human life acceptable?'

'War is brutal and the human cost to combatants and civilians appallingly high. Unacceptably high? War is a very blunt instrument. A few days of aching limbs and a banging head appears a better choice.' The two men stared at each other for a moment. 'A humane alternative to killing is surely worth some risk?' Broadbent paused as he smoked. 'The scientists and doctors admitted there could a very small number of persons who *might* react badly.'

'Such as Lance Corporal Mordon.'

'It is unrealistic to claim there is no risk in any military exercise. The goal of a reversible military weapon is surely preferable to the current obsession with the atomic bomb.'

'Radiation sickness and biological sickness alarm me with equal measure...' Badger was unsmiling as he lit another cigarette, but not before quelling an outburst of coughing. His field of expertise was policing railways and his men commonly dealt with crooks wielding little more than a crowbar or a set of picklocks to aid the depletion of stock in a warehouse or empty a loaded wagon. 'Be that as I may, we are not meeting to discuss the ethics of military weaponry?'

'We are not.'

Badger waved a hand holding his cigarette to indicate he was not going to debate the point further.

'We were given extensive proofs that this cultivated virus was safe, with thick files of test results on laboratory animals and some human individuals by both the MRD and the CDEE. We didn't enter into this like blind fools. However, the speed and scale of mortality go beyond anything predicted and beyond anything remotely acceptable. I will not defend the appalling attrition rate in my regiment. This is turning into a human tragedy with severe and long-lasting ramifications.' Broadbent dragged hard on his cigarette and Badger could see a slight twitch under one eye. 'If that were not bad enough, the MRD and CDEE are proving equally opaque and now retreating into their respective well-defended bunkers, leaving me with a crisis that threatens to overspill and become uncontainable.'

'How many of your men have died?'

Broadbent took a deep breath. 'We've lost nearly forty. At the last count. I expect it to be higher by the time I return.'

'Forty!' Badger sat upright in horror, but this outburst induced another fit of dry and painful coughing that made him reach for a handkerchief and smother his mouth whilst his face reddened. After about half a minute it subsided. 'Sorry. I've been smoking too much these last days...'

Broadbent eyed Badger suspiciously. 'There is worse. We have at least another sixty in poor shape. The medical centre is full.'

'Good God. These men are critical?'

'Once it takes hold it either behaves as Lombard and Urban promised and passes over in a few days, or it turns into acute pneumonia-like symptoms from which few hope to escape. There's no cure as yet and we can only offer oxygen - and our prayers.'

'You believe the virus is behaving quite differently than predicted when released from a sterile laboratory?'

'That appears to be the case.'

'Have the scientists offered an explanation?'

'They are undertaking extensive tests...'

'I'm probably talking nonsense, but perhaps something else is combining in the field to create such devastation? Combining with the artificial virus to make it more potent?'

'You are far wiser than many,' Broadbent replied. 'Your analysis could prove correct. The Porton Down team have hinted at the same. The arrival of Asiatic flu on our shores at the same time the trails commenced raises awkward questions.'

'They combined?'

'I am not a microbiologist. Can that happen? I don't know. But their virus has become a killer. A highly effective one. We've implemented a strict emergency regime to try and contain the infection; We've set up a field hospital to house those infected far away from those who have, as yet, avoided contagion. We cleanse everything rigorously and taken shipments of every respirator and gas suit we can lay our hands on in the country. There are fewer than you might imagine. Too few.' He gave a rueful smile. 'Working behind my desk in a gas mask and wearing heavy rubber gloves is not comfortable, but preferable to a slow death with lungs refusing to function.'

Badger stared back in stunned silence. His breathing was shallow and rapid.

'We've tried to contain the spread. We've tried to prevent panic from breaking out amongst the locals outside the camp, but it is hard to conceal losses on this scale.'

'And what of Lombard and Urban? What are they doing to control this?'

'Both cut and run. Once the epidemic killed twenty men and filled every bed with the sick, they dashed away taking most of their teams back to their dammed hiding holes where I can't reach 'em! Said they needed to run more tests to understand what had gone wrong and develop a vaccine. They drove off with blood samples and the best of the protective equipment. Lily-livered cowards!' Broadbent stubbed out his cigarette with an aggressive movement.

'I'm not sure I would feel safer locked away in their laboratories with the kind of toxins and viruses they handle.'

'They made unilateral tactical retreats without consultation. Waved a white flag, leaving us to pick up the pieces. We've been abandoned to firefight a worsening situation with no more guidance than what the four nurses they left behind can offer. We've resorted to deploying lorries at night and even laid on a special train to remove the corpses for immediate cremation. The lack of even basic humanity in their disposal sits uncomfortably, but the situation demands drastic measures.'

'And who is writing compensation cheques for the families?'

The comment stung. 'I'll have to take that on the chin...'

'But you take my point? You had my DCI jumping through hoops like a performing dog dancing to your tune. All of you. And for what?'

'Lombard of the MRD and some well-connected top brass within the CDEE were playing that particular tune.'

Badger gave a curt nod of acceptance and contemplated the ash burning on the tip of his cigarette. He noticed his hand was quivering slightly and felt a bead of sweat form on his brow.

Was it so hot in his office? *Hell's bells get a grip! Broadbent will think I'm in a blind panic...* 'You've not travelled here today to send us all on similar wild goose chases, I hope?'

'I have not.' The colonel took a fresh cigarette. He paused, with the lighter flame flickering before him, eyes forensically trying to read Badger's expression. 'Correct me if I'm wrong, but I sense you share my concerns about Lombard, Urban and their respective establishments?'

'If by that you mean I don't trust either as far as I can throw 'em, then yes. And I have sympathy for the family of that poor fellow Wellbeck from the Common Cold Institute. You heard what happened? He succumbed to a flu-like virus. I presume the same one that's running wild through Longmoor.'

'Yes, I heard. I understood he was worried all was not well with *Operation Chinese Bird,* but it got him before I had a chance to press him on the matter.'

'But not before he opened up to my DCI.'

'Then you are ahead of the game.'

'That's not all...' Badger felt a wave of shivers run through his body and in an effort to control them sat back in his leather chair and gripped the armrests, feeling profoundly cold when he'd been hot only minutes earlier. Badger told Broadbent about the disturbing discovery surrounding Phyllis Mordon's death.

'Then the enemy truly is within...' Broadbent fell silent as he watched beads of sweat form on Badger's brow. The telltale signs of an illness he'd witnessed close at hand. 'Are you unwell?'

'Me? Fit as a fiddle! A slight chill, perhaps... But it's to be expected at this time of year.'

Broadbent was not convinced. 'I need your help. We've closed the camp perimeter and forbidden anyone to leave. Transport off camp is undertaken only by men fumigated and masked. We've done all we can, but with so many men down we're struggling.'

Badger was eyeing Broadbent suspiciously, wondering if he'd brought the virus into the room and he'd caught it. He didn't feel at all well. Broadbent could almost read his mind. 'I was subjected to the full fumigation procedure and sprayed liberally with disinfecting liquid. If that doesn't kill me, nothing will!' They both shared a moment of wry laughter. Privately, Broadbent was more concerned he was going to catch something from Badger, who was visibly worsening by the minute.

'The pressing problem is the men we've lost off camp, as I explained over the telephone.'

'I have the Transport Police looking out for the men you identified.'

Broadbent nodded approval. 'The situation has altered. We have now rounded up all but two. Most were unimaginative idiots who were easily traced. The two still missing pose a significant threat, however. In the investigation following the mass AWOL incident, it appears several individuals made it known to their pals they were angry. One man who was prevented from leaving even discharged his rifle and wounded a sergeant major in a violent altercation. A flesh wound, but a serious breach of discipline that illustrates what we're up against.'

'Tempers boiling over as they see friends dying. These men escaped to get away from the infection?'

'A reasonable deduction and true for most. However, I suspect something worse in the case of the men still evading capture. They broke camp *not* to flee infection, but to carry it. To deliberately spread it far and wide.'

'I hope you're not serious?'

'We have confirmation from Professor Urban that a percentage of those infected become carriers. Immune and presenting no symptoms but as live and dangerous as a ticking bomb. They infect all they touch.'

'Oh, Lord…'

'Asymptomatic. Impossible to detect except by lab tests.'

'How long do they remain active?'

'I still await the blasted boffins in Porton Down to advise on that crucial detail.' Broadbent snorted with derision. 'I suspect some considerable time, or it would not exercise the scientific minds as much as it is. Combine that with angry young men intent on retribution and we have an unfolding nightmare.'

'You have two men with lethal vengeance on their fingertips.'

'I regret so. They were to be quarantined indefinitely. We suspect they learned of this and ran before we could confine them.'

Badger sighed impatiently. 'Can you blame them?'

Broadbent ignored the criticism. 'This has gone to the very top. The Home Secretary and the Minister for Defence have been briefed. I understand the PM has conceded the Asian flu outbreak is now severe enough and attracting sufficient press coverage to act as a smokescreen. He's allowed a week to find these men and permitted those involved to cloak any mention of *Chinese Bird* behind the Asiatic variant. We conflate the two into one and can perhaps at least prevent mass panic. But the clock is ticking.'

'How can I be of assistance?'

'There's a common link between the missing men. They were footplate crew. It follows that the railway is their quickest means to escape and an environment they feel confident within. If they have malicious intent, the railways are also the perfect place to cause maximum impact.'

'The effect could be devastating.'

'I need your men right across the national system to find the carriers. There is precious little time.'

'I shall have everyone on full alert within the hour, all leave cancelled.'

'There is something else. Nobody must approach or touch them. It could be lethal.'

'Then how do we bring them into custody?'

'You don't. You shoot them on sight.' A bleak silence fell. 'Shoot to kill. They must be felled, and a quarantine cordon put in place until we can get a team of properly protected men to deal with the corpses, which remain very dangerous.'

'You cannot be serious?' Badger was wiping his brow with a handkerchief.

'Do not underestimate this virus, Chief Superintendent. If these renegades are intent on spreading it to cause maximum dispersal you must consider them armed and willing to kill, albeit by proxy. Once the infection reaches a critical mass many hundreds of thousands could die. You shoot on sight. Trust me, you do not wish to take them into custody. They will touch and grab your officers, perhaps spit on them, with dire consequences.'

'I cannot agree to do what you ask. It flies against everything we stand for.'

'If I told you they were irradiated and passing this to all they encounter, how would you react?'

Badger was silent for a long time.

'The Home Secretary is communicating the same instruction to every Police commissioner in the land even as we speak. You can expect official confirmation from your ACC.'

'Then I shall need names, photographs and written descriptions. Everything you know about the two men. Their homes, their families, wives and girlfriends. Any pointers that could offer clues to their whereabouts.'

'I have everything prepared in this file...'

Chapter Seventeen
Teignmouth

Sergeant Winter had spent the night camped out in an abandoned pillbox dating from the war that guarded the entrance to Parson's Tunnel at Teignmouth.

It was small, but with enough space to stretch out once he'd kicked the worst of the rubbish outside the narrow door opening and moved the lumps of rock and house bricks that had somehow found their way inside.

He was unsure how long he and Clawson could evade capture. He supposed the alarm would have been raised by now and every effort made to haul them back for a Court Martial. They could expect the punishment to be severe. But could it be worse than involuntary isolation for an indefinite and lengthy period? Solitary confinement in a camp riddled with sickness. Forbidden to leave their cramped room whilst their pals dropped dead, perhaps right next door? It was almost too nightmarish to contemplate. Neither Clawson nor he had done anything wrong. They were innocent of bringing this killer virus into the world and had been suckered into taking the measly few quid to be experimented on by the reassuring words of men who knew they were playing with fire.

A night bivouacked in a pillbox beside the thundering trains roaring to and from the west was not the most peaceful of places, but Winter had slept soundly, finding solace in the steady rumble of trains through Parson's Tunnel and the regular, ordered world of the railways going about their business as usual.

It was an ugly concrete shelter, but it still felt better than being confined to what was a prison cell in all but name. He'd always enjoyed camping, and the Army training had honed his skills and taught him how to survive and indeed find comfort for a few hours in difficult situations. Camped out between the railway and the sea, unobserved and left alone, he was surprisingly content. He'd lit a small fire close to the crumbling red sandstone cliffs through which the tunnel bored. Heating water for tea and warming a tin of baked beans, he was seated on a lump of concrete that formed the upper edge of the marine defence wall, the sea lapping some feet below. There was little wind and the water although uninviting was not menacing his position. He was grateful the weather was relatively benign and not swamping his temporary home or washing him away to inevitable death as it so easily could when storms battered this stretch of the railway line.

Winter looked along the broad path that stretched back into Teignmouth and the low stone wall that offered a modicum of protection to promenaders from the towering presence of passing trains. It was possible to get very close and low down to the passing trains, the viewpoint exaggerating the size of even modestly proportioned 'Prairie' tanks that scurried past and making the glamorous crack express engines look even grander. As he sipped his scalding hot tea, a long freight train trundled by, hauled by an eight-coupled workhorse. If the fireman was surprised to see him camping out, he didn't show it and casually lifted a gloved hand as they chugged on with a regular heavy clonk of metal and fizzle of steam.

He really should be here in summer. The promenade would be heaving and the sun illuminating the rich bronze-green of the passing locomotives and glinting off the polished metalwork the Western Region still favoured on their engines. It was a lovely spot in the hot sun with the splashing waves and the promise of an ice-cream wafer...

Coming here was a moment of romantic folly. There were too few people for his presence to have any effect. Winter was not much given to melancholia or wallowing in self-pity but this sudden desire to return to this 'foreign land of his past' had overwhelmed him with an intensity almost debilitating.

Yesterday afternoon he'd decided to return to Barnstable to say a last farewell to his wife and little boy and spend a night together in their home. He would lie about his situation and manufacture an excuse about a training exercise close by and how he'd obtained permission for a night out. Jenny would be so delighted she'd not question the story, and as he betrayed no symptoms, she would be mercifully unaware of what he was bringing into their home.

A last hug and kiss. After all, she just might be immune and survive the other side of the pandemic. It *was* possible. But deep down he knew this was a fantasy. Similar to the lie he'd sold Private Clawson that they'd live long lives and have the pick of the unaffected young women when it was over. Once the truth was out that he and Clawson were mass murderers, courtesy of their breath and fingertips, there was little chance they could expect long lives. Death sooner rather than later was inevitable, but he hoped he could at least push such thoughts aside and step through their front door and lose himself in the company of his wife and son one last time.

However, his courage failed him when he stepped onto the platform at Barnstable. What was he thinking? He would be recognised in no time, and with a price on his head, he'd be arrested whilst the evening was still young. And why deliberately infect his wife and child? Did he want Jenny to face this unpleasant affliction alone in a hospital bed surrounded by masked medics? And what of his son? Small children seemed immune to the virus. If that was so, the boy would survive his mother and father as an orphan.

Winter felt dizzy and had to sit on a platform bench to regain his composure and within the half-hour was back on the same train and steaming out of town. He would leave the place largely untouched. One bench and a couple of carriage door handles had been his only lasting mark. He silently prayed his wife did not need to visit the station that day, and that she and his little boy might escape infection.

The maudlin mood persisted, and he found himself hankering back to a simpler time. Fond memories awakened of golden sands and burning summer sun; reddening shoulders and nose and sand between his toes; melting cornets with red 'monkey blood' dribbling stickily onto his fingers and a procession of packed holiday trains bearing armies of eager folk coming to 'take the air.'

He was surprised at the intensity of the childhood memories flooding back of holidaying in Teignmouth before the war. Between making sandcastles with a red enamelled spade and putting paper flags in the unsteady ramparts he would sit for hours on this very same promenade wall contentedly waiting for a succession of Great Western Railway 'Stars' and 'Castles' with their romantic names like *Queen Berengaria, North Star, Tintagel Castle* and *Earl of Cawdor* and those curiously stumpy but big-wheeled 'County' class engines that high-stepped their way on fast local trains, looking like Edwardian ladies lifting their voluminous skirts as they bowled along country lanes on bicycles.

Teignmouth was primarily a summer holiday spot and this bleak February morning brought only a solitary dog walker. Winter's presence would have little effect, but he'd needed this quiet moment of reflection. He watched the sea swell and listened to the pine trees on the cliff tops sigh whilst he breathed in the clean air. This might be his last moment of carefree living. They'd set something into motion that would become bigger and more dangerous as it gathered pace and he was now powerless to stop it.

He stared at his hands. Rugged and with dirt under the nails, but otherwise the hands of a typical young man, and yet he was a monster. No less deadly and unwelcome than a werewolf of legend or even that Baskerville hound stalking Dartmoor.

Winter felt anger rise inside and his gentle memories of a lost childhood were quickly erased. There was no room for foolish sentiment. If he was doomed to carry this murderous virus, then he was dammed if others were going to escape.

He studied his Bradshaw with renewed concentration and discovered that within a couple of hours he could take a train north, perhaps travelling as far as Shrewsbury if the fancy took him. Or a change of train in Birmingham might be more satisfactory? Snow Hill and New Street were bustling stations that saw tremendous crowds and he could do a deal of damage in a short space of time. He was due to rendezvous with Clawson in the 'big smoke' this evening and it would be easy to find a train to Euston from New Street.

* * * *

Private Clawson stepped off the short train that had just brought him from Newton Abbott into Exeter St David's. He made sure to give the droplight window and door handle a good rub with his bare hands.

He stopped, ostensibly, to look for a moment at the former Great Western 'Prairie' tank that hauled the train into St David's. It issued steam in a high-pitched sound and dribbled hot water onto the track. Clawson hefted his kitbag onto his shoulder then stepped closer to the open side of the cab where the driver was idly leaning.

'I don't suppose you know where I get the train across to Exeter Central?'

'Central? Easy, you just hop over the footbridge there, an' your train'll come in on the opposite platform.'

'Ta much!'

'You've plenty of time. It won't be leaving 'til the 'Cornish Riviera's' been through. Worth waitin' to see that.'

'Then I'll put my pack on a barrow and wait.'

The driver shook a glove off and extended a hand. 'You have a good trip, sir.' Clawson shook hands. The driver was going to find out later if 'footplate immunity' was just a myth.

He dumped his heavy pack on one of the flatbed four-wheel trucks porters used for carting mailbags, milk churns and heavy luggage, and lit a cigarette. He was underneath the long straight awning that protected the platform, but a pool of thin sunlight threw rectangular patterns of lemony yellow on the platform surface and the side of the bubbling tank engine. It offered Clawson some welcome warmth.

Three young boys in shorts and blazers with school caps on their heads were seated on a neighbouring barrow, notebooks, pencils and spotter's books in their hands. They were looking expectantly down the line. He idly wondered why they were not in school, but nearly every station in the land was populated with schoolboys, and even a few schoolgirls, regardless of the time of day.

'You lot waiting for the 'Riviera'?'

'You bet, mister.'

'Best train of the day!'

'Why's that?' Clawson was in the mood to talk.

'It's got a 'King' on the front!'

'They're the tops!'

'Lush…'

Clawson grinned. 'Remind me, what is a 'King'?'

Two boys raced each other to be the first to open the pages of their 'Ian Allan Combined Volumes' to show him a slightly blurred and murky black and white photograph of the Western Region's premier express steam locomotive. Clawson took one of the books and gave it a closer look. The pages were deliciously smooth and shiny, as was the cover. It would transfer the invisible killer perfectly. 'Lovely engines…' He handed the book back but could see the other lad looked mildly disappointed that his book had not been chosen. 'You've got a lot of spots in your book by the look of it.'

'Cops. We call 'em cops.'

'My mistake! Can I see it?' He was soon flipping the pages, touching as many as he could.

'Here she comes!' Another boy who had been hanging back, preferring to stay focused on the task in hand, raised the alert.

Clawson handed the book back and turned to watch the stirring sight of *King John* sweep through the station at high speed with a decorative headboard mounted on the front that identified it as 'The Cornish Riviera Express' in chocolate brown coloured letters on a cream background. The carriages swept past in a flurry of wind and a rattle and clickety-clack of wheels on steel, and was gone, leaving just a gently dissipating trail of scented steam in its wake.

Almost before the vapour had completely dissolved, a rather striking looking locomotive came into view from the same direction, only this was not on the centre line, but slowing to stop on the far platform.

'I think that's my train...'

'Seen it!' The cry was universal from the trainspotters appeared familiar with many of this class of engine.

'Just *Blackmore Vale*. We get her most days, worst luck...'

'Looks a fine engine to me.'

'Yeah, but I copped her loads and loads of times. It's boring.'

Clawson gave them a friendly wave and hiked off towards the footbridge. Kids didn't die from the virus, so the papers said, but just like himself, they could transmit it. They'd share it liberally amongst themselves then carry it home and into school and to their teachers.

He allowed himself a quiet smile as he walked. Inspired. That's what that was. Inspired. He'd use these spotting kids on the stations to do his work. Not quite the Pied Piper leading rats away from town, but something just as sinister. He was calling them to him, then sending them away into every home, carrying the plague...

Chapter Eighteen
Birmingham New Street

Sergeant Winter walked through the concourse of Birmingham New Street and along platforms as crowded as he'd hoped.

The very narrowness of this dark and tatty station gave the impression of too many platforms squeezed into the space available. It was all a bit of a shambles and gave the impression of having been assembled in stages with a cheese-paring meanness of budget each time. The architects of the primary station of Britain's second city had spectacularly failed to create an edifice with any hint of grandeur and simply forced everyone into a filthy subterranean iron and glass shed forever cold and yet, despite the permanent wind funnelling down the tunnels at each end, retained clouds of sour engine smoke to sting eyes and irritate throats. Porters continually hauled trucks of mailbags and luggage in all directions apparently without rhyme or discernible reason down the narrow platforms, forcing waiting passengers to cram yet closer together.

As such, New Street was perfect for Winter's needs. It was easy to brush past fellow travellers, place an idle hand on the handles of luggage trolleys and on the doorknobs of the many maroon painted wooden doors that punctured the sooty brick to ensure he spread the invisible killer. It could not be long before a pair of lantern-jawed thugs in white helmets appeared to arrest him, so was eager to cover as much of the station as possible.

He stood and watched as a 'Patriot' class locomotive named *The Royal Pioneer Corps* rolled into platform seven on its way towards York from Bristol. The regimental name reinforced the feeling that perhaps it might be time to ditch his fatigues and change into 'civvies' and even indulge in a little disguise.

Chapter Eighteen

Winter was known to do a few comic 'turns' in the annual Christmas revue the Regiment liked to stage to give everyone an evening of belly laughs and ridiculous merriment, washed down by numerous pints of beer. As a result, he knew how to create a passable imitation of a moustache and even had a pair of dusty sunglasses lying at the bottom of his kit bag in hope of a rare sunlit day. With a new hat, these glasses and a fake 'tache, he might buy himself a few more days of freedom.

Feeling energised by this idea, Winter jostled, none to carefully, up and over the footbridge and along to the end of platform six, where he'd noticed a large group of trainspotters of all ages were gathered. He rested his pack on the ground and watched as *Polyphemus* steamed in from Euston with a sparkling rake of maroon-painted coaches which were now in favour.

'Funny name!'

'You're not wrong there, mister. We get 'Polly' in every day.' One of the spotters replied with a slightly dismissive shrug.

'She a local engine?'

'Bushbury shed. Quite close. I'm waiting for something more interesting.'

A work-a-day Fowler tank engine steamed in from the opposite direction and came to a halt across the tracks. It was stained and dusty from hard work.

'Seen it!' The cry of dismay went up from the younger spotters, all eager to perform to the new audience in the form of Winter. He was a soldier, which was quite exciting, but better still he was interested in trains.

'All these are new to me. I'm from down South West, see? So, all these are unusual.'

'Corr! Have you seen all the 'Merchant Navies'?'

'And the 'West Countries'?'

'And 'Battle of Britains'?'

The chorus of voices rose as the local Brummies shouted out the names of unseen classes of locomotive based on the

Southern Region and which would never steam out of the gloomy tunnels that burrowed under their city. Winter was soon being handed a succession of spotter's books to inspect, which he did with a page-turning thoroughness the lads appreciated.

After watching *Trafalgar* snort a train away and into a tunnel, Winter decided his work was done here. He'd idly contemplated a poster on the wall that offered 'Cheap days from Birmingham' to destinations like Sheffield for 9/6, or Leeds for 14/6 and what was surely an exorbitant 10/- to travel to Rotherham. This struck Winter as especially unappealing on a bitterly cold February day. He would resist the call of these northern destinations, for now.

He formally thanked the spotters for their enjoyable company by shaking hands with each. A couple of grammar schoolboys made a gentle parody of a salute by touching the peaks of their school caps. Winter smiled.

He would walk across to Snow Hill now to catch a London Paddington train and he could buy a change of clothes along the way between the two stations. He'd ditch his army kit on the train and arrive in London a changed man. He hoped Clawson was thinking along similar lines.

Winter was now enjoying this dark escapade and in no hurry to see it come to an end. He wanted to retain his liberty at least long enough to see it take effect...

Chapter Nineteen
Belgrave & Birstall

Charles and Anna Vignoles lived in a comfortable 'semi' just a walk from Belgrave & Birstall station, which allowed them both to travel the short distance to work at Leicester Central.

Theirs was a leafy outlying suburb on a hill rising due north of Leicester, though many residents argued (with some historical justification) it was not truly part of the city and jealously guarded the sense of being 'a place apart'. Whatever its status, it was notable for a fine golf course and boasted its own football team, although Birstall United FC was unquestionably overshadowed by Charles Vignoles' own Foxy favourites, Leicester City.

Belgrave and Birstall offered a gentler pace of life than within the city with leafier roads and a broader sky, free of the tall smoking chimneys that dotted the lower-lying cityscape so often shrouded in smog. The air was discernibly cleaner, and the relative peace broken only by the beat of passing trains and ever-increasing rumble of tyres on tarmac as more car-owning commuters chose to form lengthening queues along the A6.

It was Sunday morning and frost lay white on the square of grass at the front and forming pretty patterns on the greenhouse glass. A fire burned in the grate and the comforting aroma of a roasting joint of pork filled the house whilst they both studied the Sunday papers. Above the gentle crackle of the fire and the low murmur of the radiogram, there was also sound of the automatic washing machine churning in what Anna was now calling the 'utility room'.

Sunday was not a traditional day for washing, but with Anna working during the week she'd long been forced to fly in the face of convention and learn to ignore the disapproving looks and veiled comments from neighbours and open a packet of Daz to do the wash whenever time allowed, which today was Sunday.

Well, the neighbours could think what they liked, this was the 'Atomic age' and in this exciting new world of brighter than white washing powders, surely washing could be hung out on Sundays? Society was altering, and whilst both Charles and she attended church in the morning and tried to enjoy a traditional meal together in the early afternoon, Anna could see no reason not to get the laundry on the go when it involved so little work and barely intruded into their day.

The delivery of the Hotpoint 'Liberator' two weeks before Christmas had been an event on their road. It brought most of the neighbours out to watch the gleaming white machine unloaded, prompting frequent requests to be allowed inside so they could 'see it in action.' Anna had rarely done so much washing in her life, as a succession of neighbours sat and watched with looks that flickered between wonderment and green-eyed envy as the machine worked its magic.

Once the Sunday roast was eaten and the 'Liberator' had ceased its work, they would retire to the front lounge which had been freshened up only last autumn with brighter wallpaper that looked like a cross between a diagram of splitting an atom and hot house plants. The Nordic-styled armchairs and settee were as 'modish' as Anna could find. Charles had pointed out they were as expensive as anything else on the market but agreed they introduced a welcome dash of stylish comfort to their home, all the more so when angled to offer the most favourable view of their other recent acquisition.

The television.

Charles had been reluctant at first, still loyal to radio and newsprint, but as TV aerials started to appear in greater numbers strapped to chimney stacks and offering new perches for starlings and sparrows, it became harder for him to resist Anna's pleading they join the 'affluent society'.

She bemoaned the fact the office girls were forever enthusing about entertaining or instructive television shows and the modern plays and all manner of other programmes about which she knew nothing. With a double income and no children, they could afford to splash out. Anna had even taken to reading out what they were missing from *The Radio Times,* particularly highlighting programmes she suspected her husband would enjoy. Vignoles had relented last November, and then, to their mutual surprise, discovered just how much he enjoyed 'the set'.

'It is a welcome diversion from the more challenging aspects of the job. It can be quite soothing.' Especially so with Anna snuggled close on their new sofa and crystal glasses holding a 'wee dram' to warm their souls.

If there was a negative aspect to the television it was the news bulletins, which were nearly always depressing, alarming or distressing or combinations of all three. They seemed all the more visceral when brought 'live' into the sitting room. Vignoles was thinking how the day's grim news was going to be played out that evening as both he and his wife read extended commentaries on the Asiatic flu outbreak that dominated the inner pages and editorials of the Sunday papers.

The 'popular' press had been shouting about how the 'Killer Bug grips India' and warning that 'Hong Kong Flu' had reached the United Kingdom, adopting ever more strident headlines possibly in an attempt to keep up with the draw of the BBC's *Six-O-Clock News* or the rival ITV version.

The Sunday papers at least took a more measured approach. However, even the most moderate editors were becoming concerned. The word 'pandemic' was used frequently, and the articles illustrated by charts illustrating the numbers affected and known to have succumbed. With over a million cases in India and over 100,000 in Taiwan to name but two countries, it was not comfortable reading and the citizens of the United Kingdom had good reason to be worried.

Vignoles was studying a map of the United Kingdom indicating the biggest spikes in infections and subsequent deaths. The stark black and white graphics encouraged comparisons with similar maps that had appeared during the last war to show the advances and retreats of frontlines during the conflict. It was starting to look as though battle lines were once again being drawn, with demarcation lines plotted in blood-red dots.

Over the past ten days, Vignoles had tasked PCs Blencowe and Howerth to create just such a map, in duplicate, using the largest Ordnance Survey's they could get their hands on. Spanning two giant sheets and Sellotaped together, they made an impressive sight in the Detective Department, one of which now occupied the greater part of a wall in his office. Using red or black markers that eerily echoed the map in *The Observer*, the constables were painstakingly translating every reference they could find to a flu outbreak in black, and flu-related deaths in red.

As far as the constables were concerned it was the *Asiatic H2N2* strain they were tracking, both as yet unaware of the man-made *coron56-N4* variant. Vignoles had decided that for now, he would limit the extent his department knew about this unwelcome development. Both sets of maps told a worrying tale.

There was no escaping the data and Vignoles felt an uneasy sense of brooding menace attached to anything relating to *Operation Chinese Bird,* made all the worse by the alarming task Badger had set them. Hunting down and killing two men accused of deliberately spreading the man-made virus was disturbing and weighing heavily on his shoulders.

It was no consolation, but at least offered confirmation this disturbing task was essential, that the spread of infection and consequent deaths was undeniable and following a steep upward curve in specific areas of the country. The evidence appeared to back up the belief the virus was following discernible corridors that mirrored railway lines.

It was perhaps a testament to how powerful and secretive the State could be when it felt the need that the public was as yet oblivious to the existence, let alone escape, of this man-made *coron56-N4* now seeping out along some of the main trunk lines of Britain.

There had been some rumblings and tentative attempts by several papers to write stories about the significant levels of flu infections within the Longmoor Military Railway, but these had been efficiently headed off as the Army closed ranks and offered vague references to 'the usual Winter outbreaks' and the ease of transmission amongst men in confined quarters. The alarming death rate amongst the soldiers based there had been suppressed, although Vignoles wondered for how much longer. Distressed families would soon start to rise up in collective anger and dismay. Once they refused to stay silent and went to the press, the lid would be blown right off. However, it appeared the Home Office and the Ministry of Defence were doing a clever job of masking *coron56-N4* with the Asiatic virus. Even the Army code name was looking like a stroke of genius. Any leaks of '*Chinese Bird*' would serve to reinforce the dominating story of a pandemic from the Orient thought to have originated amongst birds. Another week of this exponential rate of infection and the human misery at Longmoor could be revealed without attracting anything other than a wave of public sympathy. It would be just one more tragedy amongst so many others. The British Army operated across the far corners of the Empire and it took little imagination to visualise men returning from a foreign posting and unwittingly bringing something nasty along for the ride.

Vignoles stared into the little flames licking around the coals and his mind was whirring with uncharacteristic thoughts of conspiracy and officially approved lies and obfuscation.

Anna had just read aloud a passage from *The Sunday Times* implying the Government had been warned last October about the flu problem. However, the ongoing fallout from the Suez Crisis and change of Prime Minister perhaps explained their inaction to various ministerial warnings that it was 'highly probable' it would leap to Hong Kong and thence back to the United Kingdom.

Had Porton Down appreciated rather than ignored this warning and chosen to undertake a risky experimental trial knowing that if it got out of hand they could 'bury' the news beneath the anticipated arrival of Asian flu? Cloak and dagger stuff of a kind Vignoles would ordinarily laugh it away as fanciful nonsense. The kind of crazy imaginings of 'Angry Young Men' in the Student Union bars of Northern red brick universities. Or was it…?

The Mordons were dead, one murdered in a most sinister manner. Badger was becoming uncharacteristically agitated and hinting that even Colonel Broadbent was starting to suspect a cover-up. Wellbeck had offered his own warning before succumbing to one or other of the viruses. As the names and numbers grew, Wellbeck was already consigned to the margins of history. Just a name in a list of thousands. His article in *The Times* crowded out by so many more recent offerings all promoting different theories and solutions.

Vignoles had at least placed the bottle of disinfecting alcohol in their kitchen and explained to Anna why they should start taking extra care of their health and sanitation. She'd been sceptical, but over the past few days less so and started making enquiries about how they could obtain further stocks for her parents to use at their Italian restaurant.

'Should we be worried, Charles?

'It's nasty and there's nothing that can stop it - for now.'

'They say Asian flu targets those between 14 and 39, so we should be fine…'

'Cold comfort to those under 39.'

'Of course. But it does mean that we have a chance of evading sickness.' Vignoles did not reply. As yet, he had been given no clear indicators about any age range preferences for the Porton Down variant, although they had claimed it was targeted at younger adults. Anna continued. 'Can be we sure that you and I are immune?'

'I don't think we can.' Vignoles was agonising about whether to mention the new strain. But why? Both were potentially deadly, and the precautions would be the same in either case. It might only cause her further alarm. 'We shall take extra care. These viruses are prone to acting oddly and we won't hide behind our age as a safety net.'

Anna put her painted fingernail on a passage in the paper folded on her knee. 'Listen to this, a GP in Winchester sounds terribly worried. "*We are amazed at the extraordinary infectivity of the disease, overawed by the suddenness of its outset and surprised at the protean nature of its symptomatology.*" A senior clinician in London thinks he's detecting signs the virus is not acting in the same way they have learned from countries with more experience of the symptoms.'

'What is he saying?' Vignoles felt a cold chill down his upper back. He saw an image of Wellbeck huddled in his winter coat against the wind and the look of something inscrutable behind his watery eyes.

'The language is typically medical; '*There are increasing incidences of complications in 30% of cases with over 60% mortality. Pneumonia and bronchitis accounted for 50% of these, the rest being Cerebro- and cardiovascular disease brought on by the flu. The incidence of post-influenzal pneumonia is increasing and is proving unresponsive to known treatments. It is clear we know insufficient about H2N2, but the more exposure we have to its effects, the more concerning it is becoming.*' I don't like the sound of that!' Anna looked across at her husband. 'Did you say that soldier died due to complications?'

'He had asthma. If patients have lung or heart weaknesses, they struggle to get over the infection.' But Vignoles was not appeased by his explanation. His knowledge of medicine and science was basic, but it was blindingly clear that if the man-made virus combined with the Asiatic in some kind of biological pincer movement, the situation would become desperate.

The telephone rang.

Chapter Twenty
Sheffield

'Vignoles?' Bernard Minshul barked down the line. 'That you? Had a devil of a job getting your number...' Minshul was seated in an empty porter's lodge in Sheffield Midland station and there was a crescendo of noise outside as a train prepared to depart for Manchester, with doors slamming and metal wheeled trolley's trundling with an unpleasant grating sound that caused the ground to quiver. There was little chance of being overheard but he'd still taken the precaution of locking the door to ensure privacy.

'I'm on a line nobody would think I'd use and judging by how hard it is to find yours, there's a chance you're not being tapped.'

'Our number is unlisted and not a party line. You have something?'

'Aye, I've hot news. We've got a witness. Given us a good description of two men seen a minute or so before the same witness met Mrs M walking the opposite way down the canal path. He was walking his dog.'

'How did you find the witness?'

'He knew 'er. Not as a friend but as fellow regulars along the canal path. They'd got into the habit of noddin' an' sayin' "how do?" Once or twice she'd stopped and said summat to his dog, who's a bit old and grey. The man recognised her face in the paper.'

'How confident are you he's genuine?'

'Sheffield born and bred and lived in the same place most of his life and there's nowt bad against his name. Used to be a house painter, now retired. His dog walking routine is regular, and he seemed right shook up over the death of young Phyl. He were horrified she'd gone in the water and not heard owt.'

'Odd that he didn't hear anything?'

'We reckon not. If she were needled in the arm and dying as she fell, she'd probably didn't have time to cry out before hitting the water. If a train were passing overhead whistling an' chuffing as they do, it could mask the sound. My sergeant and I stood there a while to test the theory and it's plausible.'

'And the two suspects?'

'The less good news is they sound like anyone. Medium height, dark coats, dark trousers, dark hats low to obscure their faces and both wearing gloves.'

'Good luck with that...'

'But one man looked him right in the eye as he passed and remembers he had startling blue eyes. A proper Frank Sinatra.'

'That could lodge in someone's memory.'

'Right you are, and the other fella had a distinctive emerald green tie and a thin moustache.'

'Which could be shaved off by now and the tie changed...'

'Don't be so negative, Charles. I'm doing my best!'

'What's the strategy? It's your patch, so you call the shots.'

'I've got men making enquiries at Victoria and Midland and along the lines out from each. We'll identify all train staff on departures out of Victoria for a couple of hours after she hit the water and interview them. Someone will remember these two.'

'Has Badger give you the green light?' Vignoles was sceptical.

Minshul swigged some sweet tea. 'Yep. He's told me to find these bastards and throw everything at it. But he's got something bigger for you. Expect a call.'

'What sort of job?' Vignoles was puzzled.

'Put it this way, are you a good shot?'

'Not really...'

'The Army has admitted two men are on the run and carriers of this bug thing. Immune, but still live and dangerous and out to spread mayhem. The Home Secretary's sanctioned all forces to stop them. Stop them dead.'

'Is this a joke?'

'It's no laughing matter, Charles! But you'll hear it from the horse's mouth soon enough, just thought it best to tell you straight off, because, between you and me, the old man's not in the best of health.'

'He seems under the weather.'

'I hope it's not what I think it is.'

Vignoles agreed. 'The two hitmen. I can't see them sticking to the railway. You could be pulled off of your area of responsibility. Deep into Met or City of London territory, I hazard.' Vignoles was deliberately avoiding mentioning either secret service.

'I'm not letting niceties of jurisdiction stop me. An' besides, everything's turning on its head as we speak. There's talk of shutting a lot of the Big Smoke down and clearing the streets. A curfew, shops and schools and factories to close. Can you believe it? I heard a rumour the Army could be called out to help keep law and order. Whatever the truth of that, I want justice for Phyl.'

'If the killers are working for whom we suspect, they're going to be hard to trace and harder to bring to justice.'

'I have my own thoughts about that.'

'That sounds ominous.'

'Leave them to me. I'll follow this up and you go after those men with a virus on their hands. I feel happier tracking assassins. I know what I'm dealing with. Divide our resources for the common good?'

'Very well,' Vignoles' voice was quiet. 'Be careful, Bernard.'

'And you Charlie boy. Remember, your real enemy is invisible...'

Minshul replaced the handset and sat back in his chair and eyed the gleaming pistol lying on the desk. He then looked out of the grubby window onto the platform as a long train of coal wagons snaked past hauled by a filthy ex-War Department engine. The usual run-of-the-mill fare on this line. The train passed unnoticed and taken for granted. Just the railway going about its business as usual, as it did last week and would the next. But would it be the same next week? Next month? The country was becoming jittery, the Government alarmed about the worsening health crisis.

Even Minshul was starting to feel it. Here he was sitting in a familiar station on his home patch, armed and ready to shoot to kill.

He watched the guard's van at the end of the interminable string of coal wagons trundle past the window. He imagined what it would be like to be the guard in that little wooden box on wheels on a runaway train hurtling down a gradient, the brakes burning and the engine shaking herself to pieces as they failed to bring it under control and now facing the inevitable smash ahead. Perhaps they were all about to find out.

He needed another mug of tea.

Chapter Twenty-one
Between Nottingham and Leicester

It had been an intense morning on the Police firing range in Nottingham for the British Railways Detective Department.

The just issuing of weapons alone was a sobering experience. Each numbered firearm exuding a scent of oil and machined metal as it was removed from the greased paper and hessian wrappings, with the slight whiff of cordite in the air of the range reminding them of the purpose of these objects. The weight of the handguns and the solid clunks and clicks as the precision-engineered parts engaged whilst their unsmiling instructor talked them through the correct method of cleaning, loading and firing was compelling - and repelling - in almost equal measure.

PC Simon Howerth's eyes were like saucers with youthful excitement. This was quickly tempered once he struggled to handle the fierce kick-back of the percussive detonations and appreciated the latent danger of a loaded pistol. His bubbling enthusiasm for 'doing some shooting' mellowed into quiet reflection as he chewed over the grim implications of being called upon to fire a gun against a living being.

PC Blencowe remained almost silent throughout, but his measured calm won the approval of their instructor and he managed a creditable score. Everything he did was considered and correct. Vignoles knew he could rely on Blencowe keeping his head in a fraught situation.

DS Mellor in contrast was supremely confident from the start of the session and impatient to commence shooting. Perhaps too much so and the instructor was unforgiving, keen to rein in some of Mellor's cockiness. He was pedantically pulled up on every point during the breaking apart, loading and handling, but demonstrated previous experience with firearms and mutual respect slowly developed with the instructor. Mellor proved an excellent shot. There could be no questioning his ability to accept the challenge and stood a more than an odds-on chance of putting a round exactly where he chose. Mellor would shoot to kill if required.

There had been a robust exchange of views over the WPCs; The instructor initially refusing to accept that women could bear arms and was vociferous in his insistence that to do so flew in the face of Home Office ruling. He tried to dismiss the two women from the session, suggesting they limited themselves to providing cups of tea.

Vignoles fought his corner hard however, arguing not only had the two WPCs proven themselves previously, but the present emergency demanded he must call upon the greatest number of officers as possible. 'This is a matter of National Security, driven by the need to protect countless innocent citizens. Arming the Transport Police is proof enough we are looking at exceptional circumstances that demand exceptional interpretations of the rule book…'

He finally won agreement that WPC Lansdowne could step forward and take up one of the pistols. She was deliberately thoughtful in her approach and fully looked the model professional in her immaculate serge uniform with gleaming silver buttons and blonde ponytail hanging down from beneath her hat. Lansdowne was respectful, yet always a fraction ahead of the instructions issued in a deliberately slow and unashamedly patronising manner. Her shooting was close to perfection. The instructor fell silent as he watched, as indeed did the whole department.

After three target sessions on the range, Lansdowne turned one corner of her mouth down in dismay and apologised for a fractional miss-hit.

'That is quite exceptional, WPC Lansdowne. You have experience handling a firearm?'

'I'm dreadfully rusty, sir. Long out of practice.' She inspected the target once again and shook her head. 'I would be out of the medals with such a poor show...'

'Medals?' The instructor looked puzzled.

'Olympic bronze medallist, '48 games...' Vignoles quietly observed. 'Pistol'.

The instructor covered his embarrassment by muttering something about real-life situations being quite different from a competitive shooting range.

WPC Benson was a willing student, and her shooting whilst slow had been adequate and even gained a slight grunt of what could be taken as approval from the instructor, still reeling from Lansdowne's exhibition shooting.

Vignoles went last and held no illusions over his ability. He'd never been the best of shots and age and glasses combined with lack of practice had not improved the situation. He knew how to handle a gun and understood the responsibilities of commanding an armed force, but his lacklustre performance was politely described as 'adequate' and 'on par with many serving officers lacking specialist firearms expertise'.

With leather shoulder bags significantly weighed down by pistols and bullets, they were now headed back to Leicester in a strange mood that was a mixture of a jolly works day out combined with anxiety about what it all meant. Vignoles had remained uncharacteristically silent about the true purpose of this surprising turn of events, but they knew something serious must be brewing for them to be put through their paces on a range.

Vignoles commandeered a first-class compartment for the short ride back to Leicester to ensure his operational briefing would not be overheard. Once they were underway, with the door to the compartment closed, he explained the true reasons for arming his team.

He told them about *Operation Chinese Bird* and the subsequent death of Mordon and assassination of his wife, the death of whom especially shocked Benson. He went on to explain about the suspected breakout from Longmoor of a more dangerous virus than had been anticipated. Vignoles then explained how scientists had identified that some persons could become carriers, able to spread the virus but with no obvious effects themselves and how some men had left the camp against orders. Whilst most had been brought back, two were still on the loose.

'You are aware of the daily news surrounding the arrival of Asian flu, more accurately known as *H2N2*. We've all followed its advance from Hong Kong and Singapore through India and South Africa, felling millions along the way and the developing crisis here. I shall now tell you something that must remain between us and not shared outside this compartment.' He looked at each member of the team in turn.

'I won't attempt to whitewash this. There are agencies within the United Kingdom who wish to conceal the existence of the man-made *coron56-N4* that has escaped into the country, no thanks to *Operation Chinese Bird* at Longmoor. I shall not name them but be under no illusion they are powerful agencies and potentially dangerous. It would be wise that we only ever refer to *H2N2*. Whilst not condoning the decision made far above my head to conceal *coron56-N4,* it won't aide the protection of the citizens of this country knowing the scientific names of two competing virus strains. Idle talk can quickly sow panic and the potential for civil unrest. The revelation of the truth is for another time when the present crisis has receded. I hope perhaps then a full and proper investigation will take place into *coron56-N4*.

'Be that as it may, our task now is unambiguous. To hunt down the two carriers of *coron56-N4*. All any of us can do to slow the spread of a killer virus is end a deliberate attempt to spread the man-made variety.' Vignoles now indicated the copy of the *Daily Mirror* Blencowe had bought along. 'There is plenty enough about the pandemic in the papers as it is.' He paused a moment. 'Perhaps these lurid headlines read like scaremongering, but the news from the Longmoor Military Railway is a grim reminder of what we are up against. I was informed this morning the death count there has now reached fifty-two and will climb higher.'

What Vignoles didn't say was that Badger's telephone call had been brief, despite the serious orders he had to communicate. The Chief Super had been labouring for breath and frequently unable to continue until he'd taken gulps of air, like a fish out of water. Badger's condition was steadily worsening and Vignoles feared he was succumbing to *coron56-N4*.

Worried glances were exchanged around the compartment.

'Why use valuable time on a firing range and issue firearms if this manhunt is so pressing you might ask? Bullets are useless against the virus, but not against the men carrying it with malicious intent. The task we and other forces across the land have been set is grim but essential.' He studied the faces around the compartment to ensure he had their full attention. 'We have been ordered to find these two men and stop them. DCI Minshul, whom some of you may know, works out of Sheffield and his men will work in concert with us from now on. We are sharing resources.'

'Are the Yorkshire lads carrying guns?' Blencowe asked.

'Yes. They're undertaking the same firearms training.'

'The issuing of firearms suggests these men might be dangerous. Might they resist arrest with violence?' Benson finally broke the uneasy silence as the train rolled southward and bucketloads of white steam roiled past the window. She was clutching the shoulder bag resting on her lap and giving it odd glances whilst Vignoles was speaking.

'The two soldiers from Longmoor on the run should be considered extremely dangerous. As great a threat as any we have ever faced. There were another three who went AWOL, but all are now accounted for; one has subsequently died from the virus. That serves to underline what we are dealing with.

The two who remain at large are considered to have malicious intent to cause death on a grand scale. They are set on a course to cause maximum harm to the citizens of this country.'

Mellor now took over. 'You have your weapons and been coached on how and when to use them. When to decide to pull the trigger.' Pale faces watched intently. 'You'll be issued photographs and pen pictures of the two targets. These should be waiting at Leicester, including alternate photographs with minor facial changes created by an artist. False moustaches and spectacles, for example. We expect them to do all they can to evade us for as long as possible, whilst using the railway as their primary means to spread the infection. When encountered, you will shoot with intent to bring them down...'

'Down, Sarge?' Howerth queried.

'You will kill them. Shoot to kill. No-one must approach and attempt to arrest either man. What they carry is invisible but lethal and even their bodies must be treated with extreme caution.'

Chapter Twenty-two
Leicester Central

The briefing continued back at the Detective Department offices, where the promised information including official Army photographs of Winter and Clawson, were waiting.

'As mentioned earlier, both men are believed to be asymptomatic. Unaffected physically, but able to spread the virus to anyone or anything they come into contact with.'

'How long do they stay asymptomatic, sir?'

'Nobody knows, Benson. Presumably for some considerable time or we would not have been asked to step in with deadly force.'

'But if we shoot them and it turns out they're no longer a threat? I feel rather queasy about that.'

'Not your job to worry,' Mellor snapped. 'You have your orders, let others debate the ethics.'

Privately, Mellor shared Benson's concerns but was not going to betray that to the team. 'Our targets: Sergeant Alan Winter and Private Thomas Clawson.' He indicated the black and white glossy prints pinned to a board mounted on the wall. 'Police are presently stationed outside their family homes and those of known relatives and close friends. However, neither man has made any attempt at contact nor shown their faces. Not even a phone call to wife or girlfriend...' Mellor sucked on his fag. 'Winter is married and has a two-year-old and not a word to her.' He paused to let this sink in. 'Both last seen in army fatigues with kit bags. They are believed to be unarmed.'

'That makes lethal force even harder to stomach,' Benson looked unhappy.

'They're armed with something worse...' Muttered Blencowe.

'A gun is lethal, but precise and limited in its effect,' Mellor continued. 'What they carry is like a time bomb with a quite limitless potential. Understand that and act accordingly. Talk us through the work you and Howerth have done, Blencowe.'

PC Blencowe walked across to the giant map on the wall. 'This is Longmoor...and here...and here...are the respective hometowns of Winter and Clawson. Like the sarge said, both locations being watched by the relevant local forces. We've now got the larger stations across the railway network on high alert, so it can't be long before we get sightings - assuming, of course, they stick to rail. But they're railwaymen and railways are the best way to cause maximum damage, therefore it seems reasonable to assume they will use this method of transport.' Murmurs of assent around the room. 'Every stationmaster is tasked with providing us each morning with any information they can glean via local press, radio bulletins and telephone calls to hospitals about flu-type outbreaks and deaths. Not exactly scientific, and far from perfect, but stationmasters are conscientious types and will do a thorough job as possible. Their reports and any others we can glean ourselves, are plotted on this map. We reckon it's about twenty-four to forty-eight hours behind. Bad news as that means they steal a march on us, but it gives us a sense of where these men may have been and possibly, and more useful, indicate where they could be headed next...' Blencowe looked unhappy. He knew this to be a woefully imperfect tool.

'I doubt anyone has a better system,' Mellor was encouraging. 'What have we learned to far?'

'London is a key location. That makes sense any way you look at it, as they can cause maximum harm there. We should work on the idea London is where they will operate from, able to take trains to every corner of the land.'

'And abroad...'

'Good point, Lansdowne,' Mellor replied. 'The channel ports are on alert as we don't want this shipping into the Continent on the boat trains.'

Blencowe continued. 'We've got strong traces suggesting they first went west. Right down to Penzance, stopping off in strategic locations such as Exeter, Bristol, Newton Abbot and a number of the Devon and North Cornwall coastal towns. Winter is from Barnstable, but he's not seen his missus or kid and the town seems to have only a few cases showing so far.'

'You think they made a concerted effort to cover the West Country first?' Benson asked.

'Looks that way. If these upward trends are a result of their travels it proves the efficacy of *coron56-N4*.' Vignoles added. 'It was designed to take effect within 12 hours with acute properties of transmission. The only positive is that we can quickly map the spread.'

'If we are to believe the Government's official line, the *Asiatic flu* has reached the major port cities but not yet made any significant gains inland,' Blencowe added. 'It is not unreasonable to consider what you see on this map as being trails left specifically by our men.'

Everyone stared at the mass of red and black pins. It made for sobering viewing.

'We can see significant clusters around Longmoor and the surrounding area. Then clearly defined corridors into London, which presumably show Winter and Clawson escaping camp. Then into the west country as mentioned, and then we have Birmingham.' The mass of red and black clustered there was disturbing.

'Not exactly a port...' Howerth observed.

'Right. So, it could be one or both men went there.' More heads nodded agreement. 'The density of population plays into the hands of the virus. Easy to reach from places such as Bristol, where there is another nasty flare-up, and of course with good links to London.'

'How many have died so far?' Lansdowne asked.

Mellor picked up a telegram. 'We get twice-daily reports. Currently over eight thousand deaths and upwards of forty-five thousand struck down, but these are hospital numbers and there will be many more at home as yet unrecorded.'

'The Prime Minister will make an announcement this evening about measures to control movement and personal liberty within London and many of the southern counties. Perhaps also around Birmingham. What is perhaps more worrying, is a telephone conversation I had immediately before this meeting. The Chemical Defence Experimental Establishment and the Microbiological Research Department, both of whom were behind *Operation Chinese Bird*, have reason to believe their virus and the Asiatic version have mutated to create a deadlier variant. It is at least an admission of their culpability and they are expected to brief the PM. It is possible Winter and Clawson are carrying this version, which poses a yet more significant threat to everyone. Hence the need for immediate and decisive action.' Vignoles looked grey and his voice sombre as he delivered the news.

Mellor stubbed his cigarette out. 'This won't be easy nor pleasant, but we cannot be soft on Winter and Clawson. So, listen up…'

Chapter Twenty-three
London

Benson was back in London. It made sense. Someone had to place themselves in the heart of the infection zone and with Hawkes living there she had personal reasons for volunteering for this unwelcome posting.

The infection rate was alarmingly high in London and rising daily, but Benson was prepared to take her chances. 'I'll do it, sir. I'd rather share the risk beside someone I care for. I hope I find Winter and Clawson and can keep my aim steady before my time is up...'

It sounded melodramatic. As though she were speaking lines from a cheap B-movie, but no-one laughed. If anything, there was a subtle exhalation of breath from Blencowe and Howerth, both glad to have ducked out of being sent South.

Benson stepped out of her train at Marylebone, one of just a handful of fellow passengers. Whilst readily finding and retaining an empty compartment had initially been a joy when she joined at Leicester Central, this had altered into an uneasy sense of being quite alone in the whole carriage. There had been a discernible hollowness to the sound of the train and no distant chatter or murmur of voices. No laughter of children, a baby crying or even footsteps along the corridor and doors slid open and closed; just the whoosh of air around the corridor connections, the click of the wheels and a mournful rattle of a partially secured lavatory door. There was no buffet service, as was the ruling for all trains including the premium expresses, whilst the guard had not once walked the train, preferring to stay safe in his little compartment. At the stops along the way, just one or two doors had slammed shut and often there was no sign of life on deserted platforms.

Although doing her best to lose herself in a recently

purchased book, by the time she noticed they were entering the hinterland of London's north-western sprawl, she was starting to wish a gregarious family would spill into her compartment. She would even forgive them unpacking mounds of fish paste sandwiches or pungent pies to stink out the compartment, passing around a Thermos flask lid of sweet tea that slopped on the floor whilst the kids bounced noisily on the seat cushions. Silence was not always golden.

Walking down the platform Benson paused for a moment beside the 'V2' class locomotive that had hauled the 4.05 pm from Manchester into Marylebone, taking a few precautionary breaths of sulphurous smoke and steam.

The driver was leaning on the cab side, cigarette in hand. He'd noticed her inhaling deeply and winked.

She shrugged her shoulders, 'You never know…'

He laughed.

'Will you be heading back to Nottingham?'

'Dead right! Don't want to be here longer than I can help it.'

'Safe journey then…'

'We'll be fine, but you take care, me duck.'

Benson gave him a grateful smile, pulled her scarf across her face and hefted the shoulder bag with its ominous content into a better position on her shoulder, counter-balancing her small case in the other gloved hand.

Hawkes was not meeting her. Another alteration from the normal run of things and she would have to make her way doubly laden on a bitterly cold night with snow on the ground. On the telephone, Hawkes had given no reason for his absence. He'd sounded distracted and his voice lacked the usual bounce.

As Benson approached the covered concourse, populated by just a few figures in winter coats and scarves, she felt quite dispirited. The flower sellers were gone and instead of their buckets of bright scented cut flowers, there was just an empty skeletal framework that held the buckets and a pool of water with a few wilted leaves.

Where *was* everyone?

A long line of back cabs under the porte cochere greeted her. At least these were in abundance. The drivers looking at her with heightened levels of expectation of a fare. No queues for once. No one waiting for a bus either and few vehicles roaring along the Euston Road. It was a weekday, early evening, and yet felt more like 4 am on a Sunday. Benson started to feel disorientated. At least a newspaper hawker was still broadcasting his usual indecipherable call.

She looked at the placard on the front of his little stand.

CITY SHUTS DOWN!

She stepped closer to read the subheading on the folded copies of the London Evening Standard.

Flu kills 800 in a day as panic grips London.

The hawker held out a copy, eager for a sale and Benson passed some coins into his gloved hand. She was not sure if she wanted to read more but tucked it under her arm, then approached a cab. This was a night to get home as fast as possible.

Hawkes was at home, although judging by the desultory fire in the grate which was only just catching alight, he'd only been in a few minutes. The house felt oppressively cold and dark and lacked the usual heady smells of hot food and the noise and chatter of the others. Just like with the train, she could immediately sense that something was different.

Hawkes smiled when he saw her and offered her a kiss and a comforting embrace, although he soon stepped back to enquire what was in the heavy shoulder bag that dug into his ribs.

'A pistol.'

'A what? But why?'

'A job we must do. Not for discussion and you tell nobody. Sorry. What about a cup of tea, eh love?'

Hawkes just took her case and waved her towards the back kitchen as he walked toward the stairs. 'The others... are all in there...' He paused on the bottom stair. 'Jane...'

She looked up at him, curious at the tone of his voice.

'About this afternoon...' Hawkes was uncharacteristically tongue-tied. 'We buried Malcolm. The flu thing took him from us.'

'Oh God, no!' Benson was aghast. 'Poor Miriam...'

* * * *

The motley collection of glasses chipped cups and tin mug were refilled with generous measures of rum. The fire now blazed, and its light played over those gathered around, the tiny dancing flames bringing a measure of vivacity to dark eyes that glistened. A record player was quietly spinning a stack of 45's in the corner and a huge cooking pot with the remains of a piquant stew sat on the stove. A bowl of this goat stew had given everyone courage and energy after what had been a bleak and soulless afternoon.

'We could not see 'is coffin! They jus' told us to keep away like we was somethin' *bad*!'

'I could not even lay my hand on his coffin and say goodbye!' Miriam's tears were replaced by indignation.

'What kind of service was it?' Benson asked.

'Service? There was no *service* as you or I would understand. Just a short prayer, a few words you couldn't even hear, a drop of holy water, an' that was that!' Miriam shook her head, still struggling to understand what had happened.

'No mourners allowed. Everyone supposed to stay away or stand outside in the cold. Just two allowed inside and to keep their distance,' Hawkes explained. 'It's the same for everyone.

But that's no comfort.'

'An' you can imagine what they thought about myself goin' inside,' Miriam's eyes grew even bigger with emphasis. 'Huh... No blacks allowed. They don't want us at no funeral.'

Benson downed more rum. It was hard to take it in. Malcolm, the band's drummer and a dear friend, was now dead. But that was not the end of it, Arthur the trombonist was lying upstairs with a raging fever and an unstoppable cough, though mercifully he was sleeping at present. His girlfriend Angela refusing to leave his bedside. What chance did she have of evading catching it?

Whatever name or number someone chose to give this affliction, it was striking hard. In the space of a week, the effect was devastating on this one household. Benson squeezed Hawkes' hand. How long until they caught it? How long until the unsympathetic and aggressive landlord demanded the empty beds were filled with fresh lodgers, only for them to get it in turn?

Benson shivered. She'd told Vignoles she'd stay alive long enough to draw a bead in her gun sight on Winter and Clawson. There truly was no time to waste.

Chapter Twenty-four
Sheffield Victoria

'Boss, we've got something.'

'Tell me.'

'A bar steward. A man called Johnson who might have seen the two men. He was working a Manchester service on the evening in question and remembers two gents in the bar.'

'Where is he now?'

'On the train standing in the station. He's clearing and cleaning the galley and bar following the directive to shut all food and drink outlets -.'

'What? They're shutting the blummin' buffets an' bars?' Minshul was outraged.

'Yep. In this morning's operating directives,' DS Ashbury explained.

'That's bloody terrible,' Minshul was shaking his head as he plonked his trilby on his head. It was a short walk to the train, but the icy rain was hammering down aided by a vicious wind off the Pennines. 'Peter, you tellin' me I have to live off the sarnies my missus makes and nowt else?' He looked pale at the thought.

Derek Johnson was polishing glasses before carefully stowing them inside the tiny corner bar. The tables fixed to the carriage sides below the windows bore hand-written tent cards that advised 'This table is no longer in use.'

Minshul eyed these with suspicion. 'Why can't you sit at the tables?'

Johnson looked up. 'Regulations. Everything to close forthwith until further notice because of the outbreak.'

'And we can't even sit at a flippin' table?'

'Spreads infection…'

'I can sit on a platform bench!'

'Perhaps they should be closed as well?' Johnson continued in his work unflustered by the sudden appearance of the blustering detective. His long years of experience had rendered him immune to any kind of verbal abuse.

'Don't tell me, we'll have uniform moving' folk on who just want to sit on a bench...' Minshul gave another shake of his head. 'Right. My sergeant here says you've got summat for me?'

Johnson carefully placed the last glass away, then equally carefully folded the white tea towel before laying this on the countertop. A fastidious and careful man, and whilst his unhurried manner was testing Minshul's patience, the DCI could recognise these as the mannerisms of someone who might make a reliable witness. He bit his tongue and waited for Johnson to speak. 'The sergeant was enquiring about two gentlemen you have interest in. With trade effectively killed off, it was a slow evening in here. Added to which, working in this job it pays to have a good memory. During a busy service, I find it useful to recall a drinks order attached to a specific face, so when I catch them waving or trying to fight their way to the bar, I can repeat their order.'

'That could be useful,' Minshul was eyeing the beer pump handle and wondering if he should take the opportunity for a last pint.

Johnson gave a slight nod of the head, 'I can bring these two gents to mind vividly. One had arresting eyes. Pardon the pun.' He gave a cheeky smile.

'In what way?'

'Piercing. Bright blue and a way of staring at one that was a little unnerving.'

'What else?'

'About five-ten, slim but not skinny. Charcoal grey suit, a matching hat with no contrast to the hatband. A pale shirt. Not much else I can say.'

'So, a dark suit and hat without distinguishing details and, just like about half the population, has blue eyes. Sod all then!

What about the other? Tell me he was in a clown suit with a big red nose, so we stand a chance of recognising him in a crowd!'

'Hardly…' Johnson played it calmly. 'But his tie was distinguished, quality. And emerald green.'

'That it?'

'He had a North Walian accent.'

Minshul chewed this over for a moment. 'It's not a lot…'

'Both were cleanly shaven in sober clothes of reasonable quality. Two businessmen who wouldn't stand out in a crowd, but they were the only two in here, so that's why I remember them.'

'They boarded here, at Victoria?'

'Correct. They stepped out at Manchester.'

'Did you overhear anything they talked about?'

'It is not my job to eavesdrop…'

'Pull the other one. Tell us everything you heard.'

'They spoke quietly. Men who know what volume to maintain to make it hard to catch a word.'

'Are you laid off after today? With no work in the bar?' Minshul suddenly changed tack.

'Correct. Stood down until further notice.'

'Unpaid?'

'Also correct.'

The DCI laid a fresh ten bob note on the bar. 'Give us a whisky. I need something to cheer meself up - and keep the change.' He winked.

Johnson gave him a level stare. 'I'm not to serve anyone…'

A pound note followed. 'Make it two doubles and put that in your pocket. Then you tell me everything you heard. Everything.'

The notes were whisked away and glasses of scotch their place in moments.

'They looked like two businessmen who'd concluded a deal. Seemed pleased with "a job well done," as green tie said, and they toasted whatever it was with the same as you're having.'

'Go on. That's an expensive conversation that tells us nowt.'

'Blue eyes kept whistling the same tune over and over. Softly, but there for the three of us in the bar to hear. The Welsh chap after a while got annoyed and told him to stop it.'

'Memorable tune?' Ashbury asked.

'Yes. "Red River Valley". Sticks in the mind.'

Minshul knocked back most of his scotch. 'My missus likes it…'

'I got the feeling blue eyes was doing it without realising. Endlessly, like it covered his nerves or something.' Johnson was starting to warm to the theme, perhaps cheered by a welcome boost to his funds.

'But Welshy didn't?'

'I heard him say "Knock it on the head, you'll attract attention.'

Minshul and Ashbury gave each other puzzled looks. 'You sure you can't remember any more?' Minshul was wondering if it was money well spent.

'Blue eyes hailed from Chester or thereabouts. I recognised the accent and he made a mention of the city. Said something I didn't catch, but when I heard him say 'Chester' I placed the accent.'

'North Wales and Chester. They could have taken the same train from Manchester,' Ashbury observed.

'That narrows it down!' Minshul drained this glass in frustration.

Johnson, however, was a man who liked to operate at his own pace. He reached under the counter and pulled out a linen napkin folded over something and laid this before the two detectives. He opened it to reveal a metal cigarette lighter with an engraving on the front.

'This was left on the bar. It was hidden from view by that napkin dispenser. They were already off the train as we'd been stopped a few minutes before I spotted it. I told one of my lads to chase after them. He tried his best, but they'd gone…'

'Bloody hell…' Minshull cursed.

Johnson continued. 'A ticket inspector reckoned two men matching their description left the station through his gate. He said one was talking about connections to Wales, but that was all.'

'I was right!' Ashbury finished his whisky.

'Perhaps it was fortunate your lad didn't find them…' Minshul was giving the lighter scrutiny. 'This is the first good news we've had. Handled by yourself and the waiter, so we can forget finding useful fingerprints.' He glared at the steward. 'Everything's smudged.'

'I was not aware it had such significance.'

'We've got initials and a regimental crest.' Minshul studied them. 'He's an ex-paratrooper. 1st Airborne.'

'They were slim but solidly built chaps. Look like they could handle themselves. I'd say they were ex-military,' Johnson added.

'The Para's are a tough breed.'

'Perfect material to recruit for the kind of work we think they're in,' DS Asbury was being deliberately elliptical.

'Are they in some kind of trouble, inspector?'

'We just need to talk to them. I'll take this.' Minshul pocketed the lighter. 'If you see either men again, call me on this number immediately.' Minshul handed over a card. 'Don't let them know you've clocked them, and don't confront them. Just make sure we know and keep 'em sweet. DS Ashbury will take a statement and we'll want the timings of the train, all stations stopped along the way and a statement from your waiter friend who went charging after them.'

'I'm afraid the young man in question is in hospital. He was taken bad with the virus not long after we'd got to Manchester that evening. Last I heard, it was touch and go…'

'My job just gets easier and easier.'

Chapter Twenty-five
Waterloo Station

Waterloo Station was spookily empty of the usual maddening crowds for which it was notorious. Until the draconian antivirus measures had been imposed within London that cleared the grand concourses and platforms of virtually all its heaving, breathing, infection transmitting humanity, it had been one of the busiest railway stations in the United Kingdom. Before Prime Minister Harold Macmillan's emergency measures that effectively closed the city down, Waterloo had not been a place for the faint-hearted or timorous during rush hour. This station demanded you knew in advance the platform you required and not attempt to stand amidst a sea of impatient regulars whilst you puzzled at the massive departure and arrivals boards or fumbled in pockets to locate the pasteboard ticket you knew you had put somewhere safe and in-so-doing, impede the relentless flow of humanity.

Regulars knew the exact time it took to fight their way onto the platform before squeezing shoulder to shoulder in uncomfortable proximity with fellow commuters onboard the sardine-packed trains. Metal gates at each platform end funnelled throngs of humanity through the constricted openings whilst eagle-eyed ticket inspectors swiftly read the pasteboard tickets, unfailingly spotting a platform ticket masquerading as permission to travel or a thumb attempting to mask an outdated season ticket and the other clues to an attempted fare dodge.

Today, the gates guarding the platforms stood at various positions between wide open and closed shut, exactly as when the final normal service of slam-door carriage stock had disgorged its passengers. The platforms were empty save the usual litter lying between oily tracks and a clutch of disconsolate pigeons. A few platforms held rakes of empty stock that had not turned a wheel in days.

The majority of the little cabins at the platform ends where the ticket inspectors perched on wooden stools polished to a glossy shine, were unoccupied. The single electric light bulbs within each, extinguished. All except one. One booth was faithfully manned by a character with a face deeply scored by wind and rain and hands turning knobbly after too many years in the chill of the wind that blew across the many platforms.

Ernie Best was part of the small team retained in work whilst the others were furloughed at home on short rations and pay; told to stay indoors and stay healthy and wait for a time when the station could once again become alive with electric multiple unit trains and gleaming steam engines bearing glamorous names.

Best was almost a token gesture by British Railways, giving the impression to the few individuals who strayed into the echoing empty concourses that the railway was still open for business. A skeleton service was operating, but the infrequency of the trains and constant Tannoy announcements demanding everyone 'travel only when strictly necessary,' served to keep all but the hardiest travellers away. He was a lonely figure, hunched on the unforgiving seat reading the emaciated, emergency powers newspaper that told of encroaching doom and gloom, illustrated by a map that showed the enemy's silent advance up the country from the south-east. Different styles of dotted line with dates dishearteningly close together marked the frontline which now lay across the northern edge of Birmingham, straggling westward through the Black Country until it dropped down towards Worcester and Bristol, halted for now by the wide waters of the Severn, facing a Wales that waited for the inevitable. Best read that Norfolk was still a safe haven. There was talk of hordes clambering onto the last trains heading East. Scuffles, some violent, had to be quelled. The police and harassed Government ministers unpractised in dealing with outbreaks of civil disobedience called for calm and urged everyone 'to maintain a safe distance and wear a face covering,' whilst watching in despair as the hospital beds filled to capacity.

Each day seemed to bring new pronouncements, new orders and instructions, the closing of more aspects of city life but all to no avail. London was falling to the relentless and tireless efforts of what was still being called 'Asiatic flu', but which some observers were hinting, darkly as being something far worse and far more deadly. Whatever the truth of it, people were scared and quite reasonably wanted to run from a murderous enemy stalking the empty streets of their city. Londoners were still crowded into poor Victorian terraces, or perhaps worse, rehoused in new tower blocks of concrete and steel with the only access via tiny lifts and narrow stairwells. 'Modernity Britain' had neither designed nor built this brand-new housing stock to prove helpful in quelling a pandemic that delighted in proximity.

Best tossed the paper aside and the wind caught the outer page and whipped it away to dance and float and swirl along the platform before dropping to track level and entangling amongst the electrical pick-up shoe of the EMU ticking quietly in the one bay holding an operational train. Best had read the same disheartening news every day and stared uncomprehendingly at the ominous black-edged box in the corner of the front page that kept a running tally of the dead. He was sick of hearing about it. Tired of the whole fuss and panic. The lack of even the most basic provisions made the daily drudge of staying alive just that bit harder. He practically lived off porridge oats and cups of hot Bovril as these were about the only two things he could find to buy. And then there was the lack of rolling papers for his smoke.

Sold out! Why? Why are people stockpiling rolling papers, for Chrissake! He grumbled to himself as he fumbled tobacco into one of his last precious papers and urged his aching fingers to form it into a cylinder. As he licked the gum and tamped it down, he caught sight of the man.

He was on his own. But they usually were these days. A group had little chance of evading being challenged by the police or the Civil Defence Volunteers, demanding to see proof their journey was essential or evidence they were health workers or otherwise employed in a vital service. A stern ticking off or even a severe fine could follow failure to produce a satisfactory reason for roaming the streets. However, a solitary man dressed in black in the gloom of winter twilight could slip down the empty side streets undetected. Hustlers, dealers and crooks for the most part. Flitting from one address to another to service the needs of those with the money and confidence to trade with these shifty men who seemed to have neither fear nor respect for the virulence of the virus.

The railway was still one of the best sources of potential goods to trade. Goods 'lifted' (often aided by a substantial bribe) from the nocturnal supply trains the railway operated in their attempt to keep the city supplied with bare necessities.

Stealing cigarette papers, I bet... That thought alone made Best glare at the man with an unsympathetic, rheumy eye.

Or the man was a pimp. The prostitutes still slunk in the shadowed doorways, stockinged legs showing below unbuttoned winter coats as they shivered and watched their skin turn blue and waited for the lonely punters who snuck out to buy some company. The oldest trade in the world, and despite mass graves and impersonal burials by masked officials and the debilitating effects of those still clinging to life in hospital beds hooked to oxygen tubes and masks, these men still went out looking for the girls compelled to work by their violent and unscrupulous masters.

Best wasn't alarmed by his presence. These characters didn't like to be recognised and as long as you didn't prevent them from going about their nefarious business they would try to attract as little attention as possible. They cared nothing for the virus but were the most assiduous in wearing scarves or other face coverings. They were exploiting the fact they could conceal their identities and yet attract little or no attention despite bandit-style masks.

The ticket inspector lit his cigarette. He was bored and cold and the next departure was not for another thirty minutes. 'Come on, son, let's have a proper look at yer, then.' He sniggered as he lit the paper and inhaled. He was in the mood to cause some mischief 'Hey mister! What you lookin' for?' That usually sent them scurrying like a cockroach evading a light.

The man in black had been motionless, but in response to the hail, he approached Best. Private Clawson was now in a dark suit and coat and wearing the pair of National Health prescription glasses he sometimes wore for reading. These rested low on his nose in an attempt to alter his appearance. The new hat concealed most of his Army haircut. His step was confident, but not overly so. None of that arrogant swagger of one of the East End knife boys or West End drug dealers and pimps.

'I don't suppose there's any chance of a train?'

Best almost choked on his smoke. 'Hardly. Where you bin hidin'?'

'I know there are problems.'

'You're not kiddin'!'

'I need to get to the coast.'

'You 'an all? There's plenty who've gone for the sea air. They reckon its good against the killer bug. A bit of salty air in the lungs...'

'Exactly! I was rather hoping for a boat train...'

'Ger away wiv yer! You're behind the times.' Best laughed and shook his head. It never ceased to amaze him how some people didn't have a clue about anything. Didn't they read a paper or listen to the radio? 'I wouldn't bother even if I could find a ferry. It's no better there than 'ere.'

'I thought France was in the clear?'

'Nah, it's the Channel ports, see? The virus got on the boats and that was it. Loads of passengers on the ferries got it then piled off into Calais, Dieppe and the like. Spreadin' like wildfire...'

'Oh, I see.' Clawson was privately cheering. He'd already travelled on two boat trains to the coast and back before the services were severely curtailed. It was working. The crowded trains had been perfect, and the ferry ports a fertile ground to spread the virus without even stepping on a boat. 'Still, they must be a few weeks behind, and France is big. Plenty of space to escape.'

'Dunno. Never bin.' Best eyed the man suspiciously. He looked healthy enough, but you could never be sure. 'How d'you escape from summat you can't see?'

'True enough.' Clawson pretended to consider this profound thought as if he'd not spent almost every waking hour thinking about the destruction and misery he was sowing by the slightest touch of his fingers. 'But you *do* have trains? I mean, you wouldn't be sitting here otherwise, and I saw some men over in the far side with baggage trolleys and sack trucks. Waiting to unload something by the look of it.

'Nuffin' passes you, sir.' Best grinned.

'Just curious.' Clawson opened a new pack of cigarettes. A quality brand and Best, despite rolling his own because they were more economical, made little attempt to conceal the hungry look on his face as he saw the maroon and gold carton flip open. They were a type too rich for his meagre wage. 'Go ahead, take one...'

Best reached out. Placing his undernourished rollie on the edge of the desk in his hut to fizzle out due to lack of attention. He could return to it later.

Clawson fired up a Zippo lighter and Best instinctively leaned forward. The wind flattened the flame and the man cupped his other hand around it. Their hands touched momentarily and Best realised he'd made a mistake. The days when a friend or stranger lent you their lighter or guarded a flame as you drew intimately close for a moment were just memories. A momentary lapse, but he would have to trust to good luck to keep to lurgy away.

'We've got that one leavin' in twenty minutes... We get a few more in the mornings, otherwise, it's like a flippin' morgue.'

'I've never seen it so quiet...'

'That one's a shuttle to Clapham Junction via Waterloo East. They prefer folk to board up the junction. Keepin' 'em away from the city I suppose. There's a train to Guildford in ninety minutes, that any use?'

Clawson did not look impressed.

'What? This is hectic compared to Euston. They've practically shut the West Coast. Nothing beyond Rugby except the freight and twice-daily passenger trains for which you need a special permit!'

'You do?'

'Got to prove it's imperative to travel and fill out forms. You pay through the nose for the pleasure, an' all. They've even got the Army riding shotgun. It's worse than the war, I tell 'yer.'

'I suppose it *is* a war, of sorts...' Clawson smoked and quietly chuckled to himself. Winter had been tackling the north-facing termini and evidently, doing a good job. Clawson decided there was little point in loitering longer as there were too few passengers to infect. 'Well, Guildford don't appeal, so I'll be off.' He didn't specify where and Best was not sufficiently interested to ask.

As he turned to leave there was a series of shouts and a chorus of harsh laughs and jeers as a group of six Teddy Boys swung into view, their outrageously oiled and quaffed hair and peacock colours instantly recognisable.

''ere comes trouble.'

'Yeah?'

'Watch yourself and scarper! They want only one thing, and that's trouble.'

A length of heavy bike chain swung from a hand, a crowbar in another. An ominous flash of a blade. They were drunk and rowdy and idly kicked out at a litter bin, the bar was swung against a pillar and a door was booted for no other reason than a wish to lash out.

Clawson hurried away. There were too many of them to tackle, despite wishing he could find a way to smother each idiotically grinning Ted with the infection. That would wipe the smiles off their faces. Judging by the shouts of mocking abuse aimed in his direction, they didn't like his prescription glasses, cheap suitcase and 'straight' clothes.

He walked as briskly as he dared, not wanting to look back or suggest he was trying to flee. The thump of crepe soles grew louder, a whooping series of yells and curses and as he turned a corner, they caught up with him, a leg tripping and catapulting him forwards as the metal bar smashed onto his shoulders. He sprawled across the smooth floor, case skidding away and hat rolling on its brim in a curve. A foot stamped on the hat, hands grabbed the case and slung it spinning in the air until it crashed onto a mail truck.

Booted feet kicked at his kidneys and Clawson guarded his head as a crepe sole skimmed his cheek in a painful swipe. He tried to form a protective ball, but hands reached out and attempted to drag him to his feet, all the time the flashy men in their ridiculous drape jackets in pastel pinks and blues edged with black cursed and jeered and called him 'grandad!'

Clawson could smell the booze on their breath, and he could tell they didn't know why they were laying into him, or to what end. This was just an empty show of aggression and violence fuelled by booze, but it lacked real focus and bite, despite the very obvious soreness on his back and a stinging cheek.

Clawson pulled himself to his feet, aided by one very

young Ted in a lime green suit who had held off attacking him. 'Okay lads…you've had your fun.' He acted groggier than he was as if lacking the will to fight back whilst quietly sizing up how best to land a knock-out punch. The sneering and jeering continued, but already the initial buzz of violence was fading as the Teddy Boys found their victim too compliant. Where was the thrill? One of the older of the gang, a man with outrageously long sideburns was already walking away, 'Come on…he's a pussy. Got no fight!'

Clawson reckoned he could lay any one of them out with his left hook, but six was just too many. He made himself stoop and hunched his shoulders.

'Got any smokes?' The pale blue Ted asked, in a voice that flirted with being polite.

'Yeah…' Clawson winced extravagantly and fished out a now crumpled carton. Another face pushed up to close to his and Clawson could feel the breath on his face. This was good. The arrogant peacock was going to get a dose of something nasty.

The bike chain whirled in the air, but the young man wielding it lacked the gall to allow it to strike and seemed more interested in the act of making it sing out as it twirled. Hands touched the cigarettes, Clawson feigning staggering and placing a hand on a drape jacket to steady himself, only to have it rudely dragged aside. More contact.

A door opened and two railway personnel walked out, dressed in cleaner's coveralls.

'Oy lads! Look what the cat brought in!' Black sideburns saw two new victims.

'Darkies!'

'This is more like it!

The Teds roared with rage and ran at the two black cleaners who ducked around a corner and out of sight. Ugly chants of 'Kill, kill, kill!' echoing around the station. Clawson wondered why the two cleaners chose to flee and not dive back inside behind the safety of the door. This was going to be bloody. They'd toyed with him out of boredom and lacked the belief to follow through, but he could hear the raw hatred and see the malicious intent as they pursued their frightened quarry.

Not my problem. Clawson straightened his hat and walked across to retrieve his suitcase as cries and shouts and odd crashes and bangs filled the air. There was nobody in sight and he could not tell what was happening. Glass splintered. A yelp like a dog being beaten.

If nothing else, that's a few more infected. Clawson brushed himself down and started whistling a cheery tune as he walked. He'd stroll across to London Bridge and Cannon Street stations and see what was left running there. These stations existed for frequent and tightly packed commuter trains and there was bound to be something departing. He'd jump on whatever pulled in and take a ride out to some deathly dull outer suburb and work his evil magic there for the remainder of the evening. He might even find a warm pub open if he was lucky. Most had locked their doors days ago in the city, but it was supposed to be slightly better further out.

His tummy rumbled. It was getting hard to find places to eat. Tomorrow, he'd have to get out of London and head up north where the country remained largely free of infection. Otherwise, he'd either starve to death or be kicked black and blue by one of these gangs.

In the distance, he heard the ominous clang of an ambulance, or was it a police car? Either way, it was the constant soundtrack of the city, day or night.

Chapter Twenty-six
Waterloo

Mellor was at Waterloo in minutes of the shout being raised. Fortuitously he'd been quite close when summoned to the telephone.

Uniformed officers and an ambulance crew were gathered in huddles on the station concourse. Mellor was not unhappy to see two leather-jacketed members of the Flying Squad to one side, smoking fags and looking menacing. Mellor quickly established the alarm was about the beating of coloured railway employees by a gang of Teds.

Run of the mill fare and outside his remit to find Winter and Clawson, so he left the uniformed Transport Police to take statements whilst the unfortunate victims were patched up by masked ambulance crew. Bruising and minor cuts and one fractured rib would heal in time. The men claimed the Teds were carrying knives, but if this had been the case, they'd thankfully lacked the nerve to use them.

'Nah, they rarely use knives. Just for show, ain't it. They don't want blood on their fancy-dan suits, see? Cost too much...' One of the Sweeney observed. 'Pussies.'

'They prefer intimidation and fists and boots.'

'Now, the KBW's on the other hand are worse. A knife in the kidneys and leave 'em for dead...'

Mellor was having a smoke with the two Flying Squad, who had one of the younger Teds handcuffed in the back of their Jaguar outside. They were awaiting the arrival of a Black Maria to take him away for processing.

'KBWs?' Mellor queried.

'Keep Britain White,' one of the Sweeny replied.

'Whatever you think of their ideas, they mean business. They get properly stuck in and if they can get a neighbourhood out rioting, it gets bloody… Knives, you name it.'

Mellor didn't pass comment. He had a nagging suspicion the two Flying Squad, if not exactly approving, were lacking the appropriate level of disapproval at the beating the blacks had received. This was not Mellor's concern right now as none of the men involved bore any resemblance to either Winter or Clawson. He made his excuses and walked over to where Ernie Best was sitting with a mug of tea clasped between his fingerless gloved hands.

'You witnessed the assault?'

'Not exactly. But I saw what happened previous to the coloureds getting done over.'

Mellor frowned. 'How do you mean? There was more?'

'Yeah. I saw the gang arrive and how they were all boozed up an' looking for trouble, so I told the Gent to look sharp and get out of their way.'

'And did he?'

'He was walking off that way…' Best pointed. 'The Teds took it on to give chase. Before I knew it, they'd caught him and threw him to the ground, chucked his suitcase away and gave him a kicking.'

'This man was not black?' Mellor was confused. He'd heard nothing about this.

'Nah! White as the driven snow! With glasses and a hat and a suitcase. A normal sort of cove.'

'They attacked this white man - and then what?'

'They saw the two darkies and I s'pose wanted to do them more hurt than this feller. They left him and gave chase and I never saw what happened as they were out of view. I saw the bloke pick himself up. He seemed right enough…'

'What did you do?'

'I could hear shouting and it didn't sound too clever, so I telephoned to raise the alarm.'

'Where'd he go to? The white man you spoke with'?'

'I didn't see as I was in my hut and by the time I'd finished, he'd cleared off.'

Mellor nodded. Just a typical drunken night in the city, virus or no virus? He stood and looked around at the shadowy vaulted station roof and the lines of empty stock, at the bright yellow carriage lights of an approaching train threading its way in and at the locked doors and closed newspaper kiosks and wondered. Was he wasting his time here? He hefted the shoulder bag containing the pistol, so it hung more comfortably. 'Can you give me a description of the man you spoke with?'

'Nothing special to look at. NHS glasses and a black hat and coat.'

Mellor made a disappointed face. He decided to try another approach, and whilst still wearing his leather gloves fumbled clumsily inside a pocket to extract the photographs of Winter and Clawson. 'Was he either of these?'

Best, to his credit gave the photographs a close inspection. 'Yeah, I reckon that's 'im, but with glasses.' He pointed a nicotine-stained finger at the image of Clawson. 'Put glasses on his nose and he's a dead ringer.'

'Did he say where was he going?'

'Now that's the funny thing. He was a bit strange on that point. Wanted a boat train, or leastways, a train to the coast and seemed a bit surprised when I said there was no ferries sailing.'

Mellor was making notes. 'What else?'

'He seemed confused, didn't realise the services are shot to pieces and there's little running. I mentioned a train to Guildford that was due out, just in passing, kind of making conversation…'

'I don't have much time. This is important!' Mellor wanted to hurry Best along. Clawson was close and mustn't let the trail go cold.

'He wasn't interested in Guildford. Don't blame 'im! Then 'e just walked off. Soon as the Teds arrived, he scarpered. An odd one. I mean if you want to go to the coast and across to

France then you stick wiv yer plan and find a way, not just wander off all nonchalant like…'

'Nothing else? No clue where he was going or had come from?'

'Nope. He gave me a fag. A decent one.' Best grimaced. 'When he lit it for me, I think we bumped hands what with the wind blowing the flame.'

Mellor made no response. What could he say? If Clawson was as virulently infectious as they'd been told, then the ticket inspector was in trouble. He was glad he'd not offered Best one of his cigarettes. Mellor looked around and tried to think where Clawson might have gone once he'd survived the attack by the gang. He formed a sardonic smile. The gang of Teddy Boys were going to get a punishment far more severe than anything a Magistrate's Court could hand out. 'I need a telephone. With an outside line.'

'Mine 'ere is internal only. The head porter is still at work. Over that way…'

'Thanks.' Mellor hurried away in the direction indicated. He needed Benson and as many men as he could summon on full alert. Clawson was no more than an hour away, maybe less. The pistol bounced heavily against his side as he strode purposefully away. Before the night was out, he might have to use it.

Chapter Twenty-seven
Manchester London Road

DCI Minshul and DS Ashbury impatiently waited for their train to roll into Manchester London Road. Their driver was offering a textbook example of the gentle application of the vacuum brakes, easing the train into the station at a little more than snail's pace. Despite the rain slapping on his face, Minshul had lowered the droplight and stood, head and shoulder proud of the closed door, gloved hand on the handle ready to spring out.

'Just put the bloody brakes on!'

Ashbury thought his guvnor was not setting the best example for fellow passengers, but it was wiser to keep quiet. Minshul was already walking briskly towards the station building with Ashbury following as the last squeal of the brakes sounded.

'Have you clapped eyes on these men? Two passengers across from Sheffield.' A flash of his warrant card and Minshul launched straight into an interrogation of the startled ticket inspector. 'And don't tell me you weren't warned we'd be askin'!'

'Which two gentlemen would that be, pal?'

'Christ Almighty! We called through before we set off so you'd have plenty of time to get your brain workin'!'

Ashbury took a conciliatory approach. Minshul losing his temper was only going to hinder the process. After carefully explaining the date and time of arrival of the train in question, he did he his best to offer a description. 'Two men, average height, slim build but probably able to handle themselves. Smartly dressed in dark suits and hats. Look and act like businessmen. A pale blue shirt on one. An emerald green silk tie on the other. Blue shirt also had memorable blue eyes that stare at you like Sinatra in a bad mood. One of them might be annoyed because he's lost his favourite cigarette lighter along the way. One of the train crew tried to run after them with it but was too late. Maybe you remember him searching for it?'

The ticket inspector chewed the inside of his cheek for a moment. 'We get a lot of business types through here from Sheffield, Leeds, Hull. They're two-a-penny...'

'Think harder!' Minshul growled.

'But one looks just like another...'

'One might have been whistling 'Red River Valley' softly and all the time?'

'I don't think I was on duty that evening...'

Minshul was already stomping across to the ticket counter and engaging with the clerk behind the glass window. Ashbury was left to mollify the ticket inspector and think of a practical solution to the impasse they found themselves in. On the trail of two unremarkable men, long since moved on. Men who presumably knew how to evade detection...

'Guv, we're wasting our time. We know they lost no time showing their tickets because of what Mr Johnson told us. They're hardly likely to stick in anyone's mind.'

Minshul glared at Ashbury. 'And the flu thing has practically cleared the trains of passengers. There are so few faces *to* remember.'

'Alright. So, what would these men most likely do when they get here?'

'One is from Wales. He might be living elsewhere, of course. And the other from around these parts. My guess is they needed not only to change trains but change stations.'

'To help throw the like of us off the trail.'

'I reckon.' Rain splattered their shoulders as Minshul was speaking. 'What was the weather like?'

Ashbury enquired of the booking clerk. 'Typical Manchester. Like now, only worse.'

'We've heard nothing about umbrellas. So, they hailed a

cab to where? Exchange, Victoria or Central?'

'Or maybe just home in the suburbs...'

They exited the station to a road where a line of black cabs ticked over and filled the wintry air with exhaust fumes.

'Cabbies talk to everyone,' Ashbury strode confidently towards the nearest. 'And have a knack of remembering fares.'

Twenty minutes later and after a lot of talking, sharing of cigarettes that left both detectives out of smokes and listening to endless moans and groans, opinions and pronouncements about the pandemic and the fortunes of the local football clubs, they struck gold.

'I remember them. Wanted Exchange. A short run, but better than a poke in the eye with a stick!' The cabbie laughed and lit his free cigarette. He leaned on the outside of his vehicle which shuddered gently as the engine ticked over. 'The one man had unnerving eyes. He stared at me the whole time in the mirror. Ugh...it got right under my skin. Started to wind me up, with him staring and never blinking.'

'What colour were they?'

'Ice blue.'

'Why do you think he was holding you with that look?'

'No idea, pal, but he didn't seem too friendly, so I didn't say nothing.'

'What about the other man?'

'Tie. White shirt, black hat. All looked new and expensive. Smart fellow. Did you say an emerald green tie? Well, his was bright green so, yeah, could be?'

'What did they talk about?'

'Not a lot. I tried the usual on weather and this pan-bloody-demic. Tie man whistled a tune non-stop like he was nervy. The same over and over. He did stop once and asked staring eyes about the times of trains to Chester.'

'You think that is where they were headed?'

'Exchange would see 'em right if that were the case...'

'What was the tune?' Ashbury asked.

'The one The Andrews Sisters do. 'Red River Valley.' The bloody tune gets stuck in your head. I couldn't shake it off all night.'

'Anything else?' Minshul probed.

'Blue eyes were patting his pockets and getting worked up, still staring at me of course. I think he'd lost something. He even said they should turn back, but green tie advised against it. Green tie lit blue eye's cigarette with a match.'

'He'd lost a lighter?'

'Could be. Not best pleased, whatever it was.'

'Accents?'

'Green tie was Welsh. The other was probably a Woollyback.

'A what-a-back?' Ashbury queried.

'A Wool. From between Manchester and Liverpool. Neither one nor other.' The cabby laughed. 'Worst of both worlds. Everyone looks down on Woolies!' He laughed as if this was indeed the funniest of things.

'What places might fit?'

'Plenty to choose from, St Helen's, Warrington, Runcorn or down as far as Chester. You've got a big area to cover.'

Ashbury felt his spirits drop. 'That doesn't help.'

'But Chester is possible?' Minshul asked.

'Could be - at a stretch.'

'You seen either man, since?'

'No.'

'Aside from staring eyes and the whistling anything else makes them stick in your mind?'

'The tip was generous.'

'Right, you best get us to Exchange.' Minshul barked and the detectives climbed into his cab. 'Remember 'owt else on the way and you might get a generous tip.'

Chapter Twenty-eight
King's Cross

Sergeant Winter leaned against a pillar just inside the entrance to King's Cross station and lit a cigarette. There were too many police on duty for his liking. There were Transport Police and some grim, ugly types from what he thought could be the Met. At least one had a pistol in a leather holster and was patrolling outside amongst the ugly hotchpotch of cheap single-storey shops that blighted the frontage of what once must have been a fine building.

Worse still, he could see a smattering of Army boys with rifles slung over their shoulders. He didn't like the look of that. Why were they armed and on the streets of London? Were they waiting for him or Clawson to show themselves and take a pot shot? Surely not?

Winter smoked and chewed this over. Perhaps it was not so far-fetched. The two of them had visited nearly every terminus in the city and boarded a significant number of trains travelling out of this central ring of stations. They'd agreed to concentrate at first on over-loaded commuter trains where contamination would be most devastating in its effect, each packed carriage reaching deep into the densely populated south-eastern sector of the country or the dull suburbs to the north.

They knew the virus struck rapidly and felled people almost where they stood, and in just two days their efforts were having a startling effect. The city had lurched to something like a halt. Offices and shops had closed overnight, train services were suspended and taxi drivers starting to become reluctant to pick up fares whilst frightened shop girls and office workers stood uneasily some distance apart from each other at bus stops only to be forced together in contagious misery within the over-heated interior where breath and condensation fogged the windows. It would not be long before most of the new bright red Routemaster buses would remain inside their depots.

The city was already noticeably different, with just a fraction of the usual number walking the streets. Even the prostitutes, pimps and drug dealers that made King's Cross such an unsavoury area to linger in, were absent. This all made it harder for Winter to move around undetected. He'd hoped his civilian clothing might help him blend into the crowd, it looked as though he'd left it a day or so too late to travel north towards York as he'd hoped, and worried that Clawson, who'd agreed to try the West Coast Mainline out of Euston, would be meeting the same problem. It was frustrating to see each route of escape from the city being closed off.

Roadblocks were being erected on all the major arterial roads, especially those pointing north where the pandemic was still having minimal impact. The road closures were creating vast traffic jams of over-loaded vehicles filled with frightened citizens and their hastily packed possessions, all trying to escape the tightening grip of the virus. Petrol stations were either wrung dry and closed or clogged by anxious and angry horn-tooting drivers, each dreading the storage tanks emptying before their turn.

The sound of clanging bells filled the air as ambulances and police cars tried to find a way through the gridlock and avoid the frantic drivers impotently pacing around their stationary vehicles. Others vented their feelings by sounding their horns in a hideous wail across the night sky that stirred memories of the sirens during the blitz. Winter had never envisaged using roads as a means of transport, but there could be no possibility of escaping London by that means now.

The railway was his only option, but all the stations seemed to be guarded and with methodical checks on all tickets. Worse still, from his observations, many people were being turned away amidst much argument, shouting or even tears.

From what he'd gathered from a copy of the London

Evening Standard, as from tomorrow every traveller would need to have a travel warrant listing their destination address and a compelling reason for travel outside Greater London or beyond any of the key stations that now formed a loose ring around the edge of the Midlands and the border with Wales. A cordon had now been thrown across a large part of England with severely restricted travel. If he was going to get out of London on a train, then it was now or never.

Winter twisted his shoe to extinguish his cigarette and observed a family being refused access to the trains. The policeman and a uniformed railway worker were trying to be understanding, whilst presenting an immovable force that was not going to relent. Their faces were covered by cloth masks, making their actions appear sinister. The sobs of the frantic mother were pitiful as she reluctantly ushered her two children away, faces blank with incomprehension, the father's red and flushed with frustration and rage.

Winter was never going to get past these men by a direct approach. His picture must have circulated the police forces by now and it would not be long before mugshots appeared on the front pages of newspapers. With this level of scrutiny, the game would be up before he even got close to a platform.

He pretended to look at the list of cancelled football fixtures on the back of his paper whilst observing the careful loading of a long train bound for Newcastle and another in an adjacent platform destined for Edinburgh. Both would have been ideal.

A streamlined A4 class pacific huffed gently into view bringing in a train from York. Winter wondered if the mix of arriving passengers and the crowds attempting to gain access, might offer an opportunity to bunk his way beyond the barriers, but the rapid deployment of more masked officials and two armed soldiers, Scotched that idea. With one last glance at the elegant streamlined curves and gleaming paintwork of *Mallard*, he turned and walked away.

He knew a fair bit about trains and their operation and decided he would start his escape from London under the cover of darkness using either a newspaper train or one of the many night freights. Perhaps a milk train. He could use his military training to incapacitate or kill a goods train guard and then ride in relative comfort in a brake van until he'd passed through the cordon the government had thrown across the country.

Winter had a reasonable idea about the lay of the land and started walking around to the side of the passenger station and into the murky, sooty and unwelcoming streets that lay on the eastern flank of King's Cross, the air stinking of town gas, urine and rotting refuse. These ugly streets were even emptier than usual and thankfully free of the dangerous lowlife that usually inhabited the shabby dwellings. He could at least be reasonably sure of making progress unchallenged.

Chapter Twenty-nine
Leicester Central

Vignoles stood looking out of the window of his office, smoking a pipe.

Two maintenance chaps had rigged up a curtain rail and found two fusty blackout curtains dating from the war in a storeroom, and these now hung on either side of the window, offering a funereal quality to the room. A Z-bed was taking up much of the office on the far side of his desk and a suitcase of spare clothes sat on one of the chairs. As a makeshift hotel room, it lacked finesse, but it was at least warm and familiar and whilst the Detective Department washroom might lack a bath, British Railways could be relied upon to supply an unlimited stream of scalding water and a whole cupboard of those tiny and curiously pungent bars of soap the railway favoured, but nobody liked. But at least he had soap. This was one of the many everyday commodities now running short across the country. Similarly, the stock cupboard had recently been refilled with toilet paper. This had better remain locked for now if the rumours were true that toilet paper was exchanging hands on the black market. Thankfully the station buffet was still functioning, albeit not open to the public. It fulfilled an important role serving station workers and train crews both day and night now Leicester had become one of the 'border stations' in the battle against *covid57-N4*.

As the virus spread, completely overwhelming the south-west, south-east and especially London then started to take footholds in the northern ports, increasingly draconian measures were being imposed in an attempt to corral the pandemic. The Government wanted to try and prevent its spread across the whole nation and was treating this task in the same way it might with an invading army. Roadblocks were erected in a ragged line running from Bristol via Oxford to Bedford and Cambridge and thence to the coast. Travel by car was restricted to local journeys across the whole nation and airports closed except for freight, whilst severe restrictions were imposed on sea traffic in the docks in the southern half of the UK.

The railways were the preferred mode of transport under these stringent operating conditions, with coaching stock disinfected and fumigated after each trip and long-distance services no longer running into London. A shifting series of border stations had been introduced where such trains must terminate. Special services into London still ran but under controlled conditions. Temperature checks by a team of masked nurses were mandatory as was a stamped and validated temporary pass for all train travel in and out of the 'infection zone'. Any passengers passing these checks could expect a solitary and inhospitable experience, and as they passed through the cordon of masked medics and railway staff, many would critically examine each traveller, some with pity in their eyes. You needed a good reason to subject yourself to what lay ahead. It was especially bad in London and other larger southern towns and cities where countless hundreds of thousands were desperate to leave, but only a handful were permitted to escape.

The two big stations at Leicester had just become the new border, with the actual infection zone located some distance south of the city margins. Rugby had been the border point until only the day before, but a sudden outbreak and spike of deaths had seen it hastily abandoned. The unfortunate citizens of Rugby left to cower inside their homes and hope. The huge railway works at Rugby was almost completely closed, having been identified as the probable source of the infection. Any urgent repairs would have to carried out by other railway works further north, or if that was not possible, then engines and the stock would have to be laid up and left cold until better times. The buildings stood silent as the special trains now sped through either of the two stations in Rugby without pause, the buildings pad-locked and the lights turned out.

That Leicester was the new front line was not so much a source of pride as responsibility, with the Transport Police based there manning the frontline. They were tasked with ensuring that all new controls and security measures were implemented, and that law and order was maintained across the railway at a time when tensions were running high and something close to martial law imposed at the border crossings. Leicester Central was relatively easy to control at least, with its massive low-level entrance gates manned day and night by constables and the elevated mainline lofted high on bridges, viaducts and embankments for much of its way across the city, making it a hard to gain access.

Vignoles watched as a short line of passengers assembled on the platform, each standing six feet apart in a line as they waited to have their temperatures checked, papers inspected then stamped by nurses in face masks and rubber gloves before being allowed to leave the station. A soldier stood nearby, cigarette in hand, gun slung over his shoulder. They had just allowed in a 'light special' from Marylebone and those on board a collection of MPs, Government officials, a doctor and three businessmen. They were an orderly group, and nobody expected trouble. The engine steamed gently as two masked men walked the length of the train to check it was empty, in preparation for it to be hauled away for thorough disinfection.

Vignoles blew a smoke ring and thought about the telephone call he'd just answered. It had been from Miss Smolej. He was still getting used to her accent and mannerisms but had immediately noticed a change in her voice and instead of being advised to hold the line whilst she put him through to Badger, she hesitated, as if unsure how to proceed.

'Is everything alright?'

'It's the Chief, sir.' She stopped and cleared her throat,

voice wavering. 'His wife has just informed they have taken him to hospital. It was an emergency.'

Vignoles remembered Badger's cough and shortness of breath and already suspected the answer to his question. 'What was the reason?'

'The virus. Mrs Badger sounded very worried.'

'I see.' He did. He'd met Mrs Badger perhaps twice, but from memory, she was a sensible woman and her tragic understatement of being 'worried' carried more import than it might from some. She had grounds to be worried and there was nothing to be gained by offering meaningless platitudes of hope for better news. Practical matters would be the best temporary medicine for the young secretary. 'I understand. I shall leave it a day, then call Mrs Badger myself to see how the chief is doing. For now, who is stepping into the Chief Superintendent's role for the duration of his absence?'

'The ACC will take responsibility and he asked you to report directly to him. You should be ready to accept a call within the hour.'

'I shall not leave my office. I am based here day and night.'

'I shall advise him of the situation. Thank you…'

'I trust you are in good health?'

'I feel perfectly well, sir. Thank you.'

'Then take care.'

Working in the adjoining office to Badger, this was possibly a warning too late. With a heavy heart, Vignoles replaced the handset.

He turned his attention back to the map on the wall, now deeply forested with red and black dots. The concentrations were still around London, the South West, all channel ports and most tellingly, in Hampshire in a strong grouping around Longmoor. There were new outbreaks elsewhere, even as far north as Glasgow, but the trend was clear. Even this crude attempt at mapping the spread gave a strong indication of the significant trunk rail lines the fugitives had travelled thus far.

It had been agreed Winter and Clawson were choosing to travel by rail and they appeared to be taking a commendably systematic approach. It was grim viewing and the daily count of new infections hard to fathom, but if there was any glimmer of good news in their sick plan, it was their methodical approach. To date, neither man appeared to have stuck out into the North West or North East from London, although Birmingham had reported significant problems almost from the start. Vignoles was sure one or both had made the second city one of their stops, perhaps on the way to or from the west country.

It made sense the men would concentrate their efforts in the capital around the many termini, as they could expect to cause considerable harm whilst covering a small concentrated area. Every man and woman the Transport Police could call upon were deployed on the major stations in London and the Metropolitan and City police patrolled continuously, so it must only be a matter of time before they were caught. The streets of London were falling quiet as shops, offices and factories closed and the stations were seeing but a fraction of normal traffic. A quiet street or platform was that bit harder to navigate unseen.

Vignoles picked up the latest sheaf of notes intending to plot these on the map. The NHS was collating ever more accurate statistics on infection rates and deaths and in concert with the Home Office, this data was starting to feed through to their temporary telephone office set up in the now virtually redundant booking office. Extra clerks had been drafted in and the Signal & Telegraph Department had hastily rigged additional phone lines and run cables into Vignoles' office. Whilst useful for keeping the map updated, their real purpose was to maintain constant contact with the major stations across the network, all of which were on high alert.

The options for Winter and Clawson were closing down and Vignoles was sure that one of the many ringing phones was going to bring news of a sighting...

Chapter Thirty
Derby Midland

PC Blencowe was at Derby Midland, another vital hub in the national network and identified as one of the key locations most likely to see either of the fugitives as a potential location to visit.

The strategic thinking was to identify the most probable places two men intent on causing the widest spread of infection would choose to stop and change trains. His maps had given them a clue to the movements and intentions of Winter and Clawson. As the Detective Department had gathered around these, urgently digesting and interpreting every scrap of evidence, they'd tried to imagine the thinking of Winter and Clawson and second guess their next moves. All logic pointed north. The East Coast, West Coast or Midland routes were surely next.

With roadblocks and severe restrictions on all movement inside the cordon, the two men would find it hard to operate there. They would want to escape the net and spread their evil northwards before the inevitable. Winter and Clawson would either be run to ground in London or like game beaten from bushes, would spring out and make a dash north.

The problem for Blencowe and the four other constables on duty was that Derby Midland was a very big station that still saw an immense volume of traffic. It required constant patrolling up and down the lengthy platforms and frequent consultation of the working timetable with a complex emergency addendum to anticipate arrivals. None of which was made pleasanter by the vicious east wind that riffled the thin pages and demanded that Blencowe remove his gloves and froze his fingers each time he needed to make a consultation. He was known for his dependable and unflustered approach to any job and yet even he was finding his patience being tested.

The ceaseless procession of locomotives of classes less familiar to Blencowe (some almost alien in shape and design) offered some light relief at least and in the periods between trying to identify faces concealed by scarves and medical masks, he had taken to making a note of what part of the Empire was recognised on a brass plate borne on the side of an engine, or what Regiment had been similarly commemorated. Many more hours at Derby and he felt sure it might not be long before he had the pink parts of the World map ticked off. As it was, *Alberta* gurgled close by and he turned his back to the boiler to catch some radiated warmth.

Two trainspotters in school blazers and shorts with legs the colour of corned beef took down the name and number. All schoolboys below a certain age were forced to endure shorts, whatever the weather, but Blencowe wondered if this should not be considered a crime in this wind?

* * * *

PC Simon Howerth had been given Crewe as his posting. Another multi-platformed junction that funnelled the majority of traffic running down from London and much of the South-West to the North-West of England and onwards to Scotland.

The drastic curtailment of trains into London and the southern and westerly areas of the country had not yet decreased the traffic through Crewe. If anything, it was heavier than usual, certainly in the form of goods traffic which rumbled through in an almost endless procession, as the ports of Liverpool, Manchester and Glasgow accepted ships that normally would have docked in southern-lying ports. He might be a long way from the infection zone hot spots, but his task was no less onerous. It was desperately hard to observe even a fraction of the passenger traffic calling at Crewe and he spent the days restless and tired, continually pacing the platforms and fear of failing in his important task.

Howerth now ran his fingers over the strong webbing of the shoulder bag containing his weapon and spare rounds. The gun made his shoulder ache painfully. It was a nagging reminder of their deadly mission.

Could he *really* draw a loaded gun and point it at someone, let alone fire it? He understood his orders and knew he must obey, but what if he made a mistake over the identity? How could he be so sure, when adrenaline and fear were coursing through his veins? At least his role in this 'mission' kept him away from the infectious south. He was glad. He had so much to look forward to.

He was recently married and moved into one of the new houses under construction on an estate in Loughborough. Laura and he had hoped to live in Leicester, but Loughborough had proven more affordable and with shorter waiting lists. If this were not reason enough to avoid the killer infection, then the fact Laura was three months pregnant sealed the deal. Crewe was busy and so carried its risks, but he was still grateful to DS Mellor for placing him here. It was a posting that carried responsibility, as failure to stop either Winter or Clawson travelling through this gateway opened up the threat in places like Manchester, Liverpool and Glasgow. That he, PC Howerth might let either of this killer carries through unchecked and unseen was too awful to contemplate, but at least he stood a decent chance of evading the virus.

Howerth watched as another lengthy train of vans rumbled through, hauled by a black and muck coloured Stanier 8F freight engine. It was heading south. Going the wrong way. A short local stopper from Wrexham was gently steaming into a bay platform with a clutch of pre-war coaches. It was an unlikely train to bear either man so could leave it alone. He glanced at this watch and at his hefty working timetable book and studied the expected arrivals. It was so hard to keep on top of what was coming in from where, and on what platform.

Chapter Thirty

He ran his fingers through his hair and tried to summon up the energy to stay alert. He dragged his heavy feet up and over the footbridge for what must have been the hundredth time that day, ready to monitor the arrival of what once had been the Euston-Glasgow service, but which now started from Bletchley.

Chapter Thirty-one
Peterborough

Peterborough was one of several rail hubs considered vital to the supply of sufficient coal and perishable goods into London. If the curiously named New England engine shed at Peterborough succumbed to the virus and could not provide crew for the hundred or more steam locomotives needed each day, it was unlikely the voracious appetite of the many million home fires and hungry bellies could be met. Furthermore, as another busy junction, Vignoles thought Peterborough was a candidate for either Winter or Clawson to visit.

Posting WPC Lansdowne there ensured there was at least one person skilled in handling firearms on the station. However, gaining approval for her presence, especially in possession of a firearm, had tested Vignoles' nerves and patience. With Badger critical in hospital, Vignoles had found himself in conversation with the ACC on the matter.

As top brass went, Assistant Chief Constable Murray was the brightest and shiniest of the lot. A Scotsman, he was softly spoken but unmistakably not someone to cross. His air of quiet control exactly what was needed as tempers frayed. Murray had outlined the complex web of operational relationships hastily put in place by his counterparts within London following their orders from the Home Secretary. Coordinating a myriad of different police forces into something vaguely resembling a single entity with a shared goal was a bewilderingly complex and difficult task, with each force loyal to their territory and each unwilling to cross jealously guarded boundaries. ACC Murray had brought his parochial interests to bear and reinforced the presence of the Transport Police at all railway and ferry territories within the UK. Murray backed the decision to arm his men, arguing convincingly that they were as likely, if not more so than any to encounter the fugitives. Murray had taken persuading concerning the WPCs, but once Vignoles had won him over, he argued the case and an agreement was reached for WPC Lansdowne to be assigned to a sergeant based at Peterborough and to work alongside five male constables, two of whom would also be armed. After learning about Lansdowne's prowess on the firing range, Murray conceded she should be 'marksman of choice' if it came to a stand-off with either fugitive. A surprising decision perhaps, but Murray admitted to not being convinced the Peterborough men demonstrated any ability with firearms and perhaps posed more a liability, than help.

Lansdowne found the reality even less satisfactory than the ACC's cynical prognosis. The local men were openly sceptical about her abilities as a policewoman, let alone expert shot, and for her part, she found the casual manner with which the constables 'played' with the pistols to be downright alarming. It was as if they were regressing to childhood and excitedly recreating games of cowboys and Indians with cap guns, pointing their weapons and making occasional gunshot noises like children. Her sergeant was a stern man who didn't take kindly to criticism of his men, no matter how carefully worded. He liked even less having a woman on the team with a 'hotline' to DCI Vignoles and potentially the ACC. That she came with a heavily advertised ability to outshoot any man on the force won her no favours in his eyes.

The especially dreary weather in this bleak outpost on the Eastern fringes of the Midlands did nothing to make Lansdowne feel any better, her mood further depressed with the grim reality of the mission combined with the dispiriting news that constantly emanated from the radio in their mess room.

Lansdowne was feeling lonely and isolated, despite the constant bustle of railway traffic, the relentless shunting and thumping of wagons in the vast marshalling yards and the surprising number of passengers that still milled about the platforms.

She was seated beneath what was proving an inadequate platform awning whilst the wind blew the rain straight underneath and on to her legs. She watched blankly as an empty coal train chuffed through the station with a new-looking Standard 4 locomotive at the front. She could see in the far distance a fully-laden coal train held at a signal waiting its turn. The sheer volume of goods traffic going in and out of the capital was bewildering. The signalmen were forced to work trains at an intensity not seen since the build-up to D-Day. Each siding or goods loop looked to be occupied by goods trains of some description, all waiting their turn. The fish and the milk deliveries were usually given clear runs and hurtled through like expresses, but there were times when even these special loads that would be spoilt by any delay, found themselves waylaid, their engines blowing impatient fountains of steam from their safety valves.

Many of the trains would travel under the twin cover of darkness and the curfews imposed after nightfall, returning empty in daylight. However, despite the Army patrolling and the Transport Police standing guard over these marshalling yards, the level of violence along the railway once inside the infection zone was increasing. It was common for gangs to descend on stationary trains held at signals or pulled over into holding loops and break open wagons and make away with goods that would fetch a spectacular profit on the black market. Gunshots had been reported in violent exchanges, with at least three deaths in the last two evenings and many more hurt in these skirmishes with the law. Lansdowne felt like she was sitting on a bleak, windswept edge of a lawless wilderness, not on the platform of a cathedral town in England.

She pulled her coat tighter as the rain turned to sleet. Oh great! Just what she needed. She doubted her cold fingers would move freely enough to use the pistol if needed. To fail at her task would be unbearable in front of those unsympathetic colleagues. The icy splashes on her face felt like tears.

Lansdowne had not cried yet. There was time enough for that later. She just could not allow personal emotions to take hold, for fear they might impede her important task. For now, the sleet could do the job. Inside her uniform jacket pocket lay the fateful telegram. Terse and unemotional, it told in a few teletyped words how the man who'd once been her fiancé, was seriously ill in a Dusseldorf hospital. Dying alone in a far-away ward.

It was the virus, and of course, he might pull through… Some people did. He was young and relatively healthy and didn't smoke quite as many cigarettes as some… But most of the dead soldiers in Longmoor probably fitted the same description.

There was so much sorrow all around these days that Lansdowne was unable to summon up anything more than a numbing sense of emptiness. He was just another number; a statistic, just as CS Badger was now a number, one more added to a list of those critically ill in hospital. Just cold statistics and numbers. There wasn't time and space to allow each to retain an identity. So many infected, so many critical, so many dead…

It was last year they'd agreed, regretfully, slightly tearfully, to admit their differences and the impediment of the long distance between them and break their long-term engagement. Richard had wanted her to join him in Dusseldorf, or was it Dortmund? Somewhere dull with a dreary name in the Rhineland that had been comprehensively demolished by the British bombers and being rebuilt in bland concrete, steel and glass. From the photographs he'd sent, it looked unappealing. Her little rented room was no great shakes, but the lanes of Leicester and its lovely cathedral and the New Walk through the changing seasons seemed so much nicer. A place to call home. More than that, she didn't want to give up her career to become a young mother learning German whilst taking their child to a Kindergarten. She didn't doubt the locals would be as welcoming as Richard claimed. Lansdowne even wondered if his enthusiasm for young German women was based on experience, but either way, this was not the life for her.

A smart uniform with a badge of rank and the chance to do meaningful work meant everything. The pistol hard against her hip was proof enough. Hers was a grim task that carried a dreadful responsibility, but it had been placed on her slim shoulders and endorsed by the ACC himself and she was going to do it.

She narrowed her eyes against the cold and watched as a B1 engine approached with one of the few passenger trains allowed out of London. This was 'Emergency Service 5', a limited stopping passenger train to York. They'd change the engine here, and by turning about, Lansdowne could see a pleasingly clean and polished green V2 engine waiting to back down and take over. The coaching stock would soon disgorge its masked and otherwise protected passengers onto the platform, all looking faintly bewildered as though they'd been incarcerated somewhere dark and now suddenly exposed to bright sunlight. All would be thirsty and hungry after the interminable process of passing the boarding controls and then the emergency cordon along the way, which acted as a temporary border crossing on a train without food or drink.

Winter or Clawson only needed a mask, some different styled glasses and a change of clothes and it was going to be desperately hard to identify them...

Lansdowne concentrated her mind on the hissing locomotive easing smoothly into the platform beside her, the crew giving her a cheeky wave as they cruised past. They seemed happy enough in their snug cab with great cotton wool drifts of steam rising around them. They'd clocked up another run into the epicentre of the pandemic and believed they'd survived to tell the tale.

Only time would tell...

Chapter Thirty-two
King's Cross

WPC Benson had been given the task of patrolling St Pancras and King's Cross stations and the complex of railway land behind. As part of a team of twenty commanded by a grouchy Londoner by the name of DS Fox, they were spread thinly and expected to work long hours in the somewhat optimistic hope of striking lucky.

These two vital transport hubs on the British Railways network, whilst adjacent, also covered an enormous acreage of land with multiple platforms, parcel bays and unloading docks as well as complex subways leading to the underground station below. Under normal circumstances, the sheer volume of people passing through these stations would make it futile to attempt to find two individuals amongst the thronging crowds, especially when they were now expected to have altered their appearance. However, the draconian travel restrictions were starting to have an effect and numbers had dropped to less than a quarter the number usually witnessed.

DS Mellor, having left Benson to work under the temporary control of Fox, was south of the river on the tail of a 'hot tip'. Benson had not heard more since Mellor made it known he was following a promising lead. However, there was still a palpable sense that *something* was happening amongst her new colleagues. Perhaps Mellor had found one of the men? Perhaps he had already shot someone dead? Nobody knew anything, but the rumour mill was working hard, and it was making everyone jittery.

DS Fox made it clear that until told otherwise, they were on patrol and looking for the two men. 'Stay focused and stay alert. Don't take notice of idle talk and keep yer eyes peeled! Now get on with it...'

They were all wearing leather gloves, as much against the biting cold as for protection from infection, with scarves or bandanas tied across their lower faces. The smog and the cold made these welcome additions to their standard uniform. A small number had managed to source surgical masks, as indeed had some members of the travelling public, and Benson was struck by the surreal oddity of an echoing station concourse populated by what looked like surgeons and attendant nurses about to enter theatre.

With the Army posting sentries and every policeman now out on the streets of London, it was perhaps appropriate that the locomotive that just rolled to a stop under the cavernous roof of St Pancras was named *Home Guard*. Whilst referring to the voluntary defence force from the war, it seemed a suitable description for the men and women walking the platforms and subways and patrolling the streets of the city in the hope of preventing further infection in their home city. The trouble was of course, with faces covered and everyone dressed in a universal uniform of drab winter coats, Benson was appreciating just how impossible was their task. At least the Home Guard, under-resourced and elderly though they may have been, would have had a clear and unambiguous image of the enemy back then; distinctive uniforms, insignia, equipment and language would have made the enemy unmistakable. An invisible virus carried by two masked men wearing clothing probably matching everyone else's made them the equivalent of HG Well's Invisible Man.

She sighed in resignation and resumed inspecting the eyes and noses of those disembarking from the train. It had been allowed down from Derby with few stops between. She trusted PC Blencowe had thoroughly vetted those embarking in Derby. It was also highly unlikely Winter or Clawson were heading into London, but she'd better do her duty.

* * * *

Mellor hurried out of Waterloo and was immediately stopped by a constable who wanted to know where he was going. He showed his warrant card then asked the young PC if he'd seen a man leaving the station who looked like either of those in the two photographs he held up.

'Not seen anyone. I'd have stopped and questioned them. We've been told to challenge everyone.'

'Damn!' Mellor looked around impatiently, taking in the dark shapes of towering buildings and the curls of smog and freezing fog licking around the dark doorways and narrow alleyways and blurring the edges of everything. 'Too many ways to get out of here…'

'It's hard to watch over it all, sir. Like trying to stop water leaking from a sieve.'

Mellor felt a surge of frustration. So close, but in these dark foggy streets, a solitary figure could easily evade notice, even with so few people around. The constable only had to look the other way, and someone might be able to slink off in the opposite direction.

Mellor wanted to keep moving, run down one of the streets in the vain hope of catching his man - but which one? Each was as likely as another. He had to remain calm - and think. Now was the time for logic and strategy. This part of south London held a myriad of streets and a great number of railway stations, including a number on the underground. His man could be on the way to almost anywhere using the giant spider's web of railway lines available to him in this district.

He put away the photographs and fished out his cigarettes. He needed to consider his next move. 'Smoke?'

The offer was gladly accepted. They shivered and stood in companionable silence, watching the headlamps of buses scythe through the thickening atmosphere and beetling black cabs ferrying masked people to the warmth and safety of their firesides. A short convoy of three lorries with tarpaulin loads at the back growled along the road, kicking out pungent exhaust fumes as the sound of their hard-working diesel engines echoed from the buildings.

'That's lime. Been at for hours.'

'Lime?' Mellor queried.

'For the pits. They've got diggers making open grave pits for mass burials.'

'Bloody hell…'

'They still use coffins, but chuck lime down to keep the smell at bay whilst they fill up the hole…'

'Right.' Mellor watched the last of the lorries melt into the dark. Eyes narrowed in concentration. If he needed reminding why he was carrying a pistol loaded with live rounds, he just needed to think about these lorry loads of lime.

An ambulance clanged past.

'Where's the nearest Police Box?'

'Just around the corner.'

Mellor had a flash of inspiration. 'I need the Sweeney…'

'The Flying Squad? They're already 'ere. They cruise by every twenty minutes. I 'eard they've got every car circling the major stations. One is due any minute…'

'Then flag 'em down! I need a fast car. If we're going to catch this man, we've got to get our skates on…'

Chapter Thirty-three
Chester General

DCI Minshul was telephoning from Chester General. For the first time, he was getting that tingling sensation that comes with picking up a lead in an investigation.

He was like a hound sniffing the scent of his quarry and eager to give chase. Impatiently drumming his fingers on the desk as he waited for DI John Trinder to come to the telephone. The Welsh desk sergeant who'd answered the call had his particular interpretation of the word 'urgent' and taken an age to even acknowledge he would look for the DI, and longer to place the handset on the desk and shuffle off somewhere. For fidgety Minshul the wait was unbearable as he paced in a narrow circle with the telephone cord stretched to its limit.

'DI Trinder here, how may I help?'

Minshul remembered the voice and introduced himself.

'I remember our time working together. It has been some years now.'

'Congratulations are in order on your promotion, Detective Inspector...' Minshul cut off Trinder's appreciative response. He was a man on a mission with little time for the niceties. 'I need your help, and with your permission, I want to hop over to your patch with my DS to nab two especially unpleasant characters.'

'Intriguing, but I might need more information.'

'I appreciate that. A pair of hitmen. Professionals. They know what they're about and working for powerful paymasters - but best we don't mention who might be paying their wages. Suffice to say, it goes against all I stand for. An innocent young woman was bumped off by a poisoned injection and left to drown face down in a stinking canal...'

'Nobody could condone such behaviour.'

'Your old gaffer and I are working on the case…'

'Is he now?' Trinder's voice lifted at the mention of DCI Vignoles. 'Then I shall render whatever assistance you require. Fire away!'

'I knew I could count on yer! Now, this is what we know and it's not a lot. Two coves, smartly suited, probably in black with hats to match. Look like businessmen. One wearing an emerald green tie…'

'That could be replaced…'

'I know, I know, but it's what' we've got, and beggars can't be choosers. We've discovered one of the men is from Conway. We know that because he dropped a lighter engraved with his regiment and service number. An ex-para. Served with the 1st Airborne at Arnhem. We traced him over your way. Claims to be a travelling salesman these days.'

'Hence the smart appearance and the perfect cover for travelling frequently?'

'It's not much to work with, but we reckon he's headed back to Conway, perhaps the other is with him. We think they travelled together as far as Chester, at least. We've picked up a possible sighting at Chester General, from where I'm calling. The other fella might 'ave paratroop background as well, but we know even less about him.'

'Ok…' Trinder felt his heart sink.

'One identifier is that he whistles the same tune over and over, nervous like. '*Red River Valley*,' d'you know it?'

'I've got a '78 of the Andrews Sisters singing it.'

'Right you are then. That were a big favourite of the SAS lads…'

'I didn't know that. Do you have names for these men?'

'Just for one, but I doubt its worth much as he'll use an alias. For what it's worth, he's David Evans.'

Trinder laughed. 'That's about half of Wales covered.'

'I warned you it was worthless. We reckon one or both travelled from Chester to Conway earlier today.'

'There's not a lot here to work with.' Trinder sounded disappointed. He wanted to help, but this was genuine needle in a haystack territory. 'I'll get over to Conway with my DS and start making enquiries. That's the best I can say.'

'We'll join you whenever the next train pulls in...'

'Do so. It sounds like we'll need all the help we can get. Conway is small, but a change of clothes and a curbing of the nervous whistling and these two will melt away and become near impossible to find.'

'Do your best, DI Trinder...'

DS Ashton had been listening in. 'Both men could be anywhere by now, boss. And who's to say Evans will even go home?'

'Positive thinking, Peter! We're not far behind, I know it. They *could* go anywhere, but they need somewhere to stay and keep their heads down and for a while. The longer the better. Renting a room in a hotel is not ideal now, what with everything shutting down and increased monitoring of everyone travelling and booking rooms and the like. It's tricky to travel and getting harder each day for them to move around unobserved. If nothing else, the virus is narrowing options and making life easier for us. If Evans has a place in Conway it makes sense if he stays there. Nobody will think anything of it. The other could just stay inside and remain unnoticed. They're telling everyone to stay indoors, so that's logical.' Ashton made facial expressions that suggested he could see the DCI's point, if still unconvinced. 'And chin up, Wales is free of the bloody virus at least...'

'I've never been...'

'Then you've not lived! Better mountains than we've got, though just as much rain, and great fish and chips. The tea's not a patch on a Yorkshire brew, but we'll just have to drink beer.' Minshul laughed. They were doing something, and it felt good. 'Right, when's our train?'

Chapter Thirty-four
Neasden Shed

Fireman Eddie Earnshaw was banking his fire ready for the night ahead. He was shovelling coal into each corner of the white-hot fire that illuminated his face and body. With slightly bent legs, he smoothly dug his shovel into the coal, turned, then flung the black gold into the gaping fire hole. His driver, Teddy Watkins, was studying the working instruction he'd been handed. Every run seemed to have all manner of alterations and restrictions imposed that had to be understood and memorized. They both looked like figures from a Joseph Wright of Derby painting from the early years of the Industrial Revolution; all glowing whites, yellows and oranges and harsh shadows.

Neasden engine shed was full of locomotives being similarly prepared for work. Rows of steaming, hissing, dripping, snorting engines of various shapes and sizes and all ages, from the new 'Standard' classes, down to Edwardian-era freight engines still faithfully slogging away despite their advancing years. The constant metallic scrape of shovels sliding under coal; the quiet whistling of men working their way around and under their engines armed with long spouted oil cans; the clatter and boom of coal tipping into tenders from the coaling stage; the rushing hiss of drain cocks opening and the almost luminescent cloak of steam swathing the front end of a locomotive about to move off. Then a shout, a call, a hoot on a whistle and the whoosh of steam as another iron horse stirred into motion. The shed master in his office; bare windows and a single bulb on a brown cord from the ceiling revealing him seated at his desk in a spartan office devoid of ornamentation save a formal side-view of a long-scrapped engine constructed in Gorton Works hung on the wall. Hard chairs and a desk with an Anglepoise lamp illuminating small mountains of paperwork, balding head shining in the lamplight as he made notes with a fountain pen. His deputy and foreman out in the shed or walking the stabling lines, exchanging words with the crews, ensuring each knew their route and tasks for the night ahead. The usual working timetable had long gone to pot and unfamiliar emergency workings hurriedly brought in. The intense goods workings in and out of the capital would see a succession of locomotives hauling long rakes of coal trucks, covered wagons, fuel tankers or parcel vans with valuable cargoes that were now a lifeline for desperate Londoners virtually imprisoned in their homes. There were also the newspaper trains bearing freshly printed papers filled with tales of doom and gloom to whisk northwards telling lurid tales of a society rapidly unravelling as hospitals filled to overflowing. Two locomotives had been delegated to haul secretive trains rumoured to be filled with armed troops being transported in to strengthen the barricades around the capital.

Eddie laid his shovel down, clanged the fire door closed, then checked the water levels and steam pressure. He wiped his forehead with his neckerchief. This would be worn across his mouth as they approached Marylebone in line with the latest orders, but for now, it could serve to wipe away perspiration despite the cold night gathering around them. 'Reckon it's true about the Army?' Howerth asked as his driver hauled himself into the cab.

'In what way?'

'They're sending them up to form a defensive line against people trying to flee.'

'I couldn't say…'

'I heard they've got guns and live ammo. I mean, would they really shoot civilians?'

'Best not to believe everything you hear, Ed.' Driver Watkins sat on his wooden seat and looked around the cab. 'I dunno what to think anymore. Some police are carrying guns. I know, 'cos I've seen 'em, so why not soldiers?'

'Yeah. My best mate, Si, he's with the Transport Police and just been issued with a revolver. Said they all had to take a course in shooting on a range. He didn't say why, but I got the feeling he was supposed to use it…'

'What? To kill someone. Never! It's got to be to help keep order…you know, just a threat.'

'I suppose…' Earnshaw frowned. 'That must be it. Just wave it around and make people think twice about looting and breaking through the barricades?'

'Same as we have two soldiers riding in the guard's van. Just to keep the peace…'

'They've never fired a shot, that's true.' Howerth was trying to reassure himself.

Eddie Earnshaw and Simon Howerth had been friends since they were small. Growing up together in the tight-knit community of Woodford Halse, sharing a love of trains and adventures, books and riding bikes, identifying birds and whistling at girls - and even the odd scrape with the law after sticking their curious noses into places perhaps they should not have. But through all of this, never once had Eddie believed Simon held any desire to shoot more than a wooden gun in youthful mock battles against invading Nazis conjured from their imaginations. Simon had, however, been uncharacteristically subdued when they'd last met in an almost empty city-centre pub in Leicester robbed of its usual hum of chatter as folk opted to stay home and stay safe.

Before the pandemic struck, Eddie's newly increased workload offering the chance to fire bigger engines on the fast night freights to London and back would have been a topic of extended discussion, fuelled by many pints and packets of crisps. Conversely, Simon's trip to the firing range would have been worthy of an evening of happy conversation, with his new posting to Crewe to watch out for two dangerous criminals the highlight of the evening. If he succeeded in his task it could lead to a commendation and perhaps even to promotion... However, his friend had appeared distracted and almost aloof. Taciturn and drinking faster than usual as if seeking the dulling effect of the beer rather than savouring the taste of their favoured 'Tiger.'

Earnshaw leaned out of the cab of their Standard Class 4 and watched as the shed foreman shouted last orders up to the driver of a massive Austerity ten-wheeled freight engine that was to lead off the short cavalcade. There was movement at last.

Three engines at a time would now roll off the shed and being coupled together, would move as one onto the mainline and drop back into Marylebone, where they would be uncoupled, and the lead engine move over to the turntable to be spun about. The other two, which had been hauled backwards to the throat of the array of goods lines at Marylebone, could then swiftly back onto their waiting trains. It was an unusual working but proving highly effective at getting three, sometimes more, trains out of Marylebone in quick succession.

Earnshaw knew theirs was a string of box vans they had to race down to Woodford New Yard. It was a return empty working and so held no interest to the gangs of railway looters rumoured to lie in wait to spring violent assaults upon trains held at signals. The flatlands to the east of England were infamous for their many crossing gates and the stories of trains being stopped due to vehicles blocking the line, then attacked by gangs of up to twenty men, were shocking. The former Great Central London Extension line they were about to traverse was remarkable in having just one such level crossing and this was now guarded by soldiers. The line had been laid out for fast, clear running away from road traffic and fortuitously held fewer locations where gangs could spring such a trap. The unsettling conversation around the foul engine crew 'bothy' (a place already so filthy, nobody gave heed to the virus), suggested the gangs might resort instead to a deliberate derailment. A train crash would split open loaded wagons and make looting faster. It was a terrifying image that did nothing for the nerves of the enginemen. The more senior drivers jumped angrily on anyone heard repeating this (as yet) unproven urban myth. Such tale-telling was bad for morale.

Earnshaw was one of those who found it hard to push the idea out of derailment out of his head. The empty working they'd been given was unlikely to attract unwanted attention, but there was much harder work ahead that night. Once in Woodford Halse they would drink sweetened tea and eat a sandwich, top up the water and coal in the bunker, turn the engine on the triangle of track in Woodford shed then collect a line of fully laden coal wagons. This working was known on their line as a 'windcutter.'

A train of valuable coal to be hauled faster than any similar workings anywhere in the land and unlikely to be held at signals along the way. Their powerful new locomotive was up to the job, and Driver Watkins was experienced on 'Windcutters' and would risk opening her up to set an alarming pace. The steel-bodied wagons thundering like gunfire behind as the chimney spat sparks whilst Eddie worked his aching shoulders and back ever harder to feed the hungry fire. A 'windcutter' was a stirring sight and its thunderous roar and churning engine gave ample warning of approach, and well it might, as once up to speed it was well-nigh impossible to stop. They expected a clear run and had been told to work the train to the limit. A couple of sleepers across the track could spell a spectacular and deadly smash...

The driver gave an answering toot to an enquiring one from the engine in front and with a wave to further indicate they were all set. The signal light glowed green as the Standard Class 4 started to roll back as their lead engine took their weight.

Chapter Thirty-five
King's Cross

Winter ducked into a pool of darkness behind a small ramshackle hut. There was a little light cast by towering yard lamps, but these were widely spaced and what light they threw was minimised by veils of smog and smoke collecting over the sprawling railway yards at Kings Cross. Their proximity to the Regent's Canal was indicated by a ribbon of pale vapour pooling above its filthy water. The air quality was not improved by the pungent smell and copious fumes issuing from the Imperial Gas Works.

He noticed there appeared to be a significant number of men working; Most were solitary shunters walking between the lines, working in unison with the crews on the stubby shunting engines that could be heard better than they could be seen as they puffed through the murk, adding more smoke and steam to the thickening atmosphere. These men hitched short rides on the footboards of guard's vans or clung dangerously (and surely against regulations) to the sides of the ubiquitous bauxite painted vans with a steel toe-capped boot perched on the brake rigging, but mostly they just tramped weary miles over compacted ash, grit, oil and mud underfoot. Carrying long poles with metal hooks at one end used to uncouple wagons, these tough and wiry men were used to working in conditions of poor visibility, where wagons were liable to move unexpectedly and with little warning, but even for these seasoned operators, this was a dangerous place.

Winter, however, was unpractised in navigating his way around the many trip hazards and between what he prayed were stationary wagons whilst remaining unobserved. The conditions blurred the edges and rendered anything over fifteen yards as little more than dark forms without detail.

It was like trying to find a way through an expressionistic charcoal drawing. The disadvantages were outweighed by the obvious benefit for Winter. This was an enormous site, the size of a large village, with the few open vistas effectively closed down by encroaching darkness and this aerial soup. Winter stood a decent chance of evading detection.

If he could alter his silhouette to better resemble a typical railway worker, his chances would further increase. Now he was away from the passenger side of the railway, his trilby hat and overcoat were those of someone from 'civvy street' and might catch the eye of one of the patrolling policemen or a suspicious railway worker.

The hut he was concealed behind was provided for the use of the shunters, but there was no light showing inside. He tried the door. It swung open on groaning hinges and scraped the floor. A tiny rectangle of pale lamplight from outside glowed through a filthy cobwebbed window. It was hard to discern much except the dim shapes of sacks and piles of boxes and a great lump of metal concealed by a tarpaulin, on which he painfully banged a shin bone. There was a strong smell of oil and hessian sacking.

Closer inspection revealed a pile of discarded work clothing. This was what he'd hoped for. Winter picked up a couple of stinking items that felt rigid with encrusted grime and shook them apart. Perfect. A noxious donkey jacket with a badly ripped sleeve and there, on a rusty nail beside the door, a grease top cap of classic British Railways design. It was too small, but Winter wedged it in place and shrugged on the jacket. He smelt atrocious. His dark trousers and shoes would not attract attention in the conditions. He found a short crowbar that might prove handy. He'd also seen a shunter's pole lying outside along the front of the hut and would carry this until out of the yard.

Abandoning his hat and suit jacket on the pile of clothes, he picked up his bag, which better suited the new look, and strode away confidently. *Act like you belong. Don't bend low so you look like someone trying not to be seen. Look confident...* Winter silently coached himself as he walked. There were shunters, foremen and engine crew as well as uniformed Transport Police out there and he needed to brazenly stride through the lot of them.

But where was he going? What was the plan now? He'd wanted to board a passenger train heading north and into territory as yet largely affected. Winter knew time was running out and he could not expect to see many more days of freedom. It was vital to do his deadly work where it would hurt the most and that was now north of Derby.

It was his all-consuming obsession to wreak havoc and misery on as many people as he could. He didn't care they were innocent or that they were unaware of the experiments from Porton Down or had never heard of this man-made virus. All he wanted to do was strike out and cause harm. If he felt any prick of remorse or doubt about what he was doing, it was not seeing the virus take effect. He'd touched surfaces, especially if smooth and frequently used; he'd tried to shake hands with as many people as he could or pat the shoulder of young trainspotters in a companionable manner. He'd handled cups and saucers, glasses, door handles and let his fingertips run across the gaudy covers of magazines in the bookstalls... but was any of this having an effect? The ambulance bells clanged incessantly, he'd seen the mounting death toll written on the front of the Evening Standard newspapers stands and walked past shuttered shops and schools and factories that were now silent.

All indicators that something was taking effect, but he'd not once witnessed his touch striking someone down. Nothing that came close to seeing a friend in Longmoor collapse. A fit and healthy man in the prime of his life and his legs gave way as he fell in a sweating, crumpled pile like a marionette with cut strings. That poor blighter never recovered. A week in the hospital with a breathing mask on his face then mysteriously shipped off in the night to God knows where. No goodbye. Nothing. Winter wanted to see someone else suffer like this. He wanted to watch them collapse, or at the very least see sheeted bodies awaiting removal in hastily made coffins.

He needed to get away from London. If he could get to an outlying suburban station, he stood a better chance of slipping through the net, perhaps bunking onto a freight train like they were supposed to do in America. It was going to be a long hike... He tried to bring to mind the geography and could remember that ahead lay long tunnels and cuttings, so that meant he'd need to strike off the railway for a bit. Find a way up and over this barrier.

He felt himself slump at the thought. Perhaps he was starting to tire of the constant travel. He was dreadfully weary, with aching legs and his breath getting short, sending pangs through his chest if he inhaled too deeply. The foul air was not doing his lungs any favours. Besides, what chance did he have of crossing these new borderlines they'd set up, even if he did find a train to board? He'd seen the soldiers and police deployed at the station barriers and heard talk of needing papers granting special permission, of which he had none. Fat chance! He was a wanted man...

Looking around, he saw a torch beam playing across the tracks. Too far away to cause immediate concern, but he needed to get on his way. The bulky shape of a tank engine suddenly approached on the adjacent line at speed, the driver intently peering into the opaque murk to watch for the line of waiting trucks. He paid no heed to the solitary figure of a man holding a shunter's pole.

Winter walked deeper into this strange hinterland of railway lines and busy engines attending lines of wagons that would suddenly ripple and chatter as they buffered up. It was like a world apart from the city and yet he was deep in central London.

Chapter Thirty-five

This was an almost private place of sickly weeds, ash piles and pools of stagnant water divided by long curving ribbons of steel rails that reminded him of silvery eels. Londoners loved their jellied eels, so that seemed about right. Somewhere ahead lay the tunnels taking the lines out of Kings Cross and away to the north country. To the far left was the giant shape of the St Pancras trainshed, glowing palely behind the etched filigree of the gasholders. He'd got his bearings now, but his legs were leaden, and he had a long way to walk.

A bicycle! He could hardly believe his luck. It had a loose rear mudguard that rattled noisily and no lights. The rear wheel had a wobble, no doubt the result of striking the many rails and half-buried sleepers and the brakes were rubbed down to the metal. It was also unchained and probably used by the shunters to get around the yard and it was just what he needed.

He threaded the shunter's pole along the frame to rest on the rusty chromed back carrier and poking out over the handlebars. He felt this helped cement his disguise. It would be sedate progress with the Sturmey Archer gears stuck in first, but as this was a treacherous surface he needed to proceed with caution and the low gear would be kinder to his legs when he climbed the hill above Copenhagen Tunnel. On his bike, he'd look like a worker on his way home after work and could cover as many miles as he needed. Perfect.

Feeling surprisingly chipper, Winter pedalled off.

* * * *

Private Clawson hurried out of Waterloo station. He knew the place tolerably well and was aware of several narrower ways in and out of the giant sprawling construction, away from the grand entrances with their fancy wrought iron gates. These gates, and the men standing guard, gave the impression the station was secure, but he knew it was leaky as a colander.

A dimly lit passage probably used by staff saw him exit into the city, on what he reckoned to be Cab Road, although the number of black cabs was greatly diminished. The cabbies would be watchful, desperate for trade and would eye him up expectantly as he walked past. Maybe the police had already handed out his photograph amongst them? No. It was too risky.

He turned his back on the taxis and hiked up Spur Road, crossed Waterloo Road and struck off at a pace, head down, face almost covered by a scarf, hands in pockets and without any real objective. All he knew was that he would take a meandering route that would hopefully lose anyone on his tail, especially those loutish Teddy Boys. They'd been distracted and rushed off before they'd done any real harm, but he could feel bruises starting to form and had no wish to meet them again.

Clawson steered clear of Waterloo East as this was too obvious as a potential route across the river and would be heavily guarded. He'd continue in an eastern direction through Bankside, where the streets were quiet, with just delivery vans and trucks making up the majority of traffic and handfuls of people on foot. Everywhere was unnervingly quieter than usual, and whilst the hum of the city was still there, as were the muffled hoots and rumbles of passing trains and road vehicles, it was so much quieter than he'd ever known it. The gathering smog was also acting as a deadening layer of insulation whilst making Clawson shiver. He quickened his pace, trying to work some warmth into his limbs. His stomach rumbled. He'd not eaten well today, concerned that his face would be recognised whilst waiting to be served. As he passed a grotty pub with warm yellow light spilling through unwashed windows onto the street he longed to step into the warmth and down a few pints. Maybe fall into conversation with a few locals. They might even offer him a game of darts...

He stood outside for almost a minute, dithering and longing for some normality, some conversation, but reluctantly walked on. They had agreed on a plan. The sergeant had told him to 'get Waterloo and at least one other of the commuter stations on the south bank boxed off, then head up north.' That was next on his plan, to go north. To Crewe, Manchester, Carlisle and maybe Glasgow.

It sounded so easy, but Clawson was losing his resolve. His feet were feeling the ache of so much walking and standing, but more than that he was longing for a hot meal and some company, then a warm bed.

Sleeping rough was exactly that. Rough and hard on the back. Kipping for an unsatisfactory hour or so in a railway carriage then trying to wash and shave in those minuscule washbasins in a carriage was a maddening experience after so many days. Lord, he was tired. Weary in mind and body and spirit.

Did he have the will to carry on? It was easy to say, 'Go North!' but the police were everywhere, and he'd even caught sight of a lorry filled with squaddies heading somewhere. Were they bringing the Army onto the streets? It was looking that way, but Army or Police it was all the same; it was harder to get in and out of stations and harder to move around in daylight. There was no escaping the fact the initial thrill had gone only to be replaced by the constant fear of being hunted.

His eyes stared ahead, ever watchful, but his body was urging him to slow down, to find a warm cafe or bar and just sit and accept whatever hand fate dealt him. They'd done their work. They'd spread mayhem, infection and quite probably death, across London. They'd done the same across much of the south and the West, and the impact from what he could glean from the newspapers was impressive. They'd made their point. Dreaming of having the pick of the French girls on the Riviera who'd found themselves asymptomatic, seemed no closer. These imaginary girls were as far out of reach as if they lived on Venus. He couldn't keep going much longer.

Perhaps he didn't want to?

What was the benefit? Even if there was a chance of dragging himself down to an exotic beach in the distant future, right now, on a bitterly cold night in London he was hunted by uniformed men (some with guns), whilst steering clear of savage gangs of angry youths. This was the harsh reality. Everything else was just idle fantasy. He had no possibility of crossing the channel now. And besides, he didn't know the lingo...

Clawson looked up at a road sign and mentally tried to orientate himself. He was not so far from London Bridge station. As busy a station as you could ask for. Crammed with commuters every day. Perhaps even now it would be thronged with enough people to make it a good choice. Such large numbers made it harder for the police to check faces and there was a chance he could lose himself in the crowd whilst spreading more of the virus.

One last roll of the dice. A commuter station where he could cause maximum damage. The sarge had asked this of him, so he'd drag his weary feet there and do his duty. He'd walk the length and breadth of the station then hopefully find a little cosy cafe that might serve him a big plate of hot food and a mug of sweet tea and then wait... Wait for the inevitable and accept it, be it in the shape of an ugly copper with a truncheon or some of his Army compatriots armed to the back teeth. So be it. He'd gone as far as he could. He was unlikely to even get to Euston or St Pancras now and almost certainly not going to board a train at either terminus. There was no getting through the cordons and security checks he knew were in place. No, he'd reached the end of the line.

His day was done.

Chapter Thirty-six
King's Cross

Benson had been redeployed along with two male colleagues from the local branch of the Transport Police away from the station itself and into the vast goods yards and locomotive sheds that formed the hinterland of 'the Cross'. Another five men were spread out across the enormous footprint of this vast area, in the hope of encountering the fugitives.

Each was carrying a hand lamp and a heavy truncheon slung from their leather belts slapping their sides. Benson was also feeling the strap of the pistol case cutting into her shoulder. She'd not admitted to carrying a firearm, conscious the constables, who were all younger, taller and somewhat meaner in disposition than herself, might not appreciate the implied slight to their manliness of an armed WPC. Benson had already endured enough derisive comment and undeserved criticism in her working life to know there was a time and place for everything, and only when she needed to draw the gun, would either constable be aware she had one. For now, it handily doubled up as a place to keep sandwiches and an apple, and this explanation both amused and pacified her colleagues.

Picking her way down the constricting lines of wagons, trying not to stub her toe or sprawl headlong into the filthy ground, Benson hoped she would not need the weapon. Visibility was worsening and she would need to be dangerously close to either man to have any chance of making an identification. The act of just pointing a loaded weapon at someone at such close range was going to be hard, but the idea of shooting them was unimaginable.

Could she do it? Should she do it? The order was clear, but her basic love of humanity recoiled at the idea. If she did her 'duty', the consequences would live with her for life. Watching an unarmed man die amidst this unlovely yard would be sordid and vile. Horrific. Yet if she didn't, then either man could manhandle her. Push her aside and without inflicting any obvious physical hurt, make their escape and in so doing perhaps condemn both herself and anyone who came to her rescue with the possibility of death or an unpleasant stay in hospital. It was a horrid situation, and a part of her hoped they would get word someone else had done the awful deed.

Benson had a bitter taste in her mouth, and not just from the stewed tea she'd hastily drunk standing beside a mobile van bravely continuing to trade. Her strong brogues clumped on the cinders and ash and small pieces of ballast skittered away as she kicked them, sometimes striking a metallic object. A locomotive hissed close by, the cab briefly illuminated as the fire door opened. The crew were rendered as black figures in a swirling fog of steam coloured yellow and orange like a vision by Dante. One called out something obscene in her direction and the hellish image was shattered. Just two Cockney lads working the night shift on a humble six-wheeler.

Benson trudged on. Torch beam sweeping from side to side. She could make out the shapes of men armed with poles and carrying hand lamps, wearing flat caps and donkey jackets. They all looked the same. How on earth was she to tell them apart?

That was a police whistle! Two short toots demanding attention. She ducked low to peer beneath the lines of wagons to see where the constable was. Not there. She hurried forward to end of the line of wagons and a more open vista of weed-infested sidings. A torch was swinging side to side as an indicator and she flashed her own in response.

'What you got?'

'I saw someone...'

'Where?'

'Can you see the hut? Behind that last wagon... A man

went in and came out minutes later.'

'What of it?'

'He never put the light on. Seemed odd. In the dark in a shed.'

They were keeping their voices muted and lamp beams switched off as they were insufficiently strong to illumine the distant hut but might alert the potential suspect to their presence. The other constable now arrived. 'Summat up?'

'Maybe. A bloke went inside that hut and never put the light on, then came out looking different…'

'In what way different?' Benson asked.

'He went in with a trilby and overcoat. Not usual around here and got my attention. He came out lookin' like all the fellas working here.'

'Just changing for work?'

'Could be. But in the dark? And this is an odd time to change shifts.'

'Not a lot to go on.'

'Still needs checking, even if it's nothing,' Benson added.

They approached and switched the light on inside. 'It works.'

Benson agreed the constable had a valid point. 'Look. Hat and coat…'

The constable reached to pick them up.

'Can you catch it from clothes?' The second constable was hovering near the door and appeared unwilling to enter.

'Dunno…' Nobody moved.

'We're wearing gloves for goodness' sake…' Benson, irritated by their hesitancy and aware that every passing moment was allowing their quarry to slip further away, picked up the coat. 'New. And yet thrown down as if discarded.' She was searching the pockets, then slipped a glove off. 'Still warm…'

The younger constable growing more confident inspected the hat. 'Not a mark on the sweatband. Also new.'

'He's bought new togs to change his appearance, then dumped them and switched to railway gear...' Benson sounded grim. 'We're wasting time. Come on!'

'I didn't get the best view, but he had a donkey jacket and flat cap like they all wear on the railway.'

'As if our job was not hard enough...' Benson grimaced. 'Which way did he go?'

'Northwards. If he gets to the edge of the yard, he could find a way out and escape...'

'I'll go after him...'

'We should call in reinforcements and alert the sarge. If I can reach him. There's a phone outside.' Benson was thinking quickly. 'Get the Met boys to send some cars around the roads to cut off escape routes as he's already stolen a march on us.'

'That makes sense...' The second constable agreed, peeved he'd not suggested this himself.

'I'll put the call in...' Benson offered.

'I'll go left and work towards the shed. I can rustle up more help there,' the first constable offered.

'I can take the right flank once I've placed the call,' Benson added.

The two constables split up and walked away, only using their lamps when it was impossible to see. Benson walked over to the telephone inside a metal box strapped part of the way up a telegraph pole adjacent to the hut.

* * * *

Vignoles sat at his desk in Leicester Central. His Anglepoise desk lamp pooling light onto a stack of fresh telegrams. As he read each, he made brief comments in a book, then struck each through and tossed them into an overflowing wastepaper bin. It was monotonous work.

Mavis Green or PC Blencowe would have been quicker and more patient at the task, but Blencowe was now temporarily posted to Derby on the lookout for the fugitives, whilst the situation with Mavis was concerning.

Her dry cough had worsened, and she was now running a temperature. She was at home, in bed and unfit for work. Her niece, Laura Howerth had only recently telephoned through with the grim news.

Vignoles had met Laura only a handful of times. Mostly, whilst still Miss Green and in her role as a signalwoman and again last year with his wife at her wedding to PC Simon Howerth in Woodford Halse. This evening her usual cheery manner had lost its edge and learning that Laura Howerth was forbidden to enter the house and see her ailing Aunt, was putting extra strain on the situation. Laura had explained that as a pregnant woman, she fell into the high-risk category and was wisely obeying instructions. This was the first Vignoles had heard she was pregnant, but what would ordinarily have been a cause for congratulations and good wishes was summarily over-looked. Both had too many pressing problems to attend, and an event still seven-months away could await happier times for a proper celebration. Hopefully.

The phone jangled. It rarely stopped, as observations and reports on virus outbreaks were called in. If Vignoles and his team were to stand the remotest chance of tracking and stopping this pair of infectious men, then this unceasing sharing of information was going to be the only way to plot their progress. Either that or luck…

'Sir?'

'WPC Benson.'

'We might have struck lucky.'

'Exactly what I wanted to hear.'

'I think we're close to one of them. We can't be completely sure but…'

'Your detective brain says so?'

'Yes, sir.'

'What have you got?'

Benson explained where she was and the circumstances leading up to a constable (now identified as number 874 PC Medhurst) sighting a man entering a shunter's cabin dressed in street clothes and leaving dressed in railway worker's jacket and a cap having abandoned what they confirmed as brand-new clothing.

'Reasonable grounds for suspicion. You tried to give chase?'

'There are just three of us and with night and bad weather closing in we have no actual sighing to the suspect. The two constables are doing their best to follow.'

'Which direction do you believe he was heading?'

'North is our best guess, which would take him towards the throat of the yard complex and the opportunity to get up and out of the yard area and into North London.'

'Any further sightings?'

'Not yet. DS Mellor brought every man he could muster into the goods and coal yards and the City police are trying to throw a cordon. The Met sent cars to patrol the streets, so it looks as though they have the area sealed off. He could have slipped the net before we had time to do that.'

'Understood.' Vignoles was thinking hard. He was fortunate in that he enjoyed studying maps, especially detailed ones of railway stations such as the various London termini. He also had a good visual memory and could form a reasonable working picture of this complex area. 'Is Mellor to hand?'

'Yes, sir.'

'Put him on.'

'Guv?' Mellor sounded out of breath.

'I want all rail traffic out of King's Cross suspended until we catch the suspect or sound all-clear. The same for St Pancras. Traffic can come in, but I don't want him hitching a ride out of town.'

'Understood.'

'What's your hunch?'

'Probably it's one of the two geezers, guv. A suspicious

character. Could be Winter.'

'What chance of cornering and stopping him?'

'Fifty-fifty at best. The City and Met boys were on this like a ton o' bricks and got a cordon around the place. But it's huge and so many wagons, goods sheds, engine sheds, you name it...'

'Understood. And the other man?'

'Got a warmish trail out of Waterloo. We lost the scent, but he's in the area. I was not far behind when we got this shout from the Cross. I've put twenty men on this trail and the Sweeney is cruising the streets south of the river. With almost nobody around, if he shows his face, they should be on him.'

'Waterloo? One man south of the river, the other north?'

'Makes sense operationally to split up. My instinct says the geezer in Waterloo was heading East.'

'They need to escape from London. They know we're on to them.' Vignoles' mind was racing. 'Then we need all outgoing services cancelled across the city. I'll inform the ACC to get all the top brass in London pulling their weight. We need to stop everything from leaving. I'm on my way now. There's a special being prepared as we speak for a non-stop to St Pancras. Once there, I'll take King's Cross as it's closer. I want you back south of the river. Get Clawson.'

'The ACC?' Mellor was surprised. It was almost unheard of to speak with a man holding such an elevated position.

'CS Badger is out of the running for now. But we have work to do,' Vignoles put the receiver down. He had no desire to say more and now was not the time.

He telephoned Leicester Midland. 'Vignoles here. That special to London. I need it to depart the moment I get there... Yes, in the next ten minutes... Then tell him to get a move on! No, I don't have time to wait...this is an order! That train leaves the moment I'm on board and no excuses or the ACC himself will be calling for your neck! And I want as many of your men as you can spare on board.

Chapter Thirty-seven
Belgrave & Birstall

Anna stood close to the parapet of the bridge looking down onto Belgrave & Birstall station. The lights were lit inside the compact red brick building and threw a welcoming light onto a platform dusted with snow. It was just a light frosting but still rendered everything pale and sparkling in the moonlight. It was hard to imagine there was an invisible killer out there with this scene looking like something from a romantic Christmas biscuit tin lid.

It was bitterly cold, and Anna was glad to wear her woollen scarf across her nose and mouth in the prescribed manner. Her gloved hands remained in her coat pockets. Regrettably, the cold was far from ideal in halting the spread of infection, or at least, that was the viewpoint now being offered by yet another 'expert' nobody had heard of, unearthed from a research institute equally unknown. Whatever the truth, this cold snap meant more people would cover their faces and wear gloves or just stay indoors and avoid any human contact, which must be a good thing. Charles would be far safer if everyone kept away from the railway, and if they dared venture out, did so wrapped up like Santa Claus.

Anna watched the local train smoke gently as it waited in the station, the driver, gloved hands on the cab side exchanging a few unhurried words with the stationmaster. More complaints, rumours, theories or solutions shared...

There was little sense of rush. No passengers got on or off, and whilst the timetable was theoretically adhered to, there had been a noticeable slackening in pace in recent days. The usual sense of urgency had gone, and these local trains were taking on a more lackadaisical ambience. However, the night freights still hurtled through without hindrance with increasing frequency. No danger signals were allowed to prevent vital supplies from getting through, and the heavy freight engines shook the houses as these intensified services thundered south. With widespread panic-buying and southern ports either closing their wharves or reducing the tonnages accepted, commodities were becoming scarce. House coal, perishables and most especially, medical supplies were in desperate need and the yards at Immingham, Annesley, Leicester and Woodford were all in the frontline of the battle to supply the people trapped behind the steadily advancing Isolation Zone border.

Anna felt a sense of pride as she looked down on the little train as it steamed into motion along the twin silver rails that stretched away on a gentle gradient onto the lengthy embankments and viaducts that carried them across the city on an elevated course. The train would terminate at Central and leave the line clear. This was a railway built primarily to handle fast freight and it was now coming into its own, with so many passenger services stripped out or truncated to allow more room for the thundering goods wagons.

In her work as a goods dispatcher, Anna was busier than she could remember since the war ended. The work was relentless, and the hours long made no easier by the demand that the office was only ever manned by half the usual number. Their desks had been moved further apart and two taken away into storage. Now they each worked in splendid isolation with a scarf tied across their nose and mouth and all close contact forbidden. Tea breaks were rather odd affairs, with mugs tea or weak coffee brought in on a trolley, pre-poured by one of the buffet staff who dressed like a surgeon and wore gloves. Collected one at a time, this was 'enjoyed' back at the desk with whatever sandwiches could be pre-prepared at home. Despite her best efforts, these sandwiches were becoming dull and repetitive fare, consisting mainly of cheese on sliced white bread.

Trying to work long days then find time to queue (surely an unwise occupation in the current pandemic...) for what little foodstuffs were left in shops cleaned out by others who selfishly wanted to hoard it for themselves, was proving a challenge. Fortunately, her parents were better able to access fresh food and once a week left a cardboard box of appetising goodies on the back doorstep or telephoned her to call into their shop to collect something. However, their business was losing trade rapidly, and her parents feared they would soon have to close and live off their savings until things improved. Ice Cream was never a best seller in winter, but the television news showing disturbing reports of the situation in London and the south was keeping people away from the lure of fashionable espresso's and cream cakes and even the pull of the garish Jukebox they had recently installed. Even Elvis Presley could not entice in more than a handful of youthful visitors a day, and takings were plummeting.

Charles had not wanted her to continue working but appreciated the vital role she played in trying to provision those running short. Her job was desk-bound, inside an office with opaque windows that shut out the view and much of the light and with the ban on socially mixing, she felt as though she was becoming something of a recluse. Without their incessant processing of receipts and invoices, bills of lading and fielding telephone calls from dawn till dusk and beyond, the vast rakes of wagons and vans laden with goods would have nowhere to go and it would be impossible to keep track of their contents. Fraud and theft were on the increase, making Anna's detailed records and accounts ever more valuable. She was spending much of her day working with constables under her husband's control, helping them investigate missing goods. If it was tiring and lonely work, she gained satisfaction in appreciating that as a husband and wife team their work was complementary at this time of crisis.

Anna looked at the distant twinkling lights of the city, with the smoke of thousands of hearth fires drifting low over the rooftops and lying in pale striations between the chimneys and between the taller rooflines of factories. Her husband was still down there, in Central. Working late, and then taking a few uneasy hours sleep on the narrow folding bed he'd set up in his office. They'd not met for days, forced to talk from one side of the platform to another or through a closed window, or just once, seated at either end of a long station bench like angry lovers no longer wanting intimacy.

'It's too dangerous, Anna. The evidence shows this new strain to be is highly contagious. It acts rapidly, and it kills. Flu is bad, pneumonia deserves respect and to be avoided, but this man-made derivative is to be feared. We cannot run the risk of either of us catching it.'

'It would be unbearable... I'd not be allowed to visit you in hospital.'

'The idea is appalling. But it's the stark reality. God forbid you should succumb to this evil creation. We would have to abandon our vital work and at best, taken to separate isolation wards, perhaps never to see each other again...'

'Don't be morbid!'

'I'm not. This is serious. Worse than anyone can imagine. It's the Spanish flu of 1918 all over again. Let's not fool ourselves, we work in public spaces and our chances of encountering it are high. You're reasonably safe if you stay in your office and take just the one short train ride home. Sit alone if you can. Wait for the next train if it is too crowded. Go nowhere except for essential shopping and avoid contact with anyone. I think your chances of escaping it are at least even...'

Anna brushed a tear from her eye. Charles had sketched out the harsh reality of his own work. 'I need to go everywhere and anywhere up and down the line and that means inside the Isolation Zone. Right into the heart of London. The dangers are obvious, but I have no choice. I take what precautions I can, but Mellor and I are under no illusions. The probability of infection is high. I cannot allow my work to endanger your life. We must stay apart until this is over.'

'Whatever 'over' means…'

'Indeed. I won't soft-soap, it's going to be hard. To be so close yet so far apart at a time when we need the comfort of the other, is cruel. But this virus has no feelings. It is brutal and relentless and cares not one jot for emotions and relationships. I could not live with myself if my work caused you to fall ill. If I am to do my duty to the best of my ability, I must do so knowing that I am not materially risking your life.'

His cool logic was hard to take, but Anna knew her husband was right. She could see it in his face, in his eyes, in his smile that tried to communicate a flicker of hope whilst refusing to sweeten the bitter pill with empty promises and unrealistic outcomes that neither could dictate.

The train grew smaller and the signal clunked back to danger, the red light staring like a single eye through the dark. A tawny owl hooted somewhere over towards the golf course. She turned to walk home, and as she did so, saw a young vixen standing in the middle of the road, its sleek nose uplifted. There was almost no traffic now, day or night and nature was growing more confident. The vixen's long stare almost challenged Anna to move or say something. They observed each other, more as equals than perhaps at any other time, sharing a brief moment of intimacy across Station Road.

The vixen trotted on, untroubled.

*   *   *   *

At about the same time Anna Vignoles was sharing a stolen moment with the vixen, Mrs Laura Howerth was standing in the front room of their house on Willow Road.

She had gone in there to draw the curtains against the cold of the night and press the electric starter to get the modern gas fire alight. The room would be cosy in minutes and free of the draughts and ashy dust of her previous life in an old house with coal fires.

Their newly built house on the equally new estate on the edge of Loughborough town centre was well-constructed and compared to anything she'd known before, was the lap of luxury. She had a brand-new white gas stove with a high-level grill, a hot water geyser that worked quickly and efficiently and a glorious indoor bathroom with the trendiest coloured tiling and a floor covered in blue and white linoleum. They had a fitted carpet to the front room, or 'lounge' as the sales rep had insisted it was now called, and the gas fire was surrounded by a small wall of pale limestone and a set of dark wood shelves. Three Picasso prints mounted on pieces of board but unframed, as was the modern way, adorned the walls above their small collection of books and ornaments.

It was a lovely house, and neither Simon nor she could quite believe it was theirs. Technically, it was still in the hands of their bank, as they had a long mortgage, but they had the keys to the door. They had wasted no time settling in, with the smallest bedroom already part-painted and papered by Simon. This was going to be the nursery.

There was still plenty of time, but Laura wondered when her husband would be able to finish the room. He was eager and enjoyed the work, proving to be a practical and not afraid of 'doing-it-yourself,' and had bought a stack of colourful magazines filled with ideas and projects a man like Simon could tackle at home. 'We've borrowed every penny we can, so we can't afford to get decorators in. I can take all this on and save us a packet!'

Then the world had been turned upside down. From talk of a winter flu' outbreak that few took much notice of, to a worldwide pandemic of a virus with a funny name killing people as efficiently as the Spanish Flu after the Great War. Britain in a matter of weeks had lurched from just reading eye-catching headlines to becoming a divided nation on the verge of mass panic, with worrying tales of armed gangs looting, rioting, of grid-locked roads as people desperately tried to flee the infection zone. The police and the army were having to use force to hold back terrified citizens. There were confusing reports of injuries, shootings, even a fatality. The hospitals were overwhelmed and so many ambulance crews falling ill their vehicles stood idle, and all the while the death count was mounting so fast it was out of date by the time the papers were printed. Most chilling of all were the images of the mass graves in London and the convoys of lorries driven by gas-masked soldiers delivering more pitch-pine coffins...

Her husband, Simon was one of those on the front line. He was working every hour he could and forced to make the painful decision that he could not risk bringing the infection into their house.

'You're pregnant and high risk. Even if you got just a mild dose, the effect could be devastating. We can't take the risk, not with me working with people coming from London and the south...'

She knew he was right, and despite wanting to cling on to the romantic notion they were both 'in it together,' and yes, if God so chose it, would die together, this was foolish. Simon had important work to do and he could not function if worrying about her and the unborn baby. If she stayed safe, he could focus better on his work. But it was hard not to wonder if he would ever come back to their new house and the part-painted nursery. Laura Howerth had to fight hard not to give in to gloomy notions their child might be born never knowing its father...

She looked out on the silent street. Curtains were drawn and no-one stirring. It was like this whatever time of day, aside from a brief flurry of activity as men left in the morning to walk to the nearby Falcon Works and then repeat the process in the early evening. Aside from a quick trip to the local shops, everyone was staying indoors. It was a lonely existence.

Chapter Thirty-seven

Laura Howerth pulled the curtains closed and shut out the view. Perhaps she could look at what was on television? This was another thrilling new purchase and a novelty neither had yet tired of, although in the last few weeks the fare had become polarised into depressing news, equally depressing talk and analysis of this news or ridiculously inane game shows perhaps designed to cheer the nation. She vainly hoped there might be a film or play to lose herself in.

She sat on the sofa and stared at the screen. She could be very happy in her new life if it could just get back to something like they had imagined and planned for. But now? It was isolating, and the future so troubled and uncertain. She longed to be back in her little signal cabin on the edge of the West Bridge branch. Safe and secure in her lonely outpost, unvisited all day or night, she would have no fear of the virus and could keep herself busy pulling the signal levers and sending bell codes up and down the line, reading the weekly notifications on changes to the service and waving, safely, to the passing crews. She imagined her junction box was operating on an emergency footing now and seeing more traffic. It would be exciting to signal through special trains at all times of the day. Perhaps some might be transporting armed troops on their way to the 'frontline'. Alarming for those forced to confront armed troops, but compelling viewing for a signalwoman safe in her little domain.

This strange mix of emotions swirling about was causing a sensation like stomach pain. It was not acute and no cause to call a doctor. She realised it was waves of envy flooding through her in an almost physical manner. It felt like a stab of jealously in her belly, knowing that she was no longer out there 'doing her bit,' as her husband was...

Her duty now was to sit at home and never go out or see anyone. Perhaps this was correct, and it was hard to think what else she could meaningfully offer but knowing this didn't make it any easier.

She turned the TV on, but once the valves had warmed up and the little screen came alive, her heart slumped. 'Hancock's Half Hour.' It was a clever comedy and better crafted than much of what they showed, but the main character was a depressive and his hangdog expression and eternal sense of life's misery was not what she needed right now.

Chapter Thirty-eight
Conway

DCI Minshul and DI Trinder stood side by side under the sun awning optimistically opened over the window of a small bakery. The rain splattered noisily on the canvas now bowing from the collecting rain. Across the road lay the entrance to Conway railway station, with the massive stone walls of Edward I's castle forming a dramatic backdrop. Its keep a dominating presence and the defensive towers dotted with croaking black crows and complaining seagulls amongst the crenellations.

'The awning is not to stop the cakes overheating in the windows but to keep customers dry...' Trinder observed, wryly.

'Not so different from Sheffield.' Minshul was watching DS Ashbury and Trinder's DS, a man called Griffiths, standing in the teeming rain alongside a gaggle of the local constabulary, locked in a heated discussion, the rain making their capes glisten like ravens. 'What the heck's going on?'

Trinder took a moment before answering. 'They're having robust conversations about jurisdiction. Constabulary versus Railway. But you will be familiar with that perennial problem. If either man remains within railway curtilage, we move in for the take. If they exit the station, the local force wades in and we observe - and eat Welsh cakes. The debate seems to be about where exactly the demarcation line lies...'

'Ridiculous!'

'We're transport police and that carries little weight around here...'

'But the men are inside the bloody station! That's your beat - end of discussion!'

'Agreed...' Trinder looked pained. He'd had plenty of experience of this territorial in-fighting in his time serving under Vignoles and was all too aware the Transport Police were always treated as the lesser of the forces, apparently to be pushed aside and relegated to basic roles of standing guard over cordoned off areas or empty doorways or checking empty platforms and sidings after the local force had done the exciting work before filling in mountains of tedious paperwork after the event was over.

Trinder was still relatively new to his job in North Wales. He was considered a 'stranger,' as they would insist on calling him, and every day it was made clear he carried this unwelcome status like a brand across his forehead and there was nothing he could do to mask it. He was not one of them. 'You're not from around here, see?' and whilst treated with deference and painstakingly observed respect, it was obvious that if he could be sidelined, he would be.

Once the alarm had been raised that they had identified the two hitmen Minshul was after, the local Constabulary had arrived in force, brimming with menace and eager intent, instantly swamping the small town enclosed within its encircling stone walls with their physical presence. This promised to be the most exciting event in years.

The local constabulary moved around with the ease and confidence of men born and bred in the town or surrounding area. Their own DI had been brusque with Trinder, explaining how his men 'knew every last inch of the, castle, station and all. We'll ensure every last way out is covered. Oh, they won't get past my boys. We'll bring this to a satisfactory conclusion for you and the man from Sheffield. Now, you just leave it to us...'

His men were deploying even as he was speaking. He was effectively taking over the operation and his confidence and hard, unflinching expression did not invite argument. Minshul and his sergeant when they arrived, received little more than a perfunctory handshake and a nod of the head.

Minshul was now smoking in an agitated manner, seething inside at how he'd been made nothing more than a spectator.

'For God's sake, get on with it...'

'This is a public space and the men might be armed.'

'Nowt we heard to suggest they're carrying guns.'

'Best to be careful. My understanding is, the local lads will look to infiltrate plainclothes officers onto the platform and if the men appear unwilling to come quietly, they'll flush them outside where the sting will take place. Hence why we're standing here.'

Trinder shared Minshul's frustration, but he knew there was a limit to how far he could push his complaints without adding to the delay. Arresting the two men seen entering the station, was the priority. The only consolation in this unsatisfactory arrangement was that Minshul would take the men into his care once captured and duly process them.

'We could go up on the ramparts and watch the operation at least. If my status carries any weight, it will get us past the constable guarding the castle.'

'Might as well.' Minshul shrugged his shoulders, then adjusted his hat to better repel the rain and they hurried towards the high rain-slicked castle walls that offered spectacular views of both town and estuary. A few minutes later and despite the increased attention of the Welsh rain, the two detectives had a grandstand view of the curving platforms of the station that huddled close against the castle and built from matching stone in a complimentary style, almost as if commissioned by Edward I himself.

'Like a train set...'

'With a pair of killers included in the box?' Black humour helped lift the mood between the two detectives. 'Get a move on! How long is it taking them?' Minshul growled.

Trinder had brought a pair of field glasses and studied the tiny figures on the platform. 'One is spot on for one of your targets... But the other? Here, see what you think...' Trinder handed the glasses across. 'Looks more like a local tradesman than a hired gun...'

'I don't think he's our man...'

'They're moving in!'

Minshul tracked the approach of two men in plainclothes and noted at least six uniformed officers lurking in the background. A silent charade unfolded as, taking a man each, the police spoke to the two suspects on the otherwise deserted platform, uniformed constables close to hand ready to grasp arms and place cuffs on their wrists.

One of the men remained unflustered and spoke calmly. Had he expected this? There were no histrionics nor attempts at fleeing, although this would have been futile. He seemed to accept the situation with disarming equanimity. The other suspect was going through all the motions of outrage and making it clear he was both offended and insulted by the actions of the police. A shout or two, an arm batting away a constable's hand, a few choice words of insult in both English and Welsh could just be heard, despite the wind. He was manhandled away, hands clasped together behind his back in handcuffs, head twisting to add extra invective to the salty air.

'Either he's the wrong man or we've been sold bad information...'

'The other is a cool customer.'

Minshul handed the glasses back and hunched against the castle wall, cupping his hands to light a cigarette. He threw a curse into the wind.

'One out of two is good. The other can't be far away...'

Minshul inhaled deeply and squinting against the wind and rain as he waited for the nicotine to take effect. 'He's playing it calmly. Too bloody calm! He knows how to handle this. Handle us. He'll act the gentleman travelling salesman and won't flinch or give 'owt away. Even if we could give him a pasting in the cell - he's a pro. It would take the flippin' Gestapo to get him to confess. So, what does that leave us with? Circumstantial evidence at best.'

'You have a witness.'

'Not that will help. An elderly man saw two men in dark overcoats and hats walking down a towpath after dark. A jury won't buy a word o' that... Get a good lawyer, and his paymasters can afford one, and he'll walk out of the custody suite!'

Trinder watched the final scenes on the platform and the signal finally lifting to allow a much-delayed train to Holyhead to approach with a reproachful wail on its whistle. 'You did what you could...'

'Aye...'

'You did well to track them here.'

'To what end? No, he'll wriggle out of this, just you see.' Minshul leaned on the metal railings that lined the inner edge of the rampart walkway, placed there to prevent hardy visitors from tumbling to almost certain death on the flagstones far below. 'Hang on... Don't look around. I'm going to point towards the water as if showing you something, OK? Follow my hand then take a peek to the right of that nearest tower.'

Trinder casually turned about as instructed, smiling and acting as if he was a fellow sightseer sharing the view. 'Suspicious gent lurking in a doorway? A better fit.'

'That's the other killer. And he's cornered. There's no way out of here as they've got men on the only entrance.'

'You sure he won't have a gun?'

Minshul was not. 'Carrying a shooter in a public space is a risk and I'd vouch he won't.'

'But if the evidence we gathered is correct, they were making a move to escape to Ireland.' Trinder was privately proud of some excellent detective work he and his team had managed in little time. Local knowledge in a small and close-knit town had worked against the hitmen who'd perhaps not expected to have been tailed. 'Would he not take the tools of his trade with him?'

Minshul nodded. 'Perhaps, but they didn't use a gun on that lass. He's seen us.'

'Drop down the steps to the left and pray he's not in the mood for shooting practice. He could pick us off easily.'

'I want to look him in the eye. He won't shoot. He'll do like the other, act cool as ice and the innocent and trust to a good lawyer.'

'We'd best raise the alarm and coax him down?'

'As you wish, but I want to get up close. Smell his aftershave. Look into his eyes. I know he killed that lass and I want him to know I've got his card marked.' Minshul strode off along the stone walkway and down a set of ancient steps. After just a moment's hesitation, Trinder followed. It looked like the Transport Police were going to get the last word after all. It would be a feather in his cap to deliver this man at the same moment the local force was seeking to extricate themselves from a wrongful arrest.

The man's startling blue eyes fitted the description. He remained where he was, adopting a posture of studied nonchalance, hands in his coat pockets. He was whistling softly.

'Nice tune…'

'What's it to you?'

'*Red River Valley*,' Minshul stared at blue eyes.

'Want to get past? Not good to get too close these days...'

'Dangerous, is it?'

Blue eyes scowled. 'It can be.'

'Well, I'm not worried. Think I'll stay here and pass the time of day.'

'I'm not in a talkative mood.' He stood up straight and pressed himself against the wall. 'Go past. Both of you.'

'Your mate Evans is in the clink. We just watched them take him away.'

'Don't know anyone of that name.'

'No? You have a poor memory. You travelled with him from Sheffield.'

'Is that so?' He resumed his nervous whistling before

stopping himself.

'Do you recognise this?' Minshul held up the lighter. 'Your friend's name and number and regiment.'

'I told you I don't know anyone called Evans.' The blue eyes narrowed a moment and his Adam's apple moved, but he held his nerve.

'Then maybe it's yours?'

'Never seen it before.'

'That's a shame. We wanted to return it to the lad who lost it on the train. The one who travelled from Sheffield with you. You know, the journey you can't seem to remember making. Thought it might have sentimental associations...' Minshul was starting to enjoy this.

'Sod off!'

'What you doing up here? Sightseeing? Wah' in this wind and rain?'

'Same as you.'

'I don't think so...'

Minshul was gently tossing the lighter into the air and catching it again, the metal bright despite the heavy cloud. 'I had high hopes I could find the rightful owner, but seeing as you can't help, I might as well toss it over the wall!'

'You can't do that.'

'Why not?' Minshul stretched his arm out over the edge of the wall, fist clenched around the lighter. He stepped up closer. 'I can do what I want. Shove it down your gob, if yer prefer? Just a bit of worthless metal - unlike that young girl you pushed in the canal.'

Blue eyes held the gaze, unblinking. 'You talk a lot of rubbish. Now walk on and leave me be.'

Trinder walked past the two men and stood inside the tower doorway, where he could see the tight curve of a stone spiral staircase descending into darkness. 'Leave him, Bernard. He's got no way out. This place was made to repel attackers, but a castle can keep people prisoner just as easily.'

Minshul sneered. 'Aye, you're right.' He stepped back. 'Stay and enjoy the view. You can join your chum Evans, later...' He turned and joined Trinder, aware there were now shouts and whistles and the sound of heavy feet on stone coming from deep inside the castle tower. Reinforcements were on the way. At the last moment as Minshul stepped inside the doorway he called out. 'Hey! Catch!' He tossed the lighter towards the man but aimed deliberately off-target so when he instinctively reacted, he had to lunge forwards and stretch his arm way over the metal security rail. The whirling oblong of metal glanced off his fingers then dropped from his grasp and after a what felt like an age clattered on the stone flags.

'Clumsy idiot!' He snarled like a cornered dog.

'Ah, so it was yours?'

Something dull and metallic appeared in the assassin's other hand, but Trinder had already swung the heavy wooden door closed, narrowly missing Minshul's nose in doing so. They both smelt fresh wood and cordite as two bright white scars bloomed in the door as the bullets pinged from the inside wall.

'Down the stairs!' Trinder realised there was no locking bar and they could not lock the door. They both clattered downwards, their long overcoats in danger of tripping them and the deepening dark inside the spiral of stone making it hard to see where they were stepping. The stairs were vertiginous and whilst slow to negotiate, the constricted space at least offered little in the way of a target, but a bullet could ricochet many times before it's force was spent and the smell of cordite and the metallic smell of scorched stone was strong in their nostrils as another round was released.

They came to a landing and Minshul grabbed Trinder and hauled him against a wall. He had a pistol in his hand. 'I'm not taking a bullet in the back,' he hissed. 'Keep low...'

Trinder noticed something shiny and dark was starting to stain Minshul's left shoulder. He'd been hit.

Feet pounded down the stairs and the man appeared,

pistol in hand.

'Put the gun down! We're armed!'

Trinder wished he was. He held his breath and wondered how good a marksman an injured and bleeding Minshul was, even at short range.

Old Blue Eyes span about and fired without looking, the bullet sang off the stone with an ear-splitting note.

Minshul's gun blazed and their ears rang in pain. It was deafening. Another screaming explosion added to the confusion and in the momentary muzzle flash, Trinder could see a body flung backwards and twisting in the air. Minshul remained crouched, with both hands on his gun in the approved manner. Blue eyes lay sprawled in an ungainly position with his cheek to the stone flags, unmoving.

'He turned it on himself... The bloody coward!' Minshul was outraged.

'You got him?'

'He shot himself.' Minshul shook his head in disbelief.

Trinder was rubbing his ears and shaking his head, trying to clear it of the fizzing noise. 'You're hurt...'

'Winged. Nothing a pretty nurse, a bandage and a double scotch won't heal.'

'He shot first... I saw it. It was legitimate to return fire.'

'He never gave me a chance.' Minshul stood up, somewhat shakily, his skin pale. He stared at his pistol as he put the safety catch back in place. 'I wanted to him to take a bullet for that lass...'

'You did well, sir.'

'It's one up for us railway coppers, I suppose. Oh, come on, find me that dark-haired Welsh nurse...'

Chapter Thirty-nine
King's Cross

Hawkes was in a grotty part of London that lay some way behind King's Cross station, not so far from the busy mainlines, yards and sheds that sprawled across a vast area lying lower than most of the surrounding streets.

The band were finding bookings increasingly hard to secure, as the larger venues bowed to pressure and closed their doors. The appetite and hunger for live music, for dancing, smoking and drinking in convivial warmth and proximity, however, clung on. Despite the dire warnings on the radio and the television and splashed across the newspaper headlines about the escalating pandemic, there were still those who were desperate for a good time in an evening - and the virus could 'go hang.'

The band just needed money and the health risk was irrelevant when set against the need to eat and pay the rent. Making music was their livelihood and the hollowness in their rumbling bellies and the men with slavering pit bulls sent to collect the rent drove them across London on an unappealing night to play for just shillings. It was a shoddy dive, called the Western Star Domino Club on a miserable backstreet close to a derelict railway station of sinister design and history.

The session had been organised through Lawrence, the band's guitarist, and whose cousin knew the owner. It paid poorly, but they were promised five bottles of beer each as a sweetener. Five beers didn't pay the landlord's thugs but knocked the edges off what had already been a dreadful week.

The Western Star Domino Club at least welcomed black musicians and clientele, which was a rare blessing. Lawrence's cousin was a fellow Barbadian and so the club was almost exclusively frequented by West Indian immigrants and whilst not exclusive, care was taken to avoid admitting groups unsympathetic and looking for trouble.

The club was a converted corner shop with the picture windows bricked up to form solid walls and the front door was plated over with a sheet of tin. A little sliding cover opened in response to a knock to reveal an eye set in a craggy black face that silently surveyed those seeking entry. Only when they approved of what they saw was the door unbolted and they could file down a corridor and musty steps into the basement.

A single room with packing cases and beer crates around the edges for seating and a wallpaper pasting table serving as a bar was the only social space. The lighting was rudimentary and the sound system although simple, was loud. The back kitchen upstairs produced plates of sandwiches and the former shop floor provided storage for beer crates and liquor bottles and the boxes of valuable vinyl records used when live bands were not engaged. It was a hot and sweaty place with condensation dripping from the ceiling and running down the walls, but the atmosphere was convivial and happy. There were usually at least four or five people on the tiny dance floor. For all its obvious failings, Hawkes loved it and had hoped to bring Jane there one evening. Tonight, however, was not the night.

The club was full, but there was a strange and nervy undercurrent and Hawkes noticed two younger men had joined the ancient doorkeeper at his post. Extra muscle, in case of trouble. The barman explained that some Teds had come knocking the night before and only departed after an upstairs window had been broken and bricks hurled at the door. The vile graffiti they daubed along the front wall was still bright and raw.

'It's getting worse every day. They more confident, 'cos the police won't help us. They're not interested.'

Hawkes grimaced as he thought of Jane in her police uniform. It pained him to hear how the City police were

271

turning a blind eye to what was going on. He'd left Jane to patrol the terminus that lay less than a mile or so away, with a gun slung across her shoulder. These were strange times and he couldn't imagine where it would end.

It was not just the threat of violence that altered the mood that night. The band were worried, with yet another in bed and in a bad way and every expectation they could be next in line. Hawkes could count himself in the firing line as well. It was a sobering thought that had counter-acted the dulling effects of the free beer.

Hawkes was now standing outside the club. The performance over for tonight and his trumpet packed in its case. Old snow lay on the ground, much of it stained black or brown by pollution. The air bit into his lungs. He wrapped the scarf around his face and walked, head down, hat pulled low over his brow. The rest of the band were having a last drink, but Hawkes, uncharacteristically, wanted some time alone to think. He was not his usual ebullient self and felt a yearning to escape the sweaty, cramped club that he realised must be a fertile breeding ground for the virus. Worse than that, whilst playing his trumpet he'd felt his chest tighten and had to cut short some improvisations due to sudden shortness of breath. He knew he was tired and had smoked a lot recently. That must be it. Whatever the explanation, his performance had fallen short. If he couldn't blow the horn all evening, then his income stopped. He needed to cut down on the fags…

He stepped into the recess of a Gothic-styled brick doorway that surrounded heavy doors, not unlike those of a church and dug out his cigarettes. What the hell, he'd have a last one for the night. He turned to face the doors to put his back to the wind, and as he dragged it alight and shook the match out, noticed the doors had been given attention by vandals. One was ajar, opening inwards. A fusty smell of damp brickwork, dry rot and sour urine assaulted his nostrils. The interior was pitch black and uninviting. It was a large building, rather like a shoebox and profoundly ugly.

Hawkes had no desire to step inside and turned about and pressed himself into the corner of the doorway to gain the most protection from the elements.

A man was now cursing nearby, bending over to inspect the rear tyre on his bike. It was as flat as a pancake.

'Bad luck, mate!' Hawkes called out.

'Eh?'

'You've got a flat tyre.'

'I know. Last bloody thing I need!'

'And on a night like this...'

Sergeant Winter was trying to repress a surge of frustration. He'd hardly gone a few hundred yards and now a flat.

'Got far to go?'

'Far enough.'

'Me too. I'm headed over to West London, worst luck. A right drag...'

Winter leaned the bike against rusting railings that edged the derelict building. 'I'll collect it in the morning.' He felt the need to explain his actions whilst trying to think what his next move should be.

'If it's still there!'

'Yeah... Shank's pony will have to get me home tonight and see what tomorrow brings...' Winter's head was swimming. The cold and tiredness were getting to him.

'Smoke?' Hawkes proffered his cigarettes.

A moment's hesitation, then Winter stepped forward, standing companionably close. 'Ta.' He might as well infect one more...

A police car sped past a junction at the end of the road and the sound of a heavy train labouring with its load could be heard from behind the ugly building.

'Are we close to the railway?' Hawkes asked.

'Yep. Just come off shift there. I work the yards behind this place.' Winter decided to keep the illusion alive.

Hawkes studied the man. His face was uncovered. Hawkes said nothing as he tried to get his eyes used to the poor light but he seemed familiar. Jane had shown him the photographs of the men the police were hunting. She'd made him study the pictures and urged him to be alert in his travels and in the clubs and Shebeens he played. There was a similarity...

'Worked long on the railways?'

'All my life.'

'Dangerous work for you, these days?'

'How d'you mean?'

'In the dark, with trains everywhere.'

'I'm used to it.'

'But then there's two dangerous men on the run...'

'Dunno anything about that.' Winter narrowed his eyes.

'They didn't tell you about the two fellas carrying the virus? Spreading it around to kill as many as they can? They're using the railways to get around.'

'No...'

'They're searching King's Cross now...'

Winter shuffled his feet. Was this man on to him? He said nothing.

'What's your name?'

'What's that to you?'

'Just being friendly...' Hawkes continue to scrutinise the face. 'Save your breath. I know who you are, anyway...'

'What's your game?'

'I know who and what you are.'

Winter lunged forwards, one hand grabbing Hawkes by the throat. 'Reckon so, eh? Then if you're right - you're dead!'

Hawkes was pinned to the wall, but both his hands were free, and he easily brought them upwards in a sharp movement and broke the connection to his throat. He wriggled free.

'Sergeant Winter, you need to improve your hand-to-hand fighting!'

'I could snap yer legs and yer arms if I wanted. But I don't need to.' Winter laughed. 'One touch from me and you're a dead man.' Winter made a strange grin followed by a hollow laugh. 'So, I reckon that's yer lot mate.'

'I'll take my chances. Anyway, I might be wrong. You might be someone else.'

'Just a railwayman with a punctured bicycle?' Winter stood at the ready, arms slightly lifted and apart, ready to counter any attack, cigarette still smoking between his fingers. A dangerous point of heat that Hawkes was mindful of. 'That's your only hope now.'

Hawkes took a step back. He was not going to fight this man. 'Can't be much of a life. On your own. Hunted like a fox on the run. Shunned by everyone.'

Winter swore but didn't know what else to say. He'd had no meaningful interaction with anyone except a few sentences with Clawson. He was surprised to realise he felt in the mood to talk.

A gust of wind whipped around them, rustling dry leaves and litter around their feet. Both men shivered.

'It's too cold out here. It's open...' Hawkes pushed hard against the door which groaned and issued a painful squeal.

Winter meekly stepped inside without a word, not even thinking to protect his back as he walked into the dark. He was feeling all the fight and anger drain out of him and desperately wanted to sit down. Hawkes lit a match, which flickered for a few seconds and did little more than burn his retinas in the profound blackness, before dying out.

Winter snapped on a torch. 'Always be prepared...'

'Like a Boy Scout?'

'Like a fucking soldier!' Winter fired off another insult then flicked the beam around.

They looked at the stone floor with Gothic shaped arches vaulting above their heads at intervals along the great length of the building. It was like a cloister in a monastery. Pointed windows on the far wall offered a weak light and a glimpse of pale billows of engine steam and smoke through wire protected and soot-stained glass. Their eyes were getting used to the dark and slowly more was being revealed.

'What is this place?' Hawkes was questioning why he'd suggested they enter.

'A kind of church? But it's a strange one. What are those signs on the wall?'

'"Mourners this way." Cheery...' Hawkes walked a few yards and stopped at what looked like a lift. 'There's something here. Shine a light.'

'Access to the platform. Maximum capacity one coffin and eight bearers.' Winter read the painted sign.

'It's a funeral parlour?'

'With a railway attached?' Hawkes shrugged his shoulders.

'Just my bloody luck... I shelter in a station for the dead.' Winter looked horrified.

'How ironic!' Hawkes looked at the mounds of litter, at the stained and sour mattresses and evidence of fires that had been lit on the smooth flags. Others had done the same before them.

Winter walked across to one of the massive supporting buttresses and without taking any notice of Hawkes, slumped down, legs outstretched before him and rested his head against the stone. The torch shone its beam along the floor in a series of uneven highlights and shadows.

'Look...' Hawkes looked at a large wooden board screwed to the wall, lighting a match to read. 'It says here it's the Great Northern Cemetery Station.'

Winter gave a mirthless laugh. 'I've heard of this. Used to ferry coffins to New Southgate Cemetery. And I have to end up here of all places!'

Hawkes let the match die. 'I'd not be able to hack it on my own. I crave company.'

A long silence. 'You think I don't?' Winter closed his eyes. 'I had men to look after. A company. We were a team. A gang.

We didn't all get on of course, but some were my mates...' He paused to regain his breath. 'But we rubbed along together and mucked in and got the work done. And had some banter and good times along the way.' He hung his head. 'I probably killed 'em all without even knowing...'

Hawkes carefully laid his trumpet case down, then sat beside Winter. He'd probably already got the virus. It was too late to take precautions now. He fished out two more cigarettes and passed one to Winter.

'I've got a family I can never see. Not now.' Winter continued. 'And a mum, dad, a kid brother... But what's left for me now? I get to talk to you and then what?' He smoked and stared into the fog.

'I die.'

'And I live.' Winter spoke the words with bitterness.

'It's no life.'

'It's not. I'm alive and yet I don't have a life. Sitting in a flippin' morgue waiting for a death train that won't arrive...' He forced an ironic laugh that turned into a cough.

Hawkes smoked in silence. He didn't feel threatened by Winter. Far from it. The harm was done, and he would have to face whatever it did to his body. Perhaps he'd say a little prayer, though he realised it had been too many years since he'd last done so. By rights, he should feel anger, even hatred towards the man beside him, but instead, Hawkes was surprised to realise he felt sorry for him. Winter had done wrong and caused so much pain and suffering from his actions, but the man was having some kind of mental breakdown.

And who could blame him? He was not acting rationally and lashing out in fury and distress. It was indefensible. But was it? And who knew what the truth was these days? The papers were full of conflicting information and contradictions and there were even rumours two different viruses were going around and how one of them was a cover-up. A sinister plot engineered by secret agencies.

Hawkes felt sadness for Winter. Perhaps the soldier was just a pawn in someone else's horrid game? Winter was going to die soon, that much was for sure. Probably with a bullet in his heart, possibly fired by Jane...

Hawkes would be next, as might all his friends in the band. They were starting to show signs of infection. Had they caught it because of Winter? Or was this Asiatic flu the real culprit? Or was there any truth in the dark conspiracies flying about? Did it even matter?

Too many questions he could not answer, but Hawkes could not find it in himself to blame Winter for his friend lying seriously ill in their overcrowded house in Notting Hill. He could have contracted it without any help from Winter.

Hawkes shivered violently and his head felt light and fuzzy. He closed his eyes and listened to the distant bells of emergency vehicles and the occasional sharp whistle. The pitch could be that of a railway guard but sounded more like a police whistle. Like the one Jane carried... A steam engine chuffed and wagon buffers sang out. Somewhere out there, beyond the Gothic arched windows of this faintly sinister building, his lovely, curvy, gentle girlfriend was searching for the man now silently smoking a Player's slumped beside him.

Perhaps those whistles meant the net was closing in?

Chapter Forty
38c

Persimmon stood forward of the entrance to the brutalist form of the engine shed.

Known by the code 38c, Leicester Central engine shed was no beauty. Concrete beams, red brick infill walls and copious layers of soot and grime defined the building. Inside it was bleak and rugged with rows of lamps in enamelled shades suspended from the blackened roof beams. A coaling tower loomed over a line of locomotives waiting to have their tenders filled, whilst on the other side of the shed yard lay sidings occupied by wagons branded 'locomotive coal' in front of a small mountain of stored coal that formed the strategic reserve. The shed roads were partially occupied, but many of the heavy freight engines that lodged here were still out at work in the drive to the keep the shelves stocked and fires burning in London.

Persimmon was one of a number of the glamorous A3 class express engines in the care of the men at 38c and was cosseted, cleaned, polished and oiled to perfection. Even on this bitter night, she shone with a satisfying gleam in the light spilt by the yard lamps. The cab was glowing a rich orange as another round of coal was fed inside, the fireman a moving silhouette. The driver was leaning deep into the link motion with a long-spouted oil can in a gloved hand, feeding the oiling points before firmly thumbing the little corks back into place to keep the road dirt from entering and grinding the motion to failure.

He always took the greatest care in this work. Some of these oiling points were hard to reach, but Driver Evinson was an old hand. One of the top-link and he knew that taking time and care was vital. His engine needed to be in tip-top condition so she could safely haul the train up to speeds of 90 mph, perhaps a more, without grinding her joints or shaking herself to bits. He watched for tell-tale dribbles in places where there should be none or escapes of steam where steam should not escape. The hands of his trusty pocket watch moving inexorably forward and the shed master anxiously awaiting the time he could see this beauty roll off the shed and back onto her waiting train. Driver Evinson however, was not going to cut corners. Speed was essential tonight, but hastiness could prove fatal.

Across the divide stood another engine in steam. Edward Earnshaw was the fireman, partnered with a young driver by the name of Partridge. Ricky Partridge was eager and liberal with his use of the regulator and this demanded a lot of steam and extra work from his fireman. However, Eddie was also young, and they made a decent pairing. Given the chance to take a 'windcutter' south, they made sprightly running that gave the poor guard at the rear a fairground-style ride that was either exhilarating or terrifying, depending on the guard's personality.

This evening, instead of being sent off to pick up a line of loaded vans, Partridge and Earnshaw had been told to collect a rake of coaches and place them in readiness to form a special high-speed service into the Capital hauled by *Persimmon*. Hastily arranged, there was an aura of mystery about this service, made all the more so by the barked orders from the shed master who made it clear they'd 'better get on with it!'

Their task complete and awaiting their next instructions, Earnshaw leaned on the cab side sheet, content his fire was in good order and making steam nicely. He watched as the beautiful Sir Nigel Gresley-designed engine was given its last-minute preparations. He felt a touch of envy as the top link fireman rested his shovel in the coal heaped high in the tender before giving his neck and brow a quick wipe before retying his neckerchief. No face masks were worn on the footplate.

Chapter Forty

Everyone knew the virus didn't like the heat and smoke. Was it true? Maybe not, but no fireman could shovel tons of coal with fabric across his mouth.

Earnshaw could feel a sense of anticipation in the air. *The Master Cutler* express had been cancelled since the exclusion zone had been introduced and the stock reserved for the line's most glamourous express now stored in the carriage sidings at Leicester. The coaches were maintained in tip-top condition, specifically for special use such as this. However, what piqued Earnshaw's interest when pulling this stock into place had been the presence of soldiers at Central. Four of them, and all carrying guns!

This was the first sighting of armed soldiers in Leicester, although Ricky told him that rumours were flying that the exclusion zone was moving to the outskirts of their city. 'I heard the Army are stockpiling fencing and stuff to make barricades and my uncle Ernie saw a convoy of army lorries full of soldiers heading towards Oadby. Makes yer think summat is going on?'

It certainly did. Neither Earnshaw nor Partridge had met any trouble when they'd travelled south, but there were more frequent reports from the East and West coast mainlines of violent attacks. Soldiers had been seen posted in the larger goods yards, although so far, the former Great Central line was evading this unwanted attention.

'What's up? Have you heard anything about the special?'

'Something to do with the police. I heard they've laid it on for a Detective Chief Inspector.' Partridge replied. 'A lot of train for one man! It was supposed to go out in a few hours but was brought forward as an urgent request.'

Earnshaw chewed this information over. 'Could be DCI Vignoles. He's one of the best! And has the authority to get this train to run to his needs.'

'You know him?' Partridge was sceptical.

'I've met him a couple of times. My best mate works for

him in the Detective Department.'

'You're a dark horse!'

'I get to hear about him. I know he'll like seeing *Persimmon* on the front. He loves a Gresley Pacific.'

'Who doesn't?' Partridge looked longingly at the gloriously poised machine as it gently hissed luminous steam from the drain cocks and with a gentle series of breathy huffs, moved forwards.

* * * *

DCI Vignoles showed his warrant card, and his stamped and counter-signed letter permitting entry into London. Without this, he would be denied access and removed from the train at whatever station was now the frontline. This was Rugby at present, but liable to change at short notice. The soldiers stood a respectful distance away whilst the Station Master indicated which carriage he was to enter.

'All to yourself, inspector. All we ask is that you do not walk down the train.'

'Of course. Are others travelling?'

'Five in total. We managed to hurry them along to suit the new departure time. Some unable to reschedule will have to wait until tomorrow's special. They didn't like it, but needs must, inspector.'

'They must. Thank you for arranging this so quickly.' He tipped his hat and stepped aboard. He'd selected the first class dining coach because this gave him a larger table to work at and comfy armchairs not bolted to the floor. There was neither food nor drink served aboard, but the presentation was still immaculate with white cloths and little lamps lit at each table. As he took his seat, the lack of any other passengers gave the coach something of the atmosphere of a seaside dance hall on the last Sunday afternoon of the holiday season before mothballing until the following spring.

Chapter Forty

A door closed, a barked order given, probably to the armed soldiers. A whistle and they were off. Vignoles had noticed an 'A3' had been coupled at the front and he fully expected a sprightly non-stop run to Marylebone at the upper limit of the approved line speed limit. It was a virtually empty train so the big engine upfront was likely to put on an exhilarating performance.

He sat back in the chair and stretched his legs, tossing his hat onto the chair beside him. He removed his glasses and placed them on the starched white cloth and closed his eyes. He was feeling a wave of weariness suddenly wash over. The swiftly increasing rum-tiddy-tum of the wheels and the rumbling roar of their passing across bridges was soothing. He was going to be busy from the moment he arrived in London and unsure of what he was going to discover when he got there. It might be good to grab a nap.

He should have taken the special from Leicester Midland which would have brought him conveniently into St Pancras, but as with so much these days plans changed by the hour. There had been a nasty incident that blocked the line near Bedford. An armed hold-up, with reports of gunshots and a fatality. A train guard felled whilst defending his train. It was desperately worrying, but he'd had no time to make enquiries as his focus had to be on finding the quickest way of joining Mellor and Benson, both of whom were now engaged in their own potentially deadly mission. Leicester-Marylebone at least offered a swift route into the city, and Mellor's friends, the Flying Squad, would be waiting ready to speed him to Kings Cross along almost deserted streets.

A deadly mission? Vignoles knew this was no exaggeration. They were closing in on their quarry and the order to shoot to kill was sitting uneasily. It knotted his stomach and he'd been unable to eat all day. It was unthinkable they must shoot these men in cold blood. There had to be another way... But even if they managed to take the men into custody without recourse to this officially endorsed assassination, the medical evidence was clear that in handling them, they were effectively signing their own death warrants - and those of anyone who came close. Nobody should be placed in that danger. Cold logic determined that two lives lost against many was a price worth paying.

His stomach lurched unpleasantly once again, and a cold sweat formed on his brow. He shifted uneasily in his chair. Could he arrest these asymptomatic carriers and then, in all good conscience, travel back to Leicester, back to his house and kiss and embrace his wife? Carry this killer into the sanctity of their lovely home?

His head pounded and with eyes still closed he felt for the solid weight of the service pistol by his side. There was a good reason why they had been told to take these men at long distance, with a bullet. When he weighed up the ramifications of close contact, he knew what they must do. Then so be it. However, the inescapable reality of the situation was that these two named carriers were almost the least of his worries. They had names and identities and could be lined up in the sights of a gun, but the real threat was the invisible virus felling innocent people in the many hundreds each day. Too many bodies for the authorities to deal with respectfully and properly, as society expected.

The images of mass graves and the lime tipped on the coffins were a sight he never thought he'd witness.

Chapter Forty-one
Great Northern Cemetery Station

Winter was breathing fast and shallow. His energy ebbing fast. He'd remained in the same position since they'd stepped inside the ecclesiastically designed building. Slumped against a pillar, arms draped loosely to lie on the floor. Yet he didn't feel the cold seeping out of the stone, indeed he craved their cooling effect, with beads of sweat now trickling down his back and forming on his brow.

'I'm bushed… Walking for days with thin rations… I just need to rest up.' Winter's eyelids heavy and dropping. 'Always on the move, you see… A night's rest…and I'll be right as rain…' It was becoming harder to get his breath between the short sentences. Winter suddenly started coughing, his tired body flung repeatedly against the pillar as his chest was wracked by the painfully dry cough. Eventually, the attack subsided. 'Must have picked up a cold…' He gulped like a koi carp.

'You don't look well.'

'And you care?'

'You need a doctor. We should get you to a hospital.'

'Don't kid me.' Winter tried to laugh but abandoned the effort in another coughing fit. 'You said you knew who I am?' He looked at Hawkes through dropping eyelids.

'Yeah, a sick man who needs medical help. A warm bed at least.'

'No! I'm a bloody carrier. A walking death warrant!' He managed a few angry retorts. 'I can't get it, see? Won't touch me, but I give it to others. Lots…of others…' He gave a lop-sided grin. 'I'm your worst nightmare, matey.'

'You're so sure you can't get it? You look terrible…'

'Just a head cold. I'll shake off in a day or two.' The clamminess of his skin reflecting the faint cold glow from the railway outside. 'Take me to hospital and everyone gets it.' He stared into the distance, jaw slack. 'Maybe I should...'

'Or you've just got flu. Looks like the flu, if you ask me. You need to be off that cold floor and out of this God-awful place, that much I do know,' Hawkes was trying to convince himself. The man looked dreadful and needed medical help.

Hawkes studied the face. Despite being unshaven and deathly pale with sunken cheeks and rings under his eyes, he was unmistakably one of the virus-spreaders. Hawkes should raise the alarm. Maybe he should have cut and run the moment he first made the connection, but it was too late now. He must be infected as well. He was now just as dangerous as the dying man. His heart was pounding. With apprehension, or was that a symptom? How soon did it take hold?

He should seek help for himself, and yet he couldn't just leave this man to die alone like a sick stray dog. No matter what he'd had done, he was a fellow human being and in distress. If Hawkes got up and just walked away and left him to rot, what did that say about him? 'If you're immune, why are you sweating like a pig?'

Winter said nothing and concentrated on trying to regulate his breathing, head against the unforgiving stone.

'Who told you, you were a carrier? How can you be sure?' Did it matter now? Probably not, but Hawkes knew he couldn't leave. The best he could do now was raise the alarm and bring help to the building and stay fit long enough to warn them to keep their distance. He felt a pang around his fast-beating heart as he realised a rescue party might include Jane. The police whistles had intensified in recent minutes and he sensed they were closing in. He had to forbid her to come close. She mustn't even enter the building, let alone kiss or hold him...

He closed his eyes to hold back a sudden sting of tears. He had to keep her as far away as possible. *Damn this virus!* Hawkes slapped the flags with the palm of his hand, almost welcoming the sting of pain.

'I overheard...The doctors at Longmoor, talking...' Winter had gained enough strength to continue. 'They had to quarantine me and the others. For months...a year. As long as it took to find a cure. Like we were criminals. A life sentence for being alive and well...'

'They didn't tell you directly?'

'They were going to, but we hopped it. Lads were dropping like flies all around. Falling where they stood.' He paused for almost a minute as he regained his breath. 'A few were unharmed, and we realised what the future was going to be like...' He stared at the floor. 'It made me angry. Spitting mad! I was spared. Sounds good, doesn't it? But what happens then?' He gulped some more air and Hawkes waited as the minutes passed. 'Nobody can come near me. Never kiss a girl, never have a pint with mates, never have a life to live.'

Hawkes considered this. 'Fit and well, yet deadly to everyone else. You'd be locked in quarantine until they developed a vaccine.'

'And how long's that?'

Hawkes had no idea, but he'd read the endless debates in the papers. 'Nine months... a year? Longer?'

'I'd rather be dead than in solitary. Do you know how awful it is?'

Hawkes fell silent. A few months alone might be a price worth paying? He no longer had even that choice. Would he choose immunity whilst leaving Jane to fend for herself, unable to ever see her? He could see Winter's point of view.

Hawkes undid the latches on his trumpet case and took out the instrument. He fitted the mouthpiece and gently blew into the cold metal to warm it. His lungs still felt good, if a little tight now he'd rested from the evening performance. He felt no symptoms of illness, just the insidious chill of a frozen February night in a frigid mausoleum. If he survived the virus his lungs might still be damaged. He may never blow the horn again. Maybe he wouldn't want to if the band were lost. He'd best make the most of it whilst he still could.

He tested a note, then launched into a slow, powerful rendition of 'The Last Post.'

'You can play… But play something more cheerful. I'm not dead yet!'

Hawkes grinned. 'Seemed to fit the mood!' It was a strong and unmistakable tune, permanently linked with death and mourning and specifically with the armed forces. He was sure the police would hear it down in the railway yard. Was it possible they might make the connection? Perhaps Jane had heard it? That was the idea. He'd play something she liked. She was sure to recognise his style. A trumpet could carry its note a great distance, even across a noisy goods yard and the East Coast Mainline.

Hawkes stood up, the better to fill his lungs, and strode over to the nearest leaded window and smashed the tiny panes with the bell of the trumpet. It would be dented but would still play.

He launched into 'Singing the Blues', then improvised around this popular tune with his tell-tale signature styling. A short pause, then into 'Rip it Up', a recent favourite with the band. Jane knew both were in their current repertoire.

'That's more like it. Play another…'

Hawkes tried 'Hound Dog' then ad-libbed this into something hot and West Indian influenced. He'd learned a lot of exciting new tunes in recent months, imported fresh and hot from Barbados, Trinidad and Jamaica…

* * * *

'Is that a trumpet?'

'There's no jazz club 'round 'ere!'

'Playing 'The Last Post?' Funny sort of jazz club…'

The constables stopped and played their torches around the railway tracks with puzzled expressions. Benson joined them. 'We're too far from any night club down here?'

'It's all railways or empty buildings, nothing else.'

'Well someone's blowing a trumpet. Where from?'

Benson felt a strange tingle down her spine. 'I think…No, it can't be…'

'Can't be what?'

Benson frowned and played her torch around, but the beam showed her nothing but steel rails and sleepers and the high wall of an ugly and forbidding building. 'Forget it…'

The soloist was now playing 'Singing The Blues', the clear notes ringing incongruously above a slow-moving line of empty wagons rolling off a siding.

'Oh! Wait! I know who's playing that…'

'Come off it, darlin'! We've work to do, not waste our time…'

'I know that man!'

'Then tell him to knock it on the head and lend a hand!'

But despite the dismissals, all three found themselves walking closer as if pulled by the sound like the Pied Piper of Hamlyn. They were beside the main running lines. A dangerous place to stand, especially in the dark, even with torches. The bulk of the abandoned Cemetery station now looming ahead like the flank of a huge black freighter appearing through the fog at sea.

'He's up there. Inside that building.' Benson knew the personal signature Hawkes brought to whatever he was playing.

'There's an echo. Probably why the geezer chose to practice inside.' The youngest constable was intrigued, but he still dismissed Benson's observation. 'There's nothing here.'

'But I know who's playing.'

'Then you keep funny friends, but that don't help us catch our man.'

'I want to know why he's in there. He shouldn't be there. If nothing else, Max, the trumpet player, might have seen

Winter...'

'Pull the other one! Trying to bunk off to see the boyfriend, eh?'

'No!' Benson was indignant.

'Look, if it stops us being cut down by a train, that suits me. Worth a quick look at least?' One of the other constables was tiring of tramping the goods yards. Anything for a change.

Chapter Forty-two
London Bridge

A plan was coming together. Mellor was feeling a sense of relief that his hastily sketched operational plan had not only been accepted by others who outranked him, but who were part of more powerful police forces than his own. But this was no time to pat himself on the back.

Time was of the essence and if the suspect presently pacing in circles around one of the elevated platforms of London Bridge railway station was confirmed as Clawson, then he was one of the two 'most wanted men' in the land.

Mellor's bold idea was persuasive, but the fact Clawson was carrying the virus and willing to pass it to anyone he could touch probably did more than anything to help Mellor and the Transport Police win the day. Nobody was eager to draw close and even fewer wanted to make that final decision of when to pull the trigger. Doubt and apprehension lurked behind the eyes of every officer carrying a gun. An order issued from an office deep in Whitehall was all well and good, but someone was going to have to live with the consequences, trusting the order would still be considered just and legal once the weapon had been discharged and the inquest began.

Mellor had already studied the man in question through field glasses from an adjacent tall building. The station occupied an elevated position on a viaduct and was blessed with expanses of an uncovered platform that offered a reasonable view aided by station lighting that offset encroaching nightfall. After comparing the subject with the photographic prints and seeking a second opinion from an especially brusque officer from the City Police, they concluded this was Clawson. All trains were now held at adjacent stations up and down the line and officers guarding every access route in and out of the station, turning away potential passengers. The dramatic reduction in passengers was fortuitous. If the station was as crowded as usual in the days before the pandemic it would be mayhem and impossible to consider using a weapon. 'Black Maria' vans brimming with more men were parked along some neighbouring streets, all of which were being cleared of traffic and roadblocks erected to create a sterile area.

An eerie semi-quiet now descended around the usually bustling commuter station. It was still occupied by a handful of staff who'd been told to remain inside their offices, as a small clutch of passengers impatiently puzzled at the non-arrival of their trains, as yet unaware they were effectively marooned. Some distance away, the solitary figure of Clawson continued his circular pacing, round and round.

'He can't leave by foot or train. He's penned in,' Mellor took a drag on a cigarette to steady his nerves.

'There's still folk up there. I don't like that.'

'Neither do I. We've got to shepherd them off the platforms whilst cutting him out. Our men need to work like sheepdogs - holding the one back, but driving the others down the stairs and to safety...'

'What if he's already touched them? Rubbed against clothing and their possessions?'

'Fair point...' Mellor thought hard. 'We create holding pens on the ground. Everyone into these and tell them to stay calm and not bunch together until we can get medical staff to check them over. We'll need a fleet of ambulances...'

'You'll be lucky! They're all out on calls, non-stop these days.'

'Try...'

Orders were given, men moved away, eager to work on tasks far away from Clawson.

'Once we have the station cleared, I want a train to pull in. It will be empty and made up of stock with a door to each compartment. No corridors. Small and confined spaces to pen him inside.'

'Didn't you say there's a stack backed up the line in both directions?'

'Yeah. He's on the down platform. Presumably thinking to leave the city. We'll send one along that. I want him inside a compartment. The arrival of a train after this delay might encourage him to enter, if only because it's warm.'

The scar-faced detective gave Mellor a puzzled look. 'Thought the orders were to shoot on sight. Clear the station and our marksmen can pick him off. We've two of our best up here.'

'In this light? It's getting darker by the minute and bad weather promised on top. Look, snow!' They could see the first swirls of flakes falling. 'Even the best would struggle in these conditions. We get him into a closed space and lock him in. Then we can open a dialogue without him being able to run or for us to get close.'

'He's dangerous!'

'Not locked in a single compartment in an empty train. He'll be isolated. We'll pull the train out a short way from the station and take it from there.'

'Your DCI approved this?' Scarface was sceptical.

'We hold him alive and contained until my DCI gives orders as to what we do next. The man's unarmed and I want to be sure he *is* who we think he is before anyone starts shooting. I want to understand him. I want to know what's going on in his head.'

'Infecting millions and causing thousands to die. He's a psychopath.'

'You reckon? We can't prove that standing' here on a roof. I've no evidence of a crime committed other than he went AWOL from his regiment. Can you pin one death on him that would stand up in court?'

The officer narrowed his eyes and hid his expression behind a cloak of cigarette smoke. 'We do what the guv' tell us.'

'And I want him contained. Excluded from harming the public whilst we make sure.'

'Just fell him now. We can say he was endangering the public.'

'But he's not! Look. He's standing well apart.' Mellor stared through the binoculars at Clawson. 'I don't know if I believe half what I'm told. The scientists let this thing out and for all I know, they're blaming a poor soldier who's terrified out of his wits. Shooting him in cold blood is not justice. Even Himmler got a trial…'

'We're to stop him before he gets too close.'

'Then stay away!' Mellor threw his cigarette on the ground. 'Watch my back and tell your men to keep their trigger fingers in their pockets.'

The plan worked. Clawson showed no desire to approach the clutch of passengers who were ushered down the stairs by two constables and a porter. Clawson must have seen the uniforms and possibly Mellor and two plainclothes accompanying him, and yet he didn't react nor show interest.

He just stood. Unmoving. Snow gathering on his shoulders and hat with the snowflakes illuminated in a dizzying downward fall by the station lamps, face partially shadowed. He cut a lonely figure. Like Sinatra in the 'Wee Small Hours,' with hands in his pockets, an unlit cigarette growing damp on his lip. Kitbag on a nearby bench.

Mellor fingered the pistol now lying in his coat pocket and wondered what to do next. He'd been given unambiguous orders, but he left the safety catch on. There had to be a more humane way out of this mess.

The colour signal lights changed to green and this made Clawson's skin turn sickly; the colour of a man infected by a deadly bug in a science fiction film. But this was not a film. Mellor felt a twinge of nerves. He was wearing gloves and trying to avoid contact with any surface, but the apprehension of knowing the virus was lurking so dangerously close played on his mind.

The hum and whine of a green electric multiple unit increased as the slab-sided coaches with a plain flat front approached. The driver's face could be seen as a pale oval through a narrow driving cab window. He was accompanied by another standing in the shadows at the back of the cab. Mellor had ordered an officer to be aboard.

The train came to a halt and made a series of random clicks and clacks and whirring sounds as these machines seemed to do for no discernible reason. Other than these small sounds, the station and indeed the city, seemed to fall almost silent as if holding its breath.

Clawson stared at the train. Nobody got on or off and the platform remained empty. He approached and opened a door, then turned to look back towards where Mellor was standing. 'Joining me, officer?'

Mellor only just caught the words across the distance between them. 'Not my train.'

'No? I thought it was a special. Just for us two...'

Mellor was unsure how to respond. Clawson was no fool. He'd worked out there was some kind of plan and knew who was behind it. Well, He'd hoped for dialogue with Clawson and now he'd got it. But the soldier was still on the platform and an active danger.

'I hope the heating's on,' Clawson climbed inside and slammed the door closed.

Mellor exhaled in a stream of pale breath. He now had to approach and lock the door using the metal T-shaped key he'd been provided with. The two uniformed officers accompanying him also had a key each. 'Walk briskly, but don't run. Don't spook him, but get the door locked,' had been his advice.

The window dropped down as they drew close and Clawson's face appeared. It was impossible to reach forward to lock the door without the risk of being touched. Clawson grinned. 'Nice try!' He waved a bare hand. 'Touch me not!'

Mellor stopped and the others were glad to obey his gesture urging them to do the same.

'What do we do now?'

'What do you want to do?' Mellor asked. 'You cannot leave this station. We have it surrounded and there are marksmen above.'

'I suppose this train won't leave unless you give permission?'

'Correct.'

'I don't have a gun.'

'It would do you no good even if you had. We're armed.'

'At least I'm in the warm and you, gentlemen, are in the cold. Looks like I got the better deal.'

Mellor smiled. The man was not what he'd expected. But what *had* he expected? 'I have orders to shoot you on sight.'

Clawson ducked out of the window, stood up straight and lifted his arms above his head 'Go on then!'

'I don't believe you deserve that.' Mellor did not attempt to draw the pistol. 'I want to help you.'

'You can't help me. Nobody can. I've got it and can't die from it and all I can look forward to is confinement to the end of my days. And I'm 19, so that's a long wait.'

'They'll find a cure.'

'Yeah? You reckon they'll give me a dose and set me free? Pull the other one.'

'There's much we don't know about it. They might have it all wrong and you can be cured. Perhaps you don't even have the virus and you've done no harm? I want to keep you isolated until medical teams can run tests, establish what the situation is. Treat you fairly. Let me lock this compartment and we'll fetch some tea and hot food and wait for a medical team in protective gear to arrive…'

'A sit down and a brew! Bloody hell, you can't beat the British. A nice cuppa solves everything…' Clawson peered out of the window again and laughed.

'Step back and let me lock the door. You are under arrest, but I will see you are treated decently.'

'Yeah, yeah, yeah…' Clawson placed a hand on the opened window and dangerously close to the keyhole. 'Tell you what, I'll play ball but on one condition. I want to see how much you trust me. How about a last cigarette for the condemned man? Join me.' He fished out a carton of Players and shook it, so the cigarettes stood proud. 'I've not touched 'em…Take one.'

Mellor felt his throat dry. The man was mad. Perhaps he should have let the marksmen do their job and not let himself be drawn into this insane situation.

'It's the least you can do. We share a smoke. Then you lock the door and I sit and await my fate.'

Mellor stepped closer, his heart pounding. The carton was offered through the opened window. Clawson's hand was steady, steadier than Mellor's, who could feel shivers through his limbs. He reached for a cigarette and expected the worst, but Clawson remained still and controlled in his movements as he slowly selected his own cigarette. 'Do the honours, officer.'

Mellor struck his lighter into flame and proffered it. Clawson leaned even closer. An oddly intimate moment with the two men just inches apart. Eye to eye, the flame dancing between them.

'I could infect you. I didn't hesitate until now.'

'I know…' Mellor could barely speak, let alone smoke. He was holding his breath.

A puff of smoke blown from the side of Clawson's mouth. 'I'm bored with it. I've had enough. Nothing happens. No reaction. No one drops dead. There's no satisfaction.'

'Go on…'

'I mean, you point a gun and bang! There's a result.'

'You might not be a carrier.'

'Might? You didn't stop a busy station and fill it with armed men because I *might*.' He winked, then drew back inside. 'Take a breath Mr Policeman. You'll expire!'

'DS Mellor.' He took half a step back and gratefully drank in some snowy air. He had been holding his breath.

'Thanks for sharing a smoke. Decent of you. It gets lonely.'

'I can imagine. Leave the window open but let me lock the door. We'll keep talking.'

Clawson gave a weak smile. 'I appreciate the thought. But talking from inside a locked cell is not nice. Because that's what this is, now. A cell.'

'Think of it as a quarantine space…'

'A never-ending one. Thanks, but no thanks.' Clawson spun the lit cigarette expertly through the air with a flick of his fingers, the glowing tip like a tiny Catherine wheel as it flew past Mellor's ear. He turned and strode to the far side of the narrow compartment, delightedly flinging the door open. 'Unlocked!'

'Bloody hell!' Mellor cursed. He'd ordered all the doors to be locked on the far side.

Clawson leapt out of the door and onto the up line, deliberately stretching himself to form the arc of a leaping diver to he would be sure to span the six-foot between the tracks. The scream of agony was longer than Clawson and anyone within hearing could have wished, as the blue flashes of electricity lit the compartment ceiling whilst he fried on the live electrical third rail. The flashes and arcs and screams continued until a merciful gunshot from the train cab brought silence.

Mellor stared bleakly at the platform surface and watched the snow falling whilst trying to hide the smell of roasting flesh behind the sharp taste of tobacco.

Chapter Forty-three
Great Northern Cemetery Station

'Who's in there?' Vignoles addressed a lantern-jawed detective and his colleague, both standing outside the doors of the Cemetery Station. Neither looked pleased to see him, both scowling and fingering the weapons in their hands with something like deadly intent. The armed officers were impatient to enter the building and considered the delay whilst waiting for a railway detective, DCI or not, as unnecessary and pointless.

'You the railway dick?'

'DCI Vignoles, British Railways Detective Department.' He batted back the disrespectful insult. Another time and place, and he'd take them to task and give them an earful they wouldn't forget in a hurry. They mumbled names and rank through clouds of cigarette smoke, but all he understood from their unwilling replies was they were with the City Police. Vignoles took heart in having struck up some kind of rapport with the two equally unprepossessing chaps from the 'Sweeney' who'd whisked him there in minutes. The Flying Squad now glowered over his shoulder. A battle over jurisdiction was liable to break out.

'WPC Benson, one of my officers, raised the alarm and as this is railway property, I shall direct the operation.'

'This ain't railway! Just an old church an' it's on our manor and we're going in. Besides, we've more experience with dangerous criminals than you and your choo-choo trains!'

'This is not a church, gentlemen. It was a railway station and remains British Railways property. That places it firmly within my jurisdiction.' Vignoles had not verified this last point but was confident he was not far from the truth. He'd spotted a small 'no trespassing' sign fixed high on the sooty brickwork that had the font and design of British Railways. That would do for now. 'Benson, who is inside?' He made a point of addressing the WPC who was standing a few feet away. She'd been ignored by the detectives and overshadowed by the presence of the uniformed constables in their tall helmets who'd had arrived with her.

'Winter, sir. And Mr Hawkes. Max Hawkes...' She hesitated. 'Who is known to me.'

'The bloody boyfriend...' snarled one of the City detectives. 'What's he doin' in there then, luv?'

'And why's he playing that blasted trumpet?'

'He's a musician...'

'Can't have her entering the building, Viggles,' grumbled one of the Sweeney. 'Personal connection. It's going to be messy and we don't need her getting' hysterical all over the shop.' His dismissive outburst didn't prevent him from eyeing her up.

Benson's mouth formed a line, but she remained silent.

Vignoles raised a hand to stem to flow of invective.

'What is your understanding of the situation, Benson?'

Their conversation was rendered surreal by the unmistakable sound of a lone trumpet playing a complex jazzy re-working of 'You Couldn't Be Cuter' carried to them on unpleasantly dank air emanating from the opened door.

'The constable and I were working together on the far side of the building, moving across the goods yards that lie beyond the main running lines, searching for the suspect in question. We heard the sound of the trumpet, which struck us as unusual. I recognised the style as that of Mr Hawkes....'

'So, you went to find yer boyfriend for a sneaky kiss an' cuddle?'

'My colleagues and I agreed the sound was coming from this abandoned station, which was surprising. It could offer a suitable refuge for the suspect to evade the search parties. When I heard 'The Last Post' from within I had the idea that this was a coded message…'

A snort of derision.

'I've 'eard it all now…'

'Correctly interpreted as such,' Vignoles silenced the complaint. 'Carry on…'

'Once we discovered this door had been forced, I hailed them. There are two men inside, one of whom I can confirm is Max Hawkes and the other appearing to fit the description of Sergeant Winter. Officers Weeks and Moloney were passing at that moment, so we sought their support.'

Vignoles at least had names for the unpleasant detectives. 'What condition are the men in?'

'Winter is poorly and unable to stand…'

'All the more reason we stop gassin' and finish the job…'

'Once I have assessed the situation,' Vignoles snapped back. 'We have a civilian in there who's safety is paramount - as is our own. Winter is carrying the virus and could infect us.'

'Then we use the shooters…'

'Not with a civilian present. Where is Hawkes?'

'In the same area as Winter,' Benson replied, betraying no emotion.

'Is he held hostage?'

'I don't believe so. They seem to have struck up a rapport.'

Vignoles nodded. 'Then we approach and open a dialogue. We seek to first remove Hawkes. Nobody discharges a single round unless I give clear orders. Is that understood? Nobody draws close to either man. Keep them at a distance until we can bring in suitable help.'

'Since when did railway coppers handle guns?'

Vignoles hefted his pistol in a gloved hand. It was not loaded, but no-one was to know that. 'Don't push it, detective. I'm in charge. You follow my lead.'

Vignoles pushed the door, the hinges protesting. They needed nothing more to make it known they were entering. 'Mr Hawkes? Can you hear me?'

The trumpet continued.

'Mr Hawkes! This is DCI Vignoles and WPC Benson. Please advise your situation.'

They continued to walk slowly into the echoing vault of the entrance hall, the pungent air filling their nostrils. Torch beams played across the floor and arches, sending shadows over the glossy tilework of intertwined foliage and white lilies.

'Mr Hawkes!'

'Over here. I'm fine.' The trumpet stopped. Beams of light converged on his standing figure beside the window. 'Jane? That you? Best keep well back. All of you stay back!'

'Why's that Hawkes? You wantin' trouble?' One of the Sweeney was chomping at the bit.

'Not a bit of it. But this fella's not well. If he's got what I think he has, I'll be joining him soon enough, but there's no need for you to do the same.'

There was a low groan followed by a hacking cough from behind a pillar. Vignoles stepped forward, a hand urging the others to hold back. Their torchlight locating the outstretched legs of Winter.

'Winter?'

'Who wants to know...' His voice was weak.

Vignoles eased closer until he was about three yards away. 'Sergeant Winter?'

'Not for much longer...' His skin was wet with perspiration and his chest heaved in short, painful movements.

'You're ill? Is it the coronavirus?'

'I guess...'

'We were told you were immune...'

'Joke's on me then.' Winter's head lolled to one side and he looked at Vignoles through half-closed eyes. 'Doctors can be wrong... don't know anything...' He paused. 'Thought I was going to live forever...Just...me...and the lucky few...'

Malone, or perhaps it was Weeks, now drew close, against the orders of Vignoles, a pistol trained on Winter's chest.

'Put that away! He's not going anywhere.'

'We've got orders.'

'You will not shoot a dying man. That is an order. He can hardly breathe. Put your weapon down!' Vignoles barked.

Winter mumbled something but the words were hard to decipher. He was slipping away.

'Mr Hawkes. I must ask you to step to the far side of this room and wait there.' Vignoles barked the order. 'Keep your distance until we can get you into quarantine and hospital.'

Benson was taking measured breaths, controlling her emotions as best she could, her eyes never leaving Hawkes.

'WPC Benson; maintain a safe distance but keep Mr Hawkes company until assistance arrives.' Benson gratefully obliged.

Vignoles now called across to the Flying Squad. 'You have a car. We need two ambulances and personnel in full protection gear, and we need it fast.'

'Just finish him off...' Ugly face butted in.

Vignoles glared at him, then back at the Flying Squad 'Jump to it! These men need help. We all might...'

The Sweeny retreated to the front door quicker than they'd entered. The two mean-faced City detectives also took a few steps back whilst maintaining their disapproving scowls. 'We should secure the perimeter.'

'Yes, why don't you do that!' Vignoles was glad to see the back of them. 'Mr Hawkes. How about another tune whilst we wait?'

Vignoles could not draw close to Winter to check for a pulse, but he knew the man was dead. At least there was no need for a bullet.

Chapter Forty-four
On the road

Mark Lombard drove from the Microbiological Research Department on Thursday evening. He told his staff he'd booked a long weekend away with his wife and children in Scotland and they were not to expect him back until Monday.

'In March and during school term time?' one of his colleagues queried, but Lombard countered by pointing out that the schools were already talking about closing for the duration, perhaps even by next Monday. 'What difference will it make? We might all be forced to stay at home and never go out save for essentials and only once a day. Stuck inside for as long as it takes. Muriel and I thought we'd have a last road trip before we're confined to quarters! Scotland is almost untouched so, where's the harm?'

It was said flippantly and made to sound like it was going to be a splendid adventure, but his colleague remained unconvinced. He was not sure that travel permits were being issued for journeys as far north as Shrewsbury, let alone Scotland. It seemed implausible and a long way to go for three nights.

'Are you sure it's safe? You must have seen the news stories about the roving gangs? And soldiers demanding payments to allow you through the roadblock even if you have the correct permits. It sounds like Dorset is turning into the Wild West...'

Lombard laughed these off as scare stories. Probably deliberately spread by the Government to encourage people not to travel.

'Exactly my point, old bean!'

That was the end of the conversation. Well, it was Lombard's problem. If he wanted to spend a whole day and most of the night driving and negotiating the headaches and dangers of what might lie ahead, so be it…

The car was loaded to the gunwales. Suitcases and blankets and the eiderdown from the marital bed filled the boot, whilst the two children, Paul and Samantha crammed into the back seat along with various items of kitchenware, a gas ring and canister and a heavy canvas tent. It was uncomfortable and cramped, but the sense of adventure was winning the battle for now. With pocket torches and spare batteries in their pockets and a new book each to keep them occupied, they drove off with the suspension groaning.

Muriel Lombard was surrounded by bags of provisions, her feet in a well of produce. Until the last moment, she fretted they didn't have enough, and her face had become lined by anxiety. She constantly fidgeted and then ran back into the house for one last thing that was unlikely to prove indispensable.

Lombard tried to focus his mind on practical matters such as checking the tyre pressures and the oil level, whilst silently practising how he was going to bluff their way through the roadblocks. He had some papers that looked impressive and struck something close to the right tone, but none were correct for their needs and none made mention of the whole family in an over-laden car. He had to hope he could bluff his way through using his status and the names of anyone and everyone in a position of influence he could think of.

They were running away. Running from the humiliation and torment of the abject failure of *Operation Chinese Bird*. It was a disaster now unfolding in the ghastliest manner imaginable. Slow, tortuous and painful. However, it was not just his guilty part in the catastrophe that drove them to pack the car and point it north. He was but one cog in a great number of wheels and if they all worked in concert, ensuing plenty of obfuscation and white lies, conveniently losing communiques or altering documents they could surely wriggle out of anything too dreadful when it came to an official investigation.

No, they were fleeing because they were scared. Scared of

the virus he'd helped create and scared of what it could do. He wanted to get as far away as possible from the infection. Lombard was no hero and not about to leave his wife and children to the dubious mercy of fate or the faint possibility of a sudden discovery of a vaccine. Scotland was far enough away and sufficiently underpopulated to offer the ideal place to weather the storm.

The railway crossing gates were white with a red metal disc fixed in the centre, staring back at them like an unblinking eye. Lombard drummed his fingers on the steering wheel. 'The train is taking its time.'

'A long signal section I expect.' Young Paul knew a bit about trains.

'Of course, quite right!' But Lombard was feeling the anxiety mounting. Fingers drumming on the steering wheel. Just forty miles covered and already a holdup. A minor one, but it played on his mind. He wanted to get as far north as he could before tiredness overcame him.

'Oh?'

Four men in masks suddenly appeared out of the night, each holding a hunting gun of some description. One had a barrel saw off short. The doors were flung open and a muffled voice ordered them out of the car. 'Leave the engine running! Leave it!'

They were all so shocked, they just stumbled out in stunned silence. Lombard was about to say something when he found a double barrel pointing at his chest and clammed up.

'You and the kids! Over to the ditch! Now!' They were hustled to the roadside and made to lie flat, a heavy boot pressing between Muriel Lombard's shoulder blades keeping her face in the cold wet grass. 'Don't look!'

Lombard was told to throw his wallet onto the car seat. He was then spun about and two shots thumped into the night air.

A rough shout followed. The boot removed its weight and crunched across the loose gravel on the roadside. The gates had now been opened by one of the masked men. Doors slammed. The car accelerated into the night.

A pool of blood leaked from beneath the dead shape that had been Mark Lombard.

*   *   *   *

Behind the air-locked doors in a windowless laboratory in the heart of the Porton Down Chemical Defence Experimental Establishment, Professor Urban was working into the night. His white lab coat clammy as the sweat trickled and it made his glasses steam up.

Between twelve to fifteen hours every day, he was in there. He rarely left the building, taking hurried meals in the staff canteen but more often than not, calling for a research assistant to fetch him a plate of sandwiches and more tea, to be consumed whilst seated at his workbench. For weeks he'd not been seen outside the heavily guarded perimeter fence, only taking a short stroll around the complex to get a breath of cooling fresh air whilst he waited for test results to come through or for another culture to grow.

He was urged by colleagues to take a rest. To take time away from his mountain of notes and rows of test tubes and the Petri-dishes filled with unpleasant looking spores. To get away from the locked vault containing thousands of phials with their dreadful contents and from the rubber articulated arms that reached inside air-sealed cabinets where deadly organisms thrived.

Despite the air filtering and cooling system, it was hot work. The rubber gloves, the masks and protective visors making the scientists suffer from the heat and the laboratories always retained a whiff of old sweat. Urban seemed to be feeling the heat worse than others, but he was insistent it was 'my impatience making me sweat. I need to find a vaccine and find it fast! None of us can have the luxury of time off until we stop this cursed virus.'

Coron56-N4 was proving a tricky customer, skipping from one variant to another, tantalising and frustrating them in equal measure. Always refusing to lie down and die when faced with what looked like a promising antidote and the pressure was telling. Lack of sleep, sunlight and fresh air was started to take its toll on everyone deep in the heart of the CDEE.

However, in the last weeks, Urban had started to notice a set of promising results. Very early days, of course, far too early to dare to presume he'd made a breakthrough. They'd all suffered too many false dawns to raise their hand and declare a solution, but quietly, sweatily, Urban was tracing a pattern than implied the virus was being suppressed by his latest concoction.

Laboratory tests however offered just one means to exploring the promising vaccine formula, and they all knew to their cost how the controlled and artificial conditions in the lab were far removed from a living human being with all manner of other ailments and complications that came with the real world. He needed a willing human guinea pig. A genuine human lab rat in the first throes of corona infection who was prepared to be experimented on. And prepared to accept that, more likely than not, their trial would fail. Such persons were hard to find. Nobody wanted to be infected knowing they stood but an outside chance of survival.

As it happened, fate was about to play them a hand.

The barbed-wire fences and armed guards, barking Alsatian dogs and constant security checks and tags, were all for nothing when faced with a silent and undetectable intruder that sneaked inside this secret establishment on the greaseproof paper wrapping on one of the new sliced white loaves that were proving popular in the canteen.

A set of fingers marks from a lackadaisical bread factory employee in the bakery loading bay carried the virus into the canteen, where the loaf was unwrapped and tossed into a bin. The sous chef neglected to wash his hands despite the warning reminders on the walls, and after assembling the sandwiches, placed them on polished plates that proved the perfect transmission ground, only for the infected plate to be selected by Urban's assistant. The professor would later fumble around to find the sharp triangular cut sandwich by touch alone and then take a bite. When a drop of sweat later trickled into his eye, he impatiently wiped it away with the same hand.

Urban was about to find out if his vaccine worked…

April

Chapter Forty-five
Leicester

Leicester was a city under siege. Roadblocks sealed off all roads south and east. As with other cities and towns on the edge of the critical infection zone, written permission had to be sought to leave the city boundaries and obtaining this, even if the need was legitimate, was a fraught process perhaps designed to dissuade most from even trying.

Meanwhile, the country was learning that the best way to survive this crisis was to stay indoors, to stay away from schools, factories and offices and avoid groups - and especially crowds. Train travel north of Leicester was not forbidden, but few attempted to secure the requisite permission to travel as the journey was on trains without any food or drink and to stations and indeed towns, lacking the same facilities. Face masks were mandatory throughout, and there was no guarantee any of these precautions would be enough to prevent infection.

The city hunkered down and the weeks crawled. The clothing and shoe factories fell silent one by one, their chimneys no longer smoking whilst desks in countless offices gathered dust. The buses still growled around the city but usually bearing just two or three brave souls seated in splendid isolation. The pretty lanes of shops so loved by the locals, were silent, as most were ordered not to open or running restricted hours with limited produce. Even the Cathedral had locked its doors.

Chapter Forty-five

Leicester Midland and Central stations were both key lifelines to bring in and deliver vital supplies and operated special trains deep into the infection zone. Each train was fumigated and cleansed, each traveller allocated their own compartment and given strict instructions to follow or risk a hefty fine. The masked and gloved station staff looked on without envy at those granted permission to board. Soldiers bearing arms patrolled outside and along the platforms, but they kept their distance and tried to avoid contact. Just occasionally, tempers flared, and they were forced to approach when someone railed against the multiple restrictions and raised their voice whilst calling anyone and everyone terrible names, but the heavy booted tread of a masked soldier or policeman soon quietened them. For the most part, the stations operated in an oddly hushed manner, with voices muted by cotton coverings, the hubbub of passengers no longer present and even the steam engines seemed to sense there was a need for less noise and fuss, gently hissing and puffing into position, followed by a gentle rhythmic scrape of the shovel into coal. An occasional word from engineman to guard. The briefest of whistles set a train in motion.

*   *   *   *

Since returning from London, Vignoles had not displayed any symptoms, but he was not prepared to take risks and chose to remain within his office and see as few people as possible. Conversations were either over the telephone or through his office window or with his team at distance through the opened office door. There was no question of travelling to Belgrave and Birstall to join Anna. A crackly telephone line sufficed as their means of communication the last thing at night. It was better than nothing and they had to make the best of it, although when the evening commuter trains prepared to leave Central (half full as the Government demanded) it was desperately hard not to cross the platform and step aboard and join Anna.

It was a lonely and dispiriting existence, but he'd managed to borrow a gramophone and a box of his favourite discs had been delivered one afternoon off the all stations stopper via Belgrave & Birstall with a note from his wife, so he could at least have some light entertainment. Anna travelled alone each day, seated in self-imposed solitary confinement in the guard's section of the train in an arrangement Vignoles had pre-arranged. Sharing the space with only the guard, was the safest option. She was trying to keep their home warm and welcoming ready for the day when they could share it again. It was a strangely surreal existence, working each weekday in the same station and a half-empty office, so close to Charles yet forced to talk through a window. It was especially painful for Anna to stand on the platform at the end of the day and blow a kiss to her husband as he stood at his office window.

It was an undeniable fact Vignoles was walking a tightrope whenever he was called out on a case and liable to fall sick any day. He was aware that once the infection frontline broke and the city was over-run by hospital cases (as so many already had) he would be in the thick of it, day and night. He and his officers would be expected to try and maintain law and order and do anything they could to help the over-worked ambulance and medical staff. The worst part would be forcing panicked and angry citizens from boarding trains heading north, desperate to flee like refugees to areas as yet unaffected.

These tidal waves of people were creating havoc and Vignoles was dreading having to look people in the eye, seeing their fear and tell them they couldn't leave. As it was, most of his team were doing just that, working south of Leicester, repelling people from boarding passenger and freight trains heading out of the zone. Many would resort to violence and he'd seen many officers hospitalised in the line of duty. It was never-ending and the strain was starting to tell on them all.

Mellor had become almost nocturnal, spending the nights patrolling yards and depots or riding out of the city, usually as far as the London suburbs which were a favourite place to attempt to board northbound trains. When they got a chance to talk, Mellor looked exhausted. Nevertheless, he was the man for the task, maintaining a core of five officers with him and co-operating well with whatever local constabulary or Army unit was to hand. If there was any consolation in this unpleasant task, it was that Mellor had replaced the live rounds in his pistol with blanks. 'A gunshot in the air can do more to scare people than anything else. Goods yards are huge, and we just can't cover the distances, but a gunshot it cuts right through. Most are crooks, black marketeers exploiting the situation for their own gain and they understand the sound of a gunshot,' Mellor had explained.

There were times in the very early hours of the morning when Vignoles was awakened whilst a train was loaded with mail or milk churns, and as he lay awake, he wondered if he was cut out for this. If he had what it took to get through it. It felt as though the virus was circling the city and making exploratory incursions to ensure nobody slept soundly or felt at ease. The Detective Department was only small, but it was feeling the strain and causing Vignoles ever more sleepless nights and troubled days.

Lansdowne had been brought low by a telegram informing her that her former fiancée Richard had now died from the virus. Asiatic flu was cited, but perhaps nobody would ever know which strain was responsible. Did it even matter? A letter from a work colleague had followed a week later and described how he'd had died alone in a hospital and that nobody had been able to attend his funeral. Although the engagement had ended the year before, Lansdowne still felt the loss deeply. She was struggling with a sense of guilt that perhaps she'd been selfish in refusing to join him in West Germany, choosing instead to remain a WPC in Leicester. That she would have probably died along with Richard if she had done so was a chilling thought, but it brought no comfort that she'd survived, whilst he'd left this world alone.

It was obvious Lansdowne was also missing the presence of Jane Benson, with whom she shared a close friendship both in and out of work, but Benson was still in the last days of the most recent quarantine period in her rented room in Leicester. Benson frequently operated deep into London as this was territory she had come to know and feel almost at home within, but she was expected to isolate for two weeks at a time after each fortnight posted down south. It was a wise precaution but proving a trial. In a recent communique, she declared the virus had to better than cooped up with just her landlady's vile food and the radio for company.

Benson's boyfriend, Max Hawkes, remained ill in hospital in London. Another reason for Vignoles to post Benson to the southern reaches of their line. Hawkes was at least proving strong as an Ox, with good lungs that were bearing up. A consequence of blowing a trumpet most of his life. He stood a chance of pulling through, although it was still too early to be sure and the virus was proving reluctant to release him from its grip. There was a very real fear he might never play to a crowded room again.

Benson and Hawkes might escape from their proximity to a known carrier, as indeed had Vignoles, but Mavis Green, his indomitable secretary 'had taken bad' in recent days. She had been struggling for weeks and hopes had risen that she had shaken off a mild dose of whatever virus it might be, but then had taken a turn for the worse. They were all awaiting news from the Green household, praying it would be a false alarm.

The news from Marylebone House last month, however, had been bleak. Karolina Smolej's voice had wavered and she was audibly holding back tears whilst telling Vignoles about the awful news. Chief Superintendent Badger was dead.

The news had hit Vignoles harder than he'd expected. Badger and he had not always had the easiest of relationships, but despite his acid tongue and differing opinions of aspects of their work, 'The Badger' had been a decent 'copper' at heart and a decent man. He'd retained a strong sense of public service despite a zealous appetite for golf club membership and emptying the public purse on shiny motor cars. He'd often publicly backed Vignoles, despite voicing disapproval of some of his methodology, and Badger's loyalty to his team had been fierce. Vignoles had stared at the telephone long after he'd replaced it on the cradle and realised that he would miss the hissed warning from Mavis that 'the Super was waiting', and miss watching the man preen and make adjustments to the lie of his crisp and expensive uniform whilst deciding what hole to pick in Vignoles operational strategy. He already missed the old man.

The call to Mrs Badger had been desolate. There could be no official send-off for them to discuss. No shared discussion on the number of uniformed officers who might be present or who should bear the coffin or what readings might be suitable. The usual safety net of organisation and planning masking the lack of words that would make a difference. It was to be the hollowest and loneliest of goodbyes. Vignoles could perhaps arrange a wreath? But even these were discouraged. A few more hollow words then that was it.

He wondered if he would speak with Mrs Badger again. He didn't know her. She had always been a vague presence, obliquely referred to, if at all. She and Vignoles had no common ground other than his death and his work.

And who would replace him?

Vignoles dreaded the call from the ACC asking if he might put his name forward. Or was he just fooling himself? Vignoles detested golf and repeatedly refused invitations to the 'right' sort of events that oiled the wheels of personal advancement. With a bit of luck, he'd be passed over and could continue in the job he loved. Pen pushing in an office in Marylebone was not appealing.

Minshull had taken the loss of Badger very hard. As fellow Yorkshiremen, they'd shared a close bond and Badger had never attempted to hide his preference for the gruff, overweight copper from Sheffield. But Bernard Minshul had his own problems that were probably ensuring he would not be stepping into Badger's shoes. He was facing an internal enquiry over the death of a man currently identified as one Jeremy Williams, although Minshul doubted this was his real identity. Many awkward questions were being asked by shockingly expensive lawyers in Chancery into the exact circumstances of his death in that tower in Conway castle and it was all becoming both uncomfortable and time-consuming. That Minshul thought this was just a smokescreen for concealing the man's true identity and upon whose orders he'd been working, was not offering much comfort. The other alleged hitman, the one known as Evans, was proving as slippery as an eel and represented by the same lawyers. Evans had walked free without bail and Minshul doubted he'd ever be brought to trial.

Vignoles slowly filled his pipe and sat and watched a train being prepared for another run to London. The pale dawn light glinted off the engine as two men in formal suits, but with faces so heavily covered by scarves, it was impossible to tell who they might be. Politicians or ministers? Most had been moved out of London to counties less ravaged by virus and Leicestershire had gained a share. He glanced at the station clock. Another hour before Anna was due to step off her morning train. He'd wait for her today. Enough was enough. The hell with this dratted virus! He'd be there, standing alone on the platform and then gently usher to one side to where it was quiet and far away from everyone. He needed to see Anna, to put his arms around her and smell the scent she loved on her warm skin…

Chapter Forty-six
Along the line

Fireman Earnshaw was leaning on the cab of his engine *Impala* as they chuffed steadily northwards out of London. They'd survived yet another visit and he felt elated. Perhaps this is what the British bomber crews had felt like once they'd dropped their bombs and survived long enough to turn their aircraft about and head back home? As each mile rolled by, they could feel a bit more secure.

Not that he and his driver, nor even the guard in his van at the end of the train knew if they were safe. Nobody did, but after so many weeks of this routine they'd become less anxious and it felt familiar. As each trip was completed and they remained fit and well, the fear of the virus receded.

Things were slowly improving, or was it they were numb to it all and busy getting on as best they could? The almost other-worldly sight of the deserted metropolis had become normal, and at times Earnshaw needed to remind himself this was not in the least 'normal' and one day he would look back and remember the time they'd steamed in and out of the 'Infection Zone' with soldiers 'riding shotgun.' He would tell of hearing gunshots and perhaps exaggerate how many, although usually they just encountered semi-silence and a spooky emptiness.

It was surprising how quickly he'd adapted. How they all had. A 'new normal' way of living was evolving and the virus no longer a constant theme of conversation. They were happier discussing the erratic attempts to restart the football season or the chances of cricket being played in the summer. They gave time to dreaming of escaping in the summer for a holiday to somewhere nice. Probably a seaside resort in the north, where the virus was still having minimal impact. His driver even wanted to talk about whether the dahlias would have survived the harsh winter and what veg he was going to plant out. Gloriously mundane subjects that helped the working day pass pleasantly.

As they chugged along behind the suburban house backs and gardens, the dawn light glowed in a clear sky and lights came on behind curtains and people awoke. At Princes Risborough they passed a train of lime wagons waiting at a signal, to be invited into the city with another delivery. Lime was being stockpiled, but the mass graves had closed. There was even talk of reburials once the virus was beaten, with proper services, as the death rate had dropped significantly in the last week. Whilst the numbers of mourners were still limited, a measure of dignity had returned to these farewells. Small steps it helped make everything feel that bit more bearable.

As the sun rose, its golden light skimmed the countryside, throwing undulating shadows as they steamed through the verdant countryside of middle England. Not all trees were in full leaf, but Earnshaw caught glimpses of trees festooned in a blossom of pinks and whites against the fresh greens of leaves and it was cheering sight. He turned on the steam injector to put water in the boiler and was pleased it worked the first time. Their engine was running smoothly, being one of the no-nonsense Thomson B1s and proving a dream. He liked *Impala* and she was running nicely today. He even had time to open his snap tin and extract a well-filled sandwich.

Life was not so bad after all.

*   *   *   *

In Leicester Central, the radio was on in the Detective Department office and the news encouraging. There were hints the rate of infection was slowing and the border zone set to retreat deeper south within the next week. Vignoles nodded with satisfaction at hearing public acknowledgement of what he'd been advised the day before. He looked at the map of Leicestershire and the red dotted line that was to dip to the southern limits of the county. Leicester had held firm. They'd done their bit and won. He just hoped the news about Mavis Green would be as equally upbeat. She was at least 'stable' and not worsening, so there was room for optimism.

As Anna listened in to the same bulletin in their house, she decided the bright weather, the first they had in weeks, deserved to be properly appreciated. Although unable to share the day with her husband, she would not to let this deter her and dusted off her bicycle, put air in the tyres and took a ride out to Bradgate Park. It was a wise decision.

The park was speckled with daffodils that nodded cheerily in the sunlight. Some were even starting to go over and she regretted not having cycled out there earlier, despite the rain. Ducks and geese were abundant and full of noise and the trees filled with birdsong. Anna took deep breaths of the fresh air. It was easy to forget the doom and gloom when away from the radio and television and the unnaturally quiet streets of the city. Things no longer seemed so hopeless when life was so obviously abundant within the park, nature was almost visibly stretching and yawning as spring took hold.

Anna was about to remount her bike and cycle further on when she caught sight of a glorious vixen, her coat the most beautiful coppery red in the sunshine. Her tail was bushy and full and her poise confident in the way she lifted her long snout and sniffed the air.

'Hello, Mrs Fox...' The romantic in Anna wondered if this could be the same as she'd met on the road in Birstall. Unlikely, but she liked the idea. There was no doubting this vixen shared the same arrogant poise, giving Anna a long stare as if questioning why she was in the park. *Her* park, a place no longer overrun by noisy humans. Anna revelled in the sight of this beautiful creature and surprised herself by hoping the fear of contagion would keep the rolling fields of Leicestershire free from the call of the hunting horn and thunder of chasing hooves for many more months. In the time since the pandemic had arrived, it had been a chance for nature to reaffirm its place and for humans to be reminded their foothold on life was more transient than they had previously believed.

The vixen's copper fur rippled in the sunlight as she trotted away, and Anna felt a strange sensation; unfamiliar, unpractised and almost forgotten.

She felt happy.

The End

The next arrival will be the much delayed
'The Signalman's Daughter,' late 2021.

Author's note

This book takes inspiration from the real Asiatic Flu pandemic of 1957-58, mixed with the on-going Covid19 pandemic that needs no introduction. The difficulties we are all experiencing demanded I write a book that helped me find my way through this oddest of times.

I hope it can do the same for yourself. Whilst we cannot confidently forecast the end of the covid19 pandemic, the book hints at sunnier times to come

This is, however, a work of (Science) fiction, owing more to John Wyndham than reality. If you want proof this is fiction, then the fact it is played out over just four or so months says it all…

The former Prime Minister Harold Macmillan is mentioned, but purely to help create a sense of historical verisimilitude. Any similarity to persons living or dead is unintentional.

Similarly, the Microbiological Research Department and Chemical Defence Experimental Establishment at Porton Down and the Common Cold Unit, Harnham Down all exist or existed, and there is neither factual nor implied involvement in the themes touched upon in this story.

*

For all those working hard to keep us fit and well.

And to the memory of those who didn't make it.